William Hepworth Dixon

Lady Morgan´s Memoirs Autobiography, Diaries and Correspondence

William Hepworth Dixon

Lady Morgan´s Memoirs Autobiography, Diaries and Correspondence

ISBN/EAN: 9783742857194

Manufactured in Europe, USA, Canada, Australia, Japa

Cover: Foto ©Raphael Reischuk / pixelio.de

Manufactured and distributed by brebook publishing software
(www.brebook.com)

William Hepworth Dixon

Lady Morgan´s Memoirs Autobiography, Diaries and Correspondence

COLLECTION

OF

BRITISH AUTHORS

TAUCHNITZ EDITION.

VOL. 638.

LADY MORGAN'S MEMOIRS

IN THREE VOLUMES.

VOL. 2.

LEIPZIG: BERNHARD TAUCHNITZ.

PARIS: C. REINWALD & Cⁱᵉ, 15, RUE DES SAINTS PÈRES

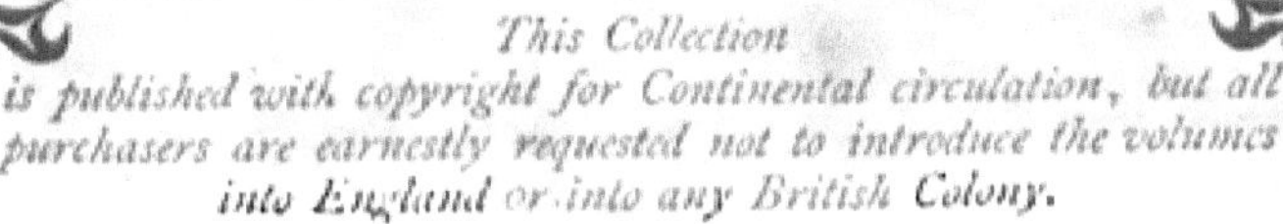

COLLECTION

OF

BRITISH AUTHORS.

VOL. 638.

LADY MORGAN'S MEMOIRS.

IN THREE VOLUMES.

VOL. II.

LADY MORGAN'S MEMOIRS:

AUTOBIOGRAPHY,

DIARIES AND CORRESPONDENCE.

COPYRIGHT EDITION.

IN THREE VOLUMES.

VOL. II.

LEIPZIG

BERNHARD TAUCHNITZ

1863.

CONTENTS

OF VOLUME II.

LADY MORGAN'S MEMOIRS.

CHAPTER I.

DR. MORGAN AND DR. JENNER.

As yet, Miss Owenson had not met the man who was to win her from the vanities of her own fancy. At this date of 1809, Thomas Charles Morgan, doctor of medicine, was mourning over a dead wife, tenderly nursing a little girl, the child of his lost love, helping Dr. Jenner to make people believe in vaccination, struggling into London practice, and proceeding to his degree of doctor in medicine. Morgan had been born in London, in 1783, being the son of John Morgan, of that city, and his early life had been spent in the neighbourhood of Smithfield. He was several years younger than Miss Owenson; in later life Lady Morgan confessed to having two years of disadvantage over Sir Charles: but the unromantic truth may be set down without exaggeration at five or six. From the Charter House, he was sent to Cambridge, where, in 1801, he graduated at St. Peter's, and, in 1804, took his degree of M. B.; thence he removed to London, set up in his profession, became a member of the College of Physicians, and entered heart and soul into the controversies about cow-pox and small-pox. Handsome, witty, prosperous, with a private income of about £300 a-year, and the prospect of a great name in his profession; he was not long left to the miseries of a bachelor's life. Miss Hammond, daughter of Anthony Hammond, of Queen's Square, then a fashionable part of town, the residence of judges, privy councillors, and bankers, became his wife, but died in about a year, in giving birth to her child. Little Nannie was left the Doctor's chief playmate; while his serious study was bestowed on his profession, little dreaming of the brilliant distraction then preparing for him in Dublin.

Jenner's letters to him are well worth reading; and there will be no need for any apology in introducing some of them, episodically, at this early stage. They show the difference between the condition of a hero, after he has been accepted by posterity, placed in his niche, and his reputation rounded into "one entire and perfect chrysolite," in which nobody sees any flaw, and the same man when he was alive — his views misunderstood, he himself painfully struggling against ignorance and calumny, and his heart nearly broken by petty vexations and hindrances. Jenner is now an acknowledged benefactor to the human race, he has a statue in London; but it was scant reverence that "hedged him," and small justice he obtained in the days of his life. Dr. Morgan was the friend and supporter of Jenner in the time of contradiction, and it is pleasant in the correspondence which passed between them to remark the tone of cordial respect in which Jenner addresses him.

Dr. Jenner to Dr. Morgan.

BERKELEY,
December 20, 1808.

MY DEAR DOCTOR,

There is nothing enlivens a cottage fire-side, remote from the capital, so much as a newspaper. The *Pilot* of last night was particularly cheering, as it told me you had finished your academic labours and received your honours. Allow me to congratulate you, and to assure you how happy I shall ever be in hearing of anything that adds to your fame, your fortune, or to your general comforts.

The horrid fever my eldest son has undergone, has left him quite a wreck; but I don't despair of seeing him restored. I should be quite at ease on the subject, if a little cough did not still hang upon him, and too quick a pulse.

The Regius Professor of Physic in the University of Cambridge, corresponding with the contemptible editors of that miserable catch-penny Journal, the *Medical Observer!!!* What phenomenon, I wonder, will vaccination next present to us? Atrocious and absurd as this man's conduct has been, there will be a difficulty in punishing him, as he seems insensible to everything but his own conceit. However, he is in able hands, and my excellent friend Thackeray (to whom I beg you to remember me most kindly) I know will not spare him.

Sir Isaac has certainly out-blockheaded all his predecessors. Pray tell me what is going forward. Alas! poor thing! He has been too daring, and I tremble for his fate. The scourge is out, and I don't see that

1*

he erased a single line that was pointed out to him as dangerous. This venomous sting will produce a most troublesome reaction, and injure the cause it was meant to support. You know the pains I took to suppress it; but all would not do.

I have not heard anything of the new Vaccine Institution since my arrival here, except a word or two from Lord Egremont, who says the Ministry are so incessantly occupied with the affairs of Spain, that matters of a minor consideration cannot at present be attended to. I shall thank my friend in Russell Square, for the communications which, through you, he was good enough to make to me, but am of opinion that the proper time to object will be when anything objectionable rises up. Whatever is going forward either in the College or out of it, is at present carefully concealed from me. The proposition hinted at by Dr. S—, respecting an equal number from both Colleges to form the Board, I mentioned to Sir Lucas as the certain means of keeping off those jealousies which otherwise I thought would show themselves.

It affords me great pleasure to assure you that your pamphlet is *much* liked by all who have read it in this part of the world, and by no one more than by myself. A few trifling alterations will be necessary for the *next edition.* I think you may be more copious in your extracts from some of those letters of which Murray availed himself. By the bye, it might not be amiss, perhaps, if, by way of firing a shot at the head of your knight, the extract from Sacco's letter (see Murray's Appendix) and that from Dr. Keir, at Bombay, were to appear in the Cambridge newspaper.

With the best wishes of myself and family, believe me, dear Doctor,

Most faithfully yours,

EDW. JENNER.

Mr. Jenner to Charles Morgan.

BERKELEY,
March 1st, 1809.

MY DEAR SIR,

I ought to make a thousand apologies to you for suffering your last obliging letter to remain so long unanswered. Did my friends whom I serve in this manner but know the worrying kind of life I lead, they would soon seal my pardon. However, I feel myself now more at ease than for some time past, having crept from under the *thick*, *heavy* Board, which so unexpectedly fell upon me and crushed me so sorely. To speak more plainly, I have informed the gentlemen in Leicester Square, that I cannot accept of the office to which they nominated me. Should the business come before the public, as I suppose it will, I am not afraid of an honourable acquittal. Never was anything so clumsily managed. If Sir Isaac himself, instead of Sir Lucas, had taken the lead, it could not have been worse, as I shall convince you when we come to talk the matter over. By the way, what is become of this right valiant knight? Thackeray, I hope, has not done exchanging lances with him, unless he is ashamed of the contest. I was glad to see your pamphlet advertised on the *yellow cover*. Give it as much publicity as you please, and remember, you are to draw on me for all costs. Does it go off, or sleep with the pages of Moseley? Opposition to vaccination seems dead — at least in this part of the world we hear nothing of it. Through a vast district around me, I don't know a man who now ever unsheaths that most venomous of all weapons — the variolus lancet; and the small-pox, if it now and then seizes upon some deluded infidel, soon dies away for want of more prey.

I have not written to my friend Dr. Saunders a long time, but if you see him, assure him he shall hear soon from me. If he considers the business between me and the Board, and looks steadfastly on all its bearings, I am confident he will not condemn my conduct. If it should be thought of consequence enough for an inquiry, I shall meet it with pleasure; but, though I say "with pleasure," I had much rather they would let me alone, and suffer me to smoke my cigar in peace and quietness in my cottage.

My boys are better. How is your little cherub?

Adieu, my dear Sir,
Most truly yours,
EDW. JENNER.

Mr. Jenner to Charles Morgan.

BERKELEY,
11th July, 1809.

MY DEAR SIR,

You have some heavy accusations I know to bring against me on the subject of my long silence. I have no other excuse to offer you than that of pecuniary bankrupts, who have so many debts, that they discharge none. However deficient I may have been in writing, I have not been so in thinking of you and your kind attentions. If you have seen your neighbour Blair lately, he must have told you so.

You supposed me at Cheltenham when you wrote last. Unfortunately, I have not yet been able to quit this place, and have been detained by a sad business, the still existing illness of my eldest son, the young man who was so ill when I was in town. His appearance for some time past, flattered me with a hope that he was convalescent, but to my great affliction he was seized on Saturday last with hæmorrhage from the lungs, which returned yesterday and to-day exactly at the same hour, and almost at the same minute — seven in the morning. This is a melancholy prospect for me, and I scarcely know how to bear it. The decrees of Heaven, however harsh they may seem, must be correct, and the grand lesson we have to learn is humility.

I wrote two long argumentative letters to Dr. Saunders soon after I received your hint, on the subject of the new institution; but from that time he has dropped his correspondence with me. When next you fall in with the doctor, pray sound him on this subject. Have you seen the last number of that infamous publication, the *Medical Observer?* There is the most impudent letter in it from the editor to me that ever was penned. I think our friend *Harry* would at once pronounce it grossly libellous. The thing I am abused for, the effects of an epidemic small-pox at Cheltenham, is as triumphant as any that has occurred in the annals of vaccination. A child that had irregular pustules, and was on that account ordered by me to be re-vaccinated, which order was never obeyed, caught the small-pox. This is the whole of the matter, and

on this foundation Moseley, Birch and Co., have heaped
up a mountain of scurrility. Between 3,000 and 4,000
persons have been vaccinated there and in the circum-
jacent villages, *who remained in the midst of the epidemic*
untouched. This *trifling* circumstance, these worthy
gentlemen did not think it worth their while to mention. Adieu, my dear Sir, I hope you are very well
and very happy.

Most truly yours,

E. JENNER.

Mr. Jenner to Charles Morgan.

BERKELEY,
9th October, 1809.

MY DEAR SIR,

You may easily guess what a state of mind I am
in, by my neglecting my friends. This I was not
wont to do. I am grown as moping as the owl, and
all the day long sit brooding over melancholy. My
poor boy still exists, but is wasting inch by inch. The
ray of hope is denied only to a medical man when he
sees his child dying of pulmonary consumption; all
other mortals enjoy its flattering light. You say nothing
of your little girl in your letter from Ramsgate. I
hope she is well and will prove a lasting comfort to
you.

If Dr. Saunders is displeased, his displeasure can
have no other grounds than caprice. I never did
anything in my life that should have called it up. I
wrote twice to him in the spring, and since that time
he has not written to me. Why, I am utterly at a
loss to know. In one of these letters I went fully

into an explanation of my conduct with regard to the National Vaccination establishment. Depend upon it neither Mr. B. nor Sir Lucas will ever make it the subject of public inquiry. They know better. I have always treated the College with due respect. They made an admirable report to Parliament of vaccination; but in doing this they showed me no favour. It was founded on the general evidence sent in from every part of the empire. I love to feel sensible of an obligation, where it is due, and to show my gratitude. If the College had published the evidence, which they *promised* to do, then I should have been greatly obliged to them. Why this was not done, I never could learn, but shall ever lament that such valuable facts should lie mouldering on their shelves, as they must from their weight have lain too heavy on the tongue of clamour for it ever to have moved again. I wish you had been there, and that I had first made my acquaintance with you. Our strenuous friend in Warwick Lane would have effected everything by filling up this lamentable chasm. I enjoyed your dialogue. *Poor* Sir Isaac! Your pamphlet is highly spoken of, wherever it is read. After this *spice* of your talents in lashing the anti-vaccinists, I hope you don't mean to lay down the rod. Moseley, as far as I have seen, has not taken the least notice of it. A proof of his tremors; for he has not been sparing of his other opponents. And now my good friend let me request you, without delay, to let me know the expenses of printing, advertisements, &c., &c. I don't exactly know where this may find you, but shall get a cover for Ramsgate. If you are not there it will pursue you. Dr. Saunders's throwing me off, I assure you, vexes me; but I have the consolation of knowing that it was unmerited. Remember me kindly to our friend *Harry*. He will soon climb the hill, I think. He may be assured of not reaching the top a day sooner than I wish him. Will you have the goodness when in town to order Harward to send the *Annual Medical Register* with my next parcel of books? I have not seen it, but shall, of course, turn to the article "Cow-pox" with peculiar pleasure. Do you recollect my exhibiting some curious pebbles which I had collected during my stay in town, to some friends of yours in your apartment? By some mishap they were left behind me. They were good specimens of wood and bone converted into silex. I don't think there is a corpuscle of the globe we inhabit that has not breathed in the form of an animal or a vegetable. Adieu!

Believe me, with best wishes,

Most truly yours,

EDWD. JENNER.

We must leave the two doctors to their controversies and incriminations. The story of the introduction of vaccination into this country is one of deep interest, and especially to female readers; but that story is not the property of Lady Morgan's biographer. We shall not see Mr. Morgan again for a year or more.

CHAPTER II.

OLD FRIENDS AND NEW.

MISS OWENSON's visit to Lady Abercorn has been mentioned. It was in her hospitable house that Miss Owenson received the riotous letter from Barrington. Lady Charleville refers to this visit, congratulating her young friend on "acquiring" the favour of Lord and Lady Abercorn's protection. Lady Charleville's good sense and strong affection for Miss Owenson, and her total freedom from the jealousy that old friends too often feel privileged to indulge, is very pleasant.

The Countess of Charleville to Miss Owenson.

CHARLEVILLE FOREST,
December 12th, 1809.

DEAR MISS OWENSON,

I am extremely sensible of the politeness of your inquiry for my health, which remains nearly stationary, or if any ways changed, certainly not for the better. It is such as to preclude any idea of town amusements mixing with my scheme of enjoyment; but, indeed, at all times I greatly prefer Charleville Forest to residence in any city.

I congratulate you very sincerely on your acquiring the favour of Lord and Lady Abercorn's protection. It is not always that both parties accord to approve of the same person's character and abilities, or indeed, to make due allowances for them. As I believe the noble lord to be, like many others, omnipotent in his own family, I am to suppose HE acknowledges the existence of those charming talents, which certainly must be improved by the intercourse of highly educated people; and once more I congratulate you on the enjoyment you must find in such society.

I am glad you write for every reason of emolument and amusement; and I do hope your next publication may have as beautiful fancies interspersed, and give less room to the gentlemen to criticise Englishmen's *sang froid* than the last has done ! ! ! !

I believe you will find Lady Costre settled in London, and very happy to do you service in her way.

I am grieved to find Mrs. Henry Tighe is very ill; I know how good she has been to you; and I think her taste should bias every creature who has a heart to feel for her, or soul to acknowledge her, as the first genius of her day . . . . . .

I am, Dear Madam,
Your very faithful servant,
CATH. MARIA CHARLEVILLE.

Sir Jonah Barrington to Miss Owenson.

MERRION SQUARE, *Thursday.*

DEAR MISS OWENSON,

I hasten to acknowledge what I value — a note from you. But why remind me of my advancing years by supposing me capable of *forgetting* a promise to Miss Owenson, which, at the period of my second climacteric, would have been a suspicion of my honour and an insult to my gallantry. Think you, that because I approach my year of *jubilee*, — because the freezing hand of Time has checked the rapid course of my circulation, and seized in his cold grasp a heart whose ardour would once have bid defiance to his icicles, — that, therefore, my memory and truth must have taken flight with my passions and left your unfortunate correspondent a mere *caput mortuum* — if you think so, you err, for my *vanity* has survived and could not be more highly gratified than by your acceptance of my labours.

The book, such as it is, is the true and unadulterated offspring of Irish feelings, and as such too congenial to your own, not to excite your attention and demand your indulgence. Our works differ, however, in a point the widest in the world — yours much the most difficult — all the talent of *inventive* genius must be cultivated by you — anything in the nature of invention would destroy my reputation. You must invent incident, I need only tell it; you must combine events, my events are already combined, and I have only to recite them. You must describe passions which you never felt; I felt all the passion I have to describe. You write to *please;* I write to reprobate; and in *that* alone *you* will find the less difficulty.

However, my vanity is not like other people's, for it is perfectly *candid*, and desires me to tell you that I think you will like the book — at least, I like it myself, and that is all that can be expected by any author.

The second part will rise from the dead, I trust, in January next; and a most flattering letter received from the Prince of Wales, at once feeds my ambition and promotes my courage — so on I go — and heaven send me a good deliverance; there will be ten parts, one hundred portraits, thirty vignettes, all comprised in two volumes — eleven engravings, *very superior*, to those you see, will honour the next number; but I do not think anything can much exceed Bush and Curran in the last, except Durginan and Napper Tandy in the next part. You see, gentlemen must keep bad company on those occasions.

You greatly mistake if you suppose the *ravenous appetite* you mention can be at all sated by my morsel — it will only be a mere lunch; I hope, however, it may increase your appetite, and give you relish for the second course which I am cooking for your table.

I wish you a happy Christmas, as I entertain no doubt you will have a merry one; and if the good wishes of Lady B— &c., can add to your pleasures, be sure you possess them.

I am, with real sincerity,

Your affectionate brother author,

Vive Irlandois.   JONAH BARRINGTON.

The following letter is from "a sound divine," and a dignitary of the Church, who was one of what her sister used to call "Sydney's Army of Martyrs;" at that period a tolerably numerous train! It would be curious to speculate on the effect it might have produced on the orthodoxy of this ardent admirer, had his prayer been granted and Sydney Owenson had become an Archdeacon's wife instead of Lady Morgan!

Archdeacon King, to Miss Owenson.

DEAR MISS OWENSON, *1810.*

Enclosed is the elegant trifle* you were desirous to obtain. I have lost no time in executing the little commission with which you have honoured me. Oh that I were destined to contribute to your felicity in the serious and important circumstance which was the subject of this evening's conversation! — to contribute to your felicity and to complete my happiness. But the unfortunate Rector of Mourne Abbey cherishes the hope, that if he cannot be blest with the *hand*, he will be *immortalized* by the pen, of the elegant and interesting Glorvina.

RUPERT KING.

Mr. F— is not permitted to give a copy of the song; you must prevaricate, and pretend that you retained it in memory after having heard it repeated.

R. K.

The "white lies" recommended in this postscript are surprising in a divine; possibly, Sydney Owenson, like Sweet Kitty Clover, had "bothered him so," that the poor archdeacon was bewildered. It is not surprising that Miss Owenson should have refused to become his wife.

Miss Owenson had begun to collect materials for another novel, upon an Indian subject. Her old friend

---

* A copy of some song, by P. Fitzgerald, Esq.

— not now her lover, though some folks thought so —
Sir Charles Ormsby, lent her a number of very valuable
works of reference from which, as her custom was, she
made extensive notes.

The following letter refers to them; the date is
omitted, as generally happens in her letters.

Miss Owenson to Sir C. Ormsby.

I have, at last, waded through your *Oriental Library*, and it is impossible *you* can ever feel the weight
of the obligation I owe you, except you turn author,
and some *kind* friend supplies you with rare books that
give the sanction of authority to your own wild and
improbable visions.

Your Indian histories place me upon the fairy
ground *you* know I love to tread, "where nothing is
but what is not," and you have contributed so largely
and so efficiently to my Indian venture, that you have
a right to a share in the profits, and a claim to be
considered a silent partner in the firm. I have to request you will send for your books, as I fear to trust
them to a porter.

Yours always,
S. OWENSON.

CHAPTER III.

BARON'S COURT.

LADY CHARLEVILLE, in her last letter, congratulated her young friend on having obtained the favour and protection of Lord and Lady Abercorn. These Abercorns were very great people. John James Hamilton, ninth earl and first marquis of his line, was of kin to the ducal Hamiltons, with their triple titles in Scotland, France, and England. He enjoyed in his own person the honour of four baronies, — Paisley, Abercorn, Hamilton, and Strabane; of two viscounties, — Hamilton and Strabane; as well as an earldom and a marquisate. In one respect he could boast of an advantage in rank above his cousin, the Duke of Hamilton, Brandon, and Chatelherault, — he was a peer in each of the three kingdoms, and could take his seat in the parliaments of London, Dublin, and Edinburgh. Only two other peers, Lord Moira and Viscount Grimstone, shared with him this great distinction. His Lordship had been married three times, had been the hero of a wretched and romantic divorce, and was now living at Stanmore Priory, with a third wife and a grown up family of children. This third wife, Anne-Jane, was a daughter of Lord Arran, and the widow of Mr. Hatton. Lord and Lady Abercorn had read the *Wild Irish Girl* and *The Novice of St. Dominic*, and been pleased with them; they had seen the authoress herself, and been equally pleased with her, and they thought they would like to take the young woman of genius to live with them and amuse them in their own house.

Lady Abercorn proposed to Miss Owenson, in a very kind and flattering manner, the wish of herself and the Marquis, that she should pass the chief part of every year with them, either at Baron's Court, in Ireland, or at Stanmore Priory, their seat near London; in short, that she should belong to them altogether, and only leave them occasionally to see her other friends.

Miss Owenson was, at that time, living in Dublin, more pleasantly situated than she had ever been in her life. She was quite independent, and yet close to her father and sister, enjoying for the first time the comfort of a family position surrounded by friends and pleasant acquaintances. She did not, at first, feel inclined to relinquish all these things for the sake of accepting Lady Abercorn's offer.

The friends who had, for so many years taken an interest in her welfare, joined in representing the great advantages of the position offered to her, and induced her to consent to go to Baron's Court for a time, without, however, binding herself to remain there. It amounted to a complete banishment from her own circle of society, as the Marquis and Marchioness were far too grand to recognise Dublin society. They were, however, eager to make their proposal pleasant to her in every way, and both before and after her acceptance, nothing could be more kind or highly bred than their conduct towards her on all occasions.

The Marquis was a very fine gentleman, the type of a class now extinct. He was convinced that the people of the lower orders were of a different nature, and made of different stuff to himself.

The groom of the chambers had orders to fumigate the rooms he occupied after liveried servants had been in them; and the chambermaids were not allowed to touch his bed except in white kid gloves. He himself always dressed *en grande tenue*, and never sat down at table except in his blue ribbon with the star and garter.

He was extremely handsome; noble and courtly in his manner; witty, sarcastic; a *roué* as regarded his principles towards women; a Tory in politics; fastidious, luxurious; refined in his habits, fascinating in his address; *blasé* upon pleasure and prosperity, yet capable of being amused by wit, and interested by a new voice and face. Altogether, he was about as dangerous a man for a brilliant young woman to be brought near as could easily be found. Miss Owenson had, however, the virtue for herself which she bestowed upon her heroines; her own sentiments and romance found their outlet and exercise in her novels, and she had, for all practical purposes, the strong, hard, common sense which called things by their right names, and never gave bewildering epithets to matters of plain right and wrong. She had no exaggerated generosity, nor sentiments of delicacy about other people's feelings. The veracity of common sense had become the habit of her mind, and she never tampered with it.

The Marchioness of Abercorn was as genuine a fine lady as the Marquis was a fine gentleman. In after years, Lady Morgan drew her portrait in *O'Donnell* as Lady Llamberris. She was good-natured and *inconséquente*. She took up people warmly and dropped them easily; she was incapable of a permanent attachment except to those belonging to herself.

Her enthusiasm for Miss Owenson was, however, marked by steady kindness for a considerable period; but their intercourse was of quite a different nature to that which existed between Miss Owenson and Lady Charleville, or Lady Stanley, or Mrs. Lefanu.

Miss Owenson's letters tell their own tale of the scenes and impressions of this period of her life.

She used to say, in referring to her life at Baron's Court and Stanmore Priory, where there was a succession of visitors, how little toilette was required in those days. Whilst at the Marquis of Abercorn's, she seldom wore anything except a white muslin dress with a flower in her bosom, until after she married; ornaments she possessed none, and her hair was dressed by the simple appliance of a wet brush to her abundant curls.

Miss Owenson to Mrs. Lefanu.

PRIORY,
January 18th, 1810.

Well, I am everything that by this you have said. I am "an idle, addle-pated, good-for-nothing thing," who, at the end of three months' absence, begins to remember there is somebody whose demands upon her grateful and affectionate recollection are undeniable; and who, in fact, she never ceases to love and respect, though she does not regularly tell her so by the week, "in a double letter from Northamptonshire;" and now, I dare say, a very clever letter you will expect. Alas! madam, that which in me "makes fat the ribs but bankrupts out the wits," the *morale*, in its excellence, bears no proportion to the physique, and I am, at this moment, the best lodged, best fed and dullest author in his Majesty's dominions. My memory comes surcharged with titles and pedigrees, and my fancy laden with stars and garters, — my deep study is pointed towards the red book, and my light reading to the French bill of fare which lies under my cover at dinner; but you will say, "hang your fancy, give me facts." *Hélas! ma belle*, I have none to relate, that your philosophic mind would not turn up its nose at. What is it to you that I live in one of the largest palaces in England? and that the sound of a commoner's name is refreshment to my organs, wearied out with the thrilling vibrations of "your Royal Highness," "your Grace," and "your Majesty!" Aye, now you open your big dark eyes, not knowing all the time (as how should you, poor soul!) that I am surrounded by ex-lord-lieutenants, unpopular princesses, and "deposed potentates," (for in the present state of things, we here are in the wrong box); on either side of me I find chatting Lords Westmorland and Hardwick (poor dears!) pop, then comes the Princess of Wales, with "quips and cranks and wreathed smiles," and "anon stalks by in royal sadness," the "exiled majesty of Sweden," who certainly deserves to reign, because he boldly *affiches* himself as *not* deserving to reign and says *toute bonnement*, "that his people were the best judges, and they were of *his opinion.*" This is *fact*, not fancy. The truth is that the *wonderful variety* of distinguished and extraordinary characters who come here, make it to me a most delicious *séjour*, — and though I am now going on my *fourth month* it seems as if I was beginning my first day. It were in vain to tell you the names of our numerous and fluctuating visitors, as they include those of more than half the nobility of England, and of *the first* class; add to which, many of the *wits*, authors, and existing ministers (poor dears!) The house is no house at all, for it looks like a little town, which you will believe when I tell you that a hundred and twenty people slept under the roof during the Christmas holidays without including the under servants; and that Lords Abercorn and Hamilton have between them nine apartments *en suite*, and Lady A. four. The Queen's chamberlain told me, indeed, that there was nothing like the whole establishment in England, and, perhaps, for a subject, in Europe. I have seen a great deal of the Devonshire family; the daughters are charming, and I am told, Lady G. Morpeth very like her mother, whom they all say, actually *died* in consequence of the shock she received from the novel of *The Winter in London*. What will please *you* more than anything is that I have *sold my book*, *The Missionary*, *famously*. That I am now correcting the proof sheets, and that I have sat to the celebrated Sir Thomas Lawrence for my picture, from which an engraving is done for my work.

I was presented almost immediately on my arrival to the Princess of Wales, who received me most graciously, and with whom I have dined. The Duchess of Gordon has been particularly kind and attentive to me, and is here frequently. We have at present a very celebrated person, *Payne Knight*, and Lord Aberdeen, who has a farm *at Athens*. He is married to one of our daughters.

I swore like a trooper to Livy I *would* be back by the 1st of January, but as that is past, I will be back

before the 1*st of March*, for these folk then move
themselves for Ireland, and it will be then time to
move off myself; so I propose myself to take a family
dinner *with you* the 1st of March *new* style.   Poor
Mrs. Wallace! she held out wondrously.   The last
day I saw her I did not think she would live a week,
and she lived twelve.   I hear he is *inconsolable* (poor
man!!) (do you perceive through all this a vein of
tender pity!) I wish he would get a star or garter
that I might smile on him, as it is "*nothing under nobility* approaches Mrs. Kitty.")   The majesty of the
people!!   Oh, how we laugh at such nonsense!   My
dear Mistress What-do-ye-call'em, can I do anything
for you, or the good man, your husband? command me.
As to the worthy person, your son, I have nothing
interesting to communicate to him, but that we have
had the Archbishops of York and Canterbury, and
they have exorcised the *evil spirit* out of me, so that I
shall go back to him a saint in grain.   Have you seen
Livy?   Love to all in a lump, and pray write to
me under cover to the Marquis, St. James's Square,
London.

Yours affectionately,

S. O.

The Mr. Wallace, who is referred to in the foregoing banter, was an eminent barrister and Q.C. at
the Irish bar.   A very warm friendship and esteem
of long duration had subsisted betwixt him and Miss
Owenson.   His wife had been a confirmed invalid, who
did not go out into society.   It may be inferred by
the sagacious reader, that Mr. Wallace had pretensions
to the hand which Sir Charles Ormsby and Archdeacon

King — not to speak of the minor crowd — had not succeeded in winning. There is a sly undertone of love-making in the following note of good advice: —

J. Wallace to Miss Owenson.

[*No date.*]

I cannot tell you, my sweet friend, how much pleasure your letter has given me! not because you have been panegyrizing me to your great friends, — nor because I have any, the most remote fancy, that those panegyrics can ultimately produce benefits to your friend; but because the unsought, disinterested, spontaneous testimonies of friendship, are with me above all value! Even if they were not *rare* they would be *precious*, — but when one who has seen as much of mankind as myself, and knows, *au fond*, how seldom a heart or a head can be found that is not exclusively occupied with its own cares, or pleasures, or interests; when such a one meets an instance of gratuitous and friendly solicitude about the interests or reputation of an absent connection, he gets a new consciousness of the value of his existence, by finding there is something in his *species* better than he expected. I profess to you to feel a sentiment of that kind from this last instance of your recollection of me; for I am so far a misanthrope, that I should not have been much surprised if a volatile little girl like *yourself*, fond of the pleasure and of the admiration of society, should have forgotten such a thing as *myself*, when immersed in the various enjoyments of such a circle as you are now surrounded by; not that I doubted you had friendship for me, — for of that I would have been certain; but I would have been easily persuaded that *present pleasure* might, for a time, have superseded *memory*, and postponed a recollection of *distant* friends and *past* scenes till a more convenient season. I confess, however, my sweet friend, that I entertained some fear that your zeal may have carried you a little too far in the conversation you mention; for anything in the way of *solicitation* or *canvass* would certainly, my dear Sydney, be to me one of the most mortifying things on earth; it would be at war with all my feelings and outrage all my principles; for there is but one thing in this world of which I can be vain — and it is a source of pleasure which nothing would induce me to forego — a *consciousness* that whatever I am, or whatever little success I may have in life, it is the pure and unmixed result of my own labours, uncherished and unpatronised. *One* instance only occurred in the course of my life, in which any attempt was made to promote my interests by the solicitation of friendship, and that became a source of great vexation to me, — it was that Mr. C. adverted to when he spoke of Ponsonby. Grattan, meaning to do a kind thing for me without my knowledge, applied to T. when he became Chancellor for a silk gown for me, and having got what he considered an explicit promise, he then mentioned the thing publicly, and it was known to half the profession before I heard of it. T. afterwards falsified his promise — by pretending that the promise was not for the *next* creation of king's counsel, but for the next but one. The consequence was the open declaration of war I made upon him — which most probably will for ever prevent me and Chancellors from being very good friends; for those fellows, like other classes of men, have a certain *esprit de corps,* and make common cause.

Speak of me, therefore, dear Sydney, *as your friend* as much as you please, praise me in *that* character as far as you can, and you confer an honour on me of which I shall ever be most proud; but beware, my sweet girl, of *patronage* or solicitation. Here has been twenty times too much of myself; but *you* have made the subject valuable by the attention you have paid to it.

What is the meaning of your question, "What are you to do with the rest of your life?" Can it be possible that a mind like yours should prove itself so feeble, that the passing enjoyments of a few months in "splendour and comfort" would disgust you with the ordinary habits of the world? This would be neither reason, nor philosophy, nor good taste; for good taste is good sense directed in a particular way; and good sense has a very *assimilating* quality and always fits us for "*existing circumstances.*" I do hope, notwithstanding the horror with which you seem to look at your *descent* from the pedestal, that you will be capable of enjoying the circumscribed, social, laughing, wise, foolish, playful little suppers which Mrs. * * * has given us, and, I hope, will again. By the way, *when* will you return? Mrs. Lefanu told me, on Saturday, you mentioned to her that you would be here in a fortnight and go back; and yet Mrs. C. knows nothing of it — *nor I.* I cannot help recurring again to your question, *What will you do with the rest of life?* I put the interrogatory to *myself* when I read your letter, — indeed, I have often asked myself the question — and what do you think I am likely to do? Most probably I shall retire to some very remote spot, where a small income will be an independence — and what then? J. W.

Miss Owenson had been slyly asking Mr. Wallace
what he meant to do with the rest of his life; and the
dull gentleman had not seen her joke. It was the
fashion for all the men to adore her; Sir Charles
Ormsby, Lord Guildford, Mr. Archdeacon King, Sir
Richard Phillips, even the Marquis of Abercorn; and
the crowd of lovers who were always flying about her
was the standing comedy of Lady Abercorn. Some
weeks after the death of his wife, Mr. Wallace received
a droll and wicked note from his fair correspondent.
Voltaire himself has nothing more droll than the alter-
native consolation offered to the widower — some being
who could think and feel with him — *or* a perusal of
the Essay on Manners. The political gossip is no less
amusing than the personal.

Miss Owenson to Mr. Wallace on the death of his Wife.

[No date.]

I write to you with reluctance, in which my heart
has no share; its natural impulses are always true to
pity and affection; to solace the afflicted is in me *no
virtue*, it is at once my nature and my habit, and if in
prosperity and joy my feelings vary their direction,
and ebb and flow to the influence of peculiar circumstances, in sorrow and in sadness they become fixed
and invariable, for, "laugh with those who rejoice,"
is less natural to me than to "weep with those who
weep;" yet respecting your grief (and the grief of a
man is to me always awful), not knowing in what
mood of mind my letter might find you, I waited till
it could be naturally supposed the first strong impressions of scenes of suffering and of melancholy

might be softened if not effaced, until nothing but a tender sadness not ungracious to the feelings remained. I know not how to use the common-place language of condolence; death has broken a tie which sometimes *galled* you; but it has also taken from you a *friend*, a sincere, an affectionate and faithful friend: for myself, young as I am, I have tried long enough to know and to feel the inconsequence of *life*. To *act right* according to those moral principles which nature has interwoven with our very constitution, and from which all the moral institutions of man are derived, is, I most *sincerely* and *solemnly* believe, the *sole good*, imperishable and lasting as long as we shall ourselves last, whether here or hereafter; that all the rest is subordinate and frail, I can assert upon my own experience. To-day, glancing my eyes over the *Novice of St. Dominic*, I was struck by the ardour, the enthusiasm, the fertility of invention, in short by all the brilliant illusions of untried youth, which gleamed in every line. I opposed them by the old, tame nature of my present feelings; — my *disappointed* heart, my *exhausted* imagination, and I had the weakness to drop tears on the page as I read; but *I dried them soon*, and I could not help thinking, that while the pleasures of the senses and the fancy of youth and the world, left behind them but idle and transient regrets, the consciousness of having always *acted right* alone remained to comfort and support, to cheer and solace; it is a triumph purchased, indeed, by many temporary sacrifices; and many an imperious wish, and many a fond desire is trampled on to obtain it. This is a very *triste* style for me, you will say, but it is my prevailing tone at this moment, and, indeed, in spite of those

states of vivacity to which I am subject, my susceptible
spirits reflect back the trouble of gay and brilliant objects. My natural character is that of one who thinks
deeply, and who naturally loves to repose in the tranquillity of meditation, who "sets loose to life," and who
is almost wearied out by the harassing vicissitudes
which "flesh is heir to." This you will not believe;
for it is among the things I have most to lament, that
you have not had *tact* to come at the real character of
your friend, nor the confidence to believe her own
assertions on the subject; you would be surprised to see
me here, stealing away from the dazzling multitude,
and passing whole days in my own room, reading some
grave philosophical work; thinking deeply — and feeling
acutely — going to the *source* of some obscure subject
— or giving myself up to tender and pensive memories,
which have for their object those that are *most dear* and
most distant. Yet this I do constantly . . . and yet I
return to society — not its most undistinguished or least
brilliant member.

If I could be of the least use to you, I should not
hesitate to fly to you in your afflictions; believe me,
when I solemnly assert, *that nothing on this earth should
prevent me*, neither the *pleasures* of the world or its
OPINIONS; but you are surrounded by friends, and
I think you have that confidence in my friendship,
that you would *call* on me if *you wanted me.* My
return to Ireland is uncertain. I am pretty *weary
of the sameness* of things *here*, where there is nothing
in the least *to interest the heart*, — they are all extremely anxious I should stay till March, as they
then mean to have private theatricals; but I would
fly to the end of the world from a species of amuse-

ment to me, of all others, the most faded and egotistical; it is, therefore, most probable, I shall abide by my original intention and leave this early in February.

I hear of nothing but politics, and the manner in which things are considered, give me a most thorough contempt for the "*rulers of the earth;*" I am *certain* that the country, its welfare or prosperity, never for a moment, make a part in their speculation; it is all a *little miserable system of self-interests*, paltry distinctions, of private pique, and personal ambition. I sometimes with difficulty keep in my indignation when I hear them talk of such a person and his *eight* men, and such an one and his *five*, and so on, for there is not one of the noted demagogues you read of, who do not carry with them a certain number of followers, who vote *à tort et à travers*, as their leader bids them; it is thus we are *represented* — the order of the day is as follows, Lord Grey, *Premier*, with the *common consent* of the nation, (except the particular party going out) Lord Erskine, Chancellor; Lord Moira, Commander of the Forces; Lord Lansdown, Lord Lieutenant of Ireland; Lord Manners resigns — they *murmur* something of *Plunket* succeeding him; Lord *Holland nothing;* notwithstanding what the papers say, nothing has been laid out for *Ponsonby*, he is looked on as the captain or ringleader of the House of Commons. Sheridan is held in contempt on *all sides;* but the Prince, who is cold to him, will make him, they say, *Paymaster* to the Navy. Such are the appointments the Prince has made out; but *Lord Abercorn* thinks they will not take place, as the King is mending fast. The anxiety and solicitude in all whom I see here, and who are interested for the issue of the business, *have disgusted me* for ever with those *falsely* called the *great.* Lord Abercorn, who always votes himself a *King's man,* preserves an armed neutrality, and though, according to *my* principles and feelings, he is *decidedly wrong,* yet it is impossible not to respect his independence. All wonder at Erskine's elevation, as he is deemed *literally mad.* Your future viceroy proposed, some time ago, for my sweet new friend, whom I believe I have mentioned to you — *Lady Hamilton* (don't mention this to any one): but was refused by *Papa.* She has become a great tie to me now, and her obvious affection for me is my greatest pride. She is a most superior and charming woman, though cold in her general manner and rigid in her principles. She is, in her person, like Lord Abercorn more than any of his children; but her character is composed of firmer stuff. I hope, one day or other, to present her to you. She met lately, by chance, at Brighton, with the *Grattans,* and is an *enthusiast* in admiration of *them,* as they *must be* of her. She says she envies that middle rank of life, and would give up her own situation willingly for *theirs.*

Farewell; this is a dull epistle, but I am as little in the mood to write gay letters as you are probably to read them. I hope Clarke has made you the offer of his house till your own is made comfortable for your residence. How and where is your dear boy? How is Mr. Hande — and where? It was in a letter from *Old Atkinson* that I first heard of your loss. I was shocked and surprised, for I all along thought that, though perfect recovery was impossible, yet that *years* of life might be still enjoyed, or rather endured. To me death has little terrors. I always look to it as to a wished-for, and necessary repose; they alone know to estimate life who, like me, have known *is great extremes*, and, let me add, they alone *can despise it*.

Once more farewell.

PS. Let me *entreat* that you will take particular care of my letters. Did you receive one from me dated the 12th. I have written *five* letters to the Clarkes since Twelfth-night, and they deny getting a single letter.

Nothing, perhaps, under your present feelings would so much *distrait* your mind as an interview with some being who would *think* and *feel* with you, for sorrow *can* know no solace. With the sympathy of intellect and sensibility blended in one, but next to that, you will find most relief from a particular style of reading which *awakens*, without fatiguing, the mind. Let me, therefore, recommend to you a work in which this moment I am deeply engaged, and which is beside me. It might be called "L'Esprit de la Raison," for never was so much delicate wit, such exquisite irony, and such incomparable humour, applied to the development of the most profound subjects that Philosophy ever *called* to the tribunal of human reason. I mean Voltaire's *Essai sur les mœurs et l'esprit des nations et sur les principaux faits de l'histoire depuis Charlemagne jusqu'à Louis XIII.* Read it, if you have not already read it, or if you have! —

Ah! what a woman's postscript!!!

CHAPTER IV.

THE MISSIONARY.

WHILST at Baron's Court, Miss Owenson completed her Indian novel of the *Missionary*, and every day, when there were no visitors, she used to read aloud, after dinner, to the Marquis and Marchioness, what she had written in the morning. She said, when talking of these times in after life, that the Marquis used to quiz her most unmercifully, declaring that the story was "the greatest nonsense he had ever heard in his life," which did not, however, prevent him from listening to it with great amusement. Lady Abercorn yawned over it very dismally. Certainly, a more romantic or a more foolish story could scarcely be imagined.

When the book was completed, she purposed to go over to England to arrange about the publication, and left Baron's Court on her way east for that purpose; but she delayed her journey, loitering in Dublin to see her friends. The Marquis and Marchioness of Abercorn wrote to her whilst she was there.

From their letters, by the way, a few amusing extracts may be culled. The "glorvina," about which her ladyship writes, was a golden bodkin for fastening up the hair, after the pattern of an antique Irish ornament, and was called a "glorvina," in honour of the *Wild Irish Girl*, who, in the novel, wears one of similar fashion. The Marchioness had a passion for ordering anything she heard of, and she invariably disliked it, or grew tired of it, before it could be sent to her — a peculiarity extremely embarrassing to those whom she honoured with her commissions. The reference to *le bien aimé* is to Sir Charles Ormsby, whom Lady Abercorn still regarded as Miss Owenson's adorer.

Marchioness of Abercorn to Miss Owenson.

[*No date.*]

DEAR MISS OWENSON,

You know so well the way we contrive to find no time for anything in this house, that I am sure you will not accuse me of ingratitude in not having thanked you, either on Saturday or Sunday for two delightful letters I have of yours, as well as for the songs and French letters, and the designs for glorvinas, &c., &c.; but Saturday was so delightful, that I was out from breakfast till dinner, and yesterday, I went to church (where, *par parenthesis*, there is the most delightful singing you can imagine), and after church, my usual Sunday walk with *mon époux* filled up the morn. You also know, that after dinner, what with hot wine and hot dishes, I am never in a state to write a *clear* letter; and after this *exposé*, you will not be surprised that I have not sooner taken notice of what I neither admire or like the less for not having said so.

I hope you yourself did not suffer from fatigue and anxiety, and that you are now in as perfect health, beauty, and spirits, as you ought to be.

Now for my glorvinas. Could you not enclose the one you think "*precisely what I should like*," the price three guineas, and I can order the others after I have seen it. I think I should like to have the motto on Lady Hamilton's glorvina "Our hopes rest on thy dear black head." Now do not laugh at my way of expressing what I wish *you* to put in *better language*, and in Irish; but I think we might unite *notre espérance* and the *black head*, which we fixed upon, for this glorvina.

As to the Princess's, I intend only a glorvina, and the motto you mention would be very pretty; but that must be very handsome, and as it will not take long to make, I conclude, it shall be the last.

I should like to see a small ten guinea Irish harp; but it would not be advisable to risk sending it by post.

Before this, you will have seen Miss Butler; I did hope to have heard from her to-day. I trust she did not catch cold on the journey, and that she will find the *festivities* of Dublin repay her for the inconvenience.

Nothing new has occurred since you left us; you, and your harp, we miss in every possible way. It was a pity you did not wait till the *Councillors* returned to town, for perhaps, had you been with us, we might have invited *le bien-aimé*, who will, of course, be at Armagh this week; as it is we shall not.

Have you sent the *Luxima* to England, yet? pray tell me, for though I never wished to hear it read ten pages at a time, I am very impatient to see it all together, and sincerely anxious for its success.

Yours, dear Miss Owenson,
Very sincerely,
A. J. A.

This is a most horrible griffonnage; but if I attempted to write it over again I should never send

3*

it, and I dare not even read it for fear I should think, for my own credit, it should be consigned to the flames.

The "Jane" mentioned in Lord Abercorn's note, which follows next, is Anne Jane, his third wife and Marchioness. The "Livy," with whom Lord Abercorn threatened to fall in love, is Lady Clarke, Miss Owenson's beautiful sister.

Lord Abercorn to Miss Owenson.

Wednesday.

This, you know, is audience-day, *dear little Glo.* (what familiarity to a great Princess!), so I have not a minute of morning to myself. But, as to-morrow is audience-day too, and next day Friday, I determine to thank you for your letter, in a hurry, rather than seem ungracious and ungrateful in the first instance; for though I have made my bargain to be allowed dryness and delay in general, I must begin with sweetness and punctuality.

So here I am, with my dinner in my throat, and my coffee in my mouth (having left my arm chair and your "boudoir," to console each other in our absence), just to assure you what you know well enough, that I have not yet forgotten you; and also what I have already assured you through Jane, that I understood, and (in your own phrase) appreciated your dislike to parting words and looks. I was going on, but will stop for fear of falling into the tender and sentimental, so, once for all, assure yourself that I feel your feelings as they deserve — as our friends the Orientals say, "what can I say more?"

I think, under the various circumstances of the case, I have written as much now as I well can, or you will wish, so, till your next letter and "Livy's" postscript bring me fresh materials, bye! bye! Have you told her that I have some thoughts of falling in love with her, if we ever meet?

Need I say, that I am and ever shall be,

Your affectionate,

A.

Lady Abercorn to Miss Owenson.

[*No date.*]

Dear Miss O.,

I received the Glorvina this morning, which I do not very much admire, and as *I do know* you do not mind trouble, I sent it back to you, and wish you would ask the man what he would do one for me of Irish gold, with the shamrock on the head in small Irish diamonds, which I think would look very well.

My harp will be beautiful, and of course I chose Hawk head, and should also like the threefold honours as ornaments; it is a pity we cannot introduce the crest and the garter, that it might be perfect. I believe, when the Garter was instituted, that the wives of the knights had a right to a bracelet with the motto; if so, I do not know why I should not introduce it on my harp, as it will, I hope, be a specimen of Irish ingenuity long after I am in another and a better world, and may be the cause of considerable curiosity (to some persons unacquainted with the history of the ' noble house of Hamilton) in future ages, which is an interesting consideration to me. I hope *the groupe* will not be preserved so long, unless you write a novel in

which you introduce the modern Solyman and his
sultanas, for I confess I should never lament that such
a quiz had lived a generation before. Seriously, it is
quite a monster; I hope you did not really see him
as you drew him. Julia was quite angry that such a
thing was intended for *pretty brother*.

Why do you tell me of Mademoiselle Espinasse's
letters if you cannot get them for me? perhaps you
could get them at Archer's — pray try. *Alfieri* has
been long promised to me from England, but has never
arrived.

I do congratulate you upon the conquest you have
made of the Duchess of Gordon. If she does not *find
you in her way*, you will find her pleasant; but beware
of that.

You know I never felt much for any mortifications
the Miss G— might receive, so the present does not
make me very unhappy. I dare say the Duchess of
Gordon will be more kind to them.

We have had Captain Pakenham here some days;
he has just gone to Lifford, but is to return on Wednesday. He is a very pleasant young man; I wish
he had been here when you were, that your recollection of Baron's Court might have been more
lively.

I have got two cantos of the *Lady of the Lake* —
as beautiful as possible. You cannot write too much
or too often, so make no excuse for doing so; but do
pray fold your letters as *I do*, and put a cover over
them, as I lose half of your precious words by the way
they are put up.

I am very glad your friend Mr. Atkinson will not
give your money to the Granards; it would be too

foolish to lose one's *all* out of delicacy. When it is well disposed of, let me know, as I shall feel very anxious.

As I cannot, in any other way, copy Glorvina, I am trying to make my handwriting as unintelligible as possible, that at least in something there may be some similitude, and, therefore, scratch and blot at a great rate, and console myself, when I look at a horrid griffonnage, by the conviction that it is a proof of genius!!!

Remember, I am only joking about the garter and crest.

Yours, dear Miss O., sincerely,

A. J. A.

Lord Abercorn thinks you very foolish not to send your novel to London immediately, as the season is passing over. So mind you do.

The Missionary was sent over from Dublin; and Phillips, who was her regular publisher, put it to press. But the publisher and author began to quarrel about terms, as they were pretty sure to do; the young Irish girl being quite as sharp as the experienced Welsh tradesman. On which side the wrong lay, and on which the offence, it would be idle to enquire. Most authors quarrel with their publishers, and will probably do so to the end of time. Miss Owenson had the highest sense of her own worth, not only to the public but to the trade. She thought her right to the lion's share of profit on her book clear; a pretension which Phillips would not allow. After printing a volume, the press was stopped. The manuscript had to be recovered, and a new "adventurer in setting forth" found.   Stockdale and Miller were the rival powers in the trade; and, with these gentlemen, Lady Abercorn, on her removal to Stanmore Priory, began to negociate for her friend, who still remained in Ireland.

Lady Abercorn to Miss Owenson.

[*No date.*]

MY DEAR MISS O.,

I shall go to town in a few days, and I will call on Miller, and see whether he is worthy of introducing your *Wanderer.*   I am sorry you had anything to do with that shabby man — Phillips; I hope, however, you have recovered the manuscript, and that you will learn wisdom from experience, for I think, notwithstanding your talents — which I do not underrate, I assure you — a little worldly wisdom is one you do not possess; so pray set to work and acquire some small share of it, if you can.   If you should think coming to England will forward any of your plans, *you know where to come*, and this is a very convenient distance from London, you can get there as often as you like.

My harp, I have no doubt, will be perfect; alas! who is to play it? for Lady Aberdeen is the only one in this family who can, and she is soon going to the sea — the rest of the family will remain here till after Christmas.

You do not say to whom you have consigned my harp, nor do you mention having sent your picture, which I was to have if I liked it better than the one I now possess.

Walter Scott's success exceeds everything; the quarto edition of two thousand did not last a fortnight, and upwards of four thousand of the octavo are gone; it is liked much better than any of the others.

I have seen both Mr. Knight and Mr. Price, here, since my arrival, and many other friends; but none that you know from reputation, except those two. I think Mr. Knight more agreeable than ever. I am sorry to tell you Lord Guildford is to be married next Thursday, so you must think of some one else.

None of your friends forget you, I assure you; Julia often talks of you — she is as *violent* an Irish girl as she ever was. Her brother Charles has been here for a week, which gave her great pleasure. He is a very fine boy — or a little man, I may venture to say.

Pray who are your two new lovers?

I am not a little stupid at present, I can tell you. I want the harmony of the Irish war harp to revive me. I have felt a little *le mal du pays* since I returned here; but you must not tell, mind!

God bless you, my dear Glorvina,
Yours, sincerely,

A. J. A.

Lady Abercorn to Miss Owenson.

STANMORE PRIORY.

DEAR GLORVINA,

Your harp is arrived, and *for the honour of Ireland, I must tell you,* it is very much admired and quite beautiful. Lady Aberdeen played on it for an hour, last night, and thought it very good, *almost* as good

as a French harp, and perhaps will be quite as good
when it has recovered the *fatigues* of the journey;
pray tell poor Egam I shall show it off to the best
advantage, and I sincerely hope he will have many
orders in consequence.

The Baron's Court field flowers were very well
received; but as Frances is thanking you herself I
have nothing more to say. The harp suffered a little
in the journey; but I shall, I hope, be able to get it
repaired.

I went to Miller, the day before yesterday, and
was as civil as possible to him; paid him many compliments upon his liberality to people of genius; talked
of Walter Scott, and proposed his publishing your new
novel, saying, you expected five hundred pounds for
it; but I do not think he answered as *your proud spirit*
would quite like, for he said he would not purchase a
novel from any one in the *United Kingdom* (nor did he
except Walter Scott) without reading it first; and, in
short, I did not proceed, for I know how high Glorvina is, and I was satisfied he was not the person who
was to introduce her *Missionary*. He is, however, to
be in Dublin in three weeks, and I was to give him a
letter to you; but I did not, as I am sure he can *find
you out* in Dublin.

I shall be very happy, I assure you, to see you
when you come to England, nor do I at present see
any thing that would make it necessary for me to
say, "your hour is not come." I know of nothing
that could, except what I trust in God will not occur
— the illness of those dear to me. I have seen your
friend, Mr. Gell, and heard him speak very *prettily*
of you.

If you knew how much I am hurried, and what a pain I have in my shoulder from the rheumatism, you would say, I was *very good* to write to-day; but I had those things I wished to *express* immediately — my failure with Miller, my admiration of the harp, and that I shall have great pleasure in seeing you here whenever you come.

A. J. A.

CHAPTER V.

VISIT TO LONDON.

When Miss Owenson at length came to London to arrange with the publishers about her *Missionary*, she took up her abode with Captain and Mrs. Patterson, who resided in good style in York Place, Portman Square, a residence more convenient to her than Stanmore Priory. She mixed eagerly and freely with the best people in London, and was particularly at home with the lions and lionesses. At this time she made the acquaintance of Lord Cockrane, then just home from his glorious exploits in the Basque roads. A note to Lady Stanley will also show that she had also become an acquaintance of Nelson's Lady Hamilton — "the famous" — as she calls her, by way of distinction from the Lady Hamilton of Stanmore Priory. The letter is franked by Lord Cockrane.

Miss Owenson to Lady Stanley.

12, YORK PLACE, PORTMAN SQUARE, LONDON,
April 20th, 1810.

Your letter made me roar. I was in Berkshire

when it arrived, and only got it three days back, but as my franker is not in town, I must defer placing the *Missionary* in your hands until the same moment I kiss them, which will be this day week. I leave this the 30th (*the evening of Tuesday next*), so that is pretty plain. My trunk goes directed for your lady-ship's *to-morrow.* To-night I expect your enchanting son to sup with me; were it not *a sin to love him*, what a passion I could feel for him! I have asked Lady Hamilton to meet him — *the famous.* I will explain the mistake of the book when we meet — till that, *joyeuse revoir*, and ever

Your devoted

GLORVINA.

Will you not send for me to Holyhead?

Lady Morgan used to tell a story about herself in these early days of her first introduction to fashionable society. She had little money, and but a slender wardrobe of smart things. In those days, dress was expensive, and white satin shoes were *spécialités* that every young lady did not command. One evening, at some party, the company were practising the waltz, then very recently introduced into England; Lord Hart-ington was Miss Owenson's partner; she was dancing with energy, when her foot slipped, and in the effort to recover herself, one of her white slippers, the pride of her heart — her only pair — was split beyond retrieval. She felt so mortified at the accident that she burst into tears. Lord Hartington was distressed, and en-treated to know the cause of her sudden affliction. "My satin shoes are ruined, and I have not another

pair!" Lord Hartington did not laugh, but said very
kindly, "Don't cry for that, dear Glorvina, you shall
have the very prettiest pair of white satin shoes that
can be found in all Paris."

He was then on the point of starting for France,
and he was as good as his promise. The shoes came in
the next ambassador's bag, and were sent to her with
the following note.

*From the Duke of Devonshire, when Lord Hartington,
to Miss Owenson.*

Tuesday.

My dear Miss Owenson,

I send you the long-promised shoes, which, however, without your encouragement last night, would
not have dared present themselves to you. They are
not what I intended, being like all other shoes; but
Paris could never produce anything like the vision of
a shoe that I had in my mind's eye for you. I depend
upon your sending me Luxima, and beg you to believe
me, dear Miss Owenson,

Most truly, your obliged servant,
HARTINGTON.

In the reply which she sent to this gallant epistle,
Miss Owenson referred to the loss of her liberty —
meaning that she had made up her mind to close with
Lady Abercorn's offer, and go into her household.

Miss Owenson to the Duke of Devonshire.

Before *The Wild Irish Girl* is *mit aux abois*, and
taken alive in the snare that has been artfully laid for

her, she begs to lay at your grace's feet the last offerings of her liberty; and by whatever name your Grace may prefer of the four you bestowed on me — whether *Puck* or Glorvina, Luxima or *Mother* Goose, she invokes your acceptance of the trifle which accompanies this.

She is ignorant whether her *keepers* mean to exhibit her for her intelligence or ferocity, like the learned pig at Exeter Change, or the beautiful hyena at the Tower, which never was tamed. But whatever part she is destined to play in her cage, it is certain that she will often look forth with delight to those days of her freedom, when, untaught and untamed, she contributed to your Grace's amusement, and imbibed those sentiments of respect and esteem for your character, with which she has the honour to subscribe herself your

Obliged and obedient servant,

GLORVINA.

There is some mystery about Miss Owenson's relations to Sir Charles Ormsby at this time, which is not wholly explained in Lady Morgan's papers. Among them is a letter endorsed in her own handwriting: —

"Last farewell letter to Sir C. Ormsby, returned with the rest of my letters and my ring after his death, which took place in 1816."

Miss Owenson to Sir C. Ormsby, Bart.

Tuesday.

I am told you have had the kindness to call more than once since your arrival in town at my door. I should have anticipated the intention and endeavoured to prevent it; but the fact is, I did not wish to intrust a letter to another person's servant, and still less to send my own to your house.

It is with inexpressible regret that I am obliged to decline your visits. I have no hesitation in declaring that I prized your society beyond any enjoyment within my sphere of attainment, and that in relinquishing it for ever, I do a violence to my feelings which raises me in my own estimation, without reconciling me to the sacrifice I have made.

The only intercourse that could subsist between us, proximity has destroyed. I thought your circuit would have lasted five weeks. I thought I should have been in England before your return, and all this would have been spared me. Were I to tell you the motive that detains me in Ireland longer than I wish or expected, you would give me your applause. At least do not withdraw from me your esteem, it is the only sentiment that ever ought to subsist between us. I owe you a thousand kindnesses, a thousand attentions; my heart is full of them. Whilst I exist, the recollection of all I owe you shall form a part of that existence.

Farewell!

Have the goodness to send me my answer to your last letter, — it was written under the influence of a nervous indisposition and exhibits a state of mind I should blush to have indulged in.

The affair between Miss Owenson and the *bien aimé* had cost her a good deal of trouble and anxiety — and it had been for some time on a very unsatisfactory footing. They met in society afterwards, and he always retained a strong and friendly interest in her career.

Miss Owenson went from York Place to the Priory and remained there some little time. During this visit, Lord Castlereagh, who had been favoured with hearing some of the MS. read aloud — which he greatly admired — offered to take Miss Owenson to town in his chariot, and to give a *rendezvous* to her publisher in his own study; an offer which was, of course, accepted. Stockdale was the publisher with whom she was then in treaty.

He was punctual to his appointment, and was naturally impressed by the environments, which gave him a higher opinion of Miss Owenson's genius than he had felt before. The opportunity to make a good bargain was improved by Miss Owenson, Lord Castlereagh himself standing by whilst the agreement was signed. His lordship was, perhaps, the greatest admirer the *Missionary* ever found; it was not so popular as her other novels. She had read up a great deal for Indian customs, history and antiquities; but India was India to her; and the manners and customs, races and countries, were all confounded together in the rose-coloured mist of fine writing and high-flown sentiment. The subject is the attempt of a Spanish priest to convert a Brahmin priestess; but the flesh gets the better of the spirit in this trial; they fall in love with each other's fine eyes, and elope together. The love scenes are warmly coloured, and the situations of the Hindoo priestess and her lover are highly critical; but the reader feels disposed to say as Sheridan said, when the servant threw down a china plate with a great crash, without breaking, "You rascal! how dare you make all that noise for nothing?" Nothing comes of all the danger, and everything remains much as it was in the beginning.

Miss Owenson to Lady Stanley, Penrhôs.

PRIORY, STANMORE,
November 20, 1810.

MY DEAR LADY STANLEY,

I ought to have announced my arrival to you before this; but I have been involved, engaged, dazzled, and you who are a philosopher, and see human nature just as it is, will account for and excuse this, and say, she is not ungrateful nor negligent, *she is only human.* My *entrée* here was attended by every circumstance that could render it delightful or gracious to my feelings. A coach-and-four was sent to meet me thirty miles off, and missed me. I remained a day or two in London with my very kind friends the Pattersons. I hold my place of *first favourite*, and the favour I formerly enjoyed seems rather increased than diminished. No words can give the idea of the *extent* or splendour of this princely palace. Everything is great and magnificent. We have had some of the noble house of Percy with us — very good sort of people — Lord Bathurst, and others; at present we are *en famille*, but expect a reinforcement to-morrow. There is something so singular and brilliant in the place that we are almost independent of society. My journey was uncommonly comfortable and snug, and I was very little fagged, all things considered, and went through the two nights without drooping. We are going to drive into town. Kindest of all kind friends, remember

GLORVINA.

Among the visitors at Stanmore Priory was Sir Thomas Lawrence, who painted the exquisite sketch of Miss Owenson prefixed to this volume; the story of which is told in his graceful epistles: —

Sir Thomas Lawrence to Miss Owenson.

GREEK STREET,
December 7th, 1810.

MY DEAR MADAM,

If you knew how little at this moment I am master of my time, you would readily pardon me for the freedom I take with the Marchioness and yourself, in naming Wednesday next for my waiting on her ladyship, instead of the appointment fixed for to-morrow. The considerations you have mentioned, do, indeed, make it necessary that the drawing should be finished in the next week, and upon my word of honour to you, if the Marquis and Marchioness permit me to go to the Priory on Wednesday, the drawing *shall* be finished within the week.

You write to me with so much good humour, and so far below your claims on my thankfulness, for allowing me to attempt this gratification to your friends and the public, that I am the more vexed at my ill fortune, in dooming me to begin it with so ill a grace.

The temple you speak of is a pretty, fanciful building, but there is something very cold and chilling in that said "vestibule." If another door opens, let me go in with you!

Believe me, with the greatest respect,

My dear Madam, yours,

T. LAWRENCE.

Sir Thomas Lawrence to Sydney Owenson.

December 21st, 1810.

My evil genius does haunt me, my dear madam, but not in your shape — on the contrary, I believe that it takes you for my good one, for it is very studious to prevent my seeing you. To morrow I cannot, Sunday I cannot; but I will make it as early in this ensuing week as my distractions will admit.

"*Doldrums and bother*," are weak terms for ladies of your invention — at least, they touch not my state of misery. You tell me that any hour will do, because the Duchess of Gordon and Lord Erskine are satisfied with the likeness. It is because they are enemies of my reputation. The former because I once (as she fancies) painted an arm or a finger too long or too short in her relation's* picture. The latter, because I neglected to make an animated beauty of a dead wife (but good faith and forgetfulness of this fact, I beg of you); but still I have a great respect for him, and will try to think better of the drawing that he has liked. "*Striking and beautiful*," is certainly a most liberal translation of "*flagrant and inveterate*"; but Miss Butler's connections are always on the favorable side. If she knew but how to quiz, she would be very captivating.

I have seen Mr. Campbell,** who is more anxious than you are for the meeting. But I will tell you of his *admiration, delight, impatience*, &c., &c., &c., when

* The Marchioness of Cornwallis.
** The poet and author of the *Pleasures of Hope*.

4*

we meet, which I repeat shall be as soon in the next week as possible.

I remain, my dear madam,
Most truly yours,
T. LAWRENCE.

PS. I have written in haste, emulous of the restless rapidity of your hands; but it is Scrub's imitation of Archer — you have a happy insolence of scrawl that I never yet saw equalled.

CHAPTER VI.

LADY MORGAN PAINTED BY HERSELF AND SIR THOMAS LAWRENCE.

THE following passage is a frank confession of principle and practice from a young, much admired, and unmarried woman. It is from a diary of the year 1811. In Lady Morgan's own writing it is endorsed

"Self, 1811."

Inconsiderate and indiscreet, never saved by prudence, but often rescued by pride; often on the very verge of error, but never passing the line. Committing myself in every way — *except in my own esteem,* — without any command over my feelings, my words, or writings, — yet full of self-possession as to action and conduct, — once reaching the boundary of right even with my feet on the threshold of wrong; capable, like a *menage* horse, of stopping short, coolly considering the risk I encounter, and turning sharply back for the post from whence I started, feeling myself quite safe, and, in a word — *quitte pour la peur.*

Early imbued with the high sentiments belonging to good birth, and with the fine feelings which accompany good education. My father was a player and a gentleman. I learned early to feel acutely my situation; my nature was supremely above my circumstances and situation, the first principle or passion that rooted in my breast, was a species of proud indignation, which accompanies me to that premature death, of which it is finally the cause. My first point of society was to behold the conflict between two unequal minds — the one (my mother) strong and rigid — the other weak and yielding; the one strong to arrest dispute — the other accelerating its approach. The details which made up the mass were — seeing a father frequently torn to prison — a mother on the point of beggary with her children, and all those shocks of suffering which human nature can disdain, and which can only occur in a certain sphere of life and a certain state of society. Man, who has his appetites to gratify, which Nature supplies in his social or artificial character, has thousands of wants which suffering poverty may deny; and even their gratification is not always attended with effects proportionate to their cause. So delicately and fatally organised, that objects impalpable to others, were by me accurately perceived, felt and combined; that the faint ray which neither warmed nor brightened, often gave a glow and a lustre to my spirits; that the faintest vapour through its evanescent passage through the atmosphere, threw no shadow on the most reflecting object, darkened my prospects, and gloomed my thoughts. Oh! it was this unhappy physical organisation, this nervous susceptibility to every impression which circulated through my frame and rendered the whole system acute, which formed the basis of that condition of my mind and being, upon which circumstances and events raised the after superstructure. So few have been the days on which I sighed not that night close on them for ever — that I could now distinctly count them — alas! were they not the most dangerous of my days; the smiling and delusive preparations of supreme misery which time never failed to administer.

It may be supposed that life hastens to its close when its views are thus tinged with hues so dark and so terrific? But the hand which now writes this has lost nothing of the contour of health or the symmetry of youth. I am in possession of all the fame I ever hoped or ambitioned. I wear not the appearance of twenty years; I am now, as I generally am, sad and miserable.

SYDNEY OWENSON.

July 12th, 1811, Dublin.

This tendency to depression of spirits — which, the reader should remember, was exhibited before the whole world had learned from Byron to turn down its shirt collar, and express the elegant despair of Childe Harold, — induced her to put away sorrow as an evil thing; her cheerfulness was a reality — a habit of mind which she carefully and systematically cultivated.

Another entry in the next page is of the same tone.

"It is a melancholy conviction that all my starts of happiness are but illusions; that I feel I do but dream

even while I am dreaming, — and that in the midst of
the inebriety I court, I am haunted by the expectation
of being awakened to that state of hopeless melancholy which alone is real — and felt and known to
be so.   It is in vain that my fancy steeps me in forgetfulness.   The happy wreath which the finger of
peace wreathed round my head, suddenly drops off,
and the soft vapours that encircled it, scathe and dis-
sipate; — all in truth and fact, sad, dreary and miserable —

" 'I may submit to occasions, but I cannot stoop to persons.'

"I may not say with Proverbs — 'Wisdom dwelleth
with Prudence.'"

The position of this young woman of genius in the
household of a great family, if brilliant in outward
show, was accompanied by a thousand vexations. The
elopement of Marchioness Cecil with Lieutenant Copley
had not increased Lord Abercorn's native respect for
female virtue.   The third wife and her husband lived
on terms of excessive politeness with each other; and
poor Miss Owenson was expected to bear their tempers
and attentions; to sit in the cross-fire of their humours,
and to find good spirits and sprightly conversation
when they were dull.   Add to this, that heavy pressure of anxiety about family matters which was laid
upon her before her nerves and sinews were braced to
meet it, and before she had any worldly knowledge,
produced a feeling of exhaustion.   In the material
prosperity of her life at Baron's Court, the tension
relaxed, and the fatigue of past exertion asserted itself.

Her own ambition had never allowed her to rest; she had been wonderfully successful; but, at Baron's Court and Stanmore Priory, all she had obtained looked dwarfed and small when measured by the hereditary power and consequence of the family in which she was for the time an inmate. She did not become discontented; but she was disenchanted (for the time) with all that belonged to herself, and saw her own position on its true comparative scale. Sydney Owenson, from earliest childhood had depended on herself alone for counsel and support. There is no sign that she ever felt those moments of religious aspiration, when a human being, sensible of its own weakness and ignorance, cries for help to Him who made us; there are no ejaculations of prayer, or of thanksgiving; she proudly took up her own burden and bore it as well as she could; finding her own way and shaping her life according to her own idea of what ought to form her being's end and aim. She was a courageous, indomitable spirit, but the constant dependence on herself, the steady concentration of purpose with which she followed out her own career, without letting herself be turned aside, gave a hardness to her nature, which, though it did not destroy her kindness and honesty of heart, petrified the tender grace which makes the charm of goodness. No one can judge Sydney Owenson, because no one can know all the struggles, difficulties, temptations, flatteries and defamation, which she had to encounter, without the shelter or support of a home or the circle of home relatives. She remained an indestructibly honest woman; but every faculty she possessed had undergone a change, which seemed to make her of a different species to other women.

The portrait of Miss Owenson was at length finished by Sir Thomas Lawrence, and the romance of *The Missionary* printed by Stockdale. The portrait was to be prefixed; but Lawrence, for the reasons given, requested that his name might *not* appear.

Sir Thomas Lawrence to Miss Owenson.

GREEK STREET,
January 21st, 1811.

DEAR MADAM,

I must be indebted to your kindness (and I fear it must put you to the trouble of writing) for preventing the insertion of my name in Mr. Stockdale's advertisement.

I have an anxious desire that the readers of *The Missionary* may be gratified with as accurate a resemblance of its author, as can in that size be given, but from the drawing being so much reduced, the engraving must be comparatively defective; and besides this, I have no wish to be seen to interfere with the province of other artists who are professionally employed in making portraits for books.

There are many of them whose talents I very highly respect, and might reasonably be jealous of, did they encroach on *my* province in painting, but our present walk in art is distinct.

I will take the greatest care that the drawing be as well copied as possible; the engraver has just left me.

Let me beg the favour of you in your communication to Mr. Stockdale, to give it simply as your demand (as a condition of the drawing being lent by you for the purpose,) without stating the reason I have advanced, which might by that gentleman be made matter of offence to others.

Believe me, with the truest respect,
Dear Madam,
Most faithfully yours,
THOS. LAWRENCE.

On the publication of the book, Miss Owenson came from the Priory to London, to her old friends, the Pattersons. From York Place she wrote to Lady Stanley.

Miss Owenson to Lady Stanley.

LONDON, 12, YORK PLACE,
PORTMAN SQUARE,
April 12, 1811.

DEAREST, KINDEST OF LADIES,

By this you have received my little packet; it is near a fortnight since I sent it to be franked, and I have been rather anxious as to its fate, but perhaps at this very moment you are seated at your fireside, Poll at your feet, and Pug beside you, and *The Missionary* in your hands; but in a few days I shall cease to envy Poll, Pug, or *Missionary*, for I shall be in your arms. I leave this heaven upon earth on the evening of the 30th, so I suppose I shall be with you about the 2nd of May, and you will, perhaps, meet me at Holyhead. And, now, who do you think I am waiting at home for? only Sir John Stanley — it is all very true! Both your sons openly avow their passion for me; and Lady Stanley is the most generous of rivals! I have been now one blessed fortnight in this region of delight, and were I to describe to you the kind of attention I excite and receive, you would either laugh at, or pity me, and say "her head is turned, poor little animal;" and you would say very true. But I will tell you all when we meet, a period now not far distant. I mean to send my trunks, directed *for you*, to Mr. Spencer's, by one of the *heavy coaches*, so pray have the goodness to mention the circumstance to him, as it will ensure the safety of my poor little property. Your letter was most gracious, and received with infinite pleasure. Dearest and kindest of friends,

God keep you ever,

GLORVINA.

I am on a visit to an East Indian *nabob's*, whose wife and family are all kindness to me.

This "East India nabob and his family," were Captain and Mrs. Patterson; they admired the young authoress, and were glad to have her in their house, and they placed it and their carriage at her disposal. Sometimes Mrs. Patterson was invited to accompany her on her visits, and Miss Owenson received her friends in their house. The Pattersons were not brilliant people; but they were thoroughly kind-hearted; they enjoyed Miss Owenson's success, and also the glimpses of high society which they obtained through the visitors who called on their guest. Lady Morgan used to tell, in a most amusing way, a story of how, one evening, she and Mrs. Patterson being engaged to a grand party, were obliged to go there in — a hackney-coach; some accidental hinderance about the carriage having occurred at the last moment. The thought of this hackney-coach tormented Miss Owenson all the evening, and destroyed both her peace and pleasure;

the idea of what people would say, and, still worse, what they would *think*, if they discovered she had come in a hackney-coach!

She persuaded Mrs. Patterson to depart early, in the hope of escaping detection; but Lord George Granville, who was very much her admirer, perceived her exit, and insisted upon "seeing her to her carriage!"

Lady Morgan used to declare, that her agony of false shame was dreadful; but sooner than confess, she allowed the servants "to call her coach, and let her coach be called"; but of course it did not come. She then insisted upon "walking on to find it," and entreated Lord George to leave them to the servant, whom they had brought with them; but he was too gallant, and still insisted on keeping them company "till they should find their carriage."

The hackney-coachman, who had been ordered to wait, espied them, and followed to explain that he was there and waiting. Mrs. Patterson took no notice; Miss Owenson took no notice; the footman, who guessed their troubles, took no notice either. The hackney-coachman continued to follow them.

"What *does* that man mean by following us?" asked Lord George.

"I really cannot imagine," said the elder lady.

"I wish he would go away," said the younger one.

"What do you want, fellow?" asked Lord George.

"I want these ladies either to get into my coach or to pay me my fare."

"What *does* he mean — is he drunk?"

"No," said Miss Owenson, at last, laughing at the dilemma; "but the fact is, that we were so ashamed of coming in a hackney-coach that we wanted nobody to know it."

Mrs. Patterson proceeded to explain all about how it had happened that they were deprived of the use of their own carriage; but her representations were drowned in the peals of laughter with which Miss Owenson and Lord George recognised the absurdity of the situation.

"So you came in a hackney-coach, and would rather have walked home in the mud than have had it known. How *very* Irish!" was his lordship's comment. He put them into their despised coach, and saw them drive away.

The comparative failure of *The Missionary*, together with the troubles she had met with from her publishers, turned Miss Owenson's mind for a moment from the romance towards the drama. She had an hereditary leaning to the stage. Her father had been a manager and a comedian. She herself had written a successful musical piece. The theatre offered her many inducements to try her hand at a play; and she had so far thought of it as to consult Lord Abercorn on the choice of a hero. Lord Abercorn's answer is among her papers.

Lord Abercorn to Miss Owenson.

[No date.]

I read your letter to the person you desired, dear, and if I did not write "by RETURN" (O you Irish expression, why cannot I write the proper brogue for such a broguey expression?) you must still impute it to the penny postman's life I am living, for when you ask me a question worth an answer, I will never delay it.

What your genius for melodrama, or any drama

may be, I have no other reason for guessing than my suspicion that you have genius enough for anything that you will give proper attention to. I should, however, be sorry that the drama, in any shape, should supersede the intentions of the romance or novel production that you last professed.

Hand-in-hand with it I have no objection; and as you give me my choice of two heroes, I will so far decide that he shall not be Henry the Fourth (Henry the Fourth of France). In the first place he is hackneyed to death and damnation; in the second, between ourselves (and spite of the whole female race whose favourite hero he is) he was no hero at all; he was a brave, good-natured, weak, selfish gentleman, and had he been endowed with higher mind and nature than he was, still his infamous conduct to the Prince de Condé would have blotted him out of my list.

The qualities, virtues, and vices of Francis the First were of a more kingly kind; and though he was hardly a hero, he was a good deal more like one; his time, too, was more chivalric, and the events of it, as well as his own words and actions, having been less hackneyed, may be worked up far more entertainingly and interestingly.

So much for my wisdom with which I shall begin and end.

So bye-bye, sweet Glo.

Lord Abercorn's objection to Henri Quatre as a hero, in spite of all feminine preferences to the contrary, were probably personal. Henri's "infamous conduct" towards Condé, perhaps reminded him of Lieutenant

Copley's "infamous conduct" to the Marquis of Abercorn.

During this visit to London, Miss Owenson made the acquaintance, and won the enduring friendship of that woman of unhappy genius, Lady Caroline Lamb. Born in the highest rank, gifted with the rarest powers, at once an artist, a poetess, a writer of romance, a woman of society and the world, Lady Caroline Ponsonby had been the belle of her season, the toast of her set, the star of her firmament. Early loved and early won by a young man, who was at the same time a nobleman and a statesman, every wish of her heart, every aspiration of her mind, would appear to have been gratified by success. As Lady Caroline Lamb, and future Lady Melbourne, she was an adored wife, with a fixed and high position in society, and with everything that wealth, beauty, youth, talent and connexions can command to make life happy. But the woman was not content. Is any woman of genius ever tranquil? Is not genius, whether in man or woman, the seed of what Schiller calls "a sublime discontent?" Lady Caroline had that restless craving after excitement — after the something unattained and unattainable — which pursues all spirits that are "finely touched." Sometimes she sought this in the exercise of her pencil and her pen; sometimes in the more dangerous exercise of her affections and her imagination. She was not wicked. She was not even lax in her opinions. But she was bold and daring in her excursions through the debateable land which divides the territories of friendship from those of love. If she never fell, she was scarcely ever safe from falling. At the date when her correspondence with Miss Owenson began, she was a young wife of five or six years, and the image of Byron, beautiful and deadly as the nightshade, had not thrown its shadow on her life. When the letter, which is now to introduce Lady Caroline to the reader, as one of the most charming figures of this correspondence, was written, Byron had just returned from the East, having his *Hints from Horace* and the early cantos of *Childe Harold* in his pocket. His *English Bards*, which he found in a fourth edition, had made him famous; and his poetry, his travels, his singularity of manners, his extraordinary personal beauty, and his reputation for gallantry, made him one of the chief lions of the London season. Half the women were soon in love with him, more or less platonically; among others, at first very platonically, Lady Caroline Lamb. How far this friendship and flirtation went between the noble poet and the noble lady, has never yet, for want of full materials, or in deference to living persons, been truly told. These reasons for observing silence are no longer binding. Lady Caroline made Lady Morgan the depository of all her secrets as to this connexion; the actors in the drama have passed away, and the story of their lives is public property. The details which may now be given, mainly under the hands of Lady Caroline and Lord Byron, will complete an interesting chapter in the poet's memoirs.

Lady Caroline may now appear on the stage.

Lady C. Lamb to Miss Owenson.

LONDON,
1811.

MY DEAR MISS OWENSON,

If it had not been near making me cry, what I am going to tell you might make you laugh; but I

believe you are too good-natured not to sympathize
in some manner with my distress. It never occurred
to me that I should forget the direction you gave
me, so that having ordered the carriage, and having
passed a restless night, I was but just getting up when
it was ready. I ordered it to fetch you; where, was
the question — at York, was the only answer I could
possibly give; for York, alas, is all I remember. Now
they say there is a York lane, three York streets,
a York place, a York buildings, and York court.
I knew no number, but immediately thought of sending to Lady Augusta Leith; the *Court Guide* was
opened, it was for 1810; Lady A. Leith consequently
not where she now is, and where either of you are
I cannot think; but as I was obliged to go into the
country, I wrote this, and take my chance of its
ever getting to you. Should you receive it, pray
accept of my regrets and excuses, and do not treat
me as ill as I have you, but remember your kind
intentions some evening. I shall be back Saturday,
I believe; but General Leith goes Tuesday.

See me before you leave town, and send me your
number and street, I beg of you; the impression you
have made is, I assure you, a little stronger, but I
never can recollect one direction — do you think the
new man could teach me?

Yours very sincerely, C. LAMB.

My direction is always Melbourne House.

The two ladies soon met to become friends and
associates for ever. No contrast could be greater than
between these two women of genius; one highly born,

adored by her husband, and every whim gratified, without her own exertion; the other humble, if not obscure; adored by many, but with a dangerous kind of love; compelled to struggle for her daily bread and for her daily safety. Both played, most perilously, with the fire; yet both came from the burning bush unscathed. Lady Caroline was saved by her affections, Miss Owenson by her principles. She, too, was weaving most unconsciously her married destiny. On the death of his first wife, Dr. Morgan accepted the post of physician to Lord Abercorn. A man so handsome and accomplished, made a deep impression on the Marchioness, who set herself to provide him with a second wife. The affair of Miss Owenson with "*le bien aimé*" was now off; and Lady Abercorn's letters to Miss Owenson began to glow with praises of her young physician. Jane Butler (afterwards Lady Manners) mentions him in one of her letters in a rather droll fashion.

"We brought Dr. Morgan," she writes to Miss Owenson, "a physician, with us, who, I believe, is very clever in more ways than one, as he understands simony and all Mrs. Malaprop's accomplishments. I believe he is of your religious persuasion, and seems to think Moses mistaken in his calculations (this is *entre nous*)."

Lady Abercorn, from the beginning, had set her heart on a match between Dr. Morgan and Miss Owenson, and Miss Owenson entered readily into all the fun of such a suggestion. When Lady Aberdeen wrote to Miss Owenson a glowing account of Dr. Morgan's learning, and genius, and qualifications, and desired her to write a poetical diploma for him, Miss Owenson answered in pure *gaieté de cœur*, as follows: —

DIPLOMA NOS UNIVERSITATAS SANTÆ GLORVINA.

We learned Professors of the College,
The Alma Mater of true knowledge,
Where students learn, *in memoria*,
The philosophical amatoria,
Where senior fellows hold no power,
And junior sophists rule the hour,
Where every bachelor of arts
Studies no science — but of hearts.
Takes his degree from smiling eyes ·
And gets his FELLOWSHIP — by sighs;
Where scholars learn, by rules quite simple,
To expound the mystics of a dimple;
To run through all their moods and tenses,
The feelings, fancies, and the senses.
Where none (though still to grammar true)
Could e'er *decline* — a *billet doux,*
Though *all* soon learn to *conjugate,*
(*Eadum nos autoritate*)
We — learned Professors of this College,
The Alma Mater of true knowledge,
Do, on the Candidate *Morgani.*
(Doctissimo in Medicini)
Confer his right well earned degree,
And dub him, henceforth, sage *M. D.,*
He, having stood examination,
On points might puzzle half the nation,
Shown where with skill he could apply
A sedative, or *stimuli,*
How to the *chorda tympani*
He could, by dulcet symphony,
The soul divine itself convey,
How he (in verses) can impart
A vital motion to a heart,
Through hours which Time had sadly robb'd,
Though dull and morbid it had throbb'd.
Teach sympathetic nerves to thrill,
Pulses to quicken or lie still;
And without pause or hesitation,
Pursue that vagrant thing *sensation,*
From right to left, — from top to toe,
From head of sage to foot of beau,
While vain it shuns his searching hand,
E'en in its own *pineal gland.*

5*

> But did we all his feats rehearse,
> How he excels in tuneful verse,
> How well he writes — how well he sings,
> How well he does ten thousand things,
> Gave we due meed to this bright *homo*,
> It would — *Turgeret hoc Diploma.*
>
> GLORVINÆ OWENSONEÆ.

On leaving England Miss Owenson again proceeded to Baron's Court. She used to relate that Dr. Morgan had heard so much in praise of Miss Owenson's wit, genius and general fascination, that he took an immense prejudice against her, and being a very shy man, he disliked the idea of meeting her.

He was one morning sitting with the Marchioness, when the groom of the chambers, throwing open the doors, announced "Miss Owenson!" who had just arrived. Dr. Morgan sprang from his seat, and there being no other way of escape, leaped through the open window into the garden below! This was too fair a challenge for Miss Owenson to refuse; she set to work to captivate him, and succeeded more effectually than she either desired or designed. The following letter gives no indication of the crisis so nearly at hand; it is to Mrs. Lefanu, and the tone is rather depressed.

Miss Owenson to Mrs. Lefanu.

[*No date.*]

CHERE, CHERE,

May the event your *sweet letter* communicated, and every event in your family that succeeds it, be productive of increasing happiness. Too much the creature of circumstances as they influence my manners or my conduct, my heart, ruled in its feelings by the objects of its affections only, knows no change, and the sympathy, the tender interest in all that concerns you, my *longest, kindest friend*, which chance recently discovered to you, has always existed under an increasing power since the first moment I pressed your cordial hand — I met the kind welcome of your full eyes. If I am too apt to visit abroad, I am sure to come home to you, and the increasing kindness with which you receive and forgive me, hourly quickens my return, and extends my contrition.

Tom and his bride are now as happy as is possible for human nature to be. I rejoice in their happiness. I pray that it may long, long continue, and above all, that it may add to the sum of your's and Mr. Lefanu's; for if ever parents deserved well of their children, you both have. I was received here with the kindest and most joyous welcome. I find the people and the place delightful — there never was such a perfect Paradise; the summer makes all the difference and the magnificent outlines I so much admired in winter, are now most luxuriantly filled up.

We have got a most desirable acquisition to our circle, in the family physician; he is a person of extraordinary talent and extensive acquirements; a linguist, musician, poet and philosopher, and withal a most amiable and benevolent person; he is in high popularity, and he and I most amazing friends, as you may suppose.

Miss Butler is here, merry and pleasant as ever. She is sitting beside me, and desires her compliments, congratulations and best recollections to your ladyship. Olivia writes of nobody but you. She seems in very low spirits about our father, poor dear soul! and *misses* me sadly. I need not say a word to you on the subject.

I am sure you will see her often, and I know you cannot *help* being kind to her, and to any one who may stand in need of your kindness.

We expect the Duke of Richmond and suite the week after next. I expect Sir C. and Lady Asgill will also come at that time, so that we shall be a gay party. Olivia has been asked over and over again, but still declines the honour.

You see the king cannot make up his mind to leave us; he is *too kind!* I believe all things remain on the other side in *statu quo.* Write to me soon like a love, and tell me all that you think I most desire to know; above all, that you continue to love

Your own GLORVINA.

CHAPTER VII.

ENGAGED TO BE MARRIED.

BETWEEN the last letter to Mrs. Lefanu and the next one to her father, not many weeks elapsed. This and the subsequent letters are all the indications that remain of her feelings and thoughts upon an event so important in her life, as her first real struggle against falling into love. She used to say, in after life, how little she was then aware of the blessing that had befallen her and how near she had been to missing it, through her own perverseness. There is no doubt that she had dreamed of making a more brilliant match.

Miss Owenson to Robert Owenson.

BARON'S COURT.
August 20, 1811.

MY DEAREST DAD,

I am the least taste in life at a loss how to begin to tell you what I am going to ask you — which is, your leave to marry Doctor Morgan, whom I will not marry if you do not wish it. I dare say you will be amazingly astonished; but not half so much as I am, for Lord and Lady Abercorn have hurried on the business in such a manner, that I really don't know what I am about. They called me in last night, and more like parents than friends, begged me to be guided by them — that it was their wish not to lose sight of me, which, except I married a friend of theirs, they might, as they never would acknowledge a *Dublin husband*, but that if I accepted Morgan, the man upon earth they most esteemed and approved, they would be friends to both for life — that we should reside one year with them, after our marriage, or if they remained in Ireland, *two years*, so that we might lay up our income during that time to begin the world. He is also to continue their physician.

He has now five hundred a-year, independent of practice. I don't myself see the thing quite in the light they do; but they think him a man of such great abilities, such great worth and honour, that I am the most fortunate person in the world.

He stands in the first-class of physicians in London, having taken his Doctor's degree at Cambridge; his connexions are excellent, &c., &c., and in person very distinguished-looking. Now tell me what you wish

for I am still, as ever, all your own loving and dutiful
child,

SYDNEY OWENSON.

On the same subject, she wrote — after a few days
— to most of her old friends. The letter to Mrs. Lefanu and Lady Stanley, may be given as specimens of
the whole.

Miss Owenson to Mrs. Lefanu.

BARON'S COURT,
August 29, 1811.

MY DEAREST FRIEND,

Your inimitable letter was a source of great comfort
to me. Your eloquent and exalted theories are still less
powerful in their influence over me than your bright
example. I have seen you the Providence of your
family, and I admire and revere too much not to endeavour to imitate.

This event, the most unlooked-for and rapid of my
life, has been accelerated by my friends here, and by
the more than romantic passion of the most amiable
and ardent of human beings, so as to leave me in a
state of *agitation* and *flurry* that prevented me writing
on the subject to any human being but my family —
and even to them so incoherently as to leave them
more to guess at from inference than fact.

The business was, indeed, *so hurried*, that it was all
like a dream. The licence and ring have been in the
house these ten days — all the settlements made; yet
I have been battling off, from day to day, and hour to
hour, and have only ten minutes back procured a little
breathing time. The fact is, the struggle is almost too

great for me -— on one side engaged, beyond retrieval, to a man who has frequently declared to my friends, here, that if I break off he will not survive it!! on the other, the dreadf·· certainty of being parted for ever from a country and friends I love, and a family I adore, to which 1 am linked by such fatal ties, that my heart must break in breaking them.

Lord and Lady Abercorn will not part with Dr. Morgan for a moment, as they suppose the whole family would die if they did; so that, after my marriage, I should have no chance of seeing you all before I went to England, and I have, therefore, at last prevailed on Morgan to permit me to go up for a *week* or *two*, while I am yet a free agent. When I read that part of your letter where you say Tom and his wife were to live with you, I wept bitterly. Oh, if it were my lot to live with those I love! but I am about to leave them all. I write incoherently, for I am feeling strongly; don't read this to Livy, but just what is right and politic to mention to any one. To give you any idea of the passion I have most unwittingly inspired, would be vain; but if I had spirits, I could amuse you not a little. Tell Livy to repeat to you some of his eloquent nonsense which I wrote to her. Barring his wild, unfounded love for me, the creature is perfection. The most *manly*, I had almost said *daring*, tone of mind, united to more goodness of heart and disposition, than I ever met with in a human being. Even with this circle, where all is acquirement and accomplishment, it is confessed that his versatility of talent is unrivalled. There is scarcely any art or science he has not cultivated with success; and the resources of his mind and memory are exhaustless. His manners are too English to be popular with the Irish; and though he is reckoned a handsome man, it is not that style of thing which, if I were to choose for beauty, I should select — it is too indicative of goodness; a little *diablerie* would make me wild in love with him. To the injury of his interests and circumstances, he has offered to settle with me in Dublin, since I appear so heart-broken at parting from my family; but *that* I would not hear of. He is just thirty; has a moderate property, independent of his profession; is a member and a fellow of twenty colleges and societies, and is a Cambridge man. This is a full-length picture drawn for your private inspection. He read your letter with bursts of admiration. He says you must have a divine mind, and that if all my country-women resemble you, his constancy will be sadly put to the test. We are to live one year with the Abercorns, which will save some income for furnishing a house in London, where we are to reside. *My man* is now playing Handel, and putting me in mind of dear Tom. He does not, however, play near so well; but has more *science* than any one, and sings the most difficult things at sight. He has so much improved me in Italian and singing, you cannot imagine. Ten thousand thanks for your benevolent attention to my poor old father — never did he stand more in need of it, sick, worn down and deprived of the attentions of a child he adores, and who has hitherto lived for him. You are all goodness, and to part from you is not among the least of my afflictions. God bless you ever,

S. OWENSON.

A thousand loves to all the fire-side circle; but above all to Joe. I am quite shocked at the expense of my last letter; but as I saw you got all your letters at the *Castle*, I took it for granted they were free.

Miss Owenson to Lady Stanley.

Baron's Court,
1st September, 1811.

My most dear Friend,

It is an age since we held any communion; in the first instance, I was prevented by the fear of boring you by a *platitude* of a letter, which could only repeat what you know — that I love you. In the second, I have been prevented writing since my arrival here (now five weeks ago) by an event unexpected and critical; in a word, in this little space of time, a man has fallen in love with me, *à tête baissée*, and almost married me, before I know where I am or what it is all about. I mentioned to you before, that Lord Abercorn was to bring over with him a physician, and as they wrote me word that he was a person of distinguished talent, a charming musician, and altogether an interesting person, I sent him some comical professional problems in my letters to Lady Abercorn. He answered them by a poetical thesis — I sent him *a diploma* — and thus prepared, we met under circumstances and in scenes too favourable to the romantic feelings peculiar to his character, and which it was my lot to excite and feed. In short, almost without looking beyond the instant, his empressment, and the anxiety of Lord and Lady Abercorn to forward an event which would place me in England near them, took me unawares, and I gave a sort of consent to an event, which it is, and has ever since been, my incessant struggle to delay.

The fact is, there is much *pour et contre*, on the subject (Dr. Morgan having but a small patrimonial property, independent of his profession, in which he is still but young). The confidence his medical skill and success have inspired in this family, where there is a continual demand on his attention, have so raised him in their good opinion, that they have declared themselves his fast friends, and promoters of his interests for life. Indeed, it was at their instance, I was induced to listen to a proposal, which could have nothing in it very gratifying to my *ambition*. The man, however, is *perfection*. His mind has that strength of tone and extent of reflection, which you admire so much. He thinks upon every subject of importance with us, and is sometimes so daring in risking his bold and singular opinions, that while it raises him in my esteem, it makes me tremble for his worldly interests, so seldom promoted by this sovereign independence of principle and spirit, which throws rank and influence at such an incalculable distance. He is, with all this deep philosophy of character, a most accomplished gentleman. He speaks and writes well several languages, and is a scientific musician, a devoted naturalist, and has studied every branch of natural history with success. With these resources of *mind*, I never saw a wretch so thrown upon the *heart* for his happiness, or so governed by ardent and unruly passion, of which his most romantic *engoûement* for me is a proof. I have refused and denied him over and over again, because if it is not in worldly circumstances a very good match for me, it is still worse for him. I am still putting it off from day to day, but fear I am too far committed to recede with honour. All this is *entre nous*, and should you mention the thing, *pronez* the business as much as you can, for upon all occasions, *il est bon de se faire valoir*. We are to live the first year with Lord and Lady Abercorn, and the next we hope to be in a baby-house of our own in London, and, oh! what happiness it will be to me to have one to receive you, dear Lady Stanley, when you come to town, instead of your going to an hotel; believe me, there is not a human being I should be happier to see, than your dear self, after my own sweet sister. The worst part of my story is, that I must then have to leave my country, and father, and sister, that I adore; when I think of this, I start from my promise, and have more than once *entreated* to be off, and in short, sometimes I am almost out of my mind between contending feelings; you would pity me if you knew and saw my struggles; pray write to me soon, and love me always, Your own GLORVINA.

We expect the Duke and court here in a few days.

Lady Stanley's reply to the announcement of her friend's proposed, but not yet accomplished, marriage is both wise and kind.

Lady Stanley to Miss Owenson.

PENRHÔS,
September 18th, 1811.

MY DEAR GLORVINA,
Shall I say the import of your letter surprised me? I know not. However, I think surprise was not the

sensation predominant among the many it set afloat; that you should have met with a man who looked, listened, and entered the lists of love, *tête baissée*, was an event much of course; but that an equal to the admirable Crichton should be met at all, and moreover, that the destinies should just place him within the circle of Glorvina's influence, is truly a matter worthy of wonder, and particularly to me, who have hitherto adhered pertinaciously to a persuasion, that kindred spirits were subjected to the same laws as parallel lines, and never could meet on this ungracious planet. But, behold an exception! Receive, my dear Sydney, my sincere felicitations on your view of establishment. Yet rest assured, I do not fail of taking a part in your anxieties, but who can be married without such attendants? If every *contre* was nearly looked to, alack, poor Hymen! But in the main, establishment is good, in some lights almost expedient, since the delights of youth, of friends, of range, and frolic, are but passengers. On the subject of riches, it must be avowed, my worldly wishes are not completely gratified, but on that question, the interests of the heart must arbitrate, nor can I dispute with those sovereigns, and do they not appear with a powerful phalanx? and sweetly chime with the old song — "Et il sera toujours de même, si j'en juge d'après mon cœur." Perhaps, ere this time, the conflict is over; I wish it may be so, and every sacrifice well compensated by the acquisition of a friend and associate, *à tout épreuve.* I have been sadly tardy in writing, but were details worth while, I could show I am more excusable than usual; I have been singularly engaged by company and hampered by business at the same time, and lassitude and chagrins spoilt every little interval. And now then, farewell, my dear Sydney. Imagine, and you may well imagine (do me but justice) how much I love to hear further of an event so interesting to me, and believe me, by every name,

Most truly yours, &c., &c.,

M. STANLEY.

CHAPTER VIII.

BETWEEN CUP AND LIP.

WHEN she was fairly engaged, Miss Owenson's courage failed her. Dr. Morgan being very much in love, desired naturally that the marriage should take place with as little delay as possible. The Marchioness, to whom the drama and the *dénouement* were a pleasant excitement, had no idea that the ceremony in real life could be anything more than the last page in a novel, or the last words in a play, after the characters have grouped themselves. She sent for the marriage ring and licence, and would have proceeded to extremities, without consulting the wishes of one of the parties most interested.

Miss Owenson, however, contrived to obtain a short respite, and permission to pay a visit to her sister and father, in Dublin. Her father's precarious state of health was the plea she used. She was sent the first stage of her journey in all the state of a carriage and four horses, with Dr. Morgan riding beside the window for an escort. A fortnight was to be the term of her absence, and she promised very fairly, that if permitted to go away, she would return without fail, at the time appointed. She had no such intention. Her father was ill; his health was quite broken up. As, however, he was in no immediate danger, Miss Owenson had no idea of stopping at home to keep him company. She plunged at once, into all the gaieties of Dublin society. She was more the fashion than ever; and she enjoyed the feeling of freedom and independence after the stately restraints of her life at Baron's Court, of which she had, by that time, become disenchanted.

Dr. Morgan was retained at Baron's Court by his professional duty. Neither the Marquis nor the Marchioness would grant him leave of absence. He was extremely jealous, and knew his fair and slippery lady love to be surrounded by admirers. He was especially vexed by the attentions bestowed on her by Mr. Parkhurst, one of the gayest men about town in Dublin society; but he was unable to do more than write eloquent letters of complaint and appeal, to which the lady paid not the smallest attention. She always owned, afterwards, that she had behaved exceedingly ill, and that she deserved for ever to have lost the best husband that ever a woman had; but at the time, she only thought how she might prolong her absence, if, indeed, she did not meditate breaking loose altogether. The correspondence on both sides is characteristic, and as the subject of love and love-making, of woman's constancy and man's perfidy, is one of perennial interest, some of this correspondence may be given. The letters are printed as nearly according to their date as can be ascertained. Both the Marquis and Marchioness seem to have been kind throughout the whole period, and to have shewn great patience with their refractory *protégée*. In one of Morgan's letters,

under date Oct. 7, there is "a magic —" which requires a word of explanation. When Miss Owenson
had been particularly naughty, and wished to make
her peace, she would leave in her next note a small
blank space to represent a kiss. Morgan was at liberty
to believe that her lips had touched the paper, and to
act accordingly.

T. C. Morgan to Miss Owenson.

BARON'S COURT,
October 1, 1811.

MY DEAREST GIRL,

Here I am, again, safely returned from Strabane,
after going through a day's eating and drinking enough
to kill a horse. We had a most heavenly day, yesterday; but to-day, it has rained incessantly; we were not,
however, wet, being well provided with coats, so that
I am in no danger of dying this trip. Baron's Court
to-day is dulness personified. Lady Abercorn received
a shocking account of Lady Aberdeen from Mrs. Kemble;
and though I know how very little such accounts are
worth minding, yet her tears are infectious, and I cannot help feeling alarmed and out of spirits. Receiving,
as I do, daily marks of their kindness and good will,
I cannot avoid sympathising with them in their worst
of all domestic calamities. Yet, true to human nature,
I am selfish enough to think much of the effect a fatal
termination of this disease would have on us and our
comforts. I trust that I am not laying up for you a
winter's residence in the house of mourning — whatever
the Apostles may say, I infinitely prefer the house of
rejoicing. But to return to a more grateful theme, how

is my best beloved after her journey? I hope to-morrow
to hear a good account of you, and that you found
your father and sister better than you expected.

Have you been gadding about much? Have you
seen many people? Are you happy and comfortable?
or are you, like me, looking forward anxiously to the
happy time that will unite us for ever? Dearest Glorvina, love me as I adore you. How often I kiss the
little gold bottle, and think of the sweeter roses on
somebody's lips. Shorten time, by every means, that
separates us, if you value the happiness of

Your ever devoted,

T. C. M.

T. C. Morgan to Miss Owenson.

Monday, October 7.

DEAREST, DEAR LOVE,

Will you, can you pardon my ravings? How angry
I am with myself! I have at last got a sweet, charming, *affectionate* letter from you, and half my miseries
are over. If my two last letters gave you pain, think
what misery (well or ill-founded), what horrid depression must have been mine to inspire them. Your *rea-
sonings* are all very fine and very conclusive; but, alas,
I parted with *reason* to a certain little coquette, and I
can attend to and feel no language but that of the
heart. Still, however, I must insist upon my distinction, that while I am ready to give up *everything* to
your lovely, amiable *family feelings*, I can ill brook
your associating any unpleasant idea with that of returning to *me.* If I know my heart, neither solitude,
sickness, nor slavery would be unpalatable, if it gave
me back to Glorvina. I would seek her amidst the

plague, in an African ship, or, if such a place existed, in her *own father's* dominions. I have but one object in life, and *it is you;* and so little can I bear the idea of your preferring anything to me, that I have been angry with Olivia when she has had too much of your attention. Indeed, indeed it is *because I love*, that I cannot suppose it possible any feeling of disgust, or *ennui*, can associate itself with your return to me, and, I would fain hope, happiness. You cannot think so meanly of me as to suppose the dimity chamber could urge me to draw you from your *duties*. Trust me, love, you never win me more than when I see you, in imagination, discharging them; but when I picture to myself the *thoughtless, heartless* Glorvina, trifling with her friend, jesting at his sufferings, and flirting with every man she meets; when I imagine her more in love with the *vanities of this wicked world* than with me, I feel not *sure* of her. Do not think me cruel in reminding you that you have lost one husband by flirting, and that that makes *me* feel it is just possible you may drive another mad. I cannot, give you to the amusements of Dublin. God knows (if he takes the trouble to know) this "pile" is "dreary" enough without you; but it makes me curse the hour I threw away my love on one so incapable of returning it, when I see you looking forward to a *solitary* winter in it; trust me, dearest, a little *natural philosophy* will make time pass pleasantly enough, never fear.

I read part of your letter to Miss B——, relative to "Almighty Tact," and she laughed *tout son saoul.* She says, if there is one human being more thoroughly destitute of *tact* than another, it is Glorvina — and, indeed, I think so. In the instance of myself you have

failed utterly. If you knew me, you would not combat
my feelings by your affected stoicism; you would flatter
my vanity with the idea of the separation being as
painful to you as to me; you would soothe me with
tenderness and not shock me with *badinage*. If you
knew how much eloquence there was in the magic —;
if you knew the pleasure I felt in touching the paper
that had touched your lips! Oh, Glor.! Glor.! have
you been all this while studying me to so little purpose? In reply to *your orders*, know that I have not
opened my lips to say more than — "a bit more,"
"very good," and "no more, thank you, MY LORD,"
since you have been gone. Lady Abercorn swears she
heard me sing, "Il mio ben quando vena," and says
I am Nina Pazza. In good truth, I believe she is
right, for surely nothing but madness would distress
itself, and what it loves more than itself, as *I* do. I
assure you I have made myself quite ill, and others
present; my calmness is acquired, unnatural, and de-
ceitful. I am sorry, very sorry, for your poor dear
dad; but hope he is not seriously worse; say everything that is kind to him from me, and tell him I hope
we shall spend many a pleasant day together yet. Do
you know you shock my tenderness by the *ease* with
which you talk of Miss Butler. Surely we must adopt
two terms to express our different loves, *one* word cannot imply such different affections. I WILL think and
speak of nothing but you. As to my commissions, do
not, best and dearest, put yourself to any inconvenience
about them; when done you may send them by the
mail, the pleasure of receiving anything from you is
worth the carriage, though it even amounted to gold.
There is, however, but *one* commission about which I

am *anxious*, and that is *to love me* as I do you, EXCLU-
SIVELY; to prefer me to every other good; to think of
me, speak of me, write to me, and to look forward to
our union as the completion of every wish, for so do
I by you. Do this, and though you grow as "*ugly*"
as Sycorax, you will never lose in me the fondest,
most doating, affectionate of husbands. Glorvina, I
was born for tenderness; my business in life is *to love*.
Cultivate, then, the latent feelings of the *heart*, learn
to distrust the *imagination*, and to despise and quit the
world, before the world leaves you. How, dearest, will
you otherwise bear the hour when no longer young,
lovely, and *agaçante*, you will see the *great ones* lay
aside their plaything and forget their companion who
can no longer give them pleasure; where, but in the
arms of affection, will you then find consolation? Fly,
then, to me by times. You have much wisdom to
acquire yet, with respect to happiness; and believe me,
the *dimity chamber* is a school worth all the Portico's in
the world, Mrs. Stoic. *There* nature reigns, and you
will hear none but the language of truth. Do you recollect folding up a piece of blotting-paper with one of
your letters? I preserve it as the apple of my eye,
and kiss it, as I would you, all to pieces.

My sweetest life, I do not mean an atom of acri-
mony towards you in all this; but misery will be querulous. I determine to pass over my sufferings in
silence; but find I cannot. Do not say I am selfish;
if I were, I should have pressed you to marriage when
I could have done it effectually. I should have opposed
your leaving me; and now I should give up all to you
for comfort. I flatter myself, that *hitherto* every sacri-

fico has been on my part. My only comfort is, that
my wishes have given place to yours.

I do not wish you to *cut* any one; but I think
Parkhurst, too *particular* in his attentions; besides,
how can I bear that anybody can have the pleasure of
talking to you and gazing on you when I cannot. I
should be sorry you offended a *friend* on account of
any whim of mine; you can be civil to him without
encouraging *his daily* visits. Strangely as I show it,
I *am* obliged and grateful for your every attention, and
in this instance in particular; but indeed I do not wish
it. I have not so mean an opinion of myself to be
jealous of anybody's alienating your mind from me by
exciting a preference, *et pour toute la reste j'en sais
assez.*

I have kissed your dear hair again and again, as
I do the bottle, twenty times an hour; do not judge of
my temper by this instance, for, believe me, I am not
always, nor ever was in my married life, in the horrible state of mind I now am. You know I think ill
of life in general, and kick against calamity as if I received an affront as well as an injury in it from fate.
But trust me, no chance of life can reach me to wound
as I am now wounded; when reposed on your dear
bosom then my spirits will be calmed, my irritability
soothed. If I thought there was the remotest chance
of my giving you the uneasiness I know I now do,
when once you are mine, I would release you from
your engagement *au coup de pistolet.* No, no, my beloved, I hope, after all, we may be enabled to say, in
our age, *c'est un monde passable*, at least it *shall* be so
to you, if I can make it so. God bless you, my own

dear, sweet, darling girl; don't, don't be angry with me, for I am very wretched without that. Mr. Eliot is come at last, and I must go dress and acquire steadiness for "*représentation.*"

Adieu *ma belle*, *ma chère* Glor.

MORTIMER.

9 o'clock.

Pity and forgive a wretch whom nothing but your presence can console. God, God bless you, dear Glorvina.

T. C. Morgan to Miss Owenson.

Du Chemin de Cerbere a la Porte d'Enfer.
Mardi, October 15th, 1811.

Faut-il que je m'égaye toujours? Combien cela est triste! Mais, soyons heureux c'est encore bien plus difficile. Égayons nous pourtant. Pourquoi? — *La reine le veut!*

· The Clitheroes are just gone with Bowen for the Giant's Causeway, the latter returns in the middle of next week; the former promise to repeat their visit soon. Oglander and the Major are gone shooting; and the little tail of nobility, Miss Butler and I, are going to ride if the weather permit. I really was *glad* you were not with us last night. We played magical music, "What's my Thought like?" and many other games *equally amusing*, for three or four hours; you would have been bored to death, as was almost your poor Mortimer. They made Lord Abercorn *go out* frequently, and though he was bored as bad as man could be, he did it with an ease and grace that was very pleasing;

he certainly is thoroughly a gentleman on those points. Miss Butler seems thoroughly determined to go to Dublin, and then what will become of us? *Che farò senza mio ben*, we shall be given up to melancholy. What will become of me? *io morirò — ahi! ben mio*, how happy should I be could I behold thee and be near thee, and see thee with thy dear family, but what useless wishes, I love thee dearest! my wife, I love thee! and for thee I will do and endure anything, everything! adieu, my love, adieu!

Farewell, dearest Glorvina,

Your own, own
MORTIMER.

Miss Owenson to T. C. Morgan.

October, 1811.

"Do the P—s and Castlereaghs go to you at Christmas? when does the Butler come to town, and when do the Carberys leave you?" — answer all. I don't send you a kiss to-day, I am tired of the *diurnal act*, but I lay my head upon your bosom in a wife-like way, and suffer you to press me gently to your heart, which is more than you *deserve!* I am glad you changed your pen — I hate *poesy* —

"When this you see,
Remember me."

"*His* mouth was Primmer,
A lesson I took,
I swore it was pretty,
And then kiss'd the book."

that is the text, vide "Peeping Tom;" but I did not intend to make so free with you this three months, for you have behaved *very ill indeed* lately, and talked *like a fool* very often. Livy does not know what to make of you! but I forgive — lay by your nervousness, and get some common sense.

S. OWENSON.

Miss Owenson to T. C. Morgan.

October 31st, 1811.

I am not half such a little rascal as you suppose; the best feelings only have detained me from you; and feelings better than the *best* will bring me back to you. I must be more or less than woman to resist tenderness, goodness, excellence, like yours, and I am simply woman, aye, dear, "every inch a woman." I feel a little kind of tingling about the heart, at once more feeling myself nestled in yours; do you remember — well, dear, if you don't, I will soon revive your recollection — I said I would not write to you to-day, but I could not resist it, and I am now going off to a man of business, and about Lady Abercorn's books, in the midst of the snow and pinched with cold. God bless you, love.

S. O.

Your song is charming; you are a clever wretch, and I love you more for your talents than your virtues, you *thing of the world*. What put it into your stupid head that I would not return at Christmas? did I ever say so, blockhead?

Well, I have only the old *story* to *tell*, no more than yourself —

" And I *loves* you, and you loves me, ·
And oh! how happy we shall be."

Take care of the *whiskers* — mind they are not to grow thus — but thus. — [Here follows in the letter a couple of droll portraits of Morgan, with the whiskers grown and trimmed in the two fashions then in favour.]

T. C. Morgan to Miss Owenson.

Thursday, November, 1814.

You are a pretty pair of Paddies, you and your sister. *Only see* how you enclosed your letter for me, to Lord Abercorn, without seal and without direction. Your second letter came at the *usual* time; but judge my consternation, when Lord Abercorn gave me your *first* at breakfast, *premising he had read three sides of it*, under the supposition it was for him, till he came quite at the end, to "my dear Morgan," which rather surprised him. In good truth, the letter is so much like the *Epistle General of St. Jude*, that it will do for *any church*. Well, "the gods take care of Cato." There was not a word of *his* frolics, of the stupidity of B. C—, of Livy's not coming, or anything one would much care about his reading; but I was in a special fright till I could get an opportunity of reading it and convincing myself; for Heaven's sake be more careful. I think he must have laughed at your *jealous suspicions*, though I don't believe he has a very high opinion of my *Josephism*. I wish I had something to *confess*, just to *satisfy* you; but, ah, alas! you have the best security in the world for my fidelity, the want of opportunity for me to go astray. For unless I made love to a young diablesse or an old witch, and became the papa of an incubus, the devil a chance have I of doing wrong. I should like to know the "when and the who" of your thoughts; perhaps it would give me *an idea*. Seriously, my best love, if you doubt me, come and claim your own, for *I am* yours and only yours.

Dearest girl, how much I wish I could say anything satisfactory to you about your father. I *cannot judge* accurately, but all your accounts of him have given me an unfavourable impression of his chance of ultimate recovery. I should think the whiskey *bad* for him; at least, if not rendered *necessary* by circumstances, it must be injurious. Your low spirits distress me very, very much. Would to God I could be with you to soothe and comfort you! I am, however, not less so than yourself, as you must see by my awkward attempts at humour. I am very *irritable* at these times, and do not know whether to laugh or cry.

My yesterday's letter (written in this mood) was particularly dull and fade; I am very much pleased, flattered, delighted by your second letter; it is so decisive a mark of your tenderness and affection. Dearest Glorvina, I *have no* love for any but you; you have my *whole*, *whole heart*, and if my letters vary, it is because my spirits vary, and with them my *tone* of thinking. When, when will the day come that shall make me *yours* for ever. Glorvina, we have both suffered much on each other's account; I feel, however, conscious we shall both be ultimately happy in each other. God, God bless you! I am writing myself into dreadful spirits; I believe catching your tone.

You give a horrid picture of poor dad! He must have been *very ill indeed* to require so much blistering. I find you are quite in raptures with Dublin. Four

dinners beside evening parties in one week; that is
pretty well for a person who went there *merely* to
enjoy the society of her family for a few weeks. However, if you are amused, I am content. You must want
occasional *distraction*, and to be candid, I should be
all the better for it, if it were in my reach. Only love
me, and write good-humouredly. You do not mention
the Butler; she is, I suppose, as happy as the day is
long; give my love to her, and tell her I miss her
very much — *da l'amantissimo vero sposo.*

T. C. Morgan to Miss Owenson.

BARON'S COURT,
Wednesday, 2 o'clock, Nov. 14th.

DEAREST AND BEST,

Me voici de retour, and I have just read your dear
letter. Great God! how little able am I to bear any
crosses in which you are concerned. I cannot free
my mind from the idea of your having been *seriously*
ill. You say you are better, and I must believe you.
But once for all I implore and beseech you, in no instance conceal from me the *full extent* of any sickness
or calamity that may reach *you* or *yours*. It is only
the entire confidence that communications *are* made,
and that nothing would be hid that might happen ill,
by which absence is rendered supportable. An anxious,
fretful and *Rousseauish* disposition (like mine) will let
the imagination so much get the start of reason, that,
when once deceived, I should never feel happy by any
communication however pleasant its nature. I should
fancy ten millions of accidents, kept from me *for my
good.* I hope and trust you have acted sincerely by

me in this instance, and are as well in health and about one-*eighth* part as happy as if you really were "*on my knee.*" What an image! how lovely! My bosom swelled in reading it, and the obtrusive drops, *for once* harbingers of pleasure, danced trembling on my eyelids; *bless* you, BLESS you, dearest love! I do kiss you with my whole heart, and pat your dear *caen dhu* [black head]; and I, too, in my turn, ask your pardon for worrying you in my last but one, and for the two short hasty scrawls of Sunday and yesterday. In each case, however, I really was compelled to be so brief; I should not have written, but, judging by myself, I thought a short letter infinitely preferable to no letter at all; I have just received your parcel, but have had no time to examine anything. You have forgotten my lavender water, of which I am in great want — *mais n'importe.* The ring does *famously.* I kiss it every instant (*now*) and NOW and NOW-W-W-W. Pray take care of the mourning ring you took as a pattern, as I value it much. Lady Abercorn played me an *arch trick* about it. By mistake, she opened the muslin and found the ring; she and Miss Butler *abstracted* it. I missed the expected delight, and flew (*à la moi*) *all over scarlet*, up to her to inquire if it was amongst her parcels, and very soon discovered by her joking how the land lay. Oh! I am a great fool, and it's all along of *you*, you thing you! God bless dear *you*, though, for all that. Lady Abercorn will be obliged by the Irish extract from *Ossian;* her countenance quite brightened when I mentioned it. At this moment my imagination is wandering in delight. I kiss and press you in idea, and I am all fire, and passion and tenderness; the sensations are rather too nervous and will leave a horrible depression; but for one such "five minutes" — perish an eternity! This morning, in bed, at Sir John's, I read part of *The Way to Keep Him*, and I see now you take the widow for your model; but it won't do, for though I love you in *every* mood, it is only when you are *true to* NATURE, *passionate and tender*, that *I adore* you. You never are less interesting to me than when you *brillez* in a large party: "C'est dans un tête-à-tête, dans la Chambre de Basin que vous est vraiment déesse, mais *déesse*-FEMME." *Apropos de la déesse*, your Paphian orders are *not* from Paphos, they are from the coldest chambers of your ice-house *imagination*. Venus disdains them, and Cupid trembles and averts his arrows, fearful of blunting their points: "Je n'ai qu'une seule occupation pour tous les jours, et presque pour toutes les nuits, et c'est de penser de Glorvina." I can neither read nor work, and the weather is horribly bad; how the time passes I can't say, for except writing to *you*, curse me if I can tell you any one thing I do from morning to night.

The *whiskers* thrive, and so, too, does the hair, but you really!

I cannot write another letter, and yet I cannot bear to part for two days in anger. Imagine all that is harsh and suspicious in this letter *unsaid* — *I know you love me*, however paradoxical your conduct, and I will try to be content; I cannot bear to give you pain; God bless my dearest love.

T. C. Morgan to Miss Owenson.

November, 1811.

I am very tired and it is late, so I shall write but
a short letter to-day, and that is the better for you,
dear, as I am thoroughly displeased with you and your
cold, calculating, most truly unamiable epistle. As for
favours, whatever this tremendous favour that you
dread to ask, be, I suppose it will be granted — *if it
can.* I have never yet been in the habit of refusing
you the sacrifice of every one of my feelings and prejudices. In every instance you have done exactly
what you pleased, and nothing else; and my wishes,
right or wrong, have been held tolerably cheap by
you; but this, I suppose, is to break me into an obedient husband by times. I could, however, better
away with that, than the manner in which you have
trifled with me in the business of delay. Why could
you not at once have told me, when *you first conceived the idea in September*, as I remember by a conversation we had, that you did not mean to return
till Christmas. You would have saved yourself some
little trouble and me very much pain, besides freeing
yourself from the necessity of stooping to something
more than *evasion.* But I do not mean to reproach
you. I know this is but a specimen of the round-
about policy of all your countrywomen. How strange
is it that you, who are in the general *great* beyond
every woman I know, philosophical, magnanimous —
should, *in detail*, be so often ill-judging, wrong, and
(shall I say) little. Ah, dearest Glorvina, you know
not how I adore you; and what pain it gives me that
you think so meanly of me as to imagine this little

trickery *necessary*. Am I not worthy of your confidence? am I not always ready to live or die for your happiness? and though I may complain when I think your affections cold, and your views *merely* prudential, yet to your seriously-urged wishes I shall ever attend. Do not write harshly to me, nor go over again the worn-out theme of your last. It is mortification enough that you can be so dead to feelings that agitate *me*, almost to madness, that you can *wish* to stay from me! You do not mention how the letter missed, or whether you have gotten all mine regularly since. Dearest, I know I am cross; but it is because I *feel* strongly, and, perhaps, not always *correctly*. Believe, however, that none can be more truly devoted to you than your own, own

T. M.

Je vous donne mille mille baisers.

Miss Owenson to T. C. Morgan.

Wednesday, November, 1811.

"*Tout homme n'est pas maître de sa propre vie,*" if he has, by all the arts in his power, made that life indispensably necessary to the happiness of another — this you have done. Your life and love are necessary to my happiness. I did not seek to associate myself with either; it was you involved me, and you must abide by it. You must live to love me, and to be loved by me. Gracious God! how your letters harrow up my soul! I would not willingly, purposely, give *you* one pang for the best joy of my existence, and yet I, too, am cruel, unavoidably so. The various feelings by which I am eternally agitated and distracted, throw me into various tempers, and I pass from one strong emotion to another, almost insensible to their successive influence. I am the victim of the moment, and moments, and days and weeks, are to me but various seasons of suffering, each, in their way, too acute to be long sustained.

The gaieties I mix in, are unparticipated by others. You mistake me totally if you suppose I am the light, volatile, inconsequent wretch you paint me. Much as I am, and *ought to be*, flattered by the attention and kindness of a very large circle of respectable and distinguished friends; intimately associated as are all my feelings, and habits, and social pursuits with my sentiments for them, still, it is not they nor the festivals they give me, that could have a moment's influence with me. Oh, no, it is a far deeper feeling.

Yes, Morgan, I will be yours, I hope, I trust; God give me strength to go through with it! I mean to leave this house clandestinely; Clarke only in my secret *My poor father!* I am very ill — obliged to assist Livy, last night, with a heavy heart. The fatigue, added to a bad cold and a settled cough, has produced a horrible state of exhaustion and nervous lowness. I scarce know what I write; your letters have overpowered me; my head is disordered and wild. You distrust me, and whether I marry or reject you, my misery is certain. Still I love you, oh! more than tenderly. I lean my aching head upon your heart, my sole asylum, my best and dearest friend. I must cease to write. The physique carries it. To-morrow I shall be in better health. Adieu.

Yours,

S. O.

T. C. Morgan to Miss Owenson.

November 26th, 1811.

DEAREST LIFE,

After three days of painful, miserable discussion, welcome, welcome to the *holy Sabbath*, and to pure, *unmixed* love. I know not why, but I enjoy to-day a *triste* sort of *calmness* in regard to you, to myself, and to all that life can give, which is ease and happiness when compared with the eternal flow and ebb of hope with which I am *usually* agitated. I will take advantage of it (while it *lasts*) in writing to you, contrary to my previous intention, and I do so, because I *can avoid* at all touching on your affairs.

I should much like to have been present at your *disputation* on the influence of *mental cultivation* on human happiness. You knew *my* opinion, as I had so lately mentioned it, though in a cursory way, in one of my letters. I believe it is not very different from your own. There can be no doubt, as far as the sciences go, with which Davy is more particularly acquainted, their happy influence on human life is considerable, not only in the *aggregate* by "bettering the condition" (that is the fashionable phrase) of man, and multiplying his comforts, but *individually*, in a way not at first sight very visible. The physical sciences all consist in facts and reasoning on facts, *totally unconnected with morals*, and, as Chamfort says, "Le monde physique paraît l'ouvrage d'un être parfait et bon, mais le monde moral paraît être le produit des caprices d'un diable devenu fou." The mind, then, perpetually abstracted from the contemplation of this influence, stimulated by brilliant discoveries, and absorbed in the consideration of beautiful, well-arranged and *constant* laws, is enlarged to *pleasurable emotion*, at the same time that it rejoices in the consciousness of its increased powers over the natural world. Those pursuits, on the contrary, which have been supposed the most to influence happiness and to tame the tiger in our nature, — the moral and metaphysical sciences, *belles lettres*, and the fine arts, are, in my opinion, of much more doubtful efficacy. Though their influence, when opposed to the passions, is really as nothing (indeed, they too often but co-operate with them in corrupting the heart) yet they cast a sort of splendour about vice by the refinement they create; and render man, if not a better animal, yet certainly a less horrible animal. As to the question whether humanity is bettered by the multiplying wants, and thereby drawing tighter the social bonds and making us more dependent on each other, on police and on Government, we cannot *decide*, — the advantages and disadvantages of each state are so little comparable; most probably what is lost on the side of liberty, is gained in security and the petty enjoyments which, by their *repetition* become important, so that, on the whole, one age is nearly on a par with another in this respect. As for the influence of these pursuits on the CULTIVATOR of them, there can, in my opinion, be hardly a dispute; he is to all intents and purposes a victim immolated for the public for which he labours. In morality, the mind always bent upon a gloomy and shaded system of things, is either tortured in making stubborn fact bend to graduate with *religious prejudices*, or if forced to abandon *these*, lost in seas of endless speculation; consciously *feeling* actually *existing*

7*

evil, and perfectly *sceptical to future good*. These
sciences, too, generally are connected with a cultivated
imagination, the *greatest curse in itself* to its unfortunate possessor. Imagination, always at variance with
reason and truth, delights in exaggeration and dwells
most constantly on what most affects the passions.
Its food, its occupation is *pain;* then, again, how constant is that sickly squeamishness of taste which finds
nothing to admire, nothing to approve; that sees the
paucity of our conceptions and the endless repetition
of them. In point of fact, I have rarely seen poets,
painters, or musicians (I mean composers), *happy* men.
Fretful, irritable, impatient; guided by enthusiasm
(another word for *false conception*). [End missing.]

Miss Owenson to T. C. Morgan.

"And if I answered you 'I know not what,'
It shows the name of love."

Give me, my dear philosopher, ten thousand more
such letters, that I may have ten thousand more excuses for loving you still better than I do. I glory
in my own inferiority when you give that exalted
mind of yours fair play. I triumph in my *conscious
littleness;* I say, "*and this creature loves me.*" Yes,
dearest of all the dears, this is a proud consciousness. I think precisely with you, and argued on the
same grounds; but not with the same eloquence that
you have done. Davy (Sir Humphry), *après tout*, is
a *borné man*. I dined with him on Saturday last, and
he lectured, tolerably, till every one yawned; I said
twenty times in the course of the evening, to Miss
Butler, "how much better *Morgan* would have spoken;"

and so you would, dearest. Nothing takes a woman like *mind* in *man;* before that, everything *sinks.* When you talk *en philosophe* to me (even the Philosophy of Love) I adore you. When you make bad puns, and are "PUT IN MIND," I hate you. So, as you see, my love is a *relative,* not a *positive,* quality. You will know how to manage me, and I wish you every success, dear.

I shall not write much to you, to-day, because I am writing a long, long, letter to — to — the — Lord Mayor!!! Aye, and going to send it to the *Free-man's Journal!!* Don't look frightened to death, you quiz! I always have something to talk to the chief magistrate about, at this season of the year, and now it is about *poor children;* but I will send you the paper, and that will best inform you. Just before I sat down to write to you, yesterday, Livy and I had four naked little wretches at the fire warming and feeding, and, to tell the truth, their sufferings added to my nervousness; and *you,* joking and dissipation, had an equal share in the wretched spirits in which I addressed the dearest and the best. "Oh! Father Abraham, what these Irish be!" but so it is, — it is next to impossible to follow the quick transitions of our feelings. Just as I had got thus far, enter Professor Higgins — our Professor of Chemistry. He came to arrange a collection of mineralogy for Livy, which Clarke bought her with a cabinet, and now, here we are, in the midst of spars, quartz, ores, madre-pores, and petrifactions. I know the whole thing now, at my fingers' ends, and all in half-an-hour!!! The Professor says, I am a clever little soul! ' I have got a little collection, myself, which, with a harp, tripod, fifty volumes, and some music, constitutes all my household furniture — funny enough! Now, *coute qui coute*, no more dolorous letters; *à quoi bon?* if I were not to marry you, it would be because I loved you too well to involve you in difficulties and in distress. If I do marry you (and, like Solus, "I'm pretty sure I shall be married") I will make you the dearest, best, and funniest little wife in the world. Meantime, I prefer you to your whole sex, and so, dearest of all philosophers,

Adio,

GLORVINA.

PS. — I shall not write to you to-morrow, love, because I am going out about business for poor papa, who is very poorly; but still, if not better, he is not worse. Here is a trait of poor human nature. When his head was blistered, he would only suffer the *size of the blister* to be shaved; but when the pain came to the front of his head, he was obliged to have it all shaven. Yesterday he said to me, "Tell Morgan, my dear, that I have made a great sacrifice to health; that I have lost the finest head of hair that ever man had, and that I prided myself on, because I should like to prepare him *for seeing me in a wig!*"

I wish you would accustom yourself to write a little every day in mere authorship. I mean we shall write a novel together. Your name shall go down to posterity with mine, you wretch. The snow very deep, and the cold insupportable.

SYDNEY O.

In the next note from Morgan to Miss Owenson,

Mr. Parkhurst is again alluded to with bitterness. How far Miss Owenson went in her flirtations with this gentleman, it is hard to say; for when Lady Morgan, after her marriage, made a collection of the love letters of her old sweethearts, and presented it to Sir Charles, under the title of *Youth, Love and Folly*, she included none of Parkhurst's, if indeed she had any to include. Parkhurst had excited Ormsby's jealousy long before he disturbed Morgan's peace of mind. But there was nothing serious between them; at least, they never quarrelled and made each other miserable, as people in love usually do.

T. C. Morgan to Miss Owenson.

MY DARLING, INJURED LOVE,   *Thursday.*
I have behaved most ungenerously, most unjustly to you, and I am a beast. Do not despise, do not hate me, and I *will* endeavour to amend. I have sat building odious castles in the air about you till I fancied my speculations were realities. Do me, however, the justice to believe, that you have been a little the cause of my irritability. When you reflect that *you* told me * * * was coming to Baron's Court *only on your account*, and that I found you were not shocked at the indelicacy of his attentions — when you add to this that I found his name mentioned in *every one* of the first few letters you wrote, do you not think that a man *who really and truly loved*, might, nay must, feel anxious and uneasy. Never, for a moment, did I doubt your preference *for me*, nor dread his influence over your mind; but I was *angry* that you should indulge your vanity at the expense of my feelings and your

reputation. I *was hurt* that you mentioned to Lady Abercorn his calling on you with so much apparent delight. But no more of this distressing subject. For God Almighty's sake, for mine and your own, do not again, while you live, seek to hide a feeling or a thought from me; let us sacrifice together on the altar of truth, and communicate with unbounded confidence. Have you, indeed, been suffering and wretched, and have I added to that suffering by my conduct? You thought by hiding *your* grief to diminish mine, and you have overwhelmed me by your apparent indifference; the badinage and frivolity of tone in your letters (excuse me, dearest), have overcome me with a conviction of your indifference towards me, no kindness of *individual expression* could confute. Had you at first told me the extent of your wishes about absence, hard as they were, I *must* have yielded to you. But the little *preaching* of delay upon delay, has impressed me with the idea, that you wished THAT *delay* should terminate in *separation*. Tell me, tell me, dearest, even what you wish and *all* you wish, and I will, at any risk, gratify you if I can. Do not wrap yourself in stoicism, nor "disdain" to open your bosom to one whose *privilege* it is to share your griefs and to soothe your sorrows. When *you will* look to me for support, you *shall* find me a man capable of strong exertion, of *self-command* to act and to suffer for you. It is your indifference, your reserve, with which I cannot contend. I confess *I* cannot see any *adequate* reason for your dread of Baron's Court. They will not return to England till late in the next summer. Do you wish, do you really wish to delay my happiness so long? I do not think you can *avoid* coming

here, without positively affronting the Abercorns, nor
can you long *delay it*.   But, as far as *I* am concerned,
do whatever will contribute to your own happiness,
and leave *mine* to its chance.   You know I had set my
heart upon our being well and intimately known to
each other by marriage, before the necessity of domestic
arrangements should interfere with our enjoyments.
When we go to England we shall have much to do
and something to suffer.   I was in hopes that by the
cultivation of every tender feeling, we should have
prepared each other to go through this with cheerfulness.
But do as you will.

Sydney Owenson to T. C. Morgan.

November 1811.

I told you I would not write to you to-day, dear,
yet down I sat, determined on sending you a long letter when I had finished Lady L.'s; but, lo! a parcel of
people (the Cahirs) and their carriage seen at the door,
others were obliged to be admitted, and one moment
till this (five o'clock) I could not get, to tell you I love
you the more I *think* of you, so take it for granted,
my *life* is yours, and should be devoted to your happiness.   God bless you! "Je t'embrasse tendrement
à la hâte."   Tell Lady L. that whatever Miss Butler
may have written her — Lady Manners *seems*, at least,
in too good spirits for anything very serious to be
impending.   S. O.

T. C. Morgan to Miss Owenson.

BARON'S COURT,
Wednesday Morning, Nov. 27th, 1811.

And God bless *you*, my dear love, notwithstanding

your shabby apologies for notes. Well, well, *you are amused — e basta cosi —* only, when you *are* at leisure, write me a dear, good letter, to make amends for your last week's *slender diet.* Your views of life are so different from mine, that at first they gave me great pain and uneasiness; use, however, reconciles to many things and I have already lost the *uneasiness;* perhaps the *pain* will soon follow, at least I feel a satisfaction in submitting my will to your's, which already diminishes it. *Nonobstant,* I wish you were more *independent* in your pleasures, and did not receive the bright lights in your picture of life so much *by reflection from the world.* For myself, I am not without a large portion of personal vanity, and am as pleased with *incense,* when offered, as others, but it is not a WANT *of habit* with me; and, on the whole, I had rather be *loved* than *admired,* and, I fear also, rather than *esteemed.* This you will say, is weakness, "le bonheur n'est pour (*moi*) ni sur la même route, ni de la même espèce, que celui des autres hommes; *ils* ne cherchent que la *puissance* et les *regards d'autun;* il ne (*me*) faut que *la tendresse et la paix,* ne suis je pas un vrai St. Preux?" and so much the worse for me, if I am; a slight touch of ambition would *pepper* life; and truly, at little more than *thirty,* it is rather hard to find all "vanity and vexation of spirit." I am as convinced as of any mathematical fact, that the whole life can give is included in the four magical letters *home.* The *affections* are the only inlets to *real* satisfaction; and they, alas! are so often chilled, thwarted, or, by death and separation, *annihilated,* that I repeat, most sincerely, "*of happiness I despair.*" Ah, Glorvina! you, you have roused me from that enviable state of apathy, in which the world

passed as a panorama, — a dream; you have called
forth the violent passions into action, which, I had
hoped, slumbered for ever *with the dead.* I am again
the sport of *hopes and fears,* and you are at once their
cause, object and end. Dearest love, you have much
in your power; oh! be merciful, be merciful! nor think
it beneath your genius to strew some flowers in the
path of him who lives but to adore you! But to *descend*
to the common-place of life, Lady Abercorn *has* received
another parcel of the books, and now finds she has got
a copy of them already. She wishes, therefore, to
know if the man will take them back, giving her something else in return? she will not *send* them till she
gets your answer. The major is again returned from
his *military duties.* How much more palpable his
PECULIARITIES are after a little absence. *Have you
burned the letters yet?* Why will you not put me at
rest on that point? You complain of my temper sometimes, but you should afford the same pardon to sickness
of *mind* as to *bodily* infirmity; your absence is the cause
of it all.

T. C. Morgan to Miss Owenson.

November 29th, 1811.

How is this Glorvina? twice, already, you have
failed writing. Is it so very painful to bestow five
minutes recollection on me? though, in truth, I know
not whether your silence is not less painful than your
letters. How cold — how indifferent — what ill-timed
levity, and ill-timed animadversion! I am, and have
been, very, very ill; and you are the cause of it. I am
sure neither health nor reason could long withstand the

agonies I suffered on your account for these last twenty-four hours. I have not slept, and am now obliged to put myself under Bowen's care. The whole of yesterday was spent in answering your letter; but *I* will not *pain you by that exhibition* of my lacerated mind; I have already destroyed it. On the subject of *delay*, however, one word for all. As long as your presence is necessary to your family, so long (be it a month or a year) I freely consent to your absence from me; *but not one hour longer;* you have no *right* to demand it, and if you knew what *love* was, it is impossible you could *wish it.* But I fear you are a stranger to love, except as it affects the fancy. You may understand its picturesque effects; but of the anxious, agonizing alternations of doubt and confidence, joy and despair — of all that is tender, of all that is *heart* in it, I fear you are utterly ignorant. For what purpose can you wish a *protracted* stay? Your plea about a "respected guest and a part of the establishment," is too childish for a moment's consideration. If you do not love me sufficiently to master such fancies — if my affection is so little esteemed, and my happiness so little valued, why have you led me into this fools' Paradise? You know you will not be able to *refuse* invitations to go out; for *them*, therefore, for your *Parkhursts* and *Ormsbys* (the devil take them) and not for your family, you will leave me in all the miseries of widowhood and solitude. I repeat it, this is *not* love. You say, before you knew me you were free as air; and I, too, was free; but you cannot give me back my former self, my "pleased alacrity and cheer of mind." Seek not, then, to torture me with your *coldness* and *carelessness.* Remember that, *attachment* means *bondage,* and that we are mutually bound to promote each other's happiness by every means in our power. Remember, that *savage freedom* is incompatible with the *social affections*, and that you have no right to render a being miserable, who lives and breathes only in your love. You cannot imagine the grief of heart, the tears, this early avowal of your wish to lengthen our separation has cost me. By heavens, there is no place so vile, so infectious, that I would not inhabit it with you; and you object to share *my* love in a *place* to which another and a more worthless passion — vanity, *has* chained you for nearly a year at once, with every circumstance that should have driven you away! How every unkind word, every doubtful expression with regard to your future conduct towards me, recurs to my recollection! *If you really do not mean to marry me*, your trifling with a passion like mine is worse than cruelty. For God's sake, be candid, and let me know the horrid truth at once.

Another thing—why do you keep secrets from me? Why suffer me to learn from others circumstances which so materially affect your interest? — as those of your father's health. For my sake, for your own, let there be no mystery between us, no separation of interests. Trust me, I was rejoiced to learn that he was better again, and that *you* were the cause of it — that is the true balm, the only balm you can pour upon the wounds made by your absence — it gratifies and consoles me.

Miss Owenson to T. C. Morgan.

December, 1811.

Great God! is there to be *no end* of this? is every *idle*, every mischievous person to change your sentiments towards me, and to destroy your confidence? what *have* I done, what *have* I said? to bring down this tirade of abuse and reproach? Your letter has distracted me. I thought myself so assured of your esteem, your confidence! I cannot write on the subject. If it is Miss Butler who has done this, I will never speak to her again.

Never mind what I said about *the bond*, no matter about that, or anything else. Your answer shall determine the moment of my departure. I will throw myself into the mail the night of the day I receive it, if you command it — *by all that is sacred* — at the expense of *health* and *life*, I will do as you desire. Livy goes *to a certainty*, except some misfortune happens, and means to leave this on the morning of the 2nd, so that she will, of course, be at Baron's Court on the night of the 3rd. If I have, indeed, been the cause of much pain to you, what remains of my life shall be devoted to your happiness. How different do we feel towards each other! I am all confidence, all esteem, all admiration, you *are in love* and nothing else. Any woman may inspire all that I have inspired — passion accompanied by distrust and suspicion — still I embrace you, my beloved, as tenderly as ever.

I am far from well. I have a most painful sore throat and oppression on my chest, with some remains of my cough; this is owing to my having gone into a bath at 105 degrees, when there was a hard frost; but the country will soon, I trust, put to flight every symptom of delicacy. God bless you! may your next bring me some comfort.

S. O.

Miss Owenson to T. C. Morgan.

December 3, 1811.

MY DEAREST DEAR,

· The horrible struggle of feeling I sought to forget
in every species of dissipation of mind, is over —
friends, relatives, country, all are now resigned, and I
am *yours* for ever — from this moment be it. The study
of my life to deserve your love, and to expiate those
errors of conduct which had their source in the long-
cherished affections of the heart, by a life devoted exclusively to you. Oh, my dearest friend, passionately
as you love me, you do not yet justly appreciate me,
and know not all I am capable of when imperiously
called on by feeling and by honour.

I have gained my point in putting of our marriage
for three months, by which I have gratified the independent spirit of my character in avoiding any addition of obligation to those on whom we are already *too*
dependent. I have satisfied the feelings of my heart by
fulfilling the tender duties they dictate, to my father
and my family. I have obtained a more thorough
knowledge of your character from the development of
your feelings in your letters; and I have satisfied my
woman's delicacy, and the *bienséance* of the world, by
avoiding the appearance of rashness in uniting myself
for life to one whom I knew but a month, which, had
I listened to you, would have been the case. I have
now done with the little world, here, and shall go out
no more; all that remains of my absence from you
must be exclusively devoted to my family. I have informed them of my resolution with great firmness; it
was received in silence and in tears; but no opposition

was made, the effort is over, and I think we are all calmer, and even happier, than during the late interval of horrible suspense. I will return to you soon after Christmas-day, as we can decide upon a safe mode of travelling. Meantime, my heart and soul are with you, and as for the little body, that will come soon enough. Every moment I can spare from my poor suffering father, I am devoting to collecting everything on Irish story that can be had here. I have made out a most exquisite subject matter for an Irish novel which will help to furnish our London *baby-house*. Well, dear, we are now where we ought to be, and long, long may we remain so. Pray tell Lady Abercorn you are satisfied with me.

Here is one of my *wife-like* demands. Will you send to London for six yards of black velvet for me? Mrs. Morgan will get it, at *Grafton House*, for half-a guinea a yard, and your friend of Pall Mall, will frank it over. This, dear, is no extravagance.   S. O.

Miss Owenson to T. C. Morgan.

Thursday, 11 o'clock, [1811].

I perceive it is easier to *command* your obedience than to *endure it*. You have taken me now, *au pied de la lettre*. Three weeks back you would have made another commentary on the text and tortured it into any sense but that in which you have now taken it. However, I submit uncomplaining, though not un-repining. Ah! my dear Morgan, *les absens ont toujours tort*, and that passion which, a month past, I feared might urge on its disappointment to exile, or even per-haps to worse, has now flown lightly over, like a summer gale, which leaves on the air scarce a trace of its fleeting fragrance. Well, "*Thou canst not say 'twas I did it.*" The inequalities, the inconsistency of my manner and my letters, the quick alternation from tenderness to reproach, from affection to indifference, the successive glow of hope and chill of despair, the brilliant playfulness of one moment, the gloomy affliction of the next — these were accessory, but not final, causes of your alienation, for your love, like your religion, is a tangible creed; faith alone will not nourish it, you must have the Real Presence; you must touch to believe, you must enjoy to adore, and in the absence of the goddess you will erect the *golden calf*, sooner than waste your homage upon an *invisible object*. Dearest, I have divined you well.

You will say, "My sweetest Glorvina, I would love you if I could; but how am I to find you? catch, if I can the Cynthia of the moment." And, dearest Morgan, you say true; but am I to blame if I am unhappy? "Who would be a wretch for ever?" and if you know the objects and the interests that alternately tear my heart, you would much less blame than pity me. In the morning, when I come down to breakfast, the dear faces I have so long looked on, turned on me with such smiles of tenderness, the family kiss, the little gossip that refers to the social pleasures of the former evening, — my whole heart is theirs, — I say, "no, I will not, cannot, part from you for ever." Then all disperse; your letter comes, your reproaches, your suspicion! divided between tenderness and resentment; wanting to give you *force*, but overcome by my own weakness — I know not what I write. My feelings struggle and combat, and I sink under it. Again —

perhaps I go out — the brilliant assembly, where every member is my friend or my acquaintance, every smile pointed to me, every hand is stretched out to me, and where all is the perfect intelligence of old acquaintance-ship, mingled with Irish wit and Irish cordiality. The reverse of the picture — the dreary country, the stately, cold magnificence, and the imposed silence; the expected affliction, and where *I* too often find ridicule substituted for that *admiration* now too necessary to me. Again you rush on me, and all is forgotten. Your true, disinterested love! your passionate feelings! your patience! your long endurance of all my faults! your generous and noble feelings! your talents, your exclusive devotion to me! THEN, *my whole soul is yours!* Father, sister, home, friends, country, all are forgotten, and I enter again upon life with you; I struggle again for subsistence; I resign ease and comfort, and share with you a doubtful existence. I give up my career of pleasure and vanity to sink into privacy and oblivion; and the ambition of the authoress and the woman is lost in the feelings of the mistress and the wife.

It was thus I felt *yesterday*, five minutes after my cold letter to you. After dinner I threw myself on the couch and heard the clock strike seven, and I was transported into the little angular room! To surprise us all, the door opened, and, carried in between two old servants, appeared the dear *father — papa!* Hot cake ordered for tea, and a boiled chicken for supper. We tuned the harp and piano, and Clarke *would* play his flute in such *time* and *tune* as it pleased God! There never was such a family picture. In the midst of it all, papa said, "I am thinking, my dears, that if God ever restores me the use of my hands, I will write a treatise on Irish music for Morgan!!" Again, when he was going back to his room, he leaned on my shoulders to walk to the door, — "you are my support now, my little darling," and he burst into tears. Such dearest, are the feelings alternately awakened in a heart so vitally alive to impressions of tenderness and affection, that in its struggles between contending emotions it is sometimes ready to burst. Oh, then, pity me, and forgive me; bear with me, examine the source and cause of my faults, and you will see them in that sensibility which makes a part of my physical structure, and which time and circumstances have fatally fed and nourished. You do not expect, do not deserve, perhaps do not wish to be *bored*, with this letter, yet I shall send it; keep it by you, and when you are angry with me, read, and forgive!

When the postman knocked, I said, "Ah! the rascal, after all his impertinent, icy Strabane letter, he has written." I flew to meet it — burst it open with a smile of triumph. It was from Lord Abercorn! the smile disappeared, and, with a sigh I sat down to write this; while you, perhaps, without one thought of the Glorvina, are writing verses on the charms of Lady Carberry.

Poor dear papa! The consequence of his little frolic last night are, that he is confined to his bed to-day, and symptoms of gout in his head. I am going to see him. God bless you. S. O.

Lord Abercorn to Miss Owenson.

[Extract.]

You are not worth writing to, little fool, for though your words are fair, they are few and probably false.

8*

Have you really the presumption to think I will condescend to write to her, who instead of writing two or three for one, thinks I am going to put up with a miserable cover of another letter?

As to "Livy," alas! I thought better of her. I thought better of her. I "give her courage by a tender line!" why was not one more tender than she deserved in my very last to you? But I see too well, that your calumnies (as I thought them) against her, are truths; and that she beguiled only to deceive me. The jackal, too, has been sneaking into the forest where the lion only should have stalked. Alas! alas! what has she to say to me for herself? and when will she say it?

T. C. Morgan to Miss Owenson.

DEAREST LOVE,

I *do* pity while I *blame* you. But your great instability, whatever be the cause of it, is equally cruel in *you* and equally unbearable to *me.* It is absolutely necessary for you to exert some firmness of nerve. Review your own conduct to me and think how very *unnecessarily* you have tortured with repeated promises, all evaded; while each letter has been a direct contradiction of the last. It is not the lapse of *time* I so much regret; and in whatever way our loves may terminate, *I beg you to carry that in your remembrance.* The same effort of self-denial, which gave you one month, would have given you *three*, had you asked it seriously and firmly. It is the eternal *fiddling* upon nerves untuned by love (perhaps too romantic) for you, that I cannot bear the repeated frustration of hope.

The evident preference you give to *general society* over mine — your very dread of this place, — the instability of your affections *as depicted in your letters*, are all sources of agony greater than I can endure, and *it must have an end.* To finish this business, then, at once — of *your own mere motion* within this last week, you have fixed with me *and with your sister too*, to leave Dublin at Christmas, *and that much* I give to *nature* and to *amusement.* If you can *then* return to me freely and voluntarily (for I will be no restraint upon you) say so, and *stick to your promise.* If not, we had better (great Heaven! and is it come to this!) we had better *never meet again.* The love I require is no ordinary affection. The woman who marries me must be *identified* with me. I must have a large bank of tenderness to draw upon. I must have frequent profession and frequent demonstration of it. Woman's love is all in all to me; it stands in place of honours and riches, and, what is yet more, in place of tranquillity of mind and ease; without it there is a void in existence that deprives me of all control of myself, and leads me to headlong dissipation, as a refuge from reflection. If, then, your love for me is not sufficiently ardent to bring you freely to me at the end of a three months' absence for your *own happiness' sake*, by Heaven! more dear to me than my own, do not let us risk a life of endless regret and disappointment. Deliberate; make up your mind; and, having done so, have the *honesty* to abide by your determination, and not again trifle with feelings so agonized as your unfortunate friend's.

As to your *two* chapters on story-telling, *I am* indignant enough at them, but my mind is too much occupied to dwell on that subject — only this; you

assume *too high a tone* on these occasions. *I* set up no
tyrannical pretensions to *man's* superiority, and have
besides a *personal* respect for *your intellect* over other
women's.   I know too, that in the present instance,
you are right.   But I never will submit to an assumed
control on the woman's side; we must be equals; and
ridicule or *command* will meet with but little success
and little quarter from me.

Oh, God! oh, God! my poor lacerated mind! but
the horrid task is over, and now, dearest woman (for
such you are and ever will be to me), take me to you,
your own ardent lover; let me throw myself on your
bosom, and give vent to my burdened heart; let me
feel your gentle pressure, the warmth of your breath,
and your still warmer tear on my cheek. Think, love,
of those delicious moments! when all created things
but our two selves were forgotten; of those instants
wherein we lived eternities.

T. C. Morgan to Miss Owenson.

Wednesday, December.

MY DEAREST LOVE,

I am indeed a wretch to inflict pain on so much
excellence; but, alas! what can wretchedness do but
complain! Recollect how often my hopes in you have
been delayed a few days, the return of a post, a week,
a month for you to go to town — three weeks' delay
in your departure added to this. And now, by every
means in your power, you would delay them still further for an indefinite time. Recollect, too, the things
you have said of yourself, your "exaggeration of your
faults," the array of lovers you have dressed out; the
times you have been on the point of matrimony and

broken it off, and think what I must suffer with a mind making food for irritation even out of mere possibilities. . Indeed, I was cut to the very heart of heart, when you first hinted at your dislike of this place being a sufficient motive for keeping *from me.* But when you renewed this plea, ere the first pang of parting had ceased to vibrate in my bosom, when you talked of happiness without me too great for comparison, can you wonder that I was horror-stricken and overwhelmed with misery. I doubt not, Glorvina, if I had duties to discharge incompatible with our meeting for some time, like you, I should discharge them, but I should *feel* the sacrifice, I should count the hours till we met, and should be, as I now am, a very wretch till that time arrived. I little thought when we parted at Omagh, that you meditated to leave me for a longer time than was originally fixed. I confess to you, I should have entreated you (on my knees I should) to have married me before you went. I should have then borne your absence with less uneasiness. Now, I have a sad presentiment we shall never meet again. I read and re-read your letter to feed upon your kind expressions, but all will not do. I sink into a despondence almost too great to bear; life is hateful to me, and the possibility of a *good* agent in creation scarcely admissible. For God's sake give me some idea when you think of returning. What hopes do the medical people give you of your father's recovering his limbs? Your last letter told me you feared he *never* would. If I had never been buoyed up with hopes of our speedy union, I could have better borne your absence. I am in so horrid a state that I have already burned two sheets full written, lest I

should annoy you; and here I am writing worse than
ever. Oh, God! oh, God! can I ever bear it? Can
you forgive it? Lady Asgill too; how that woman
frightens me! She is possessed of the only weapon
you cannot resist — *ridicule.* You will never endure
the object of her constant raillery. Really I do not
see how she can affect you, now your father is ill. I
did not part with every earthly happiness, with peace,
with everything, that you might furnish out her dinner-
tables. If you can dine out, you can come to me. I
sent you home to *nurse,* and every hour taken from
your duty to your father is a double fraud to me. Indeed, if I hear of your being gay, I shall go quite
mad! — Glorvina, *I* cannot be gay.

Sydney Owenson to T. C. Morgan.

Saturday, 10 o'clock, December 11, 1811.

If you *are not, you ought to be,* very indignant at
my last chapter upon *long stories,* for I certainly treated
the subject rather *pertly;* but you know my way of
preferring any one of the *deadly sins,* to the respectable dulness of worthy *bores;* and if there is any one
thing on earth more insupportably *provoking* than another, it is to see a man like yourself full of that *stuff*
which people call "*natural talent,*" cultivated by a
superior education, enlightened by science, and refined by philosophy, concealing his native treasures,
and borne away by the bad *ton* of a bad style of society, substituting, in their stead, the "leather and
prunella" of false taste. It is thus the *Irish peasant*
plants potatoes on the surface of those mountains whose
bosoms *teem with gold!* I have seen the best and the

worst of English society; I have dined at the table of a *city trader*, taken tea with the family of a *London merchant*, and supped at Devonshire House, all in one day, and I must say, that if there is a people upon earth that understand the *science* of conversation LESS than another, it is the English. The quickness, the variety, the rapidity of perception and impression, which is indispensable to render conversation delightful, is *constitutionally denied* to them; like all people of slowly operating mental faculties, and of business pursuits, they depend upon *memory* more than upon *spontaneous thought*. When the power of, and *time* for, cultivating that retentive faculty is denied, they are then *hébête* and tiresome, and when it is granted (as among the higher circles) the omnipotence of *ton* is so great that every one fears to risk himself. In Ireland it is quite different; our *physique*, which renders us ardent, restless, and fond of change, bids defiance to the cultivation of memory; and, therefore, though we produce men of genius, we never have boasted of any man of learning — and so we excel in conversation, because, of necessity we are obliged to do the honours of the *amour propre* of others; we are obliged to *give* and *take*, for thrown upon excitement, we only respond in proportion to the quantity of stimulus received. In England, conversation is a game of chess — the result of judgment, memory, and deliberation; with us, it is a game of battledore, and our ideas, like our shuttlecocks, are thrown lightly *one* to the *other*, bounding and rebounding, played more for amusement than conquest, and leaving the players equally animated by the game, and careless of its results.

There is a term in England applied to persons popular in society, which illustrates what I have said; it is "*he* (or she) *is very amusing*," that is, they tell stories of a *ghost*, or an *actor*. They recite *verses*, or they play *tricks*, all of which must exclude conversation, and it is, in my opinion, the very *bane* of good society. An Englishman will *declaim*, or he will *narrate*, or he will *be silent;* but it is very difficult to get him to converse, especially if he is *suprême bon ton*, or labours under the reputation of being a *rising man;* but even all this, dull as it is, is better than a man who, struck by some fatal analogy in what he is saying, immediately chimes in with the eternal "*that puts me in mind*," and then gives you, not an anecdote, but an absolute history of something his uncle did, or his grandfather said, and then, by some lucky association, goes on with stories which have his own obscure friends for his heroes and heroines, but have neither point, *bût*, humour, nor even *moral* (usually tagged to the end of old ballads). Oh, save me from this, good heaven, and I will sustain all else beside!

Dad's bedroom, 10 o'clock, letter arrived.

Ah, dearest love, what a querulous letter. While I, waiting impatiently for the post, was scribble, scribble, scribble, and would have gone on till night in the same idle way, had not your letter cut me short; — dearest, suspicious Morgan, you wrong me, indeed, you do, if you think me capable of evasion or deceit. When I left you, I had no plan, no object in view, but to gratify imperious feelings which still tyrannise and lead me on from day to day. It is not *I* who entreat permission to prolong my residence here, it is a father whom I *shall never see again* — it is a sister, whom I *may* never see again. It is friends I love, and who love me, who solicit you to leave me yet a little longer among them — you who are about to *possess me for ever!* My best friend, if after all I should be miserable, would you not blame yourself for having put a force upon my inclinations? If I come *voluntarily and self-devoted* to you, then the penalty lies upon my own head, and I must *abide the issue.* I will tell you honestly, and I have often told you so, you call it caprice or weakness if you will; but *I shudder at the place!* You will understand me, I *know* the susceptibility of my spirits, and I know the train of gloomy impressions which await them. I am *sure* of you! I am only delaying a good which may be mine whenever I please, and avoiding evils which *are certain,* and which once there, I cannot escape. Still, however, I am not the unworthy wretch you think. I am always more to be pitied than blamed.

God bless you dearest, ever. S. O.

T. C. Morgan to Miss Owenson.

Baron's Court,
December [14], *1811.*

My yesterday's letter will be a sufficient answer to yours of this morning. I can only repeat, that I will no more consent to delay and trifling, and that I consider your fulfilment of your sacred promise as the touchstone of your affection, and the only means of regaining my confidence, at present, I confess, somewhat in *abeyance.* I do not mean to *accuse* you of deceit, as you have so often said, but while your wishes extend in proportion to my facility in complying with them — while your love of pleasure (now no longer disguised) exceeds your love for me, and your regard for your own honour and pledged word — while your letters alternately breathe hot and cold as to *marrying at all*, you cannot wonder that I think you *tired of your bargain*, and I am anxious to reduce to certainty my hopes and fears on points so entirely involving my complete life. Professions of love are easily made; but if you really have that regard for me which I suppose, *place* cannot make so much difference. Your hatred of this place is an insult which any, less foolishly-fond than myself, would seriously resent. You complain of my irritable feelings; they are your own creation; from the very first hour of our intimacy, either from *want of tact*, or from disregard of it, you have kept them afloat, and when the cup is full you cannot wonder if a drop makes it run over.

[End wanting.]

T. C. Morgan to Miss Owenson.

Saturday, December 16th.

Ah, dearest, what have I done? positively nothing, but what I was always *prepared* to do, what I always felt *bound* to do — given up to yourself, — and considered you entirely your own mistress, to act as you pleased; *free as air, unpromise-bound* — to the very last moment of your approach to the altar; and yet, though our relative situation is not altered, I am fretful and uneasy, that you should *deliberate*. Perhaps I am mortified that deliberation should yet be necessary; whatever it be, I have not the courage to look the possibility of losing you in the face. Surely, surely, it has not been a presentiment of *truth*, that has uniformly haunted me with the idea that you would not ultimately be mine. Do not say I am *meanly suspicious*, or that I have any *fixed notion* of your intending me unfairly; it is but the restless anxiety of a mind, naturally too susceptible of painful impressions, acted upon by circumstances *very peculiar*, and which (when once we are married) can never recur. "Je ne doute pas votre sincerité; votre amour même n'est plus un mystère pour moi, mais j'apprehende quelques révolutions; quelles, et d'où peuvent elles venir? Je n'en scais rien — je crois que je puis dire; je crains *parceque j'aime*." This is exactly my state; ah, my God! you deliberate!! and under what circumstances? surrounded by objects all acting forcibly on your senses and imagination, all opposed to my interests in you. Bored eternally by acquaintance who wish to retain you they know not why, — and no one by to take my part, to support my cause and plead with you for me. Alas! the paper can indeed carry my *complaints*, can show you the variety of my feelings, but it shows only the *désagrémens* of the passion, but the *inconvenience* to which (perhaps an ill regulated) love *appears* to threaten you. Little can it express the warmth, the tenderness of the feeling, still less can it convey the *kiss*, the sigh, the tear, the look which speak at once to the heart, and "outstrip the pauser reason;" *ah! les absens ont tort en verité*, in this case. It is vain that the cold line is traced, without the expression that should accompany its delivery, the rhetoric of the eye is dumb and the heart cannot submit to mere *calculation and debate*. Dearest, dearest girl, I *have* a friend, an eloquent friend in your bosom; call him often to council; he will tell you far, far more than *words* can express; he will remind you of moments, blissful as they were transitory, moments when the world was but as nothing, compared to the passion, the tender self-abandonment of your friend; he will whisper of instants when father, sister, all were forgotten, or remembered only as less capable of conferring happiness than he who now addresses you. You have had, I admit, but a bad specimen of *my temper*. Irritable feelings but too idly indulged; but consider the unusual situation in which I am placed. You had always assumed a volatile, inconsequent air, and before I could be *assured of your love*, you left me. Honestly and fervently, I believed you *no trifling good*, and the *weight* of the loss has always pressed on me more than the *probability*, that I should lose you. I was uneasy because I was not *absolutely* and *entirely* certain of you.

Do you understand this? If I at all know myself, and can judge by my three years of married life, I am above suspicion and jealousy. I do not know that I ever felt one uneasy moment on that head. But while fate can snatch you from me, while you are anything short of my *married wife*, I cannot help taking alarm — I know not why — and from circumstances that won't bear analysis. Cannot you comprehend a sensation of uneasiness that crossed me (for instance) when I read your *friends'* satirical account of this place. It appears as if every body were *trying* to detain you and to picture your prospects in as dark colours as possible. Such have, however, been the *bout* of every anecdote you have written me of *Dublin conversation*. Ah, my own sweet love, you cannot think

how much *more than they ought*, such *trifles* prey upon
a bosom agitated like mine. I should, indeed, be
ashamed to confess this, if I did not feel it was *nature*,
and a necessary part of a devoted affection. Our
weather, contrary to your supposition, is fine, and
Baron's Court (in my eyes) as lovely as ever. Were
you out of the question, I could live here for ever.
London and its gaieties would be forgotten.

Miss Owenson to T. C. Morgan.

December 18th, 1811.

My dear Friend,
Your letter to-day [of the 16th] came very oppor-
tunely. *Your dreadful epistle* yesterday [of the 14th]
totally overthrew me, — it found me ill and low spirited,
and left me in a high fever; in my life I never received such a *shock* — its *severity*, its *cruelty*, its *suspicion*. Oh, what a frightful futurity opened to my
view! I went to bed almost immediately to hide my
feelings from my family, but never closed my eyes all
night; I am now languid and stupefied; my cold is
very oppressive, it is an influenza going; my throat,
however, is better.

From the style of your letter to-day, I suppose, I
may stay to accompany my sister on the 2nd, that is,
next Thursday, *the day week on which you will receive
this*. Still I will go the moment your mandate arrives, *whether I am better or not*, and whether *my life
is at stake* or no. It would be much better to die than
to suffer what I did *yesterday*. I don't care a fig about
being popular or unpopular. I am sick of that stuff
and intend to be more savagely independent than ever.

I am so very unwell, particularly in my head and throat, that I cannot write much to you. I have been obliged to give up *extracting*."

PS. — Write me word how my *large trunk* can be conveyed to Baron's Court, as I would send it off directly. My dearest, do not think of coming to *meet* us — we both particularly intreat you will *not*. We shall be quite full inside the carriage and cannot admit you (*maid inside*), and what use your riding beside the carriage? I entreat most earnestly you will let our first meeting be in your own little room. I will fly there the moment I arrive — but no human being must be present. My cold is better. If Livy does not *set off* at *daylight* on Thursday morning, no human power shall prevent me setting off in *the evening* without. She will decidedly *go, and on that day*, and so, *for once*, have confidence and believe. Who could invent such a lie, that I did not mean to go to Baron's Court till the middle of January? The idea never *suggested itself* to me; the 3rd was the most distant day I ever thought of. I suspect that wretched G., for reasons I have. God bless you, dearest and most beloved.   S. O.

I will write to-morrow if the post leaves this, but I fear it does not.

Mr. Owenson to T. C. Morgan.

Dublin, December 23, 1814.

"Not know you? by the Lord *I do*, as well as he that made you, Hal;" why, I wouldn't be acquainted with any man that I didn't *find out* in speaking two sentences, or reading a couple of paragraphs of his letter. Well, then, although I know you these *fifty years*, I am at a loss whether to believe the *whole*, or the *half* of what I hear of you; to save you a blush (for I suppose you've *learned* to blush since you came to this *immaculate* country), I shall believe but *half*, and if you are but the tenth part of that half, by the Lord you are too good for a son-in-law of mine, who have been, however, half the while, little better than one of the wicked. Well, all's one for that; heaven's above all, and as we in the *south* say, "there's worse in the *north*." The cause of this saying arose from the hatred the southerns (especially the lower orders) had to the northerns, looking upon them as marauders and common robbers; and it was a common thing with nurses to frighten the children to sleep, by threatening them to call an *Ulsterman*. I remember this very well, myself. Now, if one man is speaking ill of another to a third person, that man will probably say, "Well, well, he is bad enough; but there's worse in the north."

"But hear, you *yadward*," here's a little bit of a thing here, that runs out in your praise as if you were "the god of her idolatry;" by-the-bye, you've had a good deal of patience with her lately; don't let her ride the *bald filly* too much; and if she won't go quietly in a *snaffle*, get a good *bit* and *curb* for her. But I have nothing to say to it; "among you be it, blind harpers."

For myself, here I am, "a poor old man, more sinned against than sinning." Instead of being the "fine, gay, bold-faced vil —" no, I'll change the word to *fellow*, I was wont to be — the very head and front of every jollification — I am dwindled into the "*slipper'd pantaloon*, with my hose a world too large for my shrunk shanks." I deny this, for my feet and legs swell so in the course of the day, that I can scarcely get hose large enough to fit me; but this swelling goes off in the night. "Canst thou not minister to a *leg* diseased? if thou canst not, throw physic to the dogs, I'll none on't;" time however, is drawing near, when it will be "sans eyes, sans teeth, sans everything." With me, however, although "I owe heaven a debt, I would not wish to pay it before it's due;" therefore, if I could get these legs well, and the cursed teasing pain in my head somewhat banished, I should not fear lilting up one of *Carolan's planxtirs*, in such a style as to be heard from this to the *Monterlomy mountains* with the wind full in my teeth; for the old *trunk* is as sound as a roast, and never once in the course of a ten months' illness, was in the least affected, therefore, "who is afraid."

Sir Arthur and I will be left all alone and moody in a few days, as our ladies mean to set off immediately to the hospitable mansion of Baron's Court, where, as I am informed, the good things of this world are only to he had; so, commending you to God's holy keeping, and wishing you neighbour's share of plum-pudding, this gormandizing season, I remain, then, in truth and in spirit,

ROBERT OWENSON.

PS. You have worked a miracle—for eight months back, I never could take a pen in my hand! I really am astonished at myself now, bad as it is.

Sydney Owenson to T. C. Morgan.

December 24th.

I told you yesterday, dearest, that you should have a long letter to-day, and here comes one as short as myself. The reason is, that a good old Irishman has sent me 20,000 volumes of old Irish books to make extracts from, and I am to return them directly, and here I am in poor Dad's room just after binding up his poor blistered head, and I am just going to work pell mell, looking like a little conjuror, with all my black-lettered books about me. I am extracting from Edmund Spenser, who loved Ireland *tant soit peu;* dearest, your letters are delicious, 'tis such a sweet feeling to create happiness for those we love; if we have but *de quoi vivre* in a *nutshell house* in London, *I* shall be satisfied, and you shall be made as happy as Irish love, Irish talent, and Irish fun can make a grave, *cold*, shy Englishman. Your song is divine. Here is Livy just come in and insists on saying so; but first I must tell you that poor, dear papa continues very ill and so low spirited, that it is heart-breaking to listen to him.

SYDNEY.

Postscript from Livy.

DEAR CHARLES,

I like and thank you for your pretty song, — it is quite in the *style* of Italian composition, and is the very thing for my weak natural voice, and I shall sing it with the Spanish guitar to great advantage. I suppose I may thank Madam Glo.'s loving epistles for your little *billet doux.*

I am yours, *en tout cas,*

OLIVIA.

9*

December 24.

Irish books are pouring in on all sides — anonymously, too, which is very singular, and mostly "*Rebelly*" books as you English would call them. Has Lady Abercorn *Taaf's Impartial History of Ireland?* I hear it is beautifully written, and full of eloquence. I think, to-morrow, Livy will have talked over her journey with Clarke, and something will decidedly be settled. Till then, and now, ever and ever yours in every way,

GLORVINA.

I write, as usual, in a hurry. There is a puff in the Irish papers to-day, so like Stockdale, that I could *swear* he sent it over for insertion. I'll try and get it for you before I send this.

In the next letter it will be seen that Lady Abercorn speaks of her physician as Sir Charles. He was not yet knighted, but Lady Abercorn had always proposed that when the Wild Irish Girl married she should have a title, and His Grace of Richmond was ready to lay the sword on Morgan's reluctant shoulders whenever her ladyship pleased.

Lady Abercorn to Miss Owenson.

December, 1811.

DEAR GLORVINA,

I own I think if you are not here by Christmas, you use Sir Charles very ill indeed; let me give you a piece of advice, which I know, from a long knowledge of the world, that it is very unwise for a woman, when she intends to marry a man, to let him for a moment suppose he is not her first object; for after marriage, people have more time to reflect, and *sometimes it might so happen* that a man might recollect that though he was accepted of for a husband, that past conduct proved it was more *par convenance* than from attachment; now I know you will say, that as Sir Charles is not a very great match, he cannot ever imagine you married him for ought but himself; but that will not be so considered, and I recommend you to play no longer with his feelings. I am sure Lady Clarke will be of my opinion; I leave her to decide, trusting that she has a wiser head than you have. Tell Lady Clarke I do hope she will be here before Christmas; I am sure she will not be the person to put off coming.

I should be sorry to offend Mr. Mason; I am very sensible of his great goodness to me, and if there was a chance of his taking it ill my not wanting the MS., pray have it done. My objection to it is, that it has been so long about, that Lady Charlotte Campbell will have forgotten all about it; if, however, the Schoolmaster is come up to do it, let it be done, and, above all, express to Mr. Mason my *gratitude*. I only want the bookseller to change the books for others — they are damaged, and I have a set of them, here. He might let me have No. 62, which is about the same price.

What is the cabinet? tell me. What is become of Miss Butler? bid her write to me.

Yours, dear Glorvina, sincerely,

A. J. A.

Miss Owenson to T. C. Morgan.

December, 26, 1811.

Lady Cahir has just sent me a magnificent edition of the *Pacata Hibernica*, to be returned this evening, by Miss Butler, who drinks tea with me, and I am extracting till I am black in the face, and I have scarce a moment to say how do you do? I had made up my mind before Lady Abercorn's letter, as you must have known by three letters you had previously received; but I thought it would please her to give her a little credit, &c., &c. I have written a very civil little billet to Mrs. Morgan, merely inclosing the address for Skinner, as it will save six days' delay. Are you angry? God bless you, which is all I have time to say.

Ever your own,

GLORVINA.

Miss Owenson to T. C. Morgan.

December, 27th, 1811.

"And the last *note* is shorter than the first." I totally despair of ever writing you a legitimate letter again, and you have met with a more formidable rival in O'Donnel, of Tirconnel, than all your jealous brain ever fancied in Generals, Aids-de-Camps, and Dublin LAWYERS. I have not yet got through the *Pacata*, and have obtained permission to keep it another day. I delight in my story, and my hero, and shall give myself *à tête baissée* this winter to the best of passions — LOVE and Fame. Heaven send the *latter* do not find its extinction in the *former*, and depend upon it, dear, had I asked your leave *to stay in Dublin three months*, you would have knocked me down. I will do all you desire on the subject of odious business, and I shall write to you (barring O'Donnel) to-morrow, fully on it, and if *I do not*, believe, as Sappho says, "the less my *words*, the more my love appears." Dearest friend, protector, guardian, guide, — every day draws me closer to you by ties (I trust) which Death only can break. There was so much of FORCE in the commencement of this business, that my heart was frightened *back* from the course it would *naturally have taken*. I have now had time *to reflect* myself into love for you — how much deeper and fonder than that mere *engoûment* which first possessed me; do not fear me, my dear friend, once *decided* upon rational grounds, I am *immoveable*, and I am as much *yours* as if the Archbishop of Canterbury had given his blessing to the contract; by your wishing to get all business out of the way, I suppose I am to be met at the door by *Mr. Bowen** with his prayer-book in one hand and you in the other, and "will you, Sydney, take this man," &c., &c. Heavens, *what a horror!* but you really *cannot mean* to take me, shattered and shaken after a long, dislocating journey! Let me at least, like other innocent victims, *be fed* before I am offered.

Miss Owenson to T. C. Morgan.

December 28th.

Why, I'm coming you wretch! Do you think I can borrow Friar Bacon's flying chair or Fortunatus' wishing cap? Would I could; and at eight o'clock this

---

* Lady Abercorn's chaplain.

evening in the old arm-chair in the angular room — ah,
you rascal! —

> "Have you no bowels
> For my poor relations?"

No, you are merciless as a vulture, and I am worse
off than

> "the maiden all forlorn,
> Who was tossed by the cow
> With the crumplty horn."

Well, no matter. I go on loving *ad libitum* — and
without my "vanity and ambition," literary and personal,
I cannot get on. As to our plans of travelling, they can
be determined on in an hour. I do not think Livy could
set off before the 5th of January.

Now, Stupid the First, read the following paragraph
to the best of all possible marchionesses: —

"The injured Glorvina can read and put together
as well as other people, and with respect to No. 9,
acted with her accustomed wisdom — she bought *neither*
edition until she described both to the Marchioness.
The difference lies in this — the dear one *is dear* because
it is a rare one, done upon much larger paper than the
cheap; the engravings much finer by the execution, —
and the binding splendid morocco and gold; the cheap
one would be deemed a very fine book if not seen
beside the other. The engravings are coarser, but
the work, in Glorvina's opinion, equally good. The
scarcity of the fine edition is its value. Mr. Mason is
gone this day to look at both. I bought none till
further orders."   S. O.

T. C. Morgan to Miss Owenson.

Saturday, 4 o'clock, p. m.,
December 28, 1811.

A thousand thousand blessings upon my soul's best hope for her dear letters. Oh! how welcome was the stranger joy to my heart, yet *it was* a stranger, and its first approach, almost pain. I grew sick as I read, and trembled violently — tears flowed, welcome, heavenly drops; dear as the first showers in April, when the cold east wind has long parched the fields. My beloved Glorvina, you *will* come, then! you *will* be here at Christmas? and no longer leave me to pine at your absence, and doubt your love. Yet tell me so again; tell me your arrangements; as yet I dare not trust myself with this promise of better days. I have had a long and dreary dream, and fear has not yet quitted me. How weak, how inadequate are words to express all that I would say to you on this event! the ideas crowd upon my mind, and in vain seek for utterance. I would tell you of my love, my devotion, my gratitude. I would do homage to your *virtues*, to your *tenderness*, your *affection*, by heaven more welcome to me than fortune's proudest gifts, her foremost places; but it must not be. Your imagination must befriend me; think me at your feet, my long frozen bosom thawed and melting into all that is tender, all that is affectionate. What an age of misery I have suffered! — the pain, the grief of heart to think hardly of you! Yet so it has been; you have suffered in my estimation ,more than I dare tell; and though I *feel now* that I *wronged* you, *yet was I not unjust;* but thank God, thank God, all is again peace, and I have nothing to regret, but the lingering flight of slow-winged time. My sweet love, why do you not take care of your health? Why do you suffer that odious cough to remain? be more thoughtful of yourself, for my sake; how much too happy should I be was it possible to bear your sorrows and your sickness for you — what a proud satisfaction in the endurance! The bell has just rung, and I must bid you a hasty farewell. Give my love to Livy, and tell her, if I can manage a *billet doux* for her to-morrow I will write.

Mille metti teneri amori.

MARINO.

T. C. Morgan to Miss Owenson.

Saturday, December 29th.

I could almost fancy, my dearest life, that there was something more than chance in your having inclosed the *billet douceureuse;* that *I*, too, might have something pleasant to peruse to-day, and so sympathise with you in the delight with which you are now reading my letter of Thursday last. Ten thousand thanks for it! How little do you know my temper; that small note has a power over my mind beyond comparison greater than your grave, sententious epistles; you will never *scold* me into yielding a point; but coax me, out of whatever you will, though it be my heart's blood. I cannot think of your stupid Irish post without vexation. Two whole days of torment added to your sufferings, and to my repentance. But I have *sinned*, and must bear your anger till the return of post on Monday relieves me. When I look

back at my senseless irritability, I am more than
ashamed. It was the excess of love; but I am sure
un peu plus d'indifférence, would have been more excusable. However, at last you have gained a triumph,
and I bow submissive at your feet. Enjoy your
victory with moderation, and as you are stout, be
merciful. You may partly guess what the sacrifice has
cost *me*. You have not only vanquished love, and
ardent, passionate, yet tender anxiety to possess you;
but you have overcome my fixed *principles* of conduct
and compelled me (according to my ideas) to risk
our happiness, by protracting courtship; the *whims
and caprices I* mean are those little peculiarities of
habit, which can only be known to us by the close
contact of matrimony. All the courtship in the world
will never teach them. What the conquest has cost
you, you do not know. If love had a triumph over
reason, reason has, in its turn, gained the advantage
of love. I love you certainly less than I did. It is
more T. C. M. and Miss O., and less Mortimer and
Glorvina. Yet I hope I have stock enough on hand,
to carry us through the *vale of years.* "*Such as you
are,*" you are necessary to my happiness, so I must
e'en marry you, *your "sensible men" and all.* I hope
and trust all unpleasant discussion is over between us.
Burn my "eloquence" that it may not rise in judgment
against me, and *if you can,* forget the ungenerous
reveries in which I have indulged. You must, I hope
feel, *that in spite of my nonsense,* I am ready to sacrifice every feeling of self to your happiness. I do not
wish *me faire valoir,* but you cannot conceive the con-
vulsive throes of my mind, even now, at *trusting* my
hopes into your possession. If you had asked Clarke,

he would have told you in what funds my *little all*
lies. My long *annuity* stands in my own name; my
wife's settlement is vested in the Three per Cents., in
the names (I think) of George Hammond, Anthony
H. John Buckshaw and Francis Const, the trustees to
the settlement. So ma'am you are accountable to no
one on earth but *me*. Oh, that I could now *kiss* my
thanks to you for the sweet avowal; prepare to find
in me a *rigid accountant*, demanding the long arrear of
love you owe me, and one who will not let you off
"till you have paid the uttermost farthing." Thank
your sister for her note, *she*, too, shall love me; *kiss*
her for me, "mais pas *à bouche ouverte*, ce n'est pas
encore le temps."

Miss Owenson to T. C. Morgan.

Great George's Street, Dublin,
December, 29, 1811.

Packing to be off, you quiz! Don't grumble at this
scrap, but down on your knees and thank God you get
a line. I am all hurry and confusion, and my spirits
sad, sad, and sometimes hysterically high; how much
I must love you to act as I am acting! I shall write
to-morrow; but not after. Oh, Morgan! give me all
your love, tenderness, comfort and support — in five
short days I am yours for ever. My poor father — do
write to him — flatter him beyond everything on the
score of his little

S. O.

CHAPTER IX.

LADY MORGAN.

LADY CLARKE's health was not strong enough to bear the journey to Baron's Court at such an inclement period of the year, and Miss Owenson had to go back and encounter her fate alone. In narrating this part of her history, she admitted that she felt rather doubtful of her reception. The carriage was in waiting for her; but quite empty. On her arrival, the Marquis was stately, and the Marchioness stiff, in their welcome; but Sir Charles, who had been knighted by the Lord Lieutenant, was too enchanted by her return to be able to recollect that he had ever been displeased, and in the course of a quarter of an hour, she quite convinced him that he had been in the wrong, altogether, and that her own conduct had been, not only right, but admirable. She was soon reinstated in all her former favour. The following letter from Miss Butler to Lady Clarke shows how matters stood ten days afterwards. It was an act of courtesy on the part of his Grace the Duke of Richmond to Lord Abercorn to confer knighthood on his family physician, who had done nothing to deserve it on public grounds. Morgan, himself, cared nothing about it; but to please Miss Owenson he would have been content to pass under any denomination.

Miss Butler to Lady Clarke.

BARON'S COURT,
January 1812.

MY DEAR LADY CLARKE,

The vice-regal party are here, and are all running

after the grouse, at this moment. The Duke is to make
Dr. Morgan (of the Linnean Society, and Fellow of the
Royal College of Physicians in London) a *Knight*. The
ceremony is to take place in a few hours. The coquette
has behaved very well, for these ten days past; she
really seems now attached to him. She is afraid Lady
Asgill has quizzed *Sir Charles* Morgan to you; for a
reason Miss Owenson has, she thinks every body would
rather *have the mate*. He is in as great a frenzy as ever
about her. He left me, last night most suddenly, in
the midst of an Italian duett, before the whole *Court*,
to go and listen to what *his love* said to *Mr. Parkhurst*.
I was rather offended at being so publicly disgraced
and deserted, considering that he thinks me *the first of
women*, and that I have *great capabilities*. However,
I must tell you, Glorvina is minding her P. P. P.'s
and Q. Q. Q.'s.

Yours, sincerely,
J. BUTLER.

Lady Morgan used to tell, very comically, of her
dismay at finding herself fairly caught in the toils.
Any romance she had felt about Sir Charles, was
frightened out of her for the time being, and she said
she would have given anything to be able to run away
again. Neither was much delay accorded to her. On
a cold morning in January, she was sitting in the
library, by the fire, in her morning wrapper, when
Lady Abercorn opened the door, and said, "Glorvina,
come up stairs directly, and be married; there must be
no more trifling!"

Her ladyship took Miss Owenson's arm, and led
her up stairs into her dressing-room, where a table was

arranged for the ceremony — the family chaplain, standing in full canonicals, with his book open, and Sir Charles ready to receive her. There was no escape left. The ceremony proceeded, and the Wild Irish Girl was married past redemption.

The event had at last come upon her by surprise. No one of the many visitors in the house knew of it coming on thus suddenly; nor was the fact itself announced till some days afterwards, when Lord Abercorn, after dinner, filled his glass and drank to the health of "Sir Charles and Lady Morgan."

CHAPTER X.

FIRST YEAR OF MARRIED LIFE.

Having with difficulty won his wife, Sir Charles Morgan had to encounter the greater difficulty of making their married life answer the ardent promises and protestations with which he had invoked it. His was a more than ordinary hazardous choice. His wife, accustomed to unlimited flattery, general admiration and entire independence of action, to say nothing of the deference with which she was treated by every member of her own family circle, was very imperfectly prepared for the subordination and restraint of marriage. Her strong will and great determination of character had hitherto been virtues; henceforth, they bade fair to become inconveniences in her domestic life, whilst her entire control over her own resources withdrew from her husband that power of the purse, which, in governments and in private life, is the most effective instrument of control. It required a rare mellowness of character and a remarkable combination of qualities to extract quiet domestic happiness from such perilous materials. Sir Charles had been a very ardent lover, but the probabilities seemed many, that he would be a disenchanted husband. The result, however, proved that there is no infallible judgment except that which is formed after the event! The marriage proved in all respects a remarkably happy one. Sir Charles was a man of a sweet and noble nature, generous, high-minded, entirely free from all meanness or littleness, tender-hearted and affectionate, with a vehement and passionate temper, excessively jealous of his wife's affection, but not in the least jealous of her genius and success. He was the most enthusiastic of her admirers, the most devout believer in her powers of mind, acquirements and genius; but he was also a man of great firmness of character, strength of mind, and integrity of principle. There was nothing weak about his love for her; indeed, he was greatly her superior in solidity of character and soundness of judgment. He was rather indolent, had no ambition, and as little vanity or self-love as a man could have, — and be mortal. He had every quality in private life to ensure a woman's respect; being upright, truthful, straightforward, reserved, and reticent. His very faults, and most of all, his sharp temper, gave him an advantage over his wife. Lady Morgan held him in unbounded respect, and at the bottom was rather afraid of him; he had the qualities which rule a woman, and which all women love to find in a man. She could depend upon him for guidance and control, and that to a woman is more even than affection. He was not a man of genius, but he was a great deal wiser than his wife. Nevertheless, her strong individuality asserted itself; she had much influence with him, and whenever there was a conflict of inclination between them, she always got her own way. She loved society, — distractions, — to be in constant movement, — to see everything — to hear everything — to have incessant change of scene. Possessed of an unfailing flow of spirits, and constitutionally cheerful; she had an extremely good temper which, however, did not hinder her from being sometimes wilful and provoking. The result was, that their opposite qualities, working upon each other, and controlled by mutual good sense, produced the most agreeable effect. If she did not change his nature, she modified his tastes and his habits, so that they never went anywhere without each other, and as she could not live, except in society, he went into it with her; she could always succeed in getting him to do whatever she wished, or to go wherever she liked, though not without some grumbling and occasional protest. He kept her steady, and she kept him from stagnating into indolent repose.

The first year was very stormy, not without seasons of fine weather, but not "set fair." Afterwards, the domestic atmosphere cleared, their mutual qualities adjusted themselves, and, like the people in the winding up of a fairy tale, "they lived happily ever after." The works she wrote after her marriage take a different rank to those she wrote previously, and bear the impress of her constant intercourse with her husband's sterling and highly cultivated mind. It has fallen to the lot of very few distinguished women to be so happily mated.

Miss Owenson did not come to her husband portionless; she had saved about five thousand pounds, the proceeds of her writings; this sum was settled upon herself, and it was stipulated in the marriage settlement that she was to have the sole and independent control over her own earnings, whilst the reversion of Sir Charles Morgan's fortune was settled upon the daughter of his first marriage.

The following letters to Mrs. Lefanu, give an account of her early married life at Baron's Court.

Lady Morgan to Mrs. Lefanu.

BARON'S COURT,
February, 1812.

You, who have followed me through the four acts of my comedy, seem to cut me dead at the fifth, and leave me to the enjoyment of my own catastrophe without sympathy or participation; not a single couplet to celebrate the *grand event*, not even one line of prose to say "I wish you joy." It is quite clear, that like all heroines, I no longer interest when I gain a husband.

Since you will not even ask me how I am, I will volunteer the information of my being as happy as being "loved up to my bent" (aye, and almost beyond it) can make me, and, indeed, so much is it true, "the same to-day, to-morrow, and for ever," that I can give you no other notice of my existence than that miraculous one of a man being desperately in love with his own wife, and she "nothing loath."

Though living in a palace, we have all the comfort and independence of home; besides bed-rooms and dressing-rooms, Morgan's study has been fitted up with all the luxury of a *joli boudoir* by Lady Abercorn (who neither spared her taste nor purse on the occasion.) It is stored with books, music, and everything that can contribute to our use and amusement. Here "the world forgotten, and by the world forgot," we live all day, and do not join the family till dinner time, and as *chacun a son goût* is the order here, when we are weary of argand lamps and a gallery a hundred feet long in the evening — we retire to our own snuggery, where, very often, some of the others come to drink coffee with us. As to me, I am *every inch a wife*, and so ends that brilliant thing that was GLORVINA.

N.B. — I intend to write a book to explode the vulgar idea of matrimony being the tomb of love. Matrimony is the real thing and all before but "leather and prunella."

This chapter I dedicate to Bess. Sir Charles desires me to assure you of his highest consideration: an enthusiast in *everything*, he is a *zealot* as to talent, and one of your old letters has roused all his fanaticism in your favour; he longs as much to know you as I do to see you, *et c'est beaucoup dire!* for that, I fear, for a long time there is no chance.

Lady Morgan to Mrs. Lefanu.

BARON'S COURT.

I have just learned from Olivia that you are ill; it is quite too *bad* that you, who are so much to so many, should be so often laid up, while those who are

10*

nothing to nobody, are going about with health and spirits sufficient to bore and annoy all their acquaintances; but so it is in this best of all possible worlds! My little billet crossed your kind and delightful letter, which I have not answered just because I had nothing to say worth the trouble of poring your poor eyes over my illegible scribble; and next, because I keep writing to you in store, as children do their *bonne bouches*, — the best thing for the last.

A *chance* (studiously sought for) threw it in my way to speak of dear Tom to the Chancellor. He is himself a good old Christian, upon the good old plan, and the little sketch I gave of Tom as a primitive minister of a primitive religion, as one whose vocation seemed to have "come from above," and yet as one "more skilled to raise the wretched than to rise," seemed to please him. Shortly after, he asked me if he had not married a daughter of Dr. Dobbins!

I merely mention this to you, because the Chancellor has the disposal of the patronage of the Archbishop of Dublin, and that he is to be entirely guided by the fitness of persons to fill their stations, and not by interest or influence. He is a most excellent churchman, and not at all a man to *rébuter* any application made to him on just grounds. "On this hint" you may act.

Colonel Gore is your "*slave and blackamoor.*" The day he arrived here, in the midst of a dinner, silent and solemn as the dulness of *bon ton* could make it, he cried out, "Lady Morgan, I am under more obligations to your friend than to all the world besides." "What friend?" "Why Mrs. Lefanu to be sure; she taught my Phillip to read Milton." &c., &c.

I long to hear from you; by this I hope you have seen my dear Olivia; she is England mad, would *we were all* settled there. Here or there, *partout où vous êtes, et partout où je suis*, I must always be among the number of those who respect you most and love you dearest.

God bless you ever,
S. MORGAN.

PS. — Poor, dear, excellent Bess is, I suppose, as usual, your nurse and companion. She is, indeed, the inestimable daughter of an inimitable mother, and in my opinion, her whole life has been active, useful, and of practical excellence. She is one of the sinners who devote themselves to the "nothingness of good works."

The tone of the following letter is very much softened and subdued from the "saucy Arethusa" style of former times.

It will be seen that all the kindness and luxury with which she was surrounded did not prevent Lady Morgan from wishing to have an independent home of her own.

Lady Morgan to Lady Stanley.

BARON'S COURT, NEWTOWN-STEWART,
April 28, 1812.

I never answer your dear, kind, welcome, and clever letters at the moment I wish to answer them (which is the moment they are read) both for your sake and my own, because I wish to delay the mo-

ment of *bore* to you, and to keep in view a pleasure
for myself. To hold intercourse with you of whatever
description, has always been to me a positive enjoyment since the first moment I saw you, and that was
not the least happy moment of my life. I was then
"Pleine de ces esprits qui fournissent les espérances."
I was then beckoned on by a thousand bright illusions,
and it was a delicious event to meet half-way in my
career such a creature as yourself. In short, my dear
friend, our physical capabilities for receiving pleasure
wear out rapidly in proportion to their own intensity,
and those who, like me, see life through the dazzling
prism of imagination long before they are permitted to
enter it, must, like me, find the original infinitely inferior to the fiction; still I have no reason to complain.
I have associated myself to one who feels and thinks
as I do, and this is, or ought to be, the first of human
blessings; but *his* thoughts and feelings are still of a
higher tone — they are not qualified by that light
vanity which brings my character down to the general
level of humanity. In *love* he is Sheridan's Falkland,
and in his views of things there is a *mélange* of cynicism
and sentiment that will never suffer him to be as
happy as the inferior million that move about him.
Marriage has taken nothing from the *romance* of his
passion for me; and by bringing a sense of *property*
with it, it has rendered him more exigent and nervous
about me than before. All this is flattering and delightful, and yet I do not say with Richelieu, "C'est
être bien a charge, que d'être trop aimé," yet, for his
sake, I would be almost contented to be less loved,
because I should see him more happy. He admires
the picture I have drawn of you, and often says "Of

all the persons you have mentioned to me, Lady
Stanley is the only woman I wish to know."

You will laugh at this wife-like letter; but provided
you do laugh, I am satisfied. Could you take a peep
out of your secluded Eden at the vicissitudes and
miseries of those who live in the world, you would hug
yourself in your own "*home-felt certainty*" of peace,
comfort, and competency. The worst of all human
evils you never can have known — *poverty!* As Ninon
says upon a gayer subject, "On peut se rapporter à
moi." I am, however, for the present, living upon
fifty thousand pounds a year, and shall do so for
another year *if I choose;* but although our noble hosts
are everything that is kind and charming, we prefer a
home of our own, be it ever so tiny. Since I wrote to
you, we have lost the beautiful Countess of Aberdeen,
Lord Abercorn's favourite daughter. It was *a heavy
blow*.

I am delighted your winter has been cheered by the
society of your new son-in-law, and the amiable Emma.
My dearest Olivia comes here in *June*, if her *health
permits*, and after that I must settle in England and
she in Ireland. I am at work again; but with the
sole view of making some money to furnish a bit of a
house in London, which, *coûte qui coûte*, we *must* have.
My book will be a *genuine* Irish romance of Elizabeth's
day, founded on historic facts. I would not write
another line, to add the fame of Sappho to my own
little quota of reputation, did not necessity guide my
worn out stump of a goose-quill. My imagination is
exhausted, and those *hopes* and *views* which in the first
era of life give such *spring* to mind, and such energy
to thought, are all dead and gone. At present nothing

would give me more pleasure than to meet you in London when we go there. We are daily expecting the arrival of Lord Aberdeen and his little daughters, and Lady Marian Hamilton, and shortly Lord and Lady Hamilton and their family, so we shall have a house full; but people are mistaken as to the pleasures of a large society in great houses — there is an *incvitability* about it that is a *dead bore.*

I long to hear how the dear little farm is going on, and all the improvements. Is pig alive? is Poll as brilliant as ever, and Mrs. Jones wedded to her sentimental lover? And *you?* Do you walk about with the little black silk apron and feed the pets? Pray write to me, and soon — directly; this I ask in the honesty of earnest wishes. Sir Charles requests I will say something for him. What can I say, but that he is prepared to like you as much as he has already learnt to admire you, and so I am, as ever,

Yours, affectionately,
SYDNEY OWENSON MORGAN.

The genuine Irish romance that was to furnish the little house of our own in London was the *O'Donnel.* Lady Morgan happily changed her plan. Instead of an historical novel of the days of Queen Bess, founded on facts, she wrote a delightful sketch of the Ireland she knew so well.

CHAPTER XI.

DEATH OF MR. OWENSON.

THE first heavy sorrow of her life came upon Lady
Morgan a few months after her marriage. Her father,
whose health had long been breaking, died in the early
spring. He lived to witness the happiness and prosperity
of both his children, and he died at the house of
Lady Clarke, surrounded by every care and kindness
that affection could bestow. The following letters tell
of Lady Morgan's grief. The natural position between
a parent and child had, in their case, been reversed.
Ever since her mother's death she had felt that it was
for her to take care of her father, instead of her father
taking care of her; but this did not interfere with her
own romantic admiration for him, nor the affectionate
respect with which she regarded him.

Lady Morgan to Sir A. Clarke.

May 23, 1812.

MY DEAREST CLARKE,

'Tis an excess of selfishness in me to write to you
under my present feelings, as, except to detail my own
misery, I have little else to say. To express my sense
of your benevolence, of your affectionate attention to
our dear, dear father, I cannot. I have been saved nothing in not being with you; I have not only strongly
imagined every scene and moment of misery and sadness, but I have added to it all the horrors of suspense

and anxiety. I have lived on from post to post, always hoping the best, fearing the worst, and not knowing what part to take or how to act. Still I thought this shock would prove like the last, though Morgan gave me no encouragement; but I believed, as he knew not the constitution the disease had to contend with, that *he* might have been mistaken. In short, it appeared to me impossible that my own dear father, who was my child as well as my father, *could die* — nor I don't believe it yet! it is to me as if a curtain dropped before life. I can look neither to the past nor to the future without connecting everything with him, and the present is all, all him. The tie which existed between us was not the common tie of father and child. He was the object for which I laboured, and wrote, and lived, and nothing can fill up to me the place he held in my heart. My dearest Clarke, forgive me, but my tears, the first I have freely shed, are falling faster than I can write, and I scarcely know what I say. God knows, I want not to add to your sadness. Every body here is very good to me, and my dear husband supports, comforts, and devotes himself to me; but he could not know how endearing poor papa was, or how much out of the ordinary run of fathers. You knew him, and loved him, and were his child. I am very weak and ought not to write so.

They allow me to breakfast and dine in my own sitting-room, which is a great comfort, and I have not seen a creature since my misfortune, but Lady Abercorn, who is all affection and pity. They want me to drive to Derry, or somewhere, with Morgan; but where can I go that the image of my dead, dear papa, will not follow me? What trouble, what expence, what

suffering and sadness *you* must have had? God bless
you, for all; but goodness is of no avail. If my dearest,
suffering Livy will not come to me, I will go to her,
and this scene would be a change and a benefit to her.

My dearest Clarke, I remember buying or paying
for a watch last summer, for poor, dear papa,—I wish
you would wear it! I have just had a petition from a
starving English actor and his family, travelling through
here, that almost reconciled me to an event that put
the object I loved beyond the reach of poverty or care.
I am so altered in the course of three days you would
not know me. Livy was such a blessing to the last to
her poor father. Has Mrs. Doyle, the Lefanus, or any
of her friendly friends been with her? Morgan, who
is all tenderness, and goodness, and generosity, is bent
on re-uniting me to Livy at any sacrifice. This business has fallen like a thunderbolt on me. I knew not
what step to take. It is odd, that when Livy wrote
word of papa's talking of going to the theatre, Morgan
said it was the worst symptom that had appeared yet,
and when I laughed at him, he said we all deceived
ourselves. I have not courage to ask you any particu-
lars. I know all that could be done was done. God
bless you for it. My eyes are so inflamed Morgan
won't allow me to write any more.

God bless and preserve you,

S. O. M.

P.S. by Sir Charles.

PS. — Dear Livy, she is in no condition to write
to you, and would only increase your sufferings, nor
can I say more than that the sight of her wild and
tearless eyes almost distracts me; however, you must
both give only a short season to sorrow. I would not

say to you do not lament, but bear in mind, my dearest
Livy, that after all this is a most merciful dispensation
of Providence, especially to the object of our lamentation. What is more now to the purpose, come down
and see what a good husband I am, and what an affectionate brother you have; change of scene and of
air will be of the greatest use to you, and if the most
perfect sympathy have any consolation, you will find it
in stopping with Syd. and your affectionate Morgy.

Lady Morgan to Mrs. Lefanu.

June 26th, 1812.

Your message to Sir Charles would have insured
you an immediate answer to your letter, if there were
no other inducement to write to you; and that you have
not heard from me before arises from some mistake
about being detained here or in Dublin; I have only
this morning received it. Sir Charles desires me to say
that, from all he hears and knows of you, he is become
too much interested in your life not to feel anxious for
its preservation and comfort, and that, as far as his
knowledge and ability can contribute to either, they are
devoted to your service. He says, however, that you
have given too vague an account of your symptoms for
him to form a correct judgment. He dare not risk an
opinion without being more master of the subject. He
wishes he was near you, and would be happy to do
anything for you. He is very sensible of, and grateful
for, the tenderness you express towards me, thus ad-
mitting him to the circle of your friends; and I believe
you have had few more zealous candidates for the
honour.

Everything that you say about Dublin is very seductive, but we really are in a pitiable state of hesitation at present. They have not the remotest idea that we can or will leave them as long as they remain in Ireland, and yet they talk of that being a year or two. If we (*what they would call*) desert them, we shall risk the loss of their friendship, which would indeed be a loss; but if we remain we lose time, and it is quite fit that Morgan should establish himself soon somewhere. Add to this that they, I believe, have a real affection for us; but we are dying to be in our own little shabby house, and are tired of solitary splendours, and of the eternal representation of high life, and you will then believe that we are rather in a puzzle. Morgan, in the end, will be solely guided by honour (leaving interest, and inclination, and even happiness out of the question), which he strains to a point of romantic refinement. We expect Lord and Lady Hamilton (another invalid). I showed Lord Aberdeen your critique on noble authors; he said, "had you judged differently, he would have formed a different judgment of you, from what he was inclined to do." Arbuthnot, who is coming over as secretary, I know intimately; but I am sick of the idea of place-hunting or place-asking. I suppose, by this, you are at your Sabine Farm, at Glasnevin: would I were with you for a week! *Mais pour aller à Corinth le désir ne suffit pas;* but I should like to have you alone, that is, in the midst of your own family, for if *you* don't patronize *my* Lords and Ladies Fiddle Faddle, I will vote your Miss Macguffins, and the rest of your two-penny Misses and Masters, and some few of your *good* Mistresses this, and worthy Misters t'others, *dead bores!*

I, at least, have something for my *pride*, but the
"*Damn nigger you get for your money*" is quite below
purchase! Native worth and native genius (like your
own) must always hold the ascendant in whatever circle
it is to be found, and if you find not these amongst a
certain class, you find something else with people of
rank; you get the next best thing, *education*, which,
with English people of fashion of the present day, you
never fail to find. The young people of this family
(including the son-in-law, Lord Aberdeen) have more
acquirements and accomplishments, more literary and
general *savoir* than (with the almost single exception
of your own family), all the youth of Dublin put together. The women not only speak French and
Italian as well as English, but are good Latin scholars,
and unquestionably the best musicians I know; and
yet I never heard the Ladies Hamilton particularly
distinguished for their education above other girls of
fashion. I never mean to say that the *first class* of
society have more genius or more happiness than
any other, I only insist that they have the *next
best things*, and as I find it easier to get at a countess or a marchioness than at a Mrs. Lefanu, *faute
de mieux*, I put up with their ladyships, cutting dead
the Miss Macguffins and the Mistresses O'Shaugh-
nessey's, for whom (*à la distance*) I have a great respect. The fact is, a dull worthy is not the less *dull*
to me for being a worthy and not an earl! Lords or
commons, a bore is a bore, and I think you will agree
with me that a vulgar one is worse than a polished
one, as an Irish diamond, though "a lustre-looking
thing," is best after it has received a little working.
You who are *a real* brilliant, I am sure, I should

always have discovered your "original brightness" in whatever setting I should have found it. I know your intrinsic value, and prize it at its worth; meantime, let me prefer the rose diamonds of my Lord and Lady Fiddle Faddle to the Kerry stones of the Miss Macguffins; one, at least, has a polished surface, the other retains the "laste taste in life" of the clay! I have not left myself room to say *Je vous aime de tout mon cœur.* Love to all, Joe included.

S. O. M.

Lady Morgan to Mrs. Lefanu.

BARON'S COURT,
June 7th, 1812.

MY DEAREST FRIEND,

"To each his suffering;" you have had your portion, and it would have been unfair and unjust to have written to you under the influence of my sadness, and have drawn from you an unavailing sympathy at the moment you have been so actively and beneficially engaged in soothing and comforting my dear Olivia, who feels your goodness in her "heart of hearts." You are a *true friend,* — I have always thought so, — I have always said so, and every year of our friendship has given me fresh reason to confirm my opinion. The dearest and strongest tie, which time, nature, habit, and acts of reciprocal affection can form, has been wrenched from my heart; I ought long since to have been, and yet was not, prepared for it. It was a dreadful break up to the feelings; it is so much of life broken off. A host of dearly remembered events, feelings, and associations, are necessarily gone with it. Were it possible I could ever again love anything so well, I can never again love anything so long. The best point of existence with me is over, and new ties and new affections must be light in their hold, and feeble in their influence, compared to those "which grew with the growth and strengthened with the years." My dear husband, Olivia, yourself, and one or two more objects are still left me, to whom I will cling. It is my intention to sacrifice for the rest of my life to the HEART, and to live in Ireland, if those I love cannot live with me in England, where interest and ambition equally call Morgan and myself; *he* has no *wish*, scarcely any *will*, but *mine*, and is ready to make *my* country *his*, "*my* people *his* people." As yet, our views are very misty; Lord and Lady Abercorn are very desirous we should remain with them, as long as they stay in Ireland, at least if not after; but as that will probably be for a year or two, it would be *impossible*. We have not, however, said so.

We have lately added to our party,

"The travelled Thane, Athenian Aberdeen,"

As Lord Byron calls him. He is reckoned among the "rising young men" of England, and is one of the *virtuosi* who purchased a farm at Athens, where he resided for some time. He was the husband of Lord Abercorn's lately deceased and beautiful daughter. The meeting was very afflicting, and for some time threw a shadow over our circle.

What think you of the state of public affairs? our letters to-day, from England, say that the opposition still hold out, though offered six places out of twelve in the Cabinet, or seven out of fourteen. What a *bouleversement* in the state of things when stars and

gartors go a begging!! and commoner's misses refuse
to become princesses!!* The Cabinet remains empty
because no one thinks it worth their while to accept a
place in it, and yet all this we have lived to see! If
the opposition permit themselves in their condescension
to be prevailed upon to govern an empire, your brother
will find his own level, and you will have your *levées*
and *couchées*, and we shall find with Louis the Fourteenth's courtiers that Cuff Street "est fait pour n'être
comparée à rien" (which, by-the-bye, and with deference to Mr. Lefanu, is more true than of the Louvre)
and that "il ne plait pas à Glasnevin." In the midst
of all this political *tourbillon*, people still submit to be
pleased and amused, and run after your comedy as
they would have done in the prosperous and Augustan
days of Queen Anne. Lady Abercorn tells me she
has had great accounts of its success from all sides.
As she knows your *bonne fortune* is mine, she indulges
me with hearing of the good tidings. Livy says you
think she could write a comedy; I think so too, she
has an immense fund of true comedy in her own
character, but writing is such a distinct thing from ourselves that no inference can be drawn from thence.
Lord Byron, the author of delightful *Childe Harold*
(which has more *force*, *fire*, and *thought* than anything
I have read for an age) is cold, silent, and reserved in
his manners, — pray read it if you have not. When
I was in London, Lord G. Greville read me a poem of
his own to the same subject as *Childe Harold*. The
rival lords published their poems the same day; the

* Alluding to the gossip of the day that the Duke of Clarence had been
refused by Miss Tilney Long, the luckless "great heiress" of the period.

one is cried up to the skies, the other, alas, is cried down to —!

We expect Livy here, but she seems either unwilling or unable to leave home. We have no chance of going ourselves to Dublin till winter; by that time, every one that I have known and lived with (save yourself, the Atkinsons, and the Mason's) will have left it; indeed they are almost all gone already. It is astonishing the changes that have taken place in the little circle of my intimacy within a few years, either by death or departure to England. Among my literary friends, dear Psyche (Mrs. Tighe), Cooper, Walker, and Kirwin are no more!

Sir Charles's desire to know you increases daily. Shall we ever all meet again and all be happy together? At least write to me, and under all changes and circumstances, believe I love you tenderly and sincerely.

S. O. M.

There is no letter or memorandum to show the exact time when Sir Charles and Lady Morgan quitted the family of Lord Abercorn, to begin housekeeping for themselves, nor the immediate occasion that gave rise to it. The splendid slavery of her life was a position Lady Morgan found untenable, and it is probable that after her marriage she felt less inclined to tolerate the fine ladyism of the Marchioness than when she was in the position of a young lady. The separation took place, however, without any break in their friendly relations, though the intimacy gradually subsided. Lady Morgan was always anxious that Sir Charles should exert himself and not settle down into indolent comfort. For herself, activity and independence of mind and body were indispensable, and there is no doubt she exerted all her influence over Sir Charles to induce him to give up his connection with the Marquis, and took advantage of the first opportunity to break away.

They went to stay with Sir Arthur and Lady Clarke, until they found a house to suit them. Eventually they found a house in Kildare Street — not large, but pleasant, and with some pretensions to a handsome appearance. Lady Morgan had the pleasure of fitting up her library after the fahion she had imagined and described in her *Novice of St. Dominic*, years ago, — the story that was begun when she and her sister were with their father in Kilkenny.

The prospects of Sir Charles and Lady Morgan were tolerable, but not brilliant, as Sir Charles had his practice entirely to establish. But this change from a courtly to a city life was the best event that had ever befallen him. The constant intercourse with the brilliant, active mind of his wife, quickened his faculties, and called out the capabilities which had lain dormant or had fallen into disuse. He obtained the appointment of physician to the Marshalsea, and succeeded, in a reasonably short time, in establishing a tolerable practice.

A few years after his marriage, Sir Charles published a work called *Outlines of the Physiology of Life*, setting forth psychological opinions, boldly averred, and distinctly stated, instead of being put forward as hypothesis or left to inference. It was not an age of philosophic tolerance. Science was expected to be strictly orthodox in its theology. The work provoked a storm

11*

of opposition and censure, both religious and secular; the result was, that Sir Charles retired from general practice, though he retained his appointment to the Marshalsea. He devoted himself to literary labour, and joined with Lady Morgan in efforts to extend the knowledge of the condition of Ireland, to spread liberal opinions in politics, and to create a Public Conscience to which Irish wrongs and Irish difficulties might appeal. To these objects they both devoted themselves; especially they were staunch advocates of Catholic emancipation, when advocates were an abused minority, and their exertions were recognised when that much vexed and agitated question was at last set at rest. But this is anticipating Lady Morgan's story.

CHAPTER XII.

KILDARE STREET.

ANOTHER letter from Dr. Jenner to Sir Charles; they did not often write to each other, but they knew that whilst they lived they each possessed a friend, and it is this consciousness of possession that makes us rich, not the act of "counting out our money," like the king in the nursery rhyme.

BERKELEY,
March 14, 1813.

MY DEAR FRIEND,

My epistolatory sins multiply upon me at such a rate, I am almost ashamed to face a correspondent of any description, and quite so to appear before you. Where are my congratulatory replies to your Dublin

letter, announcing your marriage? Literally *in nubibus.*
I say *literally*, for scores of them passed through my
brain in forms so airy, that they flew aloft before I
could catch one to fix upon paper. The sober truth
is, procrastination, that thief of comfort as well as time,
took an early possession of me, and it is in vain now
to attempt an ejectment. Let me tell you one thing,
by the way, that when they flew *up*, they carried with
them my best wishes for you and yours.

I have not been in town since the summer of 1811,
nor much at Cheltenham, preferring, whenever I am
permitted, the enjoyment of my cottage, in this my
native village. But don't think I spend my time in
idleness. My pursuit has lately been, when uninter-
rupted by vaccination, the morbid changes in the
structure of the livers of brutes, which has led me to
some conclusions respecting the same changes in the
human. 'Tis hard, methinks, that the poor animal
that is content with what the meadows afford for his
daily bill of fare, and whose cellar is the pond or the
brook, should perish from the same diseases as the
drunkard; but so it is. There are plants which,
somehow or another, are capable of throwing the
state of the liver into that sort of confusion which
calls hydatids into existence. These do not continue
long in their native state, but produce a great variety
of tubera, cartilaginous, bony masses, &c. In other
instances, the disease originates in the biliary ducts,
which become astonishingly enlarged, and thickened
in every part of the liver, and finally destroy it in
various ways. This is the outline of my research.
The hydatid I can call into existence in the rabbit in
about a fortnight.

I most heartily wish well to the scheme you have in
view, and shall use my best endeavours to promote it.
I know but little of the locality of Dublin; but it is
my intention to spend a good deal of the ensuing
season at Cheltenham, where I shall probably see
many Irish families of respectability;· then, be assured,
I shall think of you, and be enabled, I trust, to do
something more than merely think. Don't let me red-
den your cheeks beyond the point to which nature has
brought them, but I must conscientiously say, that if
your merits meet with their reward, your *fingers' ends*
will grow sore with professional exercise. Let me advise you to take up some scientific pursuit, which will
admit of an exhibition — why not mineralogy? You
are quite at home there. I have a medical friend who
has long ranked as the first physician in one of the
largest cities in these realms, and whose fossils were
the *stepping stones* that led him into the wide fields of
practice.

If you can bear to write to such a correspondent,
pray let me hear from you ere long, and believe me,
with every friendly wish to you and yours

Your much attached

EDWARD JENNER.

The next letter is from Lady Morgan to Lady
Stanley. It gives a pleasant picture of herself in her
new home, and the skilful ease with which she took up
her position as mistress of a house. Lady Morgan was
very practical and prided herself upon her good housekeeping. She possessed a natural gift of being comfortable, and making her house so to herself and to all
her friends.

Lady Morgan to Lady Stanley.

35, KILDARE STREET, DUBLIN,
Monday, May 17.

Vous voilà aux abois, ma chère dame!! You see I am not to be distanced; retreat as you will, I still pursue. When I am within a mile of you, you will not see me; when I write you will not answer; and still here I am at your feet, because *I will not be rebutée;* nor (throw me off as you may) will I ever give you up until I find something that resembles you, something to fill up the place you have so long occupied; the fact is, my dear Lady Stanley, it' is pure selfishness that ties me to you. *I do not like* women, I cannot get on with them! and except the excessive tenderness which I have always felt for my sister be called friendship, you (and one or two more, *par parenthèse!*) are the only woman to whom I could ever *lier* myself for a week together. *Se devancer de son sexe*, is as dangerous as *De se devancer de son Siècle*, it was no effort, no *willing* of mine that has given me a *little* the start of the major part of them; dear little souls! who, as Ninon says, "le trouvent *plus commode* d'être jolie." The principle was *there; active* and *restless*, the spur was given, and *off I went*, happy in the result that my comparative superiority obtained me *one* such friend as yourself — that is, as you *were;* but I fear you now cut me dead.

We have at last got into a home of our own; we found an old, dirty, dismantled house, and we have turned our *piggery* into a decent sort of hut enough; we have made it clean and comfortable, which is all our moderate circumstances will admit of, save *one little bit of a room*, which is a real bijou, and it is about *four inches by three*, and, therefore, one could afford to ornament it *a little;* it is fitted up in the *gothic*, and I have collected into it the best part of a very good cabinet of natural history of Sir Charles, eight or nine hundred volumes of choice books, in French, English, Italian, and German; some little miscellaneous curiosities, and a few scraps of old china, so that with muslin draperies, &c, &c., I have made no contemptible *set* out. *I was thinking, that may be Susette* could enrich my store in the old china way, if she has any refuse of that sort which you may have thrown her in with your cast-off wardrobe — a broken cup, a bottomless bowl, a spoutless teapot, — in a word, anything old and shattered, that is china, and of no value to you, will be of use and ornament to me, and Captain Skinner has promised to bring it over for me.

With respect to authorship, I fear it is over; I have been making chair-covers instead of periods; hanging curtains instead of raising systems, and cheapening pots and pans instead of selling sentiment and philosophy. Meantime, my husband is, as usual, deep in study, and if his *popularity* here may be deemed a favourable omen, will, I trust, soon be *deep in practice.* Well, always dear friend; any chance of a line in answer to my three pages of verbiage? Just make the effort of *taking up the pen*, and if you only write "Glorvina, I am well, and love you still," I will be contented. Under all circumstances,

Yours affectionately,
S. Morgan.

Sir Charles Morgan's step-mother had married, for

her second husband, William Bingley, the animal biographer; here is a letter from him about his literary
undertakings.

William Bingley to Sir Charles Morgan.

CHRISTCHURCH, HANTS,
June 30, 1813.

DEAR MORGAN,

You will think me, as you have no doubt long ago
thought me, a very miserable correspondent; but the
fact is, that of late my time has, in a most unusual
manner, been occupied. The *History of Hampshire* has
not merely been at sixes and sevens, but at sixteens
and seventeens. A certain flowery-named gentleman,
as I conceive, has by no means fulfilled his engage-
ments with me, which I intend very shortly to prove.
I mean to call for a full investigation into my whole
conduct relating to it, which I hope the trustees will
not refuse to enter into. Lord Malmesbury was with
me some time on the subject about three weeks ago,
and I firmly believe is my friend; at all events, I shall
not let the matter rest until I have a full arrangement
of the business. My evidence on the subject is indis-
putable; and I have a letter promising a compensation
in case of a failure in obtaining the requisite number
of subscriptions. It is really too bad that I should be
a loser by a work which I was positively invited, and,
contrary to my own inclination, to undertake. If all at
last goes on well, I hope to complete it in the course
of about a year and a-half. This is no trifling concern
to me, and has cost me much anxiety. When things
go on somewhat more smoothly, I hope to become a
better correspondent than I hitherto have been.

You, I presume, are by this time comfortably settled in your new residence, and, as I should conceive, find domestic pleasures infinitely to be preferred to those of pomp and bustle in a house not your own. This is peculiarly the case with me. Since I have been in Christchurch this time, I believe I have only dined from home about four times, nor do I ever wish to be from my own premises. Mrs. Bingley has been most lamentably unwell ever since our arrival. She has three times only been out of the house, nor do I at present see any immediate prospect of her recovery. It will indeed greatly rejoice me when she is again able to go abroad.

When you next write you must inform me how many patients you have got. I presume that your knocker must, by this time, be almost worn out. I am glad your packages arrived safely; but I must confess, when I was putting your chattels together, I did not conceive that I was doing it for a voyage to a foreign country.

The new edition of the *Animal Biography* has been published about three months; and Longman and Co. have just written to request that I would prepare a new edition of the *Welsh Tour*. This is what I scarcely expected, as two or three years ago I had been informed that the copies were going off very slowly. It is my present intention to throw the work into a somewhat different form, and print it in one volume instead of two.

By the way, I have been employed, during the evenings, in preparing a little introductory work on Zoology, the first sheet of which is printed. This, at present, is unknown I believe to any except the bookseller and my family. The plan is nearly the same as that of *Animal Biography*, and it has been prepared chiefly for the purpose of affording a popular view of the Linnean system. I am very anxious for its success, although I have sold the copyright. It will be in one duodecimo volume, and it is my intention to follow it up with another on the subject of Botany and Mineralogy.

Mrs. Bingley unites with me in kindest remembrances to yourself and Lady Morgan.

I am, dear Morgan,
Most truly yours,
WILLIAM BINGLEY.

PS. — Little Susan and Tom are going on wonderfully well; their progress is more rapid than I could have conceived it possible, but their capacities are greater far than those of any children I have ever yet seen.

The next letter is from Emily Lady Cahir, Countess of Glengall; and relates to an enquiry Lady Morgan had made about a man whose adventures seemed to offer a type for the hero of the novel (*O'Donnel*), on which she was then engaged. Lady Cahir was herself the model for Lady Singleton, in the same story. One almost wonders that some of the fine ladies whom Lady Morgan produced in her works, etching them in aquafortis and colouring them to the life, did not assassinate her by way of return, especially as she invariably introduced a sketch of herself in one corner of all her pictures, taking up all the wisdom and common sense going, as well as being the most agreeable character in the story!

November 6, 1813.

My DEAR LADY MORGAN,

You see that I do not lose a moment in obeying your orders, and be assured that you ought to give me some credit, as I am in general but a bad correspondent. Your inquiries as to whether you are to make Mr. Shee your hero, has amused me considerably. The *Evening Post* inserted a long list of lies upon his subject, at which I laughed heartily at the time. You certainly could not have applied to a better person than myself for information with respect to him, as I know his birth, parentage and adventures, perfectly. He is of a low family. One of his sisters was bound to a milliner, at Kilkenny, and used to bring ribbons, gauzes, &c., to the Miss Bensfords, when their father was Bishop of Ossory. Another of his sisters was married to a coachmaker. His brother was foreman to the said coachmaker, and is now elevated to the rank of gauger in the excise by Lord Cahir's interest. The hero was in the Irish brigade at St. Domingo; but as to his prodigies of valour, I never heard anything of them. He came to London starving. Lord Cahir fed him with money till he was rather tired of so doing, and offered to get him a commission in the army, which he declined, unless the Duke of York would give him a majority at once. Lord Cahir was induced to present a memorial to this effect, and the answer was, that it was then unheard of in the service, but that a cornetcy was at Lord Cahir's command. Shee declined it. He then married the daughter of a button maker, by whom he expected to get some cash. Being also disappointed in this, and fighting considerably with the lady and her buttons, he packed up his portmanteau and set off to France, where he entered the French service, and became aid-de-camp to General Clark, who is a distant relation of his. He has since been made a lieutenant-colonel of a regiment, and was mentioned in some of the French generals' despatches in Spain, as having eaten up the English army. By some extraordinary accident, however, Lord Wellington has "lived to fight another day;" and should the hero Shee be taken, which is by no means impossible, he will swing on Tyburn tree. Nothing, in my mind, can justify a man in fighting against his own country, — not even your seducing pen can make it palatable to my old English prejudices, particularly when he had a very reasonable sufficiency in this country; for I have forgotten to state that Lord Cahir gave him a farm near Cahir, out of which he at this moment receives a very handsome profit rent. Had he chosen to have gone into our service, Lord Cahir would have pushed him forward; as it is now fourteen years since he was offered a commission, he might have been as high in the English as he is now in the French service, without the stigma of being a traitor, and without the certainty of being hanged, if taken. Lord Cahir did push on another brother to the rank of major in our army, in which rank he died. So much for our hero. And now I have only to request you to burn this letter, as I have no inclination to be quoted in anything that concerns him.

Excuse me now, if from being over anxious for the fate of a work, which, coming from your pen, will, I am sure, have so much to recommend it, I venture an opinion. Do not mix anything of religious or political opinions in a work intended only to amuse, — it will lay you open to animadversion, and party may influence opinion.

Yours truly, E. CAHIR.

This was very sage advice, but felt to be impossible by the Wild Irish Girl. An Irish story, without religion or politics!

During the whole of the first year of her residence in Kildare Street, Lady Morgan was busy upon *O'Donnel*, a national tale, for which it may be remembered she gathered the materials on her visit to Dublin, before her marriage. It was published by Colburn, early in 1814, and dedicated to the Duke of Devonshire. She received five hundred and fifty pounds for the copyright. The first edition consisted of two thousand copies, and a second edition was printed in February 1815. It is an immense improvement upon all her previous works, being written in a natural style, without the high-flown rhetoric or pedantic allusions which disfigured and overlaid her earlier stories. Her own words and opinions are embodied in the Duchess of Belmont, — a sort of feminine Puss in Boots, clever, witty, sensible, and worldly, with a sufficiently good heart to make the reader take an interest in her. In the beginning she appears as a neglected governess, in the family of Lady Singleton, who is the type of Lady Cahir, whose letter has just been quoted. She is admirably drawn. The governess, by some sleight of novel-writing, becomes Duchess of Belmont, the wife of an old peer, having declined to be his mistress. He dies (off the stage), and she re-appears on the scene as a rich and brilliant widow with a magnificent title. She is the same in all her qualities as when she was Miss O'Haggerty, the governess; but every word she utters in her new character is picked up like pearls and diamonds, and every caprice admired. Lady Morgan delighted to pay any outstanding debts of insolence, slight or absurdity she might hold against the real great ladies whom she met with; and the transformation of Miss O'Haggerty, the governess, to the Duchess of Belmont, is very amusing and well managed. The hero is not a traitor, but a very charming Irish gentleman *pur sang*, whose fortunes had fallen below his merits, and the Duchess is his good angel, who incites him "to be not afraid to take his fortune up." After much romantic incident, in the course of which he narrowly escapes being hanged, he marries the Duchess, regains the estate of his ancestors, and all ends happily. In the first sketch of her novel, O'Donnel was actually hanged, and Lady Morgan wrote such a moving account of the execution, that it drew tears from her own eyes. An old friend to whom she read it, said, wiping her eyes, "Yes, my dear, it is very beautiful, but I will never open the book again, it makes me too miserable. Don't hang him." Lady Morgan profited by the advice, and every reader of the novel will rejoice that she changed his fate.

O'Donnel retains its freshness to the present day. Any one wishing to read a novel which shall produce that delightful feeling of dissipation which is supposed to make novel reading so dangerous (but which, alas, so few novels now-a-days succeed in inspiring), should read *O'Donnel*. The scope and design of the work are admirable. The Irish social questions of the day are very ably treated; and what was then more to the purpose, they were presented in an effective dramatic

shape, so as to be intelligible to the most careless
reader.

O'Donnel had a success exceeding that of *The Wild
Irish Girl.* The *Quarterly* reviewed it as bitterly as it
had reviewed *Ida of Athens*, being exceedingly indignant at the audacity of the social and political truths
contained in it. The reader who remembers the incident of the white satin shoes will be amused at the
ceremonious assurance of his high consideration with
which Lord Hartington, now become Duke of Devonshire, acknowledges the dedication of *O'Donnel.*

The Duke of Devonshire to Lady Morgan.

DEVONSHIRE HOUSE,
February 17, 1814.

MY DEAR MADAM,

Your letter was sent after me into the country,
which must be my apology for my apparent delay in
answering it, and in assuring you how very much
gratified I am by your kind remembrance and attention
in dedicating your new work to me.

It will not, I hope, be long before I have the pleasure of reading it.

Believe me, my dear Madam,
Your Ladyship's sincere and
Obliged servant,

DEVONSHIRE.

CHAPTER XIII.

FIRST VISIT TO FRANCE — 1815-1816.

In the year after the publication of *O'Donnel*, the continent being now open, Sir Charles and Lady Morgan went to Paris to see the country under the restored *régime*, and of course to write a book about it. They took with them letters of introduction, and they were admitted into Parisian society of every shade of politics. They saw all the most noted men of literature and science, and the women whose beauty, fashion, or talent for intrigue, had made them queens of society. As a picture of the feelings and passions which were struggling and seething underneath the restored *order*, her work on France is vivid and true. She paints the contradictions struggling to assert themselves — the ill-suppressed minority — the ignorant and limited prejudices of the Bourbon party; the oppressions, and triumphs, and disgusts, are all exhibited as in a kaleidoscope; — for she went from Bourbon *soirées*, where the company were singing "Vive le roi quand même," to salons where the return of "*l'autre*" was still hoped for and expected. She formed a friendship with Madame Patterson Bonaparte, with Madame de Genlis, with Dénon the famous Egyptologist, and with Lafayette. Both she and Sir Charles were intimate with the Comte de Ségur; the Abbé de Gregoire; with the Comte de Tracy, the idéologiste; with Cuvier. The women who made society as brilliant as the hues of the feathers

on a pigeon's breast, or the glancing of diamond dust,
initiated her into the feminine coquetries and fascina-
tions of toilettes, and took her to see the *trousseau* of
the Duchesse de Berri. Lady Morgan was admired
and *fêted*, and received all the intoxicating homage of
a Parisian success. The notes and letters sent to her
would be invaluable as models of graceful phraseology
and precious as autographs, and must have been delightful to receive; but the mere printed transcript of
these airy trifles would not interest the general reader.
Very different, however, is the case with the correspondence of Madame de Genlis and Madame Patterson Bonaparte. These women belong to history; they
lived with kings and princes, with philosophers and
artists; there is about them the light of courts and
palaces; a perpetual curiosity and romance.

Poor old Madame de Genlis! In her "grande"
solitude one wonders if it were in her own "Palace of
Truth;" but no, — if we recollect aright, *that* palace
Madame de Genlis declared to be uninhabitable for
mortals, and it was demolished to point the moral of
the tale! One is glad to catch a glimpse of the mother
of Pamela for the sake of the tales with which she delighted our youth. Pamela, as everybody knows, married Lord Edward Fitzgerald, and Pamela's daughter
was the charming Lady Guy Campbell, a great friend
of Lady Morgan's, and still extant.

Madame de Genlis to Lady Morgan.

CONVENT OF THE CARMAELITES,
RUE DE VAUREGARD, PARIS,
June 8, 1816.

The name of the author of such charming works is

as well known to Madame de Genlis as it ought to
be; although she lives in a great solitude she will be
charmed to know personally her, the sentiments of
whose soul she already loves and adores. She will
have the honour to let her know if her health and
mode of life will permit her to pay a visit to Lady
Morgan. As Madame de Genlis is living in a religious
house, she cannot receive visitors in the evening. Any
way, she will not be at liberty on Wednesday next,
but would be very happy if Monday or Tuesday would
be convenient to Lady Morgan. It seems to Madame
de Genlis that Thursday is a very distant day. She
entreats Lady Morgan to accept her thanks. It is Madame de Genlis who would have been the first to solicit
the favour of seeing Lady Morgan, if she had known
she was in Paris.

One of the most remarkable of the acquaintances
made by Sir Charles and Lady Morgan during their
visit to France was with Madame Jerome Bonaparte,
the American wife of the Emperor's brother, whom he
had abandoned in a cruel and dastardly way. The
lady, however, was not of the *pâte* out of which victims and martyrs are made; she was a woman of high
spirit, and held her difficult and painful position with
a scornful courage, that excites a deep pity for the
woman's nature so cruelly scathed and outraged. Her
letters to her friend will be read with interest. They
are clever, *mordant*, and amusing; but the bitter sense
of wrong cannot be concealed.

Madame Patterson Bonaparte to Lady Morgan.

PARIS,
September 23, 1816.

MY DEAR LADY MORGAN,

You have not written me a line since your departure. I hope you have not forgotten me, as I admire and love you more than any one else. I have been to see Dénon and Madame D'Houchin; they are both your adorers, and express the greatest affliction at your departure. The most agreeable thing you could do for your friends would be to return as quickly as possible. The French admire you more than any one who has appeared here since the Battle of Waterloo in the form of an English woman. The Princess of Beauveau has been to see me, and is very kind *à mon égard* as well as very judicious in admiring and loving you. Countess Rumford saw me at our minister's, invited me to a *soirée*, and came to see me. I get on very well now, but my health has been very bad since I have lost the pleasure of your society. I suffered for two weeks more than I can express from the pain of my teeth. Mrs. Marton is still in the figurative style. Her imagination is as fertile as ever, and as I am matter of fact, I avoid her society as much as possible. A friend of hers told me you had treated her harshly; I replied, "Lady Morgan has too much sense to be imposed upon, and too much truth to encourage falsehood in others; and as she had her choice of society in Paris, it was unnecessary for her to pass over impertinence in any one. That the Marton might derive pleasure and instruction from your society; but that you could gain nothing from hers." I have not seen her since, so suppose her friend related my observations. Gerard goes on as usual and talks a great deal of you. I have been there once since your departure.

Dénon has promised me an engraving of you. The Esmenards say he has not done you justice.

Baron Humboldt was at Madame Rumford's the other night. I met Mrs. Popkins at a *soirée* at Mrs. Curzon's, where was Lady Oxford who has been twice to see me since. *Fashions* continue the same. Mrs. Popkins was afraid to look at me, for reasons which you know. Every one talks of the work which you are to publish, and great expectations are formed from it. I tell every one, that I do not know what will be in it; but that I suppose it will be worthy of you. They say you are devoid of all affectation or pedantry, and that you assume less in society than any one ever did who possessed so much reputation. In short, I can assure you with truth, that I never heard any one so eulogised as you are in Paris.

I meet Madame Suard every week at Madame Rochefaucauld's. She does not condescend to take great notice of me; I suppose because she thinks I could not understand her wit, which, by the way is rather *obsolete*. My friend Miss Clagston is coming from Cheltenham to enliven my solitude this winter; I am so often ill, and my spirits are so much affected by the state of my health, that the presence of some one who loves me would be a great source of comfort. My dear Lady Morgan, you must write me sometimes to let me know how you and Sir Charles are, and what you are doing. I shall do myself the pleasure of writing you *de temps en temps*, although I was afraid

of writing to Miss Sweeney; my style not being *recherché* enough for such a *bel esprit* as she is. Adieu.
Believe me ever,
Most affectionately yours,
E. PATTERSON.

My best love to Sir Charles. Madame La Rochefaucauld desires to be remembered to you. We had a ball at Mrs. Gallatin's. I wish you had been there. I shall give you all the news.

Madame Patterson Bonaparte to Lady Morgan.

PARIS No. 14, RUE CAUMARTEN,
November 28, 1816.

DEAR LADY MORGAN,

I have had the pleasure of receiving your agreeable letter of the 29th of October, and have executed all your commissions except that *auprès de* Madame de Genlis. I have been so unwell and occupied with moving my lodgings and receiving my friend Miss Clagston, that it has been quite impossible for me to visit the penitent at the Carmelites, however, I shall certainly go to her or write her, you may be assured. Your fairy prince, the dearest little prince in the world, has been enchanted at your recollection of him, and charges me to tell you everything that is true and agreeable for him. He means to go to Dublin in the spring, and intends writing to you — bientôt en attendant ce qui arrivera d'ici au printemps. La princesse m'a chargé de vous remercier de ce que vous avez ecrit à son égard à de la conserver dans votre souvenir. In fact, if I were to write all that your admirers and friends tell me, I should never put my pen down. Ma-

dame D'Houchin, the Gerards, &c., desire me to talk
to you of them, and all think it quite absurd for you
to leave Paris. I meet the Beauveaus at Madame Rumford's every week, when there is an assemblement of
gens d'esprit, not that I mean to call myself one of
them; however, people say I am very good, and that
is my passport to these re-unions. Madame Rochefaucauld sees company every Tuesday, when I meet Madame Suard, who is *toute autre chose que bonne.* Madame
de Villette begs to be remembered to you, and always
says, "pour cela, ma chère, Milady Morgan a beaucoup
d'esprit et beaucoup de naturel." I have been asking
after the *Novice of St. Dominic*, but it has not been seen
by any of your friends, yet. The *Missionary* every one
knows, *par cœur.* Your work on France is anxiously
expected, and if it is what every one supposes it will
be, as nothing mediocre can come from you, all those
who love you will be highly gratified. Your "Muse of
Fable" has gone from Paris to make mischief in some
other place, and to torment her Jerry Sneak *comme à
l'ordinaire.* They say she throws her shoes at his head,
and tells him an old husband must bear every thing
from a young wife, particularly such a beauty and wit
as she is. Mrs. Marshall has another child; I told her
she was a great favourite of yours, and that the "Muse
of Fable" was unworthy her regard. Miss Clagston is
at present staying with me, which renders my time
more pleasant.

By the way, although I sent my love to Mr. North,
I was very angry with him; he wrote me once after I
saw him at Cheltenham, to which I very goodnaturedly
replied, and he never gave himself the trouble to acknowledge the reception of my letter. Lady Falkener,

a very bad person and a great *intrigante*, wanted to marry an old maiden sister to him, and fancied that he liked me better, in consequence of which she tormented me terribly. How is that delightful person, Miss Bessey S.? your *soi-disant* friend, who fancied that you preferred her society, and that Mr. North was in love with her. I cannot forget her ugly face and absurd pretensions, and never think of her without laughing immoderately.

Dear Lady Morgan, I have been very ill and very *triste, tout m'ennui dans ce monde et je ne sçais pas pourquoi*, unless it be the recollection of what I have suffered. I think the best thing for me to do is to return to my dear child in the spring; I love him so entirely, that perhaps seeing him may render my feelings less disagreeable. I hate the *séjour* of America, and the climate destroys the little health which has been left me; but any inconveniences are more supportable than being separated from one's children. How much more we love our children than our husbands — the latter are sometimes so selfish and cruel, and children cannot separate their mothers from their affection.

I have seen all the persons who interest you since the reception of your letter, except Monsieur Dénon; but Madame D'Houchin has seen what you have written, and will tell him everything. Adieu; write me sometimes, I entreat you, and believe me truly and affectionately   Yours, E. P.

PS. — I hope Sir Charles does not forget me, and beg him to accept my best wishes and recollections. I am going to Madame La Rochefaucauld's, with whom you are so great a favourite, this evening.

After her return from Paris to Kildare Street, and while engaged in preparing her work on France, Lady Morgan kept up a brief correspondence with many of the political personages whom she had met. She sent one of her books — most likely the *O'Donnel* — to Lafayette, who was then living a patriarchal life amid his children and grandchildren at his chateau La Grange. He had seen so much in his time from the first American war downwards, had been a courtier in the brilliant society of the old *régime*, a favourite with Marie Antoinette, whom he had helped in her whim to go to the *bal d'Opera*, had been mixed up in so many great events, and he had rubbed against so many great men, that in the latter days', one would have expected him to be a master figure himself; wise both in old experience, and with the wisdom that comes after events; but he just missed being a great man. He was thoroughly honest and good, but not of a sufficiently large type to fill his space on the canvas.

M. Lafayette to Lady Morgan.

La Grange,
October 30, 1816.

Your letter of the 21st September, dear Miladi, has been received in our colony with a sentiment which could only be surpassed by the happiness of receiving yourself. I am equally proud and happy at your partiality for our towers and for their inhabitants, whose distant admiration for you has become tender and confiding. Your short sojourn here has left an impression upon us which makes us proud of corresponding with you, and we hope to receive another visit soon; and we comfort ourselves with the pleasant thought that you have made us a promise; already we are beginning to look about to see what would please you when you come.

We show less philosophy than you about the misfortune for which we were already very sorry before we knew how much worse it was. It is vexing to think that the work which fulfilled so perfectly the expectations of your friends, should have been for you alone the occasion of a disappointment. The copy you had the goodness to send to me has not come to hand. I expect it with great impatience.

I see that you have much amusement in retracing the articles of the last royal ordinance upon the physiognomies of your different friends. The party that you have left pretty well united, finds itself cut in two, like a polypus, and makes two distinct bodies, which make grimaces at each other, *en attendant*, the moment to eat each other up. The friends of Legitimacy, however, must not confound themselves by making part of a body of a different nature. Your acquaintances of the *salons* will be able to tell you that the ministerialists are the constitutionalists of '89; it is a calumny to impute to them that they would use force. The others do not share their moderation. It is with the impartiality of a true patriot that I ought to seek to render justice to all. There are, nevertheless, in the new chamber, some of my friends whom I cannot speak of with so much catholicity. It is not down in our country seats, it is in the *salons* that you will hear the reports of this civil war. M. de Chateaubriand is become the champion of Ultraism. Since the publication of his last work he has grown ten feet

higher.   I rather like to see the Ultras making a refuge for the ministers by putting forwards the liberal
principles which we have been preaching to them in
vain for the last thirty years.   All these undulations
alter nothing of the depths of things; let us try to
turn everything to the profit of liberty.   I am only
speaking now of the underminings and *tracasseries* of
the society of the *salons*.   See! I am also doing a little
in politics myself! You know that very few of our
summer days have the inconvenience of heat, therefore
I pity you for your walk; the rains are dreadful here;
we are afraid we shall have great losses in our harvest.
The bread is bad and dear — a franc for a four pound
loaf.   Our sheep suffer also from the damp herbage
this year.   Mine, however, about which you are good
enough to inquire, have not suffered so much.   You
see that we here have also complaints to make, besides
other misfortunes, the impression of which is too deep
to be complained about.   The two last years of war
have taken away from our peasantry the provisions
which would have enabled them to meet this year of
dearth; but they have, in the course of the revolution
made a provision of energy and good sense, which
makes them stronger and more enlightened under the
strokes of fortune than they would have been thirty
years ago.   We sympathise with all our heart with the
misfortunes of your brave compatriots, so worthy of a
better fate.   We must hope that their neighbours will
occupy themselves in finding out and developing the
good qualities they possess.

My daughters, my grandchildren and all the generations here desire to offer you the expression of their
gratitude and attachment, which sentiments animate all

the inmates of La Grange. Believe me, my dear lady,
I join with them in the renewal of the tender and re-
spectful homage with which I am

Your devoted,
LAFAYETTE.

While the book on France was growing under Lady
Morgan's hands, a very sharp battle was being fought
for it between author and publisher. Mr. Henry Colburn, a young man whose fortunes were still to be
made, had brought out *O'Donnel*, and had done very
well with it; that story was already in a third edition,
and Lady Morgan was pressing him very ardently for
a further share in the profits of her success. For
France he offered her seven hundred and fifty pounds.
She thought the sum too little, insisting on, at least, a
thousand pounds. In the fear of losing his bargain,
Colburn raised his price, as will be seen. In the next
letter, from the pen of this London bibliopole, occurs
the first notice of the establishment of the *Literary
Gazette*, which was to form a new era in literature; of
course the "new epoch" to him meant another vehicle
for announcing his own publications.

II. Colburn to Lady Morgan.

LONDON,
December 19, 1816.

DEAR MADAM,

I am just returned from the city, and have scarcely
time to save the post, and say that I really considered
the offer I made you handsome, and as liberal a one
as in common prudence could be made under the particular circumstances. Without seeing the contents,

which certainly promised well, I naturally expected
the most interesting work on the subject that has appeared; but however excellent and *original*, you perhaps have no idea how great a disadvantage to the
sale is the number of works on the same topic that has
already appeared.

I should indeed be sorry that you should be compelled to arrange with any other bookseller, and whatever *apparent* advantage there may be in publishing
with any other, I am very confident, on a proper *ba-
lancing*, of its *being in my favour*. No one bookseller,
I am certain, takes the tenth part the pains I do in
advertising, and in *other* respects I do not think any
one will *in future*, cope with me, since, from January
next, I shall have under my sole control *two journals*,
viz., the *New Monthly*, which flourishes as well as possible in England, and my new forthcoming *weekly* literary journal, which is to be sent *free by the post* in-
stantly all over the country like a *newspaper*, and to
foreign parts. It is to be called *The Literary Gazette
and Journal of the Belles Lettres*. The publication will
form a new epoch in literature; it will please and
astonish the public by its novelty, and cut up the sale
of my rival reviews and journalists by the *novelty* of
its plan, the VALUE of its contents, and the *preferable
mode of publication — thirteen* numbers for one of the
Quarterly! but more of this anon, in my prospectus.

To conclude at once, though at a really great risk,
I will consent to undertake to pay the one thousand
pounds, and on my *honour* if it succeed better than expected, I will *consider myself accordingly your debtor*,
BESIDES making up to you the other *fifty pounds* on

O'Donnel that you may no longer regret the third edition.

That I may make arrangements accordingly, I will beg your ultimatum by return of post. I am obliged to conclude,

Being, dear madam,
Yours, very truly,
H. COLBURN.

Colburn's offer, as amended, was accepted, and the work went on, with some delays and hitches in its progress, the chief one of all being the illegibility of Lady Morgan's MS., which Colburn plaintively mentions more than once. There was also great delay in sending the proofs, as it is incidentally mentioned that the post only went three times a week. Colburn spared neither pains nor expense to make the work perfect, employing a careful scholar to read Lady Morgan's careless proofs, and to edit them.

Sir Charles Morgan contributed several chapters to the work on France, embodying his observations on the state of medical science, political economy, and French jurisprudence, both as it existed in that day and as it had been at the period of the Revolution. These chapters are valuable, but somewhat too heavy for the slighter and brighter portions of Lady Morgan's own share of the work.

CHAPTER XIV.

PUBLICATION OF FRANCE — 1817.

ON the 17th of June, 1817, Colburn wrote to Lady Morgan announcing that *France* was published, and that she was finely off, meaning on the swelling tide of his best puffs and preliminary paragraphs. The first edition was in two volumes, quarto; and Colburn expressed his firm assurance of being able to sell the whole of this first edition by the first of July.

The work on France made a great sensation. It was so long since France had been open to the English, that it was fresh ground to that generation; indeed, it wore a new face to all the world; for the restored France of 1816 was a different world to what had been the France of the old *régime*, or the France of the Consulate and the Empire. Lady Morgan's work was seized upon with avidity by readers of all classes, and provoked criticism as diverse as there were shades of opinion about Legitimacy, Bourbonism, Liberalism, and the Orthodox anti-Jacobin Church and State true blue intolerant Toryism.

The clamour of abuse was enough to have appalled a very stout heart. The praise and admiration, though quite as hearty, came from a less influential party. Lady Morgan was so thoroughly sincere in her liberal opinions that she did not at all realise the horror and obloquy her opinions caused. She had also the support and countenance of her husband, whom she both loved and reverenced; this was a protection and shelter which defended her from the storm to which she was exposed. The party critics treated her opinions as synonymous with all that was irreligious, unwomanly and detestable.

The work itself, which provoked all this clamour, is extremely brilliant and clever; the sketches of manners, opinions and people, are bright, vivid, and touched in with a life and vigour that impresses the reader with their truthfulness. The sketches of the French peasantry are excellent and graphic; her own experiences amongst the Irish peasants gave her a practical insight into the general conditions of this class. The notices of French society, both Royalist and Bonapartean, are charming and sparkling. She had keen perceptions, and admirable powers of narrative; but in *France*, her wit, for the first time in her published works, touches on flippancy, and she allows herself to expatiate, with more complacency than good taste, on the compliments and attentions she received. A Parisian *succès de société* such as she had achieved, was enough to turn the head of any woman, and especially of an Irish woman.

It was a pardonable vanity; but it gave her enemies a handle against her. It was easy to make "a hit, a very palpable hit," at her careless self-revelations of vanity; but the adverse party were blind and clumsy in their abuse, and in their zeal outran all truth and discretion. A more moderate style of abuse would have done Lady Morgan more injury with her public, though it might have been less injurious to herself. She was fed on flattery and detraction; and she had to receive both, without any of the mitigating influences which usually interpose between the giver and the receiver. If she were coarsely abused, she was as coarsely flattered to her face; and those who in later life observed her, could trace the scars of these long bygone years. Her notoriety was beyond what any other woman has ever had to endure "who kept her fame." That this notoriety had a scathing and deteriorating influence, cannot be denied; but in the heat of so much party scandal no aspersion was ever cast upon her personal character and prudent conduct as a woman.

The *Quarterly* assailed Lady Morgan in an article which has become almost proverbial for its virulence and bitterness. That article was eminently unjust; it was far-fetched in its criticism and unfair in its conclusions.

Lady Morgan was rather proud than otherwise of the commotion it made; and she amply avenged herself by putting John Wilson Croker, who had the credit of writing it, into her next novel, *Florence Macarthy*, — the novel being at least as likely to live and circulate as the article.

The following *jeu d'esprit* from the pen of her sister, Lady Clarke, is an amusing and not unfair version of this once famous and formidable article.

> The book we review is the work of a woman,
> A fact which we think will be guessed at by no man,
> Who notes the abuse which our virulent rage
> Shall discharge on its author in every page.
> And who is this *woman* — no *recent* offender,
> A Jacobin, Shanavest, Whiteboy defender.
> She who published "O'Donnel," which (take but our word)
> Is a monstrous wild "tissue of ALL THAT'S ABSURD" —
> Indeed there's a something in all her romances,
> Which, to tell our opinion, does not hit our fancies.

No, give us a novel, whose pages unfold
The glories of that blessed era of old,
When Princes legitimate trod on the people,
And the Church was so *high* that it out-topped the steeple:
No, give us some Methodist's maudling confusion,
RELIGION in SEEMING, in FACT, PERSECUTION;
Some strange Anti-Catholic orthodox whining,
At this age of apostacy wildly repining ! !

    This WOMAN ! — we scarce could believe when we read,
Retorts all the charges we heaped on HER head;
And leads to rebellion young authors, by shewing,
That calling *hard names* is by no means *reviewing.*
She boasts that we've not spoilt her market in marriage,
That vainly her morals and wit *we* disparage;
But surely that man is the boldest in life,
Who, in spite of OUR ravings, could take her for wife;
And therefore we now set him down without mercy
As the slave of enchantment, "THE VICTIM OF CIRCE."

    Now to come to the matter in hand — we advance
'Tis "AN IMPUDENT LIE," when she calls her book "FRANCE;"
A title that would not be characteristic,
Unless for a large Gazetteer or Statistic.
For we hold that it is not allow'd in a work,
To form our opinions by *Ex pede Here.*
She ought to have visited Lyons, Bordeaux,
And peeped into Marseilles, and Strasburgh, and Meaux;
For though the design of the Congress miscarries,
And Jacobins kick against Louis — at Paris,*
Though Freedom lies bleeding and chain'd *on the Seine,*
And the emigrants *there* mould the state upon Spain,
In the rest of the kingdom, for what she can tell,
The impudent jade, things *may* go mighty well.

    Next comes her arrangement! — (when this we denounce
We must eke out our charge with a bit of a bounce;
And o'erlook the confusion which reigns in our head,
To charge it at once, on HER book in the stead) —
Of this book, my good readers, in vain you may hope
An account of its merits, its plan or its scope;
For the tale *she* relates does not chime with the view
Which *we* take of France in our *loyal review.*
And though we should rail till our paper were shrinking,
Alas! we should but *set the people a thinking.*
On the list of ERRATA 'twere better to seize,
For thence we may conjure what blunders we please.

These mixed with the few, which the best author makes,
In a work of such length, and *our own worse mistakes;*
With some equivocation, and some "*direct lies,*"
Of abuse will provide our accustom'd supplies;
Which largely diluted with loyalty rant,
With much hypocritical methodist cant,
Mis-quotations, mis-statements, distortions of phrase,
Will set the HALF-THINKERS (we judge) in amaze,
And this "WORM MOST AUDACIOUS," this "woman so mad,"
This compound of all that's presumptuous and bad —
(Tho' we should not succeed in repressing her book,
And the youth of our land on its pages still look,)
Will perceive, with her friends, midst the people of fashion,
That the *Quarterly* scribe's in a desperate passion.
Postscriptum — we'd near made a foolish omission,
And forgotten a slur on her Second Edition.
Though perhaps, after all, she may have the last word,
And reply to our "wholesome" remarks — by a Third —
And thus, like a sly and insidious joker,
The malice defeat of an *hireling* CROKER!!

Looking to the correspondence of Lady Morgan,
we pick our pleasant way through heaps of the friendly
and familiar letters which, in those days, softened the
warfare in which she was engaged with her enemies,
and particularly with the malignant countryman of
her own who had once been her friend, and had possibly aspired to become her husband. We pass over
many tempting notes — hearty, sympathetic, eloquent.
Here, however, is something to arrest the eye from
Alicia Lefanu, whose writings are ever welcome for
her brother's sake and for her own.

Poor, graceful, gracious Mrs. Lefanu! ill in body,
anxious in mind, and worried in addition with bad
Memoirs of her brother, Richard Brinsley Sheridan!

Mrs. Lefanu to Lady Morgan.

Ash Wednesday,
February 19, 1817.

Many thanks, dear Lady Morgan, for your frequent and kind inquiries. I am very ill, and hopeless of being better. My great anxiety about Joseph made me forget and neglect myself until severe pain forced me to resort to medical aid. A severe cold, caught on Christmas day, and great uneasiness of mind, have put me in a state of continual suffering.

I wish I was able to write any satisfactory account of my brother. Watkins's history of him and my family is a tissue of falsehood. What satisfaction could it be to him to write the life of a man whom he evidently hates and basely calumniates? Of my family history he knows nothing: he must be a very impertinent fellow to take the liberties he has done with a family he could know nothing of.

But S. White did worse; for he fabricated letters from my mother, &c., that she could not have written. He was the natural son of an uncle of my mother, who left him five hundred pounds, with which, and my father's assistance, he set up a school; but he never was acknowledged as our relation, — we never were boarded with him or placed under his care, &c., &c., — all lies.

My mother's sketch of a comedy, unfinished, was put into my brother Richard's hands by my father at Bath, when we were resident there; but my father never even hinted that he had made any use of it in *The Rivals.* Of my own knowledge I can say nothing, for I never read it.

I hope your labours will soon be over and amply rewarded. Much is expected from you; and I trust you will not disappoint expectation.

Believe me, affectionately yours,

ALICIA LEFANU.

I beg my kind compliments to Sir Charles.

Our next letters are from Madame Patterson Bonaparte. With her airy manner, her beauty and her wit, she would have made an excellent princess, American as she was. One wonders that Napoleon should have been blind to her capabilities — he, whose motto was, the "tools to him who can use them." Mr. Moore is, of course, Tom Moore, the poet.

There is no need to draw attention to the passage on "the loves of the Duke of Wellington." Madame Bonaparte speaks of such things with the gaiety and ease of a perfect Parisienne.

Madame Patterson Bonaparte to Lady Morgan.

PARIS, May 8, 1817.

MY DEAR LADY MORGAN,

Your kind letter by Mr. Moore reached me, and I have been prevented replying to it by a variety of circumstances. My health has become worse than it has been, and they now say it is a disease of the liver, added to debility of lungs. I know not what it is, but I am very tired of suffering, and must make a journey to procure present relief.

All your friends are well and anxious about you as ever. Madame Suard makes many inquiries of you and your work. I go once, *par semaine*, to Madame Rochefaucauld, where I find the same society you left. It is impossible to see Madame D'Houchin, as the hours generally appropriated to visits are spent by her in sleep. She dines at half-past nine. M. Dénon has been good enough to see me sometimes, which I attribute to the partiality with which you distinguished me. I know nothing more flattering than your regard, and am very grateful, I assure you.

Madame de Villette is to me what she has always been, — a constant friend. She is equally faithful in her admiration and love of you; and never speaks of you but in the way every one who is not envious must do.

France is the country you should reside in, because you are so much admired and liked here. No English-woman has received the same attentions since you. I am dying to see your last *publication*. Public expectation is as high as possible; and if you had kept it a little longer, they would have purchased it at your own price. How happy you must be at filling the world with your name as you do! Madame de Stael and Madame de Genlis are forgotten; and if the love of fame be of any weight with you, your excursion to Paris was attended with brilliant success. I assure you, and you know I am sincere, that you are more spoken of than any other person of the present day. Mr. Moore seldom sees me, — I did not take with him at all. He called to show me the article of your letter which mentions the report of the Duke of Wellington's *loves*. I am not the Mrs. — the great man gives as a successor to Grassini.

You would be surprised if you knew how great a

fool she is, at the power she exercises over the Duke; but I believe that he has no taste *pour les femmes d'esprit;* which is, however, no reason for going into extremes, as in this case. He gave her an introduction to the Prince Regent, and to every one of consequence in London and Paris. She had, however, no success in France, where her not speaking the language of the country was a considerable advantage to her, since it prevented her nonsense from being heard. Do not tell what I have written to you of this affair, since I should pass for malicious and unfriendly towards my compatriot and relation. She writes, too, all the paragraphs you may have seen in the newspapers; and might revenge herself by saying some spiteful things of me through that channel.

The Prince de Beauveau asks me after you, and has, I believe written you. They are all going to Spa for the summer.

Madame de Genlis has had the daughter of the Duke of Orleans confided to her care for the purpose of education. I have heard this piece of intelligence, for the authenticity of which I cannot, however, vouch.

I know not a single syllable of the political news of France or any other country, nor do I even read the gazettes at present. My bad health and *ennui* more than occupy me, and deprive me of all interest in life.

Mr. Moore writes you everything you desire to know of your friends here. He goes often to Mrs. Bradshaw's. Have you seen the voyage of Madame Clairvoyante?

Adieu, my dear Lady Morgan. Do not forget me.

Write me sometimes, and believe me ever most affectionately attached to you.

How is Sir Charles? Pray give my love to him, and ask him what I must do to get well.

I shall write you a long letter when I am better. I am confined to the house at present.

Mrs. the "Muse of Fable," has come back after a tour to the south of France. Did you know she was in love with De C—e last summer, and that she attended his levees very regularly for the purpose of captivating him? I fancy, however, he scarcely knew she was in his *salon*, or dreamed of the ravage he made on her heart. His *attentions* did not flatter very much, it appears, by her falling in love with another person since. I seldom see her at present. Adieu once more.

Yours truly,
E. PATTERSON.

Madame Patterson Bonaparte to Lady Morgan.

PARIS,
August 11, 1817.

DEAR LADY MORGAN,

Sir Charles's letter of which you inquire through Mr. Warden, was received by me a long time ago. Since then I have the pleasure of writing you a long letter with all the news of Paris. Your work on France has appeared through a French translation, in which they have suppressed what they thought best, and have arranged what they chose to give the public in the way best suited to their own purposes. I read it cursorily, in English, as the person who lent it me could permit me to keep it only six hours. It ap-

peared to me, like everything you write, full of genius
and taste. Its truths cannot at this moment be admitted here, but in all other countries it will have
complete success. The violent clamour of the editors
of the Paris gazettes proves that it is too well written;
were it an insignificant production they would say less
about it. They are publishing it in America, where
your fame has been as much extended as in Europe,
and where your talents are as justly appreciated.

I have not seen Madame D'Houchin and M. Dénon
for a long time. My health obliged me to spend
some weeks in the country and Madame D'Houchin
you know, wakes when other persons sleep, which
renders it impossible to enjoy her society without
paying the price of a night's repose, and this to me is
very difficult since I have lost my health. Your old
friend and admirer, M. Suard, is dead of old age. I
met him two weeks previous, at a party, where he
enjoyed himself as much as any of us. His widow
gave a dinner the day week after, because she was
afraid of being *triste*, she said. Since then she receives as usual, and takes promenades on the Boule-
vards, because "bon ami m'a dit qu'il fallait vivre."
Her friends are encouraged to flatter themselves, that
her great sensibility will not kill her; at the same time
that it induces her to give them parties and attend
their *réunions*. She grieves in the most agreeable way
to all those who find her house convenient or her
society desirable.

Madame de Villette is exactly as you left her. Mr.
Warden and herself are my neighbours for the present;
I shall bid them adieu in six weeks.

My desire to see my child is stronger than my taste

for Paris. I really am of your opinion, the best thing a woman can do is to marry. It appears to me that even quarrels with one's husband are preferable to the *ennui* of a solitary existence. There are so many hours besides those appropriated to the world, that one does not know how to get rid of (at least one like me has, who have no useful occupation), that I have sometimes wished to marry from *ennui* and *tristesse*. You never felt *ennui* in any state, because, when absent from society, you cultivate talents which will immortalize you. I know no person so happy as yourself. Madame de Stael died regretting a life, which she had contrived to render very agreeable in every way. Her marriage with Mr. Rocca is thought very superfluous. The liberal system she pursued through life forbids us to attribute other motives to her last matrimonial experiment, — unless that of tranquillizing the conscience of her young lover may be added. All her most intimate friends were ignorant that a marriage existed, and unless her Will had substantiated the fact, would have treated her marriage ceremony as a calumny. Marrying a man twenty years younger than herself, without fortune or name, is a ridicule in France, *pire qu'un crime*. Her son, by him, is called one of her posthumous works. What think you of the *Manuscript of St. Helena* being attributed to her and Benjamin Constant? Is it possible to carry absurdity and the desire of rendering her inconsistent further? I have heard persons gravely assert that she wrote it.

Adieu, my dear Lady Morgan; do not forget me when I shall be at a greater distance from you. Your recollection accompanies me to the New World, where I wish I may meet any one half as agreeable. My son

is like you; they write me he is *pétri d'esprit*, and
promises to develope great talents. I believe *difficile-
ment* that any good awaits me, because I am constantly
disappointed and distressed. Do you think it easy to
judge of the future capacity of a boy of twelve years?
I fear he may not justify what his teachers now predict
of him, and that after exciting my hopes he will become like the generality of people, *médiocre* and tiresome. I hope Sir Charles likes me always, and that
my most *affectionate* regards will be accepted with as
much pleasure as I offer them through you. How is
the *bel esprit*, Bess Sweeney? She was a successful
impostor with many persons in Cheltenham, where she
passed herself for your friend, for a wit, and for the
object of Mr. North's preference, all at the same time.
She was a lofty pretender.

Yours, affectionately and sincerely,

E. P.

PS. — Write me addressed to my banker here.
After my departure, Warden will send you my address,
dans l'autre monde.

The next letter is from Lady Charleville. The
letters of Madame Bonaparte and Lady Charleville are
in as great a contrast as the writers in their personal
appearance, characters and fortunes. Lady Charleville
was large, stately, and imposing, with magnificent grey
eyes, a courtly, formal manner, and a deeply-toned
voice, which made her most trifling observations im-
pressive — rendered all the more so by her habit of
addressing every one as "Ma'am," or "Sir." Madame
Bonaparte was fair, dodu, and piquant, with particu-

arly beautiful arms. She had been flattered and spoiled — the idol and queen of her native city, Baltimore. She made a brilliant marriage with the brother of the First Consul, then on the point of becoming Emperor; but instead of sharing the rising fortunes of her young husband, she had been subject to the bitterest insult and outrage that could be offered to a woman. Her marriage was broken; her child made illegitimate; her prospects in life killed; and she herself, stripped of her husband's protection when little more than a girl, flung upon the world to sink or swim as she could. It is no wonder that her letters bear the impress of a life run to waste, and a heart turned to bitterness. Napoleon trampled down many things in his march through life, but the ravage made in the hearts and souls of those whose interest stood in the way of his plans, was more cruel and fatal in their effects than the mere loss of life and limbs on his fields of battle.

Lady Charleville's letters, like those of Madame Bonaparte, contain some of the news going about society, but none of the scandal of the period; there is an absence of the cruel keenness and bitter dissatisfaction—one might almost call it jealousy—that mark similar topics in the letters of Madame Bonaparte. Lady Charleville's life had been that of an invalid, and, in other respects, not free from the ills that every one born of woman is heir to in this world. When she was a young woman — not more than thirty — she lost the use of her limbs, and during the remainder of her life had to be carried or wheeled about in a large chair. Never being seen, except sitting, she had the appearance of a queen upon her throne. It will be seen from the following letter, that her strictures on men and morals were as dignified as her appearance. Whatever personal news may come to light in these old letters, is so old that it has now become historical, and merely illustrates the spirit of the time. If there be any survivors, we can only quote Lady Teazle, and say, that "Scandal, like death, is common to all."

Lady Charleville had been a steady protectress to Lady Morgan when she needed friends, and was her admirer now she had obtained a distinguished position in the eyes of the world. Madame Bonaparte's friendship for Lady Morgan was more for her own sake. She found in her a friend with some substance of character, and one who could sympathize with the romantic discomforts of her position.

Lady Charleville to Lady Morgan.

14, Terrace, Piccadilly,
November 24, 1817.

I never was more pleased to hear from you, dear Lady Morgan, than in the receipt of yours of 27th of October, as the explanation you gave me of Perney's name sliding (through natural confidence in a decent man's catalogue) into your work, did away a cruel prohibition of the higher powers, who, on their arrival at Worthing, said they knew that author to have written only indecent blasphemy! and that they who approved of it could not be my correspondent. Thank God, thank God, you did not do so; such a heart and such talents as yours should not be exposed through the idle vain-glory of seeming to have read everything, to so dreadful an imputation; and it is in the fulness of goodwill and admiration for your talent, which is superior and *improving every year*, that I rejoice all these stern readers can now say is, that you relied too hastily on the bland and decent manners of Frenchmen, and could not conceive, with a pure and honest heart, that any one could recommend an unvarnished tale of indecency to your consideration. Lord Charleville says this wicked man has *never* written but against religion and decency, and that one line of his principal work contains more shocking impiety than the folios of all the encyclopedists; he will not allow that Voltaire's *Pucelle* (giving it up as a work too free, yet rather calculated for the Romish abuses of religion than to impugn the basis of all), or Chaucer's loose tales, should do away their fame, since Voltaire's other works are highly beneficial to mankind, and highly moral; and, at least, old Geoffrey, though a libertine, is not an impious one! The parallel, therefore, he thinks unjust, and yet he would wish, in praising either Voltaire or Chaucer, that a woman should mark something of disapprobation of the loose parts of their writings. Such is the result of all he said to me; and once more your letter of the 27th has set all to right again, and I trust in heaven that your warm and amiable feelings may no more be tortured by the disapprobation of good and stupid men, or the *slanders of ruffians.*

I received your letter of the 7th; you now know why it remained unacknowledged. I knew before I received it that Mr. Croker was the author of the article, in which, some say, he was assisted by Mr. Barrow, Secretary to the Admiralty; but of that I doubt, as hitherto this gentleman has kept to the in-

vestigation of science only. I am quite of your opinion that Mr. Croker deserves all the reprobation of
candid, honourable men; but I don't think squibs will
touch him — his mail of brass, and his heart of
adamant secure him; and though I sincerely wish him
every mortification, I don't see what can afford it to
such a man. I sent the lines to Scotland* to some
clever people, who think as I do, about the general
merits of *France*. I am sure all the newspaper mention
of it was in its favour, for people do love controversy.
I hope the next edition may, somehow or other, do
away with the mention of Perney's name! which is of
more import than you can well believe in respect to
society.

The Danish Ambassador, who speaks English as
well as we do, said to me the other day, "We, in
Denmark, cannot impeach Lady Morgan's politics as
being dazzled with Napoleon!"

I agree in *toto* with your feelings of what true religion should be, "to visit the sorrower in affliction, and
keep one's self unspotted from the world;" this, with
a firm acknowledgment of the great truths of Chris-
tianity, would be the perfection of all doctrine! ! ! To
persecute is horrible, and every species of protection
that law, and liberty, and property inviolable, can bestow, is the indefeasible right of a subject of these
realms; but what has that to do with the question of
giving legislative rights to Romish persons, insomuch
as their fatal superstition has established deism on the
continent in all thinking men. Whe should dread and
deplore to encourage a worship of such baleful effect;
nor ever give them power to sap the foundations of a

* See *ante*, p. 193.

pure and holy form of worship, which, allowing of the finest system of ethics for our guide, requires no sacrifice of the understanding.

* * * * * *

I have heard since I came into town yesterday, that Walter Scott has given *Rob Roy* to the press as his own, and says he has another novel ready. Sir J. B. Burgess is publishing *The Dragon Knight* (a poem epic). Mr. Ellis has disappointed all his friends by his dull narrative about China.

Sir William Gell is gone back to the Princess of Wales, and those anxious for her honour and security are glad of it, as the wretches in whose hands she is, have already contrived to load her with debt as well as dishonour. — She, who in England (dearer than in any other spot on the globe), did not leave a debt, and refused an augmentation of income. Mr. Brougham tried, but could not break the spell; but Gell has more power with her, and equal goodwill.

M. CHARLEVILLE.

Early in July, Colburn had sold the first edition of *France*, and, on July the 14th, wrote impatiently for the new preface, that he might bring out the second edition, which was to be in octavo. The preface was to explain how the same errors were in that as in the first. He says, "I have announced the work by numerous paragraphs and advertisements, and it shall be *well* advertised *everywhere*." Colburn had always more faith in his own advertisements for the success of a work than in the genius of the author. Since furnishing the work on *France*, Lady Morgan had been busy on a new Irish novel which she had now three-parts finished.

Sir Charles had also written a scientific work in his own department. These they offered, in the first instance, to Colburn, who declared he would be charmed to publish them, as he considered "the solidity of Sir Charles would qualify the airy lightness and badinage of Lady Morgan;" but he wanted to have the MS. at a bargain, and offered a thousand pounds for the two. Lady Morgan resented the idea. She hated a bargain, except when she drove it for herself, and she threatened to go to some other publisher. Colburn complained that it would be a bad return for all his exertions, and there was a good deal of haggling, the result of which was that he agreed to give one thousand two hundred pounds for the two. This they accepted. Sir Charles's work has not remained in memory; but the novel, which Colburn called *Florence Macarthy*, is still read and admired.

It is not so romantic as *O'Donnel;* but it hits much harder upon the social and political abuses in Irish Government. In this book, Lady Morgan embodies her own views in the heroine, who is as wild, fascinating, romantic and extravagant as ever trod the stage of theatre or page of romance. Florence Macarthy appears always in disguise and masquerade — flits about like a will-of-the-wisp, mystifying everybody — setting the wrong to rights, "confounding the politics and frustrating the knavish tricks," of all who mean wrong to Ireland. Like all Lady Morgan's heroines, she is endowed with very little money, but no end of beauty, good sense, wit, and the representative of a real *ould* Irish noble family of decayed fortunes.

It is curious that whilst the story is wildly improbable, the accessories are all true, not only in spirit,

but in the letter. The heroine, Florence Macarthy, has
the mission, (self-imposed and followed, *con amore*) of
arousing a charming young Irishman to a sense of what
he owes to his country, and to stimulate his indignation
against the oppressions and abuses especially crying
for redress.

The sketches of character, the pictures of fashionable society in Dublin, the English fine ladies and
dandies of the period, the Irish characters, both of the
good and of the despicable class — in short, all the
shades and varieties of the moral and social influences
at work in Ireland at the time, are given with a
subtlety and vividness which is wonderful; they are
dashed off with vigour; they live, and move, and bear
their truth to nature stamped upon them in every line.
Mr. Crawley, the Castle hack, and all his tribe, the
toadies and servile tools of Government, embody what
were then the worst evils of English rule in Ireland.
All the Crawley sketches are supreme and inimitable
for the racy humour, the genuine fun Lady Morgan has
thrown into their portraits. They are etched with a
sarcasm that bites like aquafortis; but the humour
tempers and mellows the malice. In this family sketch
she paid her debt to Croker, who, rightly or wrongly,
had the credit of being the author, not only of the attack on *France*, but of all the other assaults upon her
in the *Quarterly*.

Lady Morgan was, before all things, an artist, and
she did not hate Croker too much to be able to make
him amusing to the general reader, who had no cause
of offence against him. There was nothing impotent in
her revenge; no wish to wound beyond her power to
strike; the strokes of her weapon were clear, keen,

incisive, and effectual. She got the laugh on her side; she left her critic transfixed on the point of her diamond pen, and she could afford to forgive him, for she had, as children say, "paid him off," and kept a balance in hand against the future.

In the end, the conversion of the hero is rewarded by marrying Florence Macarthy, whom he has loved hopelessly all along, and who has been at once his guardian angel, guide, philosopher, and friend. All Lady Morgan's novels are characterised by the same theatrical construction. Her theatrical descent and early associations account for her use of stage effects and melo-dramatic expedients. This love of mystery, disguise, and rapid changes of scene (for the heroines are all gifted, if not with ubiquity, at least with the power of being in one place in a miraculously short space of time, after having been seen in another, a long way off) give an element of romance to Lady Morgan's novels, which remove them from real life or "the light of common day." It perhaps enables readers to go patiently through political discussions and statistical details of the then existing state of things in Ireland, which otherwise would not have been tolerated, but it gives an air of trick and mannerism which, to say the best, is meretricious; but in spite of criticism and sober judgment, it makes them extremely entertaining.

14*

CHAPTER XV.

OUT OF ENGLAND INTO FRANCE — 1818.

LADY MORGAN was still engaged in completing *Florence Macarthy*, when Colburn went to press with it early in March, though it was not more than half finished. He had his own reasons for pressing forwards the publication. He had an idea. This idea was to follow up the success he had had with the work on *France*, by producing another of a similar class upon Italy.

In March, 1818, Colburn wrote to Sir Charles and Lady Morgan, proposing they should pay a visit to Italy that year, and write a work upon that country, similar in scope and design to the one that had been so successful on France; Lady Morgan to write the observations and sketches on men, manners, and the things worthy of note; Sir Charles contributing the chapters on the state of the laws, the influence of politics, and the condition of science and education. He offered them two thousand pounds for the copyright. They closed with the offer, and he wrote to thank them, declaring that their frank acceptance of his offer had put him in fresh spirits. He urged them to come to London immediately, to make their final arrangements. Sir Charles and Lady Morgan left Dublin rather earlier this year, bringing *Florence Macarthy* to be finished amid the brilliant bustle and distraction of a London season.

On their way to London Sir Charles and Lady Morgan remained one night at Holyhead, the spot she had so often visited when going to her old friend, Lady Stanley. The dear friend was dead, and here is Lady Morgan's record of her visit to the empty shrine.

"This is the first time I arrived at Holyhead without the hope of seeing dear Lady Stanley standing at her own gate, with Sir John on one side and Susanne on the other with her shawls and dog. The gates were now closed, and all looked gloomy and desolate."

Colburn had engaged rooms for them in Conduit Street, and they were soon surrounded by all the gaiety of London. Colburn was in high good humour, and so enchanted with *Florence Macarthy*, in reading the proofs, that in the enthusiasm of the moment he rushed out and bought a beautiful *parure* of amethysts, which he presented to Lady Morgan, as a tribute of admiration, and perhaps, with a little hope of keeping her in good humour. The whole of their stay in London and Paris, *en route* to Italy, has been minutely chronicled in the Odd Volume,* and there is no further need to allude to it. It was a pleasant season of visits and friends, old and new; but Lady Morgan wrote to her sister —

"You are not to suppose we spend all our time in idleness, for we study hard in our different departments. I give an hour to Italian every morning, and have began a course of history, ancient and modern, to rub up my memory before touching classic ground."

---

* Published by Bentley, 1858.

Italy was not then the accessible holiday tour it has since become. There was enough of difficulty and adventure to give the journey a dash of the heroic to Lady Morgan's imagination, which loved to set all things in theatrical array.

Whilst in London she received the following letter from Madame Jerome Bonaparte. Madame Bonaparte had returned to America, where she must have found her position more irksome than in Paris, if her wrongs had not been too great to leave room for petty vexations.

Madame Jerome Bonaparte to Lady Morgan.

May 23, 1818.

MY DEAR LADY MORGAN,

I have not received a line from you since my arrival in America, which I regret more than I can express to you. I wrote you a very long letter describing the effect your work on France produced on its transatlantic readers. The demand was so great, that it went through three editions with us. I assure you that your reputation here is as familiar and as great as in Europe, where you are so justly admired. I wish I could see and listen to you once more; but this, like all my desires, must be disappointed, and I am condemned to vegetate for ever in a country where I am not happy. My son is very intelligent, and very good, and very handsome — all these advantages add to the regret I experience at the destiny which compels me to lose life in this region of *ennui.* You have a great deal of imagination, but it can give you no idea of the mode of existence inflicted on us. The men are all merchants; and commerce, although it may fill the purse, clogs the brain; beyond their counting houses they possess not a single idea — they never visit except when they wish to marry. The women are all occupied in *les détails de ménage*, and nursing children — these are useful occupations, but do not render people agreeable to their neighbours. I am condemned to solitude, which I find less insupportable than the dull *réunions* which I might sometimes frequent in this city. The men being all bent on marriage do not attend to me because they fancy I am not inclined to change the evils of my condition for those they could find me in another. Sometimes, indeed, I have been thought so *ennuyée* as to be induced to accept *very respectable* offers; but I prefer remaining as I am to the horror of marrying a person I am indifferent to. You are very happy, in every respect, too much so, to conceive what I suffer here.

I have letters from Paris which say De Caze, the Minister of Police, is created a peer, and is to marry one of the Princesses de Beauveau, whom you know.

Qu'en pensez vous? It appears very strange to my *recollections* of the state of *political* feeling of the parties, but nothing is too surprising to believe of politicians. He is very handsome, at least, which is not a bad thing in a husband; they say, too, that he has talents, and great sensibility — of the last two I cannot judge, as I saw him only *en passant*.

Paris offers too many *agrémens*, too many agreeable recollections — among the latter you are my greatest — and I think with pain that I shall perhaps never see you again.

Mais cela n'empêche pas que je vous prie de lui dire — that I recollect him with pleasure and regret, and

that I beg to be remembered to him. I suppose you
will return to Paris, where I hope you will be happy
and pleased; it is very easy to be pleased and happy
in your situation, because every one is pleased with
you, and you are loved whenever you choose to be so.
The French admire you so much, that you ought to
live with them. Suppose you were to come to this
country; it is becoming the fashion to travel here and
to know something of us, and I assure you that if you
would spend some time here you might find materials
for an interesting work — *de toutes les manières*, you
would make any country interesting that you wrote
about. I wish I could return to Europe; but it is impossible — a single woman is exposed to so many disagreeable comments in a foreign country; her life, too,
is so solitary except when in public, which is not half
the day, that it is more prudent for me to remain here;
besides, I have at present only eleven hundred pounds
a-year to spend, which you know make only twenty-
five thousand francs — not enough to support me out
of my own family, where I have nothing to spend in
eating, or in carriages, rent, &c. I wish I could send
my son to Europe for his education; I should prefer
Edinburgh, but I know no one there to whom I could
entrust him. I should write you more frequently
were there any incidents in this dull place which
might interest you, or any anecdotes that could amuse
— there are, alas, none. I embroider and read, *pour
me défaire de mon temps* — they are the only distractions left me. Do you remember the description Madame de Stael gives of the mode of life Corinna found
in a country town in England, and the subjects of conversation at Lady Edgermon's table, which were limited

to births, marriages, and deaths? I am so tired of
hearing these three important events discussed, and
my opinion of them has been so long decided, that it
is a misery to be born and to be married, I have painfully experienced, without lessening my dread of death
— so you may imagine how little relish I have for the
conversation on these *triste* topics, and how gladly I
seek refuge from listening to it by retiring to my own
apartment.

Adieu, my dear Lady Morgan — *il ne faut pas vous
ennuyer d'avantage.* Make my best love acceptable to
Sir Charles, and ask him to think sometimes of me.
Write to me, I entreat you. J'ai plus que jamais be-
soin de vos lettres pour me consoler de tout ce que j'ai
perdu en vous quittant pour revenir dans mon triste
pays. Have you a good college in Dublin? I might
send my son there in two years, perhaps, as I cannot
send him to France, and do not wish him educated in
England, where his name would not recommend him
to much favour.

I remain, most affectionately yours,
ELIZA PATTERSON.

A letter from Lady Morgan to her sister, written
on their route to Paris, is a curious picture of what
travelling was in comparatively modern times. We
seem to be divided by a great gulf from those days,
— as wide as that which separates us from the feudal
times.

Lady Morgan to Lady Clarke.

CALAIS,
August 27, 1818.

Here we are, my dear love, after a tremendous expense at the hotel at Dover, where we slept last night, and embarked at twelve o'clock this morning, in a stormy sea. The captain remained behind to try and get more passengers, and the result was, that we remained tossing in the bay near two hours, almost to the extinction of our existence. In my life I never suffered so much. As to Morgan, he was a dead man. The whole voyage we were equally bad; and the ship could not be got into port, — so we were flung, more dead than alive, into a wretched sail boat, and how we got on shore I do not know. It rained in torrents all the time; but the moment I touched French ground, and breathed French air, I got well. We came to our old *auberge*, MM. Maurices, and the first place we got to was the kitchen fire, for we were wet and cold; — and really, in that kitchen I saw more beauty than at many of our London parties. Madame Maurice and her daughter, are both handsome women. We were obliged to have bedrooms opposite to the *auberge*, as it was quite full, but the house, Madame told us, belongs to "*mama*." She is herself about fifty, so you may guess what "mama" is. She is *admirable* — a powdered head, three feet high, and souflet gauze winker cap. Our chamber-maid is worth *anything*. She is *not* one of the kitchen beauties, *par exemple;* but here she is — an ugly woman of seventy, in her chemise, with the simple addition of a red corset and a petticoat, several gold chains, and an immense cross of shiny stones on her neck, with long gold earrings, and with such a cap as I wore at a masquerade. With all this, her name is Melanie; and Melanie has beauty airs as well as beauty name. Whilst she was lighting our wood fire (for it is severely cold) I asked her some questions about the Mr. Maurice. You may guess what a personage he is, for she said — "Ah pour notre Mr. Maurice on ne parle que de lui — partout Madame on ne s'occupe que de notre Mr. Maurice." So much for Miss Melanie and *her* Mr. Grundy. We dined at the *table d'hôte*. We had an Englishman and his wife, and a Frenchman only, for our company. The Englishman was delightful. We had a capital table, with everything good, and in profusion; but the Englishman sat scowling, and called for all sorts of *English sauces*, said the fish was infamous, and found fault with everything, and said to the waiter — "What do you mean by your confounded sour mustard?" The poor waiter to all his remarks only answered in English, "How is dat, sar?" The Burgundy was "such d——d stuff." And the *last* remark, "Why, your confounded room has not been papered these twenty years," was too much for our good breeding; and we and the Frenchman laughed outright. Is it not funny to see our countrymen leave their own country for the sole *pleasure* of being dissatisfied with everything?

We leave this early to-morrow, and shall be in Paris the next day, please God. Lafayette is to come up for us to take us to his chateau; until, therefore, I learn the post town of *La Grange*, direct to the Hotel d'Orleans, where we shall go on our arrival in Paris. I feel myself so gay here already, that I am sure my

elements are all French. A thousand loves, and French
and Irish kisses to the darlings.

S. M.

The travellers passed through Paris and Geneva
into Italy. In Florence, they met Tom Moore, then
troubled with his leg. In Lady Morgan's papers is a
little note which may be given for the sake of the
story that follows.

Sunday night, October.

MY DEAR MORGAN,

This leg of mine seems inclined to turn out rather
a serious concern, and the sooner I avail myself of
your skill, the better. Can you make it convenient
to call upon me soon after breakfast to-morrow
morning?

Yours very faithfully,
THOMAS MOORE.

This "leg" had been an ill of long standing. Moore
refers to it in several of his letters to his ·mother in
the previous year.

Lady Morgan used to tell, in a very droll manner,
a story about a visit that Sir Charles paid to Moore
whilst he was laid up with the leg of which he complains in the preceding note. Moore was a good Catholic, or at least very orthodox in his opinions; Sir
Charles was neither. On this occasion, after examin-
ing and prescribing for the leg, he sat down on the
bedside and entered into a physiological and metaphysical discussion. Moore, for a time, sustained his part,
until he became somewhat hardly pressed, when he
exclaimed —

"Oh, Morgan, talk no more, — consider my immortal soul!"

"Damn your soul!" said Sir Charles, impatiently — "attend to my argument."

Argument was not the strong point in Moore.

Moore mentions this conversation; but does not make a story of it.

CHAPTER XVI.

SOJOURN IN ITALY — 1819.

THE ground mentioned in these letters has been constantly travelled over since; but there is a freshness and vitality in Lady Morgan's description which give it a peculiar charm. It is curious to contrast the changes that have come over travelling since those days.

Lady Morgan to Lady Clarke.

MILAN, ALBERTO REALE,
May, 1819.

MY DEAR LOVE,

By this I trust you have received my letter from Geneva,* which we left with difficulty and infinite regret. We had entreaties and invitations to remain for months to come, and as a temptation to bring us back, we have the offer of a house and garden on the Lake as long as we please to occupy it. We were loaded with books and little presents at our departure, and letters and notes of adieu, with the most flattering

---

* Published in "Odd Volume." — *Bentley, 1858.*

testimonies of esteem and even of affection. They were all astonishment at what they termed *my simplicity*, as they expected to find me a learned lady at all points. The day before we departed we dined with the Prince or Hospodar of Wallachia, who is travelling with his charming family of three generations, his Prime Minister, and a number of his court! What I would have given if you had seen us in the midst of their turbans and beards! the Princesses and the sweet little children speaking nothing but Greek, and conversing with me by signs, all dressed in Greek costume and the servants in the beautiful Albanian dress! The men speak French like Parisians, and we have made up a great intimacy with Mavrocordato, the minister, who is young, handsome, and pleasant. The women had eyebrows painted like a horseshoe down to the nose. They set out for Italy the day after us, and overtook us on the road with a suite of five carriages. Our first day's journey from Geneva was through the lovely valleys of Savoy to Chambery — the capital. There we had letters, and found green peas, strawberries, and kind and enlightened people. Accompanied by learned librarians and professors, we visited the public institutions, and what interested me more, the town and country house of Madame de Warrens. For the whole of our journey, so far, see Rousseau's *Confessions.* Here we found my *France* better known than in Ireland, for although it was *mise sur l'Index*, that is interdicted by the government with Madame de Stael's last work, I was assured that it was to be found in almost every house.

Having passed two or three days in Chambery, which is not much larger than Drogheda, we proceeded the next day through scenes of romantic beauty that defy all description. At a lovely Alpine village — Aquibelle, we were so delighted, that we made a halt, and made some delightful little excursions on foot, where no carriage could penetrate. Here the *snow mountains* rose closely on us. The next day's journey all appearances of spring gradually faded into a perfect winter, the horrible grandeurs of the Alps multiplied around us, and fatigued in spirits and imagination, we reached the dreary little village of Lanslebourg late in the evening, where all presented a Lapland scene, nothing but snow and ice, and a hurricane blowing from the mountains. We found at the foot of Mont Cenis, which we were to begin to ascend the next morning, an inn kept by a good little Englishwoman, and I believe, next to finding myself at your chimney corner, this truly English inn gave me the greatest pleasure I could feel. It snowed all night, and we began our ascent in a shower of snow, with four stout horses and two postilions dragging our light carriage. My imagination became completely seized as we proceeded, and I sat silent for near seven hours, my teeth clenched, my hands closed, my whole existence absorbed in the sublime horror that surrounded me. The clouds that form your sky were rolling at our feet, and the pinnacles of the mountains were confronted with the dark vapours which formed their Alpine firmaments in stormy weather. We had a slight glimpse of what they call "*le tourmente*," which obliges travellers to employ guides to hold down the carriage on each side to prevent its being carried away. We had three feet of snow under our wheels; but the road was otherwise fine. Such a noble work, such a monument of the mighty means and great views of Bonaparte! As we descended, a slow spring gradually opened on us, the snows were melting, the trees budding, and once arrived in the lovely plains of Lombardy, the same glowing summer presented itself we had left in the valleys of Savoy. We passed a day at the first Italian town we reached, Susa, at the foot of Mont Cenis, and with the old Governor, with whom we had a delightful scene. The next day we arrived at Turin — a pretty city of palaces — took a handsome apartment in the Hotel de l'Europe, and sent out our letters of presentation by our Italian *valet de place*. The next day the whole town of Turin was down on us. Some of the *corps diplomatique*, some of the ministers and officers of the Court, the Prussian Ambassador and Ambassadress, the Prince Hohenzollern, the principal physicians and professors; — all left their cards and offers of service. The Countess of Valpergua, one of the leaders of the *haute noblesse*, took us at once to herself, and without the least form or ceremony, told us that in the first place we must command her carriages, and horses, and her box at the opera. The night after our arrival she made a ball for us and introduced us personally to the whole Piedmontese *noblesse*. The palace Valpergua, was the first Italian great house I saw, and the suite of rooms we passed through that night were, I think, more spacious and numerous than the rooms of state at the Castle, though Madame Valpergua told me she had only opened half the suite. A few nights afterwards, the Prussian Ambassadress made a ball for us equally brilliant. She told me that she had lately been at Baden, and that the Princess of Baden, hearing I was

travelling, was very anxious to see me and pay us
every attention — that they had both spent a night
crying over *The Missionary*. But what flattered us
infinitely more, was the attention of the Count de
Balbo, minister, who, as head of the University, gave
orders that all the professors should attend to receive
us. At the University, imagine my shame to see all
the learned muftis in their robes, each in his department, receiving us at the doors of their halls and colleges. In the Cabinet de Physique, they prepared all
sorts of chemical experiments for us, &c., &c. These
poor gentlemen were under arms three days for us.
I must give you one of our days at Turin. From
nine to twelve, morning, we received visits from professors and *literati* who accompanied us to see the
sights. Every one dined at two o'clock. Between
four and five, regularly, the Countess Valpergua called
for us in an open carriage, and we drove to see some
villa near the town. By seven o'clock we were back
for the Corso, where all the nobility drive up and down
till the opera begins. From thence we went to a
coffee-house and had ices, and then to the Opera,
where, during the whole night, visits were received,
and everything was attended to but the music; by
eleven we were at home. The Court was at Genoa;
but the Master of the Ceremonies showed us the palace
from top to bottom.

At last here we are, in the ancient capital of Lombardy, now under the government of the Emperor of
Austria, whose brother, the Arch-Duke Regnier, is the
lord-lieutenant here. Milan is a very fine city, and as
far as we have gone, a delightful residence for us.
The Count Confalonieri, and his lovely Countess, came

to us the moment of our arrival, and from that moment attentions, visits, friendship, and services on all sides. Madame Confalonieri began by taking us to the Corso, one of the great places of exhibition, and introducing us at the Casino, where the nobility are exclusive, and where even professional men are not admitted, and then insisting on our considering her opera-box as ours during our residence here. Thus presented, our success was undoubted; but we found it was already prepared for us by the eternal *France*, and by Morgan's work in French, sent here from Geneva.* Not only the liberal party have visited and invited us, but the Austrian Commander-in-Chief and his wife have been to see us, and we have spent an evening there. We dined yesterday at the Count de Porrio's, whose palace is celebrated for its Etruscan vases, &c., &c. The Italian dinner is very elegant; the table is covered with alabaster vases, flowers, fruit, and all sorts of ornaments; the soups and meats, are served on the side-table, cut up, and handed round by the servants, so all is kept cool and fresh — the great object of their lives here. From the only English residents here, we have received the kindest and most hospitable attentions. These are Lord and Lady Kinnaird, and Colonel and Lady Martha Keating.

The Opera-house is considerably larger than the Opera-house at London, and truly magnificent and imposing; but the stage only is lighted: the women go in great bonnets, and it is, therefore, by no means so brilliant or enjoyable as ours. The orchestra is immense, and the scenery, for beauty and taste, beyond what you can imagine; and the ballet the finest in

* Outlines of the *Physiology of Life*.

Europe as a drama, though the dancing is bad; as soon
as the ballet begins, every one attends. They have
played one wretched opera for these forty nights back,
for they don't change these entertainments ten times
a year. Last night we had a new one brought out,
and helped to damn it. God bless you all, dear loves,
and send me safe back to you!   S. M.

Lady Morgan's descriptions remind one of Beck-
ford's *Italy*, and the Italian novels of Mrs. Radcliffe;
especially of some of the pages in the *Mysteries of
Udolpho*. These scenes had not then been expounded
by Murray's *Guide Books*, or hackneyed by "summer
tourists." The freshness of "better days" still hangs
over them!

Lady Morgan to Lady Clarke.

LAKE OF COMO, VILLA FONTANA,
June 26, 1819.

The attentions of the Milanese increase with our
residence among them, and persons of all parties,
Guelphs and Ghibellines, have united to pay us attention. The Ex-minister of the Interior made a
splendid entertainment for us at his beautiful villa, as
did the Trivulgis, and a Marquis de Sylvas, of whose
villa and gardens there are many printed accounts.
We were told there was no hospitality in Italy. We
not only dined out three times a week on an average,
but we have had carriages and horses so much at our
service, that though we have made several excursions
of twenty and thirty miles into the country, we never
had occasion to hire horses but once, and that was to
go to Pavia, where we spent a few days, and made the

15*

acquaintance of old Volta, the inventor of the voltaic battery. We went with the Count and Countess Confalonieri to see Monza, and its magnificent cathedral, where the iron crown of Lombardy is kept. The difficulty and ceremonies attending on this, convince me that the travellers (not even Eustace who mentions so lightly having seen this relic), have never seen it at all. We had an order expedited the night before from the Arch-Duke to the chanoines of Monza, who received us in grand pontificals at the gates of the church, as did the Grand-Master of the imperial suite at the palace of Monza, where the Arch-Duke resides. We have also been to see the Grand Chartreuse, and in all my life I was never so entertained; but as to churches, and pictures, and public edifices, and institutions, my head is full of nothing else. To tell the truth, we became latterly quite overcome and exhausted by the life we led, for we never knew one moment's quiet, nor had time to do anything. We had been offered the use of two beautiful villas on the Lake of Como, for nothing; one of them, the Villa Someriva, one of the handsomest palaces in Lombardy. We left Milan ten days back, and have since lived in a state of enchantment, and I really believe in fairy land. I know not where to refer you for an account of the Lake of Como except to *Lady M. W. Montague's Letters*. The lake is fifty miles long, and the stupendous and magnificent mountains which embosom it, are strewn along their edges, with the fantastic villas of the nobility of Milan, to which, as there is no road, there is no approach but by water. We took boat at the pretty antique town of Como, and literally landed in the drawing-room of the Villa Tempi. The first things I perceived were the orange and lemon trees, laden with fruit, growing in groves in the open air; the American aloes, olive trees, vines, and mulberries, all in blossom or fruit, covering the mountains almost to their summits. The blossoms and orange flowers, with the profusion of roses and wild pinks, were almost too intoxicating for our vulgar senses.

The next day we set off on our aquatic excursions through regions the wildest, the loveliest, the most romantic that can be conceived. We landed at all the curious and classical points — at Pliny's fountain, the site of his villa, &c., — and after a course of twenty-five miles, reached *my villa* of Someriva, which we found to be a splendid palace, all marble, surrounded by groves of orange trees, but so vast, so solitary, so imposing, and so remote from all medical aid, that I gave up the idea of occupying it, and we rowed off to visit other villas, and at last set up our boat at a pretty inn on the lake, where we sat up half the night watching the arrival of boats and listening to the choruses of the boatmen. The next day we returned, and after new voyages found a beautiful little villa on the lake, ten minutes row from Como, which we have taken for two months, at six pounds a month. The villa Fontana consists of two pavilions, as they are called here, or small houses of two storeys, which are separated by a garden. In one reside the Signor and Signora, our hosts, with a charming family; in the other reside the Signor and Signora Morgan, with an Italian *valet de chambre.* These pavilions are on the lake in a little pyramid; the vines and grapes festooned from tree to tree, and woven into a canopy above. The lake spreads before us with all its mountain beauties and windings. To the right lies the town of Como, with its gothic cathedral. Immediately behind us, on every side, rise the mountains which divide Italian Switzerland from Lombardy, covered with vines, olives and lime trees, and all this is lighted by a brilliant sun and canopied by skies bright, and blue, and cloudless. We have already made some excursions into these enchanting mountains, which are like cultivated gardens raised into the air; and walked within a mile of the Swiss frontier. We have a boat belonging to the villa anchored in the garden, into which we jump and row off. But of all the delights, imagine that shoals of foolish fish float on the surface of the lake in the evening, and that Morgan, who ambitioned nothing but a nibble on the Liffey line, here catches the victims of his art by dozens! Our villa consists of seven pretty rooms on the upper 'floor, and four below. The floors are stone, sprinkled with water two or three times a-day, the walls painted in fresco, green *jalousies* and muslin draperies, and yet with all these cooling precautions, the heat obliges us to sit still all day. There is only one circumstance that reconciles me to your not sharing our pleasures, and that is a small matter of thunder and lightning, which comes about two days out of three, and is sometimes a little too near and too loud for the nerves of some of my friends. At this present moment it shakes the house, and the rain is falling as if Cox of Kilkenny was coming again. If, by the time we return, I don't make "Les serpens d'envie siflor dans votre cœur" with my Spanish guitar, my name is not Oliver! Morgan is making great progress on the guitar. I think it would amuse you to witness the life we lead here. We rise

early, and as our house is a perfect smother, we open
the blinds (the sashes are never shut), and paradise
bursts on us with a sun and sky that you never dreamt
of in your philosophy. We breakfast under our arcade
of vines, and the table covered with peaches and
nectarines, while the fish literally pop their heads out
of the lake to be fed, though Morgan, like a traitor,
takes them by hundreds. Except you saw him in a
yellow muslin gown and straw hat, on the lake of
Como, you have no idea of human felicity! All day
we are shut up in our respective little studies, in which
the light scarcely penetrates, for the intolerable heat
obliges every one to remain shut up during the middle
of the day, and the houses and villages look as if they
were uninhabited. At two o'clock we dine, at five,
drink tea, and then we are off to the mountains, and
frequently don't come back till night, or else we are
on the lake; but in either instance we are in scenes
which no pencil could delineate, nor pen describe. The
mountains with their valleys and glens are covered
with fig-trees, chestnuts, and olive-trees, and with the
lovely vineyards which are formed into festoons and
arcades, and have quite another appearance from the
stunted vineyards of France. The other day, after
dinner, we walked on till we came to some barriers,
where we were stopped by *douaniers*. We asked where
we were, and found it was Switzerland. So, having
walked through a pretty Swiss village, and admired a
sign, "William Tell," we walked back to Italy to tea.
We are by no means destitute of society; some of our
Milanese nobles come occasionally to their villas on
the lake, and we are always asked to join the party.
The Commandant de la Ville continues to give us tea

parties, and we have three very nice English families, of whom we see a good deal (that is, as much as we like). One consists of three sisters, heiresses, and nieces to the Bishop of Rochester, the Misses King. They are sensible, off-handed women, travel about with no protection but a Newfoundland dog, though still youngish, and are equally independent in every other respect. They were so anxious to know us, and so fearful of intruding, that the youngest (*drôle de corps*) was coming in disguise as an Italian lady (because English women, they said, have no right to force themselves on me), with some story to get admittance! Another family, Mr. Laurie's, English people of fashion, with seven children, a French governess, an Irish tutor, and an English housekeeper. Our last and most delightful is Mrs. Lock and three charming daughters; she is aunt to the Duke of Leinster, being the old duchess's daughter, by Ogilvie. She is connected with all the first and cleverest people in England, and smacks of all that's best in the best way. She was, she said, a long time negociating the business of an introduction to me, and at last effected it by getting a dinner made on the lake, to which we were invited. Since then we are in constant correspondence, either by voyages on the lake or by notes. We dined there the other day, and by way of amusing the sweet girls, who are shut up in the loveliest but most solitary site, I announced a party in my vineyard; and there were the Kings, and my Austrian commandant, and some of his officers and Spanish guitars, and a little band of music and fireworks, provided by the young Signori of my host's family; there was tea, and cakes, and all sorts of things laid on the terrace by the lake; and

Mrs. Lock's boat approached in view, and the heavens looked transcendently bright, when lo! up rose one of the lake hurricanes, the lightning flashed, the thunder rolled, tea, cakes, and fireworks were carried into the air, and poor Mrs. Lock, after tossing for five hours in a boat, which at every moment threatened to be overset, was too happy to land at midnight, two miles off, at a wretched little village, and pass the night at a cabaret or miserable public house. So much for my Como news!

The weather has been splendid; the heat was at ninety degrees of our thermometer for some days. In the midst of the glories of this beautiful clime these sudden storms burst forth, and while they last, spoil all. Among our Comoesque amusements, one is going to the festivals of the saints on the mountains, and to the churches. To-morrow we are to have an opera in Como, with a company from Milan, and the Commandant has given us his box. There has been an imperial fête at Milan, called a *carousal*, for which we had an imperial invitation; but as court dresses were necessary, we thought it not worth the expense. We are delighted with the good family of our host here; they are, Don Giorgo and Donna Teresa, the heads; he is ready for the "Padrone," and excellent in his way; she, the best woman in the world; but as they speak Milanese, and very little Italian, we get on as it pleases heaven. The chief beau is the eldest son, a major in the army, and aide-de-camp to his uncle, a general; he is "Don Gallias," and my "poor servant ever," for he absolutely watches our looks and anticipates our wishes. Then two younger sons, handsome lads, come home for their college vacation, and two

pretty, brown, black-eyed girls, Donna Giovana and
Donna Rosina — nothing can equal their gaiety and
noise. They live in the garden, and the young men
are delightfully musical. The talent for music here is
as common as speech. The children walk hand in
hand and sing in parts almost from the cradle. On
Sundays, the recreation of the peasantry is to get into
boats, and float on the lake, and sing in chorus, which
they do wonderfully, but you never hear a solo, though
there is nothing but singing from morning till night.
Such is our life, circle, and society here! Considering
the remoteness of our habitation *ce ne'st pas mal.* I
forgot to mention we have an ex-ambassador and his
gay, French wife, and some Capuchin friars, and that
I was most gallantly received by the monks of a most
famous college here — one of them, the finest head I
ever beheld. Nothing can equal the beauty of some of
the fine heads here, of our young hosts in particular;
but there is also the most hideous race, called Cretins,
that ever nature sent into the world to disgrace her
handy works; they are precisely the figure of nut-
crackers, that we have in toy-shops, not above two feet
high, with the head almost on the knees, but mon-
strously gay and self-conceited.

I labour, as usual, four or five hours a-day. I think
I shall do the best that I have done yet, and that my
great glory is to come. Lord Byron is, I hear, at
Bologna. We have read his *Don Juan.* It is full of
good fun, excellent hits, and *à mourir de rire.* His
blue-stocking lady is sketched off wickedly well, but
his shipwreck is horrible, bad taste, bad feeling, and
bad policy. I see they have put in the French papers
that I have left Italy for Vienna. I don't know the

motive. What is to be done about Moore? We were going to write to Byron about him, poor fellow!

Love to Clarke; kisses to the children — *sans adieu!*

S. M.

Moore's deputy at Bermuda had, at this time, embezzled a large sum of money, for which Moore was held responsible.

CHAPTER XVII.

LETTERS AND GOSSIP.

A LETTER, from excellent Lady Charleville, carries us back to the time when *Tales of the Hall*, *Mazeppa*, and *Don Juan*, were the "last new poems!"

Lady Charleville to Lady Morgan.

LONDON,
July 13, 1819.

MY DEAR MADAM,

Had I required to learn the uncertainty of all human projects being fulfilled, my now sad tale had taught it me. After a consultation here, a warm climate was held to be good for Lord Charleville, and I had no doubt of quitting England forthwith, but my son's illness forbids our emigration; thus sinks, for the second time, to the ground, my hope of selfish relief for myself, and advantage to my children by foreign travel, and observation of man in other climes. Upon receipt of your kind letter, *I went to Colburn*, whose answer, perfectly unsatisfactory as to fact, was to require your address, which I have sent. *Florence Macarthy* is in the fifth edition, and it has been dramatised with good effect at the Surrey Theatre, where the *Heart of Mid Lothian* was better arranged by far than at Covent Garden! Lord Byron's *Mazeppa* has a beautiful description of wild horses, that makes amends for every line of the other trifles which swell his pamphlet, and Crabbe's *Tales of the Hall* have the nature and morality of his former works, and are still more prosaic. Scott's new tales offer one very beautiful story — *The Bride of Lammermoor* — and one bloody and dull *Legend of Montrose.* Lord Byron's *Don Juan* I have not yet got; but *I hear* it is not personal, but very impious and very immoral; however, this may be as false as the other distorted account of it, and, write what he may, his is a great genius unhappily directed.

Lord and Lady Westmeath's separation for temper, and the overthrow of Lord Belfast's marriage and fortunes, by Lord Shaftesbury having discovered that the Marquis and Marchioness of Donegal were married under age by *licence*, and not by banns, which renders it illegal, and bastardizes their children irreparably, is the greatest news of the upper circles at present. The young lady had said she married only for money; therefore, for her, no pity is shown; but poor Lord Belfast, to lose rank, fortune, and wife at once, at twenty years of age, is a strong and painful catastrophe to bear properly. I hear Mr. Chichester (rightful heir now) behaves well; but he cannot prevent the entail affecting his heirs, nor the title descending to him from his cousin.

There have been half a dozen marriages, and another dozen are about to take place. Lady J. Moore to Mr. William Peele; Lord Temple, Lady M. Campbell; Mr. Neville, Lady Jane Cornwallis; Mr. Packenham, Miss Ponsonby, and so on, &c.

This letter is a true account of a most agitating, frightful state of mind, that required all the effort that I was capable of to enable me to *seem* like other people before my dear child, for he judged his state by my impressions of it as they appeared to him, and I did act a difficult and a cruel part, laughing and telling tales to him when I thought all lost!!

Farewell; and to your better pencil I consign all the glories of Italian scenery; may you, in Sir Charles's health, find a recompence and a joy such as I wish you, to sweeten life and reward your real merits.

PS. I have just finished *Don Juan* — it is beautifully written, not immoral, not personal. Farewell; I am always your Ladyship's sincere friend.

C. M. CHARLEVILLE.

Lady Morgan to Lady Clarke.

MILAN,
September 3, 1819.

Here we are again, and here, owing to the kindness and hospitality of our Milanese friends, we sojourn for two days. You never saw such lamentation as our departure from Como produced. The Locks came over in a storm to see us, and we were obliged to contrive beds for some of them, who remained with us all night. The poor dear Fontanas parted from us with tears in their eyes; the Kings said they would follow us, and we had a little crowd of friends round our carriage.

All this is very gracious in a foreign country, and, indeed, without vanity, I must say we have hitherto inspired affection and made friends wherever we have been. The moment we reached our Albergo Reale, we had all our old cronies of Milan. A large dinner party was made to day at Count de Porro's, who has been one of the kindest persons we have met with in Italy; he has two superb villas on the Lake of Como, to which he took us the day before we left Como. It was the festival of the Saint of the Lake; we went to church in the morning where high mass was celebrated by the Bishop; we had the finest opera music that could be selected — I never heard anything so imposing and splendid; in Ireland they have no notion what the catholic religion is. At night we had fireworks on the lake, accompanied by thunder and lightning. There is scarcely a note of printed music, you are obliged to have all copied; but the backwardness of this unfortunate country is incredible. We have just returned from a dinner party, after which we went to pay visits, as is the fashion here, to the Marchesa Trivulgi, who is a patient of Morgan's at present, and on whose account we remain a day longer than we intended. I will describe one visit that will do for all. The palace Trivulgi is a great dark building; we enter the court, which is surrounded by a pillared arcade, and go up a flight of great stone stairs into the waiting-room; the servants permit us to pass in silence, and we continue our route through eight immense and superb rooms, all dimly lighted, the floors marble, and the hangings silk, &c., &c. This suite terminates in a beautiful boudoir, where we found the Marchioness on her *canapé*, with a small circle of visitors. At nine o'clock, the visiting is over at home, and then the whole world is off for the Opera. Direct your next, Florence, *poste restante.* S. M.

In contrast with the tone of keen enjoyment in Lady Morgan's letters, here is one from Madame Jerome Bonaparte. She has come from America to Geneva, and finds herself almost as uneasy in one place as the other. It was as much the custom then to be ruined in America by "commercial speculations," as it has continued to be since; but whether ruined or prosperous, her letters are always pleasant.

Madame Patterson Bonaparte to Lady Morgan.

GENEVA,
October 1, 1819.

MY DEAR LADY MORGAN,

Your letter from Casa Fontana reached me yesterday. I cannot imagine the cause of this long delay, as it appears, from the direction you gave me for the 1st of September, that the letter was written previously; the date you neglected putting. I am very anxious to see you again, to assure you of an affection which absence has not diminished, to listen to you once more, and to relate to you my adventures since our separation. I had heroically resolved to support the *ennui* of my fate in America, and should never have ventured another voyage to Europe could I have found the means of education for my son which exist here; but either he must have remained ignorant or I was compelled to leave the repose of my *fauteuil*, therefore, I did not hesitate to sacrifice my personal comfort for his advantage.

You know we have been nearly ruined in America, by commercial speculations, and even I have suffered, as my tenants are no longer able to pay me the same rents, and the banks have been obliged to diminish the amount of yearly interest which I formerly received from them; these inconveniences are, however *momen-tané*, and I flatter myself that in a year or two, *tout ira bien;* it is, however, provoking enough to find one's income curtailed at a moment when I most required it; my son's education, too, demands no inconsiderable expense, and as you know, his father never *has* and *never will* contribute a single farthing towards his maintenance. We have no correspondence with him since the demand I made two years ago, which was merely that he would pay some part of his necessary expenditure; this he positively refused, therefore, I consider myself authorized to educate him in my own way. I wish I could see you again; it was so unfortunate for me that you had left Geneva before my arrival. I fear, too, that you will not return this way, and it is impossible for me to leave my son without protection in a foreign country. Your *Florence Macarthy* is the most delightful creature, and had the greatest success with us; by the way, you should take into consideration with your bookseller in London, the profits which accrue to him from the sale of your works in America, where they are as much sought after as in Europe. This town is intolerably expensive, quite as much so as Paris; there exists, too, an *esprit de corps*, or *de coterie*, appalling to strangers, — I mean to *woman* strangers, for men are *les bien venus par tout;* it is quite *apropós* that I did not contemplate amusement, or *petits soins* during my *séjour*, and that I came *seulement par devoir.* They have a custom here *parmi les gens du haut de prendre à un prix très fort des étrangers en pension seulement "pour leur agrément."* In these genteel boarding-houses there is no feast to be found, unless it be the feast of reason; the hosts are too *spirituel* to imagine that their *pensionnaires* possess a vulgar appetite for meat and vegetables, tarts and custards, but as I cannot subsist altogether on the contemplation of *la belle Nature*, I have taken a comfortable apartment for six months, *en ville*, where I hope I shall get something to eat. *La belle nature, Mont Blanc, le Lac de Génève, le beau coucher du soleil, le lever magnifique de la lune,* are in the mouth of every one here, and *paroissent tenir lieu de toute autre chose.* I am writing you all this; my letter will, perhaps, never reach you. Adieu, my dear friend; tell Sir Charles everything amiable for me, and be convinced of the sincerity of my affection for you both.

My health is entirely restored, and I am much less in the *genre larmoyant* than when you saw me, — I was so ill, *physiquement*, that I had not sufficient force to support *les maux morales.* I am so happy that I did not go to Edinburgh; the climate here is finer; living, although dear enough, cheaper, and the language, *French*, — more desirable for my son than English, which he knows; in short, *à toute prendre*, I am better here than I could possibly have been in Great Britain. Why do you persist in living in Ireland? I am sure you would be delightfully circumstanced in any other place. E. P.

The above would reach Lady Morgan in Florence, at which city she arrived early in October. Before giving her own account of her journey, we present a billet from the Comtesse d'Albany, the widow of Charles Stuart and of Alfieri! The words are little, a mere permission to visit the Ducal library, but gracefully courteous. If we could transfer the autograph to the reader, the clear, firm, round, legible writing, — he would look at it with an interest borrowed from the fortunes of the writer.

The Countess of Albany to Lady Morgan.

Ce Mercredi, October 13, 1819, à 3 heures.

La Comtesse d'Albany n'a pas oublié quelle devait procurer à Lady Morgan le plaisir de voir la bibliothèque du Grand Duc. Elle sera la maitresse d'y aller Vendredi prochain 18 du Mai depuis dix heures jusqu'a deux ou bien Lundi si ce jour ne lui convient pas. Elle est priée de ne pas passer l'heure de deux, le Bibliothécaire etant obligé d'aller a la compague. La Comtesse d'Albany profite avec empressement de l'occasion d'assurer Lady Morgan de sa consideration et de tout ce qui lui est dù.

Lady Morgan to Lady Clark.

FLORENCE, PALAZZO CORSINI,
October 28th, 1819.

We left you setting off for Florence. At the opera the Counts Confalonieri and Visconti told us we were mistaken, and that we were going with them the next morning to Genoa! Without more ceremony they ran off with our passport to the police and got it changed, and *finalemente*, as we say in Italy, we set off next day for Genoa. Our journey lay partly over the

Apennines; we began to ascend them a little before the purple sunset of Italian skies, and pursued our route by moonlight, and never did any light shine upon scenes more romantically lovely. Nothing was wanting. In the cleft of a mountain we heard a funeral chaunt, and the next moment appeared a procession of monks, their faces covered, and only their eyes seen, — horrible, but strange and new to me. We slept that night on the top of the mountain, and the next day, having walked more than we drove, we beheld "Genoa the superb" at the foot of the Apennines, and the Mediterranean spreading far and wide. Our hotel lay on its banks, and we had scarcely dined, when we were invited to go on board a British ship of war that lay in the bay (the Glasgow, Captain Maitland). Accompanied by our Italian friends, off we sailed. There never was anything to equal the *empressment* of the officers and their kindness to me. I left them my fan, and they gave me one. They had tea for us, and I was so delighted with this most magnificent spectacle, that I went down between decks and saw three hundred sailors at supper, notwithstanding the heat was at one hundred degrees. The result was that the next day I was seized with rheumatism, &c., and never knew one hour's health during the fortnight I remained there; still, I struggled against it, as I had so much to see, to learn, and to hear, — went about to visit all the palaces, — oh, such ancient splendour! Churches, hospitals, and institutions! — All the learned professors, head physicians, &c., waited on Morgan. The Commander-in-Chief himself, who came to us the moment we arrived, with his aides de camp, accompanied him to the different hospitals, and

16*

he was solicited to give his opinion of the disorder of
a young heir to a great family, which he did with success.   This family, and that of the Marchese Pallaviccini, are the first in the town; they were among the
first also to come forward. They asked us to a splendid
ball and dinner, and we took so well that they insisted
on our considering their table as ours, and dining with
them every day.   We did so as long as my health and
the fatigue of going to their villa would admit of the
thing.   But oh, that you could see us going! You
must know that the old republican streets of Genoa
are so narrow, one excepted, that carriages cannot ply,
as the town is built up against the Apennines, and the
villa Pallaviccini is perched on the steepest; there is no
going there, but being carried in sedan chairs, and this
is the way Morgan and I went every day; for nothing
but a goat and a Genoese chairman could scale those
precipices.   The night of the ball, all the officers of
the Glasgow went in this manner. Apropos, one of the
officers came on shore to see us, and sent up his name,
Mr. Marcus Brownrigg.   It was no other than "I am
your man, and I'll carry your cane," thrown into a
very charming and gentlemanly young man. I never
saw so kind a creature. He said he had orders to bring
the Captain's boat and ten men for me as often as I
pleased.   He came with this set-out twice, and was in
despair that I could not go. He wrote me an elegant
note to tell me so, but alas! after near a fortnight's
struggle, and going out every day sick and weary, I
was knocked down fairly, or rather foully, with a
bilious complaint that threatened fever.   There was
no getting a breath of air, — I suffocated; however,
Morgan was nurse, doctor, all, and himself far from

well. In fact, in despair of my recovering in this scorching climate, he wrapped me up one fine morning and threw me from my bed to the carriage, and set off with me for Bologna. The moment we began to descend the mountains and get into the fresh, delicious plains of Lombardy, I recovered, and we both got well by the time we reached Parma, where the late empress of Europe reigns over a dreary, desolate, and gloomy country town. Her only amusement is the opera, and such an opera! a narrow lozenge box, lighted with five tallow candles. We staid to see the churches and Correggio's paintings, and would have staid longer, but we were entirely hunted out by the bugs. Modena, though a royal residence, is a sad set out, and the whole of this earthly paradise broken up into little states, neglected, poor, melancholy, presents but one great ruin. We gladly escaped from these little capitals to the lovely magnificent country. The vines festooned from tree to tree, present their luxurious fruit to any hand that will pluck them. It was the vintage, and I never saw such contrasts as the comfortless aspect and misery of the people, and the enchantment and plenty of the scenery.

Arrived at Bologna, we sent out our letters, and the next day were visited by all that was delightful and distinguished in the town. The Countess Semperiva, a young, pretty, clever widow, took us at once under her wing; her carriage was at our door every morning to take us to see the galleries, palaces, &c., She made a delightful dinner party for us, so did our banker, at his villa; a Madame Martinelli, the Beauty and Wit of Bologna, was equally kind, and made two very elegant evening parties for us; at the last we found Crescentini, singing some of his own delightful compositions at the piano; and Sir Humphrey and Lady Davy; nothing could be more cordial than he was, though he is completely turned into a fine man upon town. All the cleverest professors called on Morgan, and when he went to the hospitals he was complimented on his work (*Outlines of the Physiology of Life*), which, by-the-bye, has taken wonderfully in Italy, and procured him infinite fame; a second edition of the French translation has appeared. When we arrived at Bologna, they recommended us our apartments by telling us they were well aired, as Lord Byron only left them the day before. You may suppose he came to Bologna to visit the learned body of that ancient university, or consult its famous library. Not a bit of it. He came to carry off a young lady.

The hotels at Florence are handsome, comfortable, and expensive. We set up at the Nova-Yorka, kept by an Englishwoman. Our arrival being known, some of the principal persons came to visit us *instanter;* the Prince Corsini (minister of the interior), Prince Borghese (Bonaparte's brother-in-law), the Countess D'Albany, widow of the last Pretender, and the fair friend of Alfieri. Several of the learned came to see Morgan, — Lord Burghersh, the Ambassador, and Lady Burghersh, Lady Florence Lindsay, and her charming daughters, and lots of my Paris Wednesday evening acquaintances of all nations. The Countess D'Albany, who never goes out, asked us immediately; she is "at home" every evening, and holds quite a royal circle. All her fine gold plate, the finest I ever saw, was displayed. The circle is most formal, and you will scarce believe, and I am ashamed to say, she kept the seat of honour vacant for me, next herself. It was in vain, last night (for we go to her constantly), that when ambassadresses and princesses were announced, I begged to be allowed to retreat, she would not hear of it. You have no idea the sensation this makes among the folks here, as she is reckoned amazingly high and cold. She has remains of the beauty so praised ¦by Alfieri. But the kindest of all persons is the minister, Corsini. He made a splendid dinner for us at his most magnificent palace, to which he invited all the noted literary characters in Tuscany; a *réunion*, they say, almost unknown here. We were invited to dine at the English Ambassador's, where we had a large party. Last night we went to Madame D'Albany's full of your letter, delighted with its dear, welcome contents, but quite *triste* about Moore. I had scarcely taken my seat by the legitimate Queen of England, when Lord Burghersh brought up a dashing beau, who was no other than "brave Colonel Camac," who told me that he had been all day roving about looking for us, for a friend who had just arrived; — it was no other than Anacreon Moore! Accordingly, while we were at breakfast next morning, enter brave Colonel Camac and Moore! By the advice of all friends he has taken a trip to Italy, till something can be done to better his affairs; he travelled with Lord John Russell, but parted company with his lordship to visit his friend Byron, at Venice. Moore said we were expected at Venice, and that he had heard of us everywhere. Lord Byron bid Moore tell Morgan he would be happy to make his acquaintance, but not a word of encouragement to his "lady intellectual." I never saw Moore gayer, better, or pleasanter. We have begged of him to come and breakfast with us every day, and he goes with me the day after to-morrow, to the Comic Opera, where I have Capponi's box.   He then runs off to Rome, Naples, and returns to Holyrood House, Edinburgh, where he settles down to write and arrange his affairs. What elasticity and everlasting youth! Pray call on his excellent mother and tell her all this; she will be delighted to hear of him.   He feels about Italy much as we do.   He told us Morgan's work, though attacked, has been treated with the greatest respect as an extraordinary though a dangerous book.

You will now like to know how the deuce we have got into a palace, into a suite of elegant and spacious apartments, filled with flowers such as are only found in Italy. (Moore says "how are we ever to leave it all.") The fact is we are here in the thraldom of a fairy. Everything has been prepared for us, we want for nothing.   A few days after our arrival, when we were sick of the expenses of our inn, comes a gentleman to say he is the Marquis de Capponi's *homme d'affaires*, that he has an apartment ready for us, an opera box, &c., &c., and here we are in a palace once belonging to the Prince Corsini. The palace Capponi is the finest I have seen, except the great Orsini, and a much more extensive building than Carlton House.   There are apartments for every season: those of summer open into an orangery. The actions of its historical lords are painted on the walls of the great saloon. They have eight villas round Florence, at one of which we breakfasted the other day: one immense room laid out with curiosities and antiquities. Should the handsome Marchese Capponi call on you, (for he is now on his way to Ireland), tell him how gratefully I express myself. All the English say, we are the only strangers for whom the Italians make dinners. We were the other night at a party at Mrs. Mostyn's, (daughter of Mrs. Piozzi), where we met Lord and Lady George Thynne. Mrs. Piozzi is in high health and spirits at eighty. Meantime, in spite of all my friends can say, I am growing old, and now look forward only to living in your children, to whom I trust I shall be restored early in the spring, for the moment the Alps are open we set off, please God. I think half the Irish reform is owing to *Florence Macarthy*. I expect a statue from *that enlightened and grateful people*. The first thing I saw here in all the booksellers' windows was my picture stuck up with a good translation of *Florence Marcarthy*. It is well done, and the picture pretty, but not like. Bartolini, the famous sculptor, has shown us great civility. He has dedicated to me one of his best statues, a boy pressing grapes; the original is bought by Lord Beauchamp, and a cast done by himself is to be packed up and sent to Ireland for me. I shall be like the Vicar of Wakefield and his picture. I would willingly have made a visit to Italy blindfolded to have seen only the Gallery at Florence; — we go there every day. I read to Moore *Lady Belvidere*, and it made us all die laughing. We leave this for Rome on the 2nd of November.

S. M.

Lady Morgan did not in the least exaggerate the attention she received; for Moore in his diary, dated Florence, October 17, 1819, confirms every word.

A little note from Moore, pleasant, and by no means romantic for a poet.

Thomas Moore to Sir C. Morgan.

ROME,
November 7th, 1819.

MY DEAR MORGAN,

I have only time for a line; but a line from Rome is worth a hundred from anywhere else. This place does not disappoint. There are some old brick walls to be sure, before which people stand with a delight and veneration in which I cannot sympathize; but the Coliseum is the very poetry of ruins. My leg, thanks to you and Goulard, arrived quite sound and well, and has never troubled me since.

I think of being off from here the latter end of this week. It was my intention at first to go to Naples, but Cannæ was by no means tempting, and then there is such talk of escort, &c., &c., that, what with the Colonel and the guards, I thought it much too dilatory a proceeding, and gave it up.

Love to Lady Morgan

From hers and yours truly,
THOMAS MOORE.

The "son of Hortense," so slightly passed in the next letter from Lady Morgan to her sister, was no other than Louis Napoleon, now Emperor of the French.

Lady Morgan to Lady Clarke.

ROME, VIA DEL ANGELO,
December 17, 1819.

MY DEAR LOVE,

I received your letter at the foot of Antonines'

Pillar, and have seen nothing at Rome pleased me better — and now for our journey of seven days in the middle of December. We travelled in furs and rugs like Russian bears; but the climate softened as we proceeded — we found the trees in full leaf, and the enchanting, lovely, and diversified scenery wore a fine October appearance. The romantic views are beyond description — all the towns dreary ruins, too much for English spirits to stand; we ascended to many of them (Cortona and Perugia particularly) up perpendicular mountains, and the horns of the oxen that drew us, were on a level with the top of our carriage; but oh, the inns!!! We travelled with *tea*, *sugar*, *tea-things and kettle*, but from Florence to Rome we could get neither *milk* nor *butter*. There was but one fire-place in each inn, and that kept in the heat and let out the smoke. Our precious servant (*a treasure*) took care of us as if we were children, and made a fire in a crock in our bedroom, which, with *stone floors*, *black rafters*, and a *bier* for a bed, and the smell of the stable to regale us (for it generally opened to it) was quite beyond the reach of *his* art to make comfortable. We always set off before daylight and stop before dark. Thirty miles from Rome begins that fearful desert the Campagna, and then adieu to houses and population. We arrived, however, safe and sound, without even a cold; but the fatigues of travelling, and I think the *climate*, is terribly consuming. I think I look twenty years older than when you saw me. However, I am in excellent spirits and health, *odds wrinkles!!!*

The kindness of our Florence friends pursued, or rather *dévancéd* us here. The Princes Corsini and Borghese, who have the two finest palaces at Rome, wrote to their librarians and agents to be of use to us in every way. The Countess D'Albany wrote to the Duchess of Devonshire to say we were expected, and yesterday (the day after our arrival) are their invitations sent to us. The Princess Borghese (Pauline, Napoleon's beautiful sister) has written to invite us to spend the evening, and the Duchess de Braciano, has asked us for every Thursday evening whilst we remain in Rome. To night we go to the Duchess of Devonshire', and after her *soirée*, to a concert at the Princess Borghese's. The former wrote us the kindest of notes. I think you will like to hear something of Pauline. She is separated from Prince Borghese, who was so civil to us at Florence; but she lives in his superb palace here quite like a little queen! Nothing could equal her reception. She said it was noble in me not to *fall heavy* on the *unfortunate*, &c. I confess I do not see that exquisite beauty she was so celebrated for. She is, she says, much altered, and grown thin fretting about her brother. Her dress, though *demitoilette*, very superb; and the apartments, beyond beyond! She had a little circle, and she introduced us to the son of Hortense (the ex-Queen of Holland), her nephew, and to a daughter of Lucien Bonaparte; when we were going away she put a beautiful music-book of the Queen of Holland, into our hands, to copy what songs we pleased.

The Eternal City disappoints at first entrance. I thought it mighty like an Irish town, shabby and dirty — we have yet seen nothing save St. Peter's to which we ran like mad the moment we arrived. The first impression of that disappointed too; the interior overwhelmed me! but not as I expected — but of such places and things it is impossible to speak with the little space a letter affords. The climate heavenly — orange trees in boxes out of every window, mignonette, &c.; young lamb, chickens, and salad every day. We have got into private lodgings, lots of visitors — Lord Fortescue and Lady Mary, Sir Thomas Lawrence (who has just shown us his picture of the Pope, that has left all the Italian painters in despair). I have two cardinals on my list of visitors. The Italian ladies dress as we do — the French toilette — some of them very fine creatures, a *rich beauty*, all glowing and bright — the most good-natured, caressing creatures. We get on famously with our Italian. I spoke all along the road to the common people, and got lots of information. Did I not tell you that Bartolini, of Florence, has done my bust in marble? — just as I had written so far, Canova called on us. He is *delightful*, and recalled Dénon to our recollection.

December 18. — We had a delightful party at the Duchess of Devonshire's last night; divine singing; Lord John Russell was introduced to us (brother of the Duke of Bedford), and I flirted all the evening with the Prince of Mecklenburgh! On my return home to old Dublin, I shall feel as Martha did about sifting cinders. I have had a visit from the daughter of *Monti*, the famous poet.

Adieu, S. M.

The following amusing account of a visitation from two bores is written in a journal of scraps kept whilst on her journey — this is the only finished entry. There are other things which, if finished, might have been entertaining, or if legible; but they are jotted down in memoranda as indications for her own memory, and are unintelligible to any one else. The present sketch of a morning with two Bores, has been recovered from MS., compared with which, ill-written Greek characters, or a cuneiform inscription, would be legible as fair Italian text-hand!

Bores and Prosers.

Enter Mrs. B — and her brother, who prosed me out of Spa, begged me from Lausanne, and hummed me into such a lethargy at Geneva that it is a mercy I was not buried alive! They are the best poor dears on earth — and there's the worst of it.

I had my cheek kissed by the sister, and my hand by the brother, for ten minutes at least, by the town clock — not rapid electrics, but long-drawn kisses, against all character of kissing, which, if it be not electric, is nothing.

The kissing over, the prosing began.

Mrs. B — took the lead, *comme de raison*, opened the campaign *d'ennui*, with unwonted vigour; the fun was to see her brother deliberately taking up his posture of patience, like a general on active service, his heavy lids gently falling over his heavy eyes, his very nostrils breathing stupefaction.

Observe, for it is good to know the outer and visible signs of our natural enemies, Bores have noses peculiar to themselves. The nose of a German Bore is a sort of long, broad, romantic, rather aquiline, and rather drooping nose — the drooping nose characterises invariably the nosology of a bore — in a word, it is the leading feature.

But to return; Mrs. B—— began with an account

of her journey. Not a stage, not a turn in the road,
not a cross that I had gone over six days before but
was described to me, first *en gros* and then *en détail;*
but this was nothing — at least it was fact, topogra-
phical fact — but to my utter despair, every village,
town, and house, "put her in mind" of some cottage,
town, road, street, or something, in Ireland, Scotland,
or England — something had happened to her in one
or all of the aforesaid places. But still *this* was nothing; they were graphic pictures, however ill-drawn
— it was the *moral* demonstrations, the particular
parentheses, which left me without hope, help, or resource; every beggar, post, landlord, or landlady, "put
her in mind" of her mother's housemaid, who used to
say when called to warm the bed, &c. Boots put her
so strongly in mind of her grandfather, by having a
wart on his left cheek, that I trembled lest the course
of association should carry us back to the founder of
the family of Bores, which would have thrown us back
to the memories of the Pre-Adamites, had not the entrance of a *goûté* cut her short, for ah! there is nothing
short about bores but stopping their mouths by filling
it with ice-cream. This was the moment for her
brother, who cut in nobly to open his entrenchments.
The whole family are of the breed of those dealers in
art, science, and literature, who gave rise to the caution,
"Drink deep or taste not."

The dear B——'s have drunk like sparrows and
swelled like crows, but drunk a little of everything,
"from humble port to imperial tokay," and it is this
that renders them more tiresome in their prosy scraps
than the most obdurate ignorance could ever make itself. No one could be in the room a moment after

Mr. B—— came in, without knowing that he was a geologist, botanist, archæologist — everything. He began by complaining of all he had suffered from heat, and I gave him my whole share of sympathy! But when he got upon the *causes*, and talked of the fundamental laws of nature, I started up in the midst of a diatribe on cosmogony, and in despair, exclaimed, "My dear Mr. B——, you are aware that God made the world in six days, and did not say one word about cosmogony!" It might be thought that was a hard hit; — not at all, he took it gravely and began a disquisition on the Mosaic account. The word Moses overcame all my power of face, and I burst out in a fit of laughter, for by one of Mrs. B——'s "put-me-in-minds," Moses put *me* in mind that in Ireland we call a bore "a Mosey," and there was something so utterly *Moseyish* in the look and manner of the proser, that the ridiculous application was too much for me, and I owed him, perhaps, one of the pleasantest sensations in the world, that of laughing, not wisely, but too well. I have now made out my case of bore-phobia.

CHAPTER XVIII.

STILL IN ITALY — 1820.

Lady Morgan to Lady Clarke.

Rome,
February 4th, 1820.

Dear Love,

Your letters have given us great uneasiness about
our house, but I have no room for any feeling except
joy and gratitude that you are well out of your troubles,
and that the young knight promises to do honour to
his people.

Now for Rome, and our mode of existence. Immediately after breakfast we start on our tours to ruins,
churches, galleries, collections, &c., &c., and return
late; dine, on an average, three times a week at English
dinner parties; we are scarcely at home in the evenings, and never in the mornings. The Duchess of
Devonshire is unceasing in her attentions to me; not
only is her house open to us, but she calls and takes
me out to show me what is best to be seen. As Cardinal Gonsalvi does not receive ladies, she arranged
that I was to be introduced to him in the Pope's
chapel: as he was coming out in the procession of cardinals, he stepped aside, and we were presented. He
insisted upon calling on me, and took our address.
Cardinal Fesche (Bonaparte's uncle) is quite my beau;
he called on us the other day, and wanted me to drive
out with him, but Morgan looked at his scarlet hat

and stockings, and would not let me go. We have been to his palace, and he has shown us his fine collection (one of the finest in Rome). Lord William Russell, Mr. Adair, the Charlemonts, &c., are coming to us this evening. Madame Mère (Napoleon's mother) sent to say she would be glad to see me; we were received quite in an imperial style. I never saw so fine an old lady, — still quite handsome. She was dressed in a rich crimson velvet, trimmed with sable, with a point lace ruff and head-dress. The pictures of her sons hung round the room, all in royal robes, and her daughter and grandchildren, and at the head of them all, *old Mr. Bonaparte!* Every time she mentioned Napoleon, the tears came in her eyes. She took me into her bedroom to show me the miniatures of her three children. She is full of sense, feeling, and spirit, and not the least what I expected — vulgar. We dined at the Princess Borghese's, — Louis Bonaparte, the ex-king of Holland's son, dined there, — a fine boy. Lord William Russell, and some Roman ladies in the evening. She invited us all to see her jewels; we passed through eight rooms *en suite* to get to her bedroom. The bed was white and gold, the quilt point lace, and the sheets French cambric, embroidered. The jewels were magnificent.

Nothing can be kinder than the Charlemont family. We were at three *soirées* all in one night. With great difficulty I at last got at Miss Curran, for she leads the life of a hermit. She is full of talent and intellect, pleasant, interesting, and original; and she paints like an artist.

God bless you.

S. M.

A letter from Lady Charleville contains some very amusing contemporary gossip. The charitable reader will be glad to see authentic instances of generous feeling in King George the Fourth, not generally known.

Lady Charleville to Lady Morgan.

BRIGHTON,
18th February, 1820.

A long and severe attack of my spasmodic affection, dearest Lady Morgan, must excuse and account for my silence. I am now as well nearly as before it happened; and I delay not to thank you for your very kind letter from Florence, which I received here in January. Let me assure you of the unwearied solicitude I feel that your progress through Italy, nay, let me say conclusively, through life, may be as successful and as well spent as its commencement. You know me too well to take pleasure in fulsome compliment, if I knew how to address it you; but I shall not doubt that you know I value the feelings that fill your heart — its tenderness — its fulfilment of close domestic duties — and also its deep sense of all Ireland has had to suffer, though we may differ in the causes; in short, that I admire the natural patriotism and love of liberty which inspires your lively imagination and throbs at your heart, and without which your writings had never attained their just celebrity. I understand and like you the better even when the scale and compass may not strictly bear you out; and in full sincerity I will always speak when I think they do not, because however ungifted I am, yet I am true and unprejudiced, which is the best light to common minds. I suppose

17*

you at Rome are steeped in classic lore; and I fain would know whether the remains of the glorious dead do not fill you with something more than contempt for our moderns? This and other absurd questions I would ask you, but that I am sure you would rather hear what we are about here. Well, we are going on dully enough, our Regent in love like a boy of sixteen, and the marchesa, after eight years attempts on his person, I believe in full enjoyment of her base ambition. We dined twice, by royal command, and were several evenings in a party of about twenty, where she was awkwardly enough situated, and certainly without tact or talent to get out of the dilemma. His royal highness had very cleverly left the pavilion unfit to enter, and therefore stuffed into a common lodging-house in Marlborough Row, with his one sitting-room about twenty-four by eighteen, his suite next door; and no party of the Lord Chamberlain Hertford, or Cholmondley, &c.; thus he escaped at once from the societies of eighty and their *sposas* to those of his own age, and twenty years difference, *se compte pour quelque chose*. So there we were singing, and he as gay and as happy *singing second, à gorge déployée* to the musical misses, and making love, *tout son saoul*, when his brother's death struck him to the heart; — for a heart he has depend upon it, and a generous one too. The Duke of Kent had behaved to him basely, yet he wrote tenderly to him, and forgave him. It is strange to say how much he felt the death of his father, always unkind to him; and a fact it is that he was thrown into fever by these events, and a cold brought on inflammation of the chest. Tierney saved his life by courage. One hundred and thirty-six ounces of blood were taken

from him at four bleedings, and he is safe and well
now. As soon as he was out of danger, *he sent for
the Duke of Sussex*, and said, "My father and brother
dead, warns his family to unite and live as they should
do. I can forget everything!" The duke wept much,
and the world is pleased with the king, and does him
justice. Again, the late king's Will is unsigned, and
consequently all his money-wealth goes by law to the
Crown. When the Chancellor told him so, his reply
was, "No, my lord, I am here to fulfil my father's
wishes, not to take advantage of such a circumstance;
therefore the Will will be executed as if it had been
signed." Of another amiable trait you will think as I
do. Walker, apothecary and surgeon, who has attended
him since his childhood, failed to open the vein; and
as Sir Matthew Tierney had been a surgeon, and the
danger of an hour's delay was great, he took the
lancet, and failed also; upon which His Majesty said,
"Demm it, I'm glad you fail, for it would have vexed
Walker," and turning to whom, he said, "Come man,
tie up the other arm."

Observe, if you please, the excellent feeling which,
with his life dependant on the operation, animated him
to forget himself for the old man who had often sat up
in his nursery, and you will allow it was very fine.
The report of all travellers who have had any knowledge of the Princess of Wales, renders it imperative
that such a woman should not preside in Great Britain
over its honest and virtuous daughters, and something
is to be done to prevent it. The king's wish is, that
she should be handsomely provided for; and he fain
would divorce her, but the Chancellor and others wish
only to save England from the disgrace of such a queen,

and themselves the unpleasant work of unsaying their
rash acquittal. There are only foreigners to witness
her dreadful life on the continent; and John Bull
thinks a foreigner would lie for sixpence, so a middle
line will be pursued, I imagine, on the opening of the
new parliament in May.

February 18th.

The Duc de Berri's murder; I have had such an
account of it from the Col. de Case himself to his
nephew. All parties, of course, abhor the act; but it
is feared by all wise people it will be made use of as
a plea to deprive the people of the benefit of some
law resembling our *Habeas Corpus!* All this you will
hear of better than my defective information can apprise
you. In the way of literature, we have been all
busied with Mr. Hope's *Anastatius; or Memoirs of a
Greek*, which certainly has a great deal of excellent
matter in it; but, upon the whole, it is a heavy book,
and one which bespeaks a most unhappy feeling in its
author. Walter Scott's *Ivanhoe*, with his Jewess
Rebecca is worth a world of Christian damsels. He
has got nine thousand pounds for that, and his novel
not published. Mr. Chamboulan's book is read and
admired, and Murray has given him one thousand two
hundred pounds for it. He has nobly fulfilled his duty
to Napoleon. Napoleon's own work is only worth
much as a military notice upon the battle of Waterloo.
The writing I doubt being his own, because the ex-
treme vanity of epithet is entirely unworthy of so great
a man. Yet there is something fine in the avoidance
of complaint against the party who betrayed him in
that senate which owed its existence to him, &c., &c.
Farewell; I hope Sir Charles Morgan is quite well;

and tell him from me not to expose himself to visit the catacombs, where malaria prevails at all seasons.

Mr. Becher has married Miss O'Neil, and she has nobly provided for her whole family out of thirty thousand pounds she had accumulated.

February 25.

It is now known that Leach, Vice Chancellor, persuaded the Regent there could be no difficulty in the divorce of his wife; but that upon proposing it to Lord Howe, he persisted that two ocular witnesses of English birth would be required by John Bull to divorce an English queen; and that fifty foreigners would not suffice to satisfy the country. The point is, therefore, given up, and a legal separation only resolved on. Her life might be taken for forgery; but I understand she is to be let off cheaply, and her income of fifty thousand pounds given her. Farewell. I wish you a most happy year, and as many as may smile upon you.

C. M. CHARLEVILLE.

Lady Morgan, once more in Rome, writes as indefatigably to her sister as though she had no other correspondent in the world, nor any book to prepare for, nor any travelling, or sight-seeing, or visiting.

Lady Morgan to Lady Clarke.

ROME, PALAZZO GIORGIO,
April 2, 1820.

MY DEAREST LOVE,

Here we are again, safe and sound, as I trust this will find you all. We were much disappointed at not finding a letter here on our return, and now all our hopes are fixed on Venice, for which we should have departed this day but for the impossibility of getting horses; the moment the Holy Week was over, there was a general break up, and this strange, whirligig travelling world, who were all mad to get here, are now all mad to get away. Before I place myself at Rome, however, I must take you back with me for a little to Naples. Just as I despatched my letter to you, with the account of my February summer, arrives the month of March with storms of wind, a fall of snow on the mountains, and all this in an immense barrack, called a palace, without chimneys, or doors that shut, or windows that close. In short, as to climate, take it all in all, I am as well satisfied now with my old, wet blanket, Irish climate as any other. I had nothing to complain of, however, at Naples, but the climate — nothing could exceed the kindness and politeness of the Neapolitans to us both. Every Monday we were invited to a *festino* given by the Neapolitan nobility to the English, and our time passed, in point of society, most delightfully. There is less to be seen than at Rome; but those few sights are more curious and more perfect than anything at Rome except the Coliseum. The buried town at Pompeii, for instance, is unique, — a complete Roman town as it stood two thousand years ago, almost all the furniture in high preservation; but this is beyond the compass of a letter. We left pleasant, brilliant Naples with infinite regret, and our journey here was most curious. Notwithstanding we were five carriages strong, yet at each military post (and they were at every quarter of a mile) two soldiers leaped upon our carriage, one before and another behind, with their arms, and gave us up to the next guard, who gave us two more guards, and thus we performed our perilous journey like prisoners of state. You may guess the state of the country by this. At Rome, however, all danger from bandits ends, and when I caught a view of the cupola of St. Peter's rising amidst the solitudes of the Campagna, I offered up as sincere a thanksgiving as ever was preferred to his sanctity. We arrived in Rome in time for the first of the ceremonies of the Holy Week. All our English friends at Naples arrived at the same time; but after the Holy Week at Rome, never talk of Westminster elections, Irish fairs, or English bear-gardens! I never saw the horrors of a crowd before, nor such a curious *mélange* of the ludicrous and the fearful. We had a ticket sent us for all by Cardinal Fesche, and saw all; but it was at the risk of our limbs and lives. Of all the ceremonies the benediction was the finest, and of all the sights, St. Peter's illuminated on Easter Sunday night, the most perfectly beautiful. We were from eight o'clock in the morning till two o'clock in the afternoon in the church; all the splendour of the earth is nothing to the procession of the Pope and Cardinals. Morgan was near being crushed to death, only he cried out to Lord Charlemont to give him some money (for he could not get to his pocket), which he threw to a soldier, who rescued him. I saw half the red bench of England tumbling down staircases, and pushed back by the guard. We have Queen Caroline here. At first this made a great fuss whether she was or was not to be visited by her subjects, when lo! she refused to see any of them, and leads the most perfectly retired life! We met her one day driving out in a state truly royal; I never saw her so splendid. Young Austen followed

in an open carriage; he is an interesting-looking young
man. She happened to arrive at an inn near Rome,
when Lord and Lady Leitrim were there; she sent for
them and invited them to tea. Lady Leitrim told me
her manner was perfect, and altogether she was a most
improved woman; the Baron attended her at tea, but
merely as a chamberlain, and was not introduced. Before you receive this, if accounts be true, Her Majesty
will be in England. I think you will not be sorry to
hear that if we live and do well, our next letter will
be dated from Paris.

S. M.

Sir Charles and Lady Morgan returned home in
the course of a few weeks after the above letter. They
arrived at their house in Kildare Street safe and well.
The following extract from a letter of Lady Morgan to
Mrs. Featherstone gives in a few lines a picture of herself and her husband settled down to their ordinary
avocations, and engaged on their great work, the record of all they had heard and seen during their
travels.

Lady Morgan to Mrs. Featherstone.

KILDARE STREET,
September 1820.

MY DEAR MRS. FEATHERSTONE,

I really was rejoiced to see your pretty hand-wri-
ting once more. The recollections of old friends are to
me infinitely more precious than the attentions of *new*,
and though the latter days of my life are by far the
most prosperous, yet I look back to the first (adverse

though they were), and to those connected with them, with pride and affection — you and Mr. Featherstone are two of the oldest friends I have. I thank you for the expression of friendship contained in your kind letter.

Our journey to Italy has been most prosperous, as well as the pleasantest we ever made. Nothing could equal our reception everywhere. We were particularly fortunate in such a long journey as we have made throughout Italy, not to have met with an accident, and in a country, too, part of which is infested with banditti; but the fatigue was *killing*, accommodation wretched, and expense tremendous.

Imagine, on our reaching home, we found the tenant who had taken our house during our two years' absence, had gone off with the *rent*, destroyed and made away with our furniture, and left our house in such a ruinous condition that we have been obliged already to spend three hundred pounds to make it *habitable*. I have brought many pretty things from Italy, so that we endeavour to console ourselves for our loss by enjoying what is left and what we have added. I am now writing eight hours a day to get ready for publication by December, and endeavour to keep out of the world as well as I can, but invitations pour in. People are curious, I suppose, to hear some news from Rome, and I want to keep it for *my book*. And now, dear Mrs. Featherstone, believe me,

Truly and affectionately yours,

S. MORGAN.

The following letter from Madame Bonaparte shows that lady devoured by lethargy and *ennui*.

Madame Patterson Bonaparte to Lady Morgan.

GENEVA,
September 30th, 1820.

MY DEAR LADY MORGAN,

I wish they would give us your work on Italy to rouse me from the lethargy into which I have fallen. It is only you that have both power and inclination to make me forget the ennui of existence, and only in your society that I am not entirely *bête*. What shall I do with the long mornings in Geneva? You know you laughed me out of my *maître de litterature*, which, *par parenthèse*, was very inconsiderate, unless you could have pointed out some more amusing method of killing time. Baron Bonstettin came to see me to-day; you were the subject of our conversation, nothing but admiration and regret when we talk of you.

How is dear Sir Charles? He is the only man on earth who knows my value, which has given me the highest opinion of his taste and judgment.

The Marchioness de Villette wishes me to spend a month with her in Paris. I cannot go, although it would be a great *soulagement* to converse with a person who loves me, one has always so much *sur le cœur*, and in this country they are so heartless. I do *dédomager* myself a little by uttering all the ridiculous things which come into my brain, either about others or myself. *A propos*, how do you like the Queen's trial? the newspapers here are worn out in passing from one prude's hand into another's; they are so much inquired for that the *loueurs de Gazette* have raised their price.

Do not let me forget to tell you that Mr. Sismondi

has made my acquaintance — he is married, too; I
wonder that people of genius marry; by the way, I
recollect that you are an advocate for *le mariage*. Oh!
my dear Lady Morgan, I have been in such a state of
melancholy, that I wished myself dead a thousand times
— all my philosophy, all my courage, are insufficient
sometimes to support the inexpressible *ennui* of existence,
and in those moments of wretchedness I have no human
being to whom I can complain. What do you think
of a person advising me to turn Methodist the other
day, when I expressed just the hundredth part of the
misery I felt? I find no one can comprehend my feelings. Have you read *Les Méditations Poétiques de La-
martine?* There are some pretty things in them, although he is too *larmoyant*, and of the bad school of
politics. Miss Edgworth is here; I visited her; she
came to see me with Professor Pictet, and we have
never met. She has a great deal of good sense, which
is just what I particularly object to, unless accompanied
by genius, in my companions. It is only you that combine *tous les genres d'esprit*, and whose society can
compensate me for all the losses and the mistakes of
my heart; but I shall never see you again, those whom
I love and who love me are always distant; I am
dragging out life with the indifferent. They are so
reasonable and so unmoved in this place, their mornings devoted to the exact sciences, the evenings to
whist, that in spite of myself I am obliged to read half
the day. There have been some English, but I have
seen little of them — they would not like me, I am
too *natural ou naturelle.* I believe that women are
cold, formal, and affected — just my antipodes, therefore we should not be agreeable to each other, besides,

they require a year to become acquainted, and I have too little of life left to waste it in formalities.

Do hurry, then, with your work on Italy, *pour maintenir votre* reputation, and to give me pleasure — my pleasures are so few that my friends are right to indulge me when they can.

I have seen a German Countess; — that means, seen her every day during three months; she is a practical philosopher of the Epicurean sect, a person just calculated to make something of life — unlike me as possible — she has a great deal more sagacity; to do her justice, she tried to *débarasser* me of what she called *mes idées romanesques et mes grandes passions;* but I am incorrigible, and go on tormenting myself about things which I cannot change. She had more coarse common sense, with greater knowledge of the world, than any person I have ever known. I wish I resembled her, because I should be more happy.

Adieu, my dear Lady Morgan, write me frequently; your friendship is among the few comforts left me.

E. P.

CHAPTER XIX.

THE BOOK ON ITALY.

THE book on Italy was advertised to appear simultaneously in London and Paris on the 15th of June, 1821. The English edition was announced in two volumes quarto. There had been some difficulty in completing them together. In Colburn's letters, there is a curious incidental mention of there being no post to go out to France between Friday and Tuesday!

The French edition was published by Dufour, who is several times mentioned by Lady Morgan in her *Odd Volume*. Dufour found great favour with Lady Morgan. Colburn, in one of his letters, expresses himself hurt that she should consider Dufour's gratitude as something wonderful compared with the insensibility of English publishers. He says, "Ought not Dufour to have an exuberance of gratitude, considering he has got the publication without paying anything for it? Now though *I* am paying two thousand pounds for it, which Lady Morgan calls 'a paltry sum,' but at the mention of which every one held up their hands in amaze, yet I declare that I feel happy that my sanguine temperament has enabled me to go so far towards a remuneration for a species of labour, which is, after all, not to be remunerated by publishers, but by the more pleasing acquisition of *Fame*."

Lady Morgan, however, did not consider fame any substitute for that payment; and Colburn expressed himself much hurt at a jest of hers about "authors and publishers being natural enemies."

Italy appeared nearly on the day appointed. It produced a greater sensation than even the work on France.

Comparatively little was known of Italian society, or the condition of the country. Italy had just passed from the despotic but intelligent sway of Napoleon to the blessings of the "right divine to govern wrong" of the Bourbons; and Lady Morgan's work is full of eloquent lamentation and description of the change for the worse that had come over everything. It is the work of a woman who could see what passed before her eyes, and could understand the meaning of what she saw.

There are several chapters on the state of Medical Science and Jurisprudence — contributed by Sir Charles Morgan — marked by solid judgment and good sense.

It is still the best description of the state of Italy, moral and political, as it was at the period of the restoration of the Bourbons.

Her ladyship's criticisms on the public buildings and pictures may lie open to question; but the spirit of the book is noble, and its fascination is undeniable. To the last, Colburn considered it one of the most valuable of his copyrights.

In his letters, there are curious indications of the state of journalism in those days; except the great reviews, which were governed by party politics, the literary papers were entirely in the hands of those publishers who advertised largely.

Colburn wrote with great satisfaction to Lady Morgan to tell her that the *Examiner*, the *New Times*, and the *John Bull*, had abstained from saying anything against the work, adding naïvely, "I am intimately acquainted with the editors; and *advertising with them a great deal, keeps them in check.*" Criticisms and reviews went more by clique than merit. Colburn's indignation when journals "in which he advertised largely" ventured to say a word in blame or even in question of one of *his* publications, would be comic, if it did not reveal the entire abeyance of moral courage and independent judgment on the part of those who were presumed to guide public opinion in literary matters. The machinery of literary journalism has since then undergone a change.

A letter from Colburn, three weeks after the appearance of the work, reports progress.

Mr. Colburn to Lady Morgan.

LONDON,
June 27, 1821.

DEAR MADAM,

I have forwarded to you some papers, in which the book is mentioned after a fashion, — to call them criticisms would be a misnomer. The *Times* has acted the part of traitor, after getting two copies from me. However, it only confirms me in the opinion that the *Times* is certainly the most illiberal of journals. I was much amused with the *Literary Chronicle* making a heinous offence in me keeping my author before the public! The *Press*, *Globe*, *Herald*, and *Statesman*, all speak handsomely; and whether others do so or not, will not affect the sale, which must go on according to the principles laid down for all my publications, or rather yours. It will be well, however, to hear all the remarks before the second edition goes to press. Indeed I hardly knew what I was saying when I talked of commencing immediately, as if the knowledge of a second edition got abroad (as I fear it has in Dublin), it will materially tend to *delay* the publication of it.

I had the pleasure of receiving from Lover the miniature, which is certainly well done. It was necessary to have a fresh background, made the proper size. Meyer is engaged upon it. He will take every pains. It is a pity I had it not three months ago.

The public will be quite ready for a new work in January or February next. But it is high time, I should think, of settling my account, fifteen hundred pounds; the other five hundred to remain open a little while, if you have no objection. I assure you I always wish to be square. If agreeable, instead of giving my bills, I will pay into any banker's in town.

Dear Madam, yours most obediently,

HY. COLBURN.

In another letter of later date, Colburn mentions his delight at Byron's notice of *Italy*, as he declared he saw in it "a great and profitable effect upon the sale."

Lord Byron, writing to Murray, August 24, 1821, said, "When you write to Lady Morgan, will you thank her for her handsome speeches in her book about *my* books? I don't know her address. Her work is fearless and excellent on the subject of Italy. Pray tell her so; and I know the country. I wish she had fallen in with me, I could have told her a thing or two that would have confirmed her positions." His Lordship had been at the pains to defend himself to Murray from the charge of plagiarism in general.

He says, "Much is coincidence; for instance, Lady Morgan (in a really *excellent* book, I assure you, on Italy) calls Venice an *ocean Rome;* I have the very same expression in *Foscari*, and yet *you* know that the play was written months ago, and sent to England; the *Italy* I only received on the 16th instant."

Amongst Lady Morgan's correspondence at this time, extending over a period of several years, are a series of letters, all more or less long and sorrowful, from Italian and Spanish refugees. Even clever people cease to be capable of writing amusing letters when they are in distress.

These "refugees" were men who had been mixed up in plots to attempt to gain political freedom and enlightened laws for their country, which had been condemned by other nations to return to the old Bourbon rule. Some of these men had suffered imprisonment, and, after many trials and tortures, had escaped to England to lead a life of exile in poverty, worse to bear in England than elsewhere. Sir Charles and Lady Morgan were much in advance of the political opinions of their time. They sympathised with the Italian people in their struggles, when there was as yet no public interest for them; when England cared little for these things, they nobly repaid all the kindness they had received during their sojourn in Italy, by patient untiring zeal in behalf of the Italian refugees, who came over in shoals after the unsuccessful rising of 1821. All who came addressed themselves to Lady Morgan; appealing to her to obtain for them money, employment, advice, assistance; in short, for every conceivable service which one human being can require from another.

To those who know what it is to endeavour to serve to the utmost, with necessarily limited powers, which every one persists in believing to be *unlimited*, Lady Morgan's unflagging, cheerful, exertions on behalf of the Italian and Spanish refugees will be at once a matter of surprise and admiration. The mere reading of these letters, to say nothing of paying the postage, must have been no slight effort to a woman naturally so impatient of dulness and expense as Lady Morgan.

Archibald Hamilton Rowan was a gentleman of family and fortune. In 1791 he was Secretary of the Dublin Society of United Irishmen. He was prosecuted for a seditious libel in 1794, and sentenced to two years' imprisonment in Newgate, with a fine of five

hundred pounds. Curran made a celebrated speech on
Rowan's trial. The principal witness against him was a
worthless and disreputable man named Lyster. There
is a life of Rowan by Dr. Drummond. Rowan's fortune
was originally five thousand pounds a year, on which,
however, his philanthropy made heavy draughts. "He
had always," says his friend, Lord Cloncurry, "some
adventure on his hands, and two or three of these in
which he rescued distressed damsels from the snares
and force of ravishers, made a deal of noise at the
time." During the period when he was in America, he
was often in want of money, his remittances from home
being uncertain. He was indebted for a livelihood to
his mechanical skill, which enabled him to take charge
of a cotton factory at New York. In his youth he was
eminently handsome, remarkable for his noble stature
and bodily strength. He was proud of having run a
foot-race in the presence of Marie Antoinette and the
whole French Court in jack boots, against an officer of
the *Garde du Corps*, dressed in light shoes and silk
stockings; he won with ease, to the great admiration
of the Queen, who honoured him with many marks of
regard. He kept up his strength and remarkable appearance to the last; he might be seen in the streets of
Dublin, a gigantic old man, in an old-fashioned dress,
followed by two noble dogs, the last of the Irish race
of wolf dogs.

The following letter from him to Sir Charles Morgan
was written during the period of George the Fourth's
visit, and alludes to some royal *gentilesse* not acceptable to the lady.

Hamilton Rowan to Sir Charles Morgan.

September 14th, 1821.

MY DEAR SIR CHARLES,

I did my duty to my Sov——— no, to my family. I kissed the lion's paw, but did not attempt to pull the tail of the beast. I have seen my caricatures, which are strong likenesses of the original, but until I saw George the Fourth, I never met a person who in features, contour, and general mien out-did their caricature. Hone's likeness in the House that Jack Built is a flattery.

I shall be well pleased to hear that the charms of the Hermitage give way to the boudoir and library in Kildare Street. I really am not fit to leave home for more than a few hours. I even cross the bridge with reluctance. Yet I rowed my boat down to the bay, expecting a noble assemblage of vessels of war, but I was disappointed; probably because when soldiering on South Sea Common, I had repeatedly seen the British fleet riding at Spit Head. You have heard how Mrs. Dawson drove his Majesty from her society, and Mr. Dawson, I hear, says he is not surprised at it, as she is so old and ugly, that he has not kissed her himself these seventeen years. I hear he does not think the Irish ladies remarkable for their beauty. There are to be *six feasts* a year, &c., &c., &c., which, however, are at a stand, for Hercules is cleansing the prisons.

A letter from London of the 11th, says the King is at Milford, and proceeds by land to London, where, I believe, other greetings will meet him, than he found on this side of the channel. Will all this end in smoke?

Two bad days after what we have had are bad omens for rents. Yet, I cannot think with Mr. Attwood, that an issue of notes would cure short payments. I do think the monied interest should bear a proportion of the incumbrance, but really, the taking off duty on the manufacture of grain, and supplying the deficit by seven-and-a-half per cent. on poor devils who receive one hundred pounds a-year as compensation for their services, and letting contractors for loans, &c. go free, is not fair play.

I am yours sincerely,
A. H. Rowan.

I am lithographising Mr. Wolff's prayer over the corse of the persecuted — injured Queen of England.

CHAPTER XX.

LIFE AND TIMES OF SALVATOR ROSA.

A second edition of *Italy* in two volumes octavo had been put into the press as early as August of the preceding year, but the publication had, for trade reasons, been delayed. It came out in January, 1822; Colburn going to immense expense in advertising it. During her sojourn in Italy, Lady Morgan had become enthusiastic about Salvator Rosa, both as a hero and an artist, and had collected many materials for writing the history of his life and times. The work on Italy had to be completed before she began any other work; but no sooner was *Italy* through the press than she was busy with *Salvator Rosa*. After a long correspondence

Colburn agreed to her terms for the copyright of this new work. He engaged to give her five hundred pounds, and entreated her to get on with it as quickly as possible.

With liberal good sense he sent her as a present all the books that he conceived would be useful to her in the course of her work. He also pathetically entreated her to take care of her eyes, and to have green cloth upon the table where she wrote.

In addition to her swarm of Spanish and Italian refugees, Lady Morgan had, at this time, an Irishman on her hands: a man of genius, and as difficult to help as all the rest put together. It was the Reverend Charles Robert Maturin. This gentleman was the author of a tragedy, called *Bertram*, in which Kean had appeared at Drury Lane, and of a romance called *Melmoth*, which had made a sensation, and for which he had received five hundred pounds. He was not an unsuccessful author, for Colburn, writing to Sir Charles Morgan, in 1818, says, "Maturin's tragedy has run through many editions, and has certainly made him a great name." Maturin had, since that time, fallen into great distress; he had written another tragedy and another novel, which neither managers nor publishers would take; and he wrote quires of letters to Lady Morgan entreating her to use her influence with Kean and Elliston to take the tragedy, and with Colburn to bring out his new novel. To those asking assistance and patronage, it seems very hard that they who have succeeded for themselves should fail in their attempt to help others; but neither the success nor the qualities that earn success can be transferred. On the contrary, the ill fortune seems to re-act on those who try to help them.

The difference between the position of Maturin and that of Lady Morgan was the result of the difference in their characters. That fetish of Ireland "good luck," had befriended him once. His early chances in life had been far better than Lady Morgan's; but he could not use them. Sir Charles raised a subscription for him, amounting to fifty pounds. The first use he made of it was to give a grand party. There was little furniture in the reception room, but at one end there had been erected an old theatrical property throne under a canopy of crimson velvet, where he and Mrs. Maturin sat to receive their visitors.

Once, when Mrs. Maturin was confined, Lady Morgan called to enquire after her and the baby — the Irish servant who opened the door took the enquiry to her master, and returned with the message, "Plaze, my Lady, the masther says, 'My angel is better, but my cherub has flown!'" — a piece of "good luck" for the cherub.

Melmoth the Wanderer, and another romance called *Woman*, or *Pour et Contre*, had each a success in its day. A search in any old circulating library would disinter them, and they would repay perusal. Isidora, in *Melmoth*, and Eva, in *Pour et Contre*, are female characters which deserve to be recollected amongst the ideal women who inhabit the pages of romance. A man who had made such a success ought not to have required any further help.

Maturin subsequently wrote a tragedy which was accepted at Drury Lane — called *Manuel* — Kean taking the part of the hero. Its success was not equal

to that of *Bertram* — which is still played occasionally.
After *Manuel*, he wrote another tragedy, which was
played at Covent Garden, called *Fridolfo*.   We remember to have read them both, but can only testify to
the blankness of the impression they have left.
Maturin also published a volume of sermons which
were entertaining.

He died in great poverty, feeling resentment
equally against those who helped him and those who
had not.

In December 21, 1821, Colburn wrote a formal
proposal to Lady Morgan, offering two thousand pounds
if she and Sir Charles would write a work on Germany,
similar in design to her books on France and Italy.
This proposition, however, never came to anything,
Lady Morgan being at that time engrossed with her
Life and Times of Salvator Rosa.

If Colburn's letters and memoirs were published,
they would form a chapter in the secret history of
English literature.   His letters to Sir Charles and
Lady Morgan abound in curious details of his method
of making "his authors," as he always styled them,
and their books successful.   After Sir Richard Phillips,
Colburn was the person most connected with Lady
Morgan's literary life; and he was as much fascinated
by her wit and grace as a woman, as Sir Richard
Phillips had been; but, like Sir Richard, he was afraid
· of letting his admiration interfere with a good bargain.
Lady Morgan, on her side, was perfectly indifferent to
all flattery from her publishers which did not tend to profit.

Here is a note from Lord Erskine, who, in his turn,
had been flattered by Lady Morgan's compliment on
his style.

Lord Erskine to Lady Morgan.

13, ARABELLA ROW, PIMLICO,
October 11th, 1822.

DEAR LADY MORGAN,

A long time ago, in one of your excellent works (all of which I have read with great satisfaction), I remember your having expressed your approbation of my *style* of writing, and a wish that I would lose no occasion of rendering it useful. I wish I could agree with your Ladyship in your kind and partial opinion; but as there never was an occasion in which it can be more useful to excite popular feeling than in the cause of the Greeks, I send your Ladyship a copy of the second edition, published a few days ago.

I have the honour to be,
With regard and esteem,
Your Ladyship's faithful, humble servant,
ERSKINE.

In her search after materials for her *Life of Salvator Rosa*, Lady Morgan applied to Lord Darnley, who was known to possess a number of the painter's noblest works. Lord Darnley at once replied to her request for information as follows: —

Lord Darnley to Lady Morgan.

BERKELEY SQUARE,
October 30th, 1822.

Lord Darnley presents his compliments to Lady Morgan, and loses no time in returning an answer to the letter with which he has been honoured by her ladyship.

The *Death of Regulus*, by Salvator Rosa, is, and has been for some years, in Lord Darnley's possession, having been purchased by him, together with another very fine picture by Guido, from an Italian of the name of Bonelli, who had brought them from Rome, where they were both in the Colonna Palace, till the Prince was compelled to sell them (as Lord Darnley has been informed) to enable him to pay the contribution levied by the French. The *Regulus* was always esteemed. It is believed to be Salvator's finest work. The exact price paid for it Lord Darnley cannot ascertain, as there are other things included in the bargain. It was certainly very large, but not so much as generally supposed.

There is also in Lord Darnley's collection at Cobham Hall, another Salvator Rosa, inferior in merit only to the *Regulus*, representing *Pythagoras teaching his doctrine to Fishermen*.

There is an etching of the *Regulus*, by Salvator himself, which Lord Darnley believes may easily be obtained, and which will give a much better idea of the picture than any description can afford.

Whenever Lady Morgan again visits the Continent she will find these pictures exactly in her way; and Lord Darnley hopes she will take the opportunity of convincing herself of their merit, and that their common friend, Mr. Porri, will be her *cicerone*.

Lord Darnley is rather surprised that Lady Morgan should have heard nothing of the *Regulus* in Italy, as the place it occupied in the gallery of the Colonna Palace, at Rome, is pointed out.

A letter from an old Irish gentleman who had "registered a vow;" marks the spirit of the times, and may wind up the letters of this year.

Sir Charles Molyneux to Sir Charles Morgan.

MERRION SQUARE,
24th December, 1822.

MY DEAR SIR CHARLES,

I think it necessary to inform you that when the Union Act passed, a few patriots, with myself, invoked the most *solemn imprecations on our heads* if we should ever attend levee, ball, or dinner, at the Castle until its repeal should take place!!! I have great respect for Lord Wellesley. I admire his liberality. I did all I could, leaving my ticket at the Park at Woodstock. You will explain this, if agreeable to the gentlemen of the household. With compliments to Lady Morgan,

Yours very truly,
C. MOLYNEUX.

CHAPTER XXI.

WRITING THE LIFE AND TIMES OF SALVATOR ROSA — 1823.

LADY Morgan was searching in all directions for information about Salvator Rosa's pictures. Amongst others, she wrote to Lady Caroline Lamb, who interested her brother in the subject, and to the Duchess of Devonshire. The Duchess's answer contains gossip about pictures and other matters. The writer of this letter was not Georgiana, the beautiful, electioneering Duchess, but the second wife of the Duke (Lady Elizabeth Foster) who died in 1824.

The Duchess of Devonshire to Lady Morgan.

Rome,
March 22nd, 1823.

My dear Madam,

I should not have delayed so long answering your interesting letter, if I had not been almost in daily expectation of some part of the information which you was so anxious to obtain on the subject of Salvator Rosa's writings and musical compositions. All that I have yet received was, the day before yesterday, in a letter from the Abate Cancilliari to M. Molagoni, one of Cardinal Gonsalvi's secretaries. I enclose you what he says. The answer from Baini, about his musical compositions, I have not yet received. Cammuccini told me that there only remained at Rome two undoubted pictures of Salvator Rosa, and that there were two small landscapes at Palazzo Spada. The picture which you mention at Palazzo Chigi, they seem ignorant of, or to doubt its being what you represent it. The same of *La Lucrezia*. I wish that I could have been of more use to you; and I shall be anxious to see the *Life of Salvator Rosa* when it is published. General Cockburn is still here; and I have told him how difficult it is to obtain any of the works which you mention. I was told that some sonnets were published; but I went to De Romani's and he had them not. If anybody can procure the music, it is Baini. I am very glad that you are not unoccupied; and I can easily conceive the interest which you have taken in writing the life of so extraordinary a genius.

We have had a severe winter for Rome; and even to-day, though very fine here, we saw snow on the

Alban Hill. A Marchesa Farra Cuppa has begun an excavation at Torneto, ancient Tarquinia, which has excited a great degree of interest. A warrior with his lance and shield was discovered entire, but the first blast of air reduced it to dust. She gave me part of his shield. A small vase of a beautiful form and two very large oxen are, I believe, coming to the Vatican Museum. The antiquity of them is calculated at three thousand years. Other excavations are making by some proprietors at Roma Vecchia. The first *fouille* produced a beautiful mosaic statue of a fine stag, in black marble. I feel gratified that my Horace's satire is approved of. Pray are there in it two of Pinelli's engravings and compositions to the Latin text? If not, I will send them you by General Cockburn. I beg my best compliments to Sir Charles,

And am, dear Madam,

Your ladyship's very sincerely,

ELIZABETH DEVONSHIRE.

PS. — A fine statue of a Bacchus has been discovered, about four days ago, not far from Cecilia Metella's tomb.

Lady Caroline Lamb had written to her brother, the Honourable William Ponsonby, to ask him for information about Salvator Rosa for Lady Morgan. The information contained in his letter is interesting to those who admire, or collect, his pictures.

The Honourable William Ponsonby to Lady C. Lamb.

BRIGHTON,
April 20, 1825.

DEAREST SISTER,

I send you all that I can recollect about Salvator
Rosa's pictures. I must have some account in town
of all those I have seen, or liked, abroad; but now I
can only quote from memory. Lady Morgan will, of
course, have much better information, both from books
or her own observations, than any I can send. Boydel's
engravings, and Richardson's and Pond's, give some of
the finest pictures in England. With respect to tho
Duke of Beaufort, he has no pictures of any kind now
(but family portraits); and I much doubt any of any
great reputation having, at any time, been purchased
in Italy, unless Lady Morgan is very sure of the fact.
I could easily find out by applying to the Duke, if she
wishes it. The second and third Dukes of Devonshire
were both great collectors of gems, precious stones,
books, pictures, drawings, prints, &c., and the Salvator's
at Devonshire House were bought by them: I think by
the third. *Jacob's Vision* is, I believe, reckoned the
finest; but I like the large landscape at Chiswick,
which was bought by Lord Burlington, the best. It is
the fashion now to run down all the pictures at Devonshire House and Chiswick; but I do not believe justly.
Amongst the number, there may be some bad; but I
would back Sir Joshua Reynolds' and West's opinions
and my own eye, though I am no judge, against
modern critics. My brother had two, *Zenocrates and
Phryne*, still at Roehampton, and a smaller one, which
you must recollect, *Jason and the Dragon;* the figure

in armour, spirited and graceful, like all Salvator's, and the rocks almost as natural as at Sorrento, and the cave where he studied; both have been, I think, engraved by Boydel. The former was bought by my grandfather, at the sale of the old Lord Cholmondeley; the *latter* has had rather a remarkable fate, having belonged to two of the richest men in England, in the possession of both of whom it seemed likely to remain; and, indeed, in my grandfather's it seemed tolerably secure, though he was not quite in that predicament. He bought it at the sale of the Duke of Chandos, in Cavendish Square. It was afterwards sold to Mr. W. Smith, and, at his sale, travelled back again in the possession of Watson Taylor to its old habitation in Cavendish Square, — likewise purchased by Watson Taylor. It is now shortly to be sold again with his pictures; but I hope Lady Morgan will not puff it before its sale takes place, as I have great thoughts of squeezing out all I can possibly afford, to try and get it back again, though it does seem to *porter malheur.* She, of course, knows of the *Belisarius* still at Raynham. It was given by the King of Prussia to Lord Townshend when Secretary of State. There were formerly two (if not three) very large pictures by him at Lansdowne House, left by the late Lord Lansdowne to the Dowager, and sold by her. I have some idea the present Lord Lansdowne bought them back. I only remember the subject of one of them, — *Diogenes:* fine, but not a pleasing picture. It has been etched by Salvator Rosa himself, together with three other large ones; but I forget whether either of the other two I mentioned at Lansdowne House are amongst them. The four are these, — *Diogenes; Regulus,* formerly at the Colonna Palace, at Rome, but not there now. I have seen it, but forgotten where; *the Battle of the Giants; and the Child exposed*, hanging on a most beautiful tree. They are generally bound up with his etchings of groups and single figures. Lord Ashburnham has, I believe, *St. John preaching in the Wilderness*. The *Prodigal Son* travelled to Petersburgh with the Houghton collection. Two very fine sea views at the Pitti Palace, and the *Witch of Endor*, formerly at the Garde Meuble at Versailles, and now, I suppose, in the Louvre. I find one at Lord Derby's. Prince Ramoffski showed me a card at Vienna, in the lid of a snuff-box, on it a very pretty sketch by Salvator Rosa, which he is said to have done one day that he called on a friend who was out, to show him he had been there. They tell pretty much the same story of Michael Angelo at Rome. There is, at Rome, a painter who paints Claudes and Salvators for the use of the *forestieri* in a most extraordinary manner, and has taken in numbers of us.

Your affectionate brother,
WILLIAM PONSONBY.

A letter from General Cockburn to Lady Morgan, with the result of his enquiries about Salvator Rosa's works; he was the author of a dissertation on the Passage of Hannibal over the Alps.

General Cockburn to Lady Morgan.

ROME, *May 24th, 1823.*

MY DEAR LADY MORGAN,

I have at last got into the Chigi palace. The Duchess of Devonshire was there the same day, and took Camacini with her (a first rate artist), and we saw the picture of the *Satyr and Philosopher*, and formed the following verdict —

Done by Salvator Rosa no more
Than by Jacky Poole or Lord Glandore.

From Croker's ill-natured lines on one of our poor friend J. Atkinson's plays. The *Philosopher*, not like any print I ever saw of Rosa, and there is no other picture in the palace or in Rome even reported to be a portrait of him.

The Duchess also took Camacini to the capitol to see the Magi, called Salvator Rosa's; our verdict, *a vile performance*, not worth sixpence, and certainly not done by Rosa, — and appeal against this if you please. There are two magnificent and genuine pictures of his here, one in the Colonna Palace, *Prometheus chained to the Rock*, and the Vulture devouring him, horribly well done. The other is an altar-piece in the church of St. John, Dei Fiorestini; namely, the Martyrdom of Sts. Cosmos and Damian on the pile, but the fire, instead of burning them, by a miracle, burns their persecutors, which it would not have done, had such unbelievers as you and Sir Charles been on the pile; and old *Sardinia* would willingly have you both on such a pile if he could, and *en attendant*, he *burns* your Italy whenever he can lay hold of a copy. I wish the old rascal and the two Ferdinands, Naples and Spain, were to suffer martyrdom, — but I should be content to hang or throw into the sea, — not liking torture. I saw the librarian this day, at the Vatican, and he swears as hard as any Pat ever did before *Baron Boulter* — that Salvator Rosa left no music, at least, none in the Vatican.

Now you have got all the information which Rome can produce on the subject, so go to press as fast as you can. We shall remain in dear Rome another *month*; if you answer this, direct — *Venice*, *poste restante*. I shall not be more than three weeks going there, from hence, and that will just give time for you to receive this, and for us to hear you are well, wicked, and radical as ever.

I remain,
My dear Lady Morgan,
Most sincerely yours,
G. COCKBURN.

From Lady C. Lamb and her brother, William Ponsonby, there is a joint letter, containing further information about Salvator Rosa's pictures.

Lady Caroline Lamb and Hon. Wm. Ponsonby, to
Lady Morgan.

19, ST. JAMES'S SQUARE,
May 27th, 1823.

I hope you will not impute it to me that your questions are not answered; the truth is, I am in the country, enjoying this most beautiful time of year, and my brother has written me word that he will make all the inquiries you desire, but how soon this may be I cannot tell. Lord Cowper will write down on paper *about one* only. The two at Panshanger are landscapes in the usual dark, abrupt style. The one at Chiswick, much larger, is reckoned very fine; there is a famous Belisarius there, but I do not think they know who it is by; the Soldier in Armour and the old Belisarius

19*

are quite beautiful, — can this be a Salvator? The Phryne you name, has reddish, or rather, yellow hair, and is by no means decent in her drapery. I never could endure that picture; it is not, I fancy, at Roehampton now; there was a very fine one there besides, which my brother will name to you. I must try and see the one you mention; but it is not this month that I can do anything beside staring at the flowers and trees. All this is very unsatisfactory, therefore, only consider this letter as a kind of apology for my delay. You shall hear more soon.

DEAR MADAM,

My sister sends me this letter to forward to you, and apologizes for not having done your commission earlier, because she was in the country. I must do the same, because I am in town, and really have had my time completely taken up by business; besides, as you must know, the great houses from which our information is to be obtained, are not always the most easy of access. Not to lose more time than necessary, I thought it better to write direct to you and recall to your recollection our old Dublin and Priory acquaintance, than send any little information I might be able to glean round by Brocket. As for *Phryne*, I cannot say I ever was much struck with the modesty and decency of her attire and countenance. She and the philosopher appear to be engaged in a very warm argument, but she does not exhibit herself as she did to the Grecian painter on the sea shore, nor has she recourse to the expedient she made use of to melt the stern hearts of her judges. There is nothing eloquent in the picture, however, and it is not one which I ever

thought very pleasing; this is still in Lord Bessborough's possession at *Roehampton*. The *Jason was
sold*, and was a most beautiful picture, full of all the
bold and wild character of Salvator's landscapes, and
the grace which I think he usually shows in his figures,
though Sir Joshua Reynolds says no. The Russian
prince's name is Ramoffski. The Duke of Beaufort
has a curious picture by Salvator Rosa, at Badminton,
but I do not recollect seeing it, though I have often
been there. I will enquire more particularly as to the
subject the first time I see him, but the story is that it
was painted to ridicule the pope and cardinals, and
that he was banished from Rome in consequence. I
think Phryne's hair is light. The Belisarius is still in
Lord Townshend's collection at Raynham, and was
given to the Secretary of State of that family, by the
King of Prussia. The Belisarius my sister mentions at
Chiswick, is of doubtful origin, but never claimed
Salvator Rosa as brother, and could not be listened to
in any court if sworne to him. It has been sometimes
said to be by Vandyke (and is stated so in the engraving I think) sometimes by Murillo, and is a very fine
picture. I do not know where the Giants are, nor the
Child Exposed, whom I believe to be Œdipus. I will
make enquiry concerning Lord Lansdowne's, Lord
Ashburnham's, and Lord Morpeth's pictures. Those at
Devonshire House are the *Jacob's Vision*, with the
angels ascending and descending by the ladder to and
from heaven, one of *Jacob and the Angel wrestling;*
and another, landscape, with huge trees and rocks,
with soldiers reposing on them. There is a large
landscape at Chiswick. His letters are curious, and
I believe rather difficult to be met with now. Would

not a new edition, with some observations on them, form a good second volume of his life. I fear I have but very inefficiently executed your commission, but beg leave to assure you that it is not from want of inclination.

Yours, most truly,
W. S. PONSONBY.

The Duchess of Devonshire, along with much kind interest expressed in Lady Morgan's work, gives a little grave remonstrance on her Ladyship's habit of hasty judgment and rash assertion.

The Duchess of Devonshire to Lady Morgan.

ROME,
May 31st, 1823.

DEAR LADY MORGAN,

I send you a list of the pictures which are known to be Salvator Rosa's and those that are attributed to him. You will see what you attribute to the ignorance or indifference of Prince Chigi to the treasure which he possesses, is a proof of his being neither ignorant nor indifferent, but convinced that the picture did not deserve to be classed as the performance of that great painter, and discouraging its being called his.

I have taken with pleasure all the pains necessary to procure you the information which you wanted, but do not be offended if I say that I should have felt still more pleasure in doing so were you less unjust to this country; fallen they are certainly in power, but not in intellect, or talent, or worth of every kind; and your stay in Italy was far too short to admit of your appreciating them as your own undoubted talent would have enabled you to do, had you staid longer and derived your information from other sources. You said to me once, that were you to write your journey in France again, that you should write it very differently. I am sure you would say the same were you to come again into Italy; every monument of antiquity is attended to with the greatest care, and every picture that requires it is either cleaned, or noted down to be so. The commission of five attend on every new discovery to give their opinion as to the merit of what is found, and most productive have this year's excavations proved to be in sculpture. Mosaic repairs go on, and new buildings in every part of Rome, and the Braccio Nuovo alone merits, in the Duke of Devonshire's opinion, that one should come from London to Rome were it only to see that beautiful new museum, begun and completed by a pope from the age of seventy-nine to eighty-two!

I know not any capital so adorned by its sovereign as this is. To know with certainty the different objects, there is a catalogue by Signor Camacini; of all the classical pictures in the churches, and galleries, and palaces, — of all those that deserve citation, — of all the frescoes, outward and inward, — of the different houses which are classical or rare. We are often apt to think things are unknown because we have fancied them valuable on the authority of Vasi, or a *lacquey de place*, and find the owner scarcely knowing of their existence; Vasi and the *lacquey* having given an assumed name, and the proprietor, like Prince Chigi, who is a man of taste, of science even, and of elegant literature, is called ignorant because he disclaims the assumed merit given to his picture.   Prince Chigi has a small gallery of excellent pictures and statues, and the Filosofo was shown me on my request, because *put by as not Salvator's.*   He has the famous Cicero, and a cameo with the last battle of Alexander the Great; these the Prince shows himself.

Baini is living, he is a man of great musical science, he composed a fine *Miserere,* which was sung this year; but Salvator improvised his compositions, and no written ones can be found.   Monseigneur Mai made diligent search for me, but in vain.   If I can be of any further use to you, pray write to me.   General Cockburn is still at Rome.

Events of the day are passing which may deserve blame, but the efforts, — the heroic efforts which the Greeks have made and are making, are worthy of all our admiration, and will end, I hope, by restoring that interesting country to its situation in Europe.   There is matter to animate your genius, and I hope you will turn your thoughts to something that may tend to do justice to this long oppressed and calumniated people. And, my dear Lady Morgan, I must add, in praise also of my dear Rome, that the Greek fugitives were received in Ancona, and fed and lodged there.   This is true tolerance.   .

Once more adieu, my dear Madam, and pray let me know when your life of Salvator Rosa will appear; I have no doubt of the success which it will meet with.   Very sincerely yours,

E. DEVONSHIRE.

So much for Salvator Rosa and his pictures.   Whilst Lady Morgan was busy rehabilitating the name and

character of a man of genius, she was undergoing a
very unpleasant ordeal herself.

Sir Charles Morgan had been knighted by an act of
personal favour, before he had done any thing osten-
sibly to merit the distinction, and it had been made a
handle for ill-natured sarcasm; but vague ill-nature
gave place to special hostility. Lady Morgan had made
herself too marked a personage in the liberal interest
to escape the hatred of the opposite party. The Tory
clique desired to mortify her by any means, they were
not particular about their weapon, and they certainly
hit upon a method which was likely to mortify her to
their heart's content.

The right of the Lord-Lieutenant to confer the
honour of knighthood was impugned. It was speciously
argued that since the union, the king alone in person
could confer honours. The titles of several of their
own partisans were at stake as well as Sir C. Morgan's;
but they were willing to sacrifice a few of their friends
to their hatred of Lady Morgan. The case was argued
in England before the judges at the house of the Lord
Chief Justice Dallas. Legal opinion was favourable to
the privilege, and the following letter conveyed the intelligence to Sir Charles Morgan. Lady Morgan cared
for the title a great deal more than her husband did;
but it would have been a mortification to him to have
had it declared an illegal possession.

J. Rock to Sir Charles Morgan.

OFFICE OF ARMS, WESTLAND ROW,
June 30, 1823.

In the absence of Sir William Betham, I beg leave
to state for your information, that on Tuesday last the

judges of England assembled at the house of Lord
Chief Justice Dallas, in London, in pursuance of the
royal mandate, to take into consideration and decide
upon the disputed power of the Lord-Lieutenant of
Ireland to confer the honour of knighthood. Two of
the number were unable to attend from illness; but the
other ten were of opinion unanimously that the Lord-
Lieutenant did possess the power, and that knights
created by him were knights throughout the world.

I expect the return of Sir William Betham from
England in the course of this week, when the above
solemn decision will be given to the public in a manner equally *notorious* as the doubts of the Lords of the
Admiralty which originally occasioned the discussion.

I have the honour to be, sir,
Your most obedient,
Very humble servant,
F. Rock.

Amusing letter from Lady Caroline Lamb, complains
of false reports. She suffered more than most persons
from this "common lot," though "candid friends" would
have told her she brought it on herself.

Lady Caroline Lamb to Lady Morgan.

August 8, 1823.

I have been much annoyed to-day by a paragraph
in two papers about my turning a woman out of doors
— pray if you see or hear of it, contradict it. As I
hope for mercy, it is a most shameful falsehood made
by a very wicked girl, because I sent her away. She
came to me as Agnes Drummond, a spinster, and ten

days after hid a man in Brockett Hall; the servants, in an uproar, discovered him in the evening; he said first his name was Drummond, then Fain — it was natural we should desire him to walk out, in particular as Agnes Drummond had confided to me, only the day before, that she had been married, when sixteen, to a thief of the name of Fain, who had married her and carried away her watch and property. I trouble you with this, as I see my name as having *beaten* her and turned her out of doors *without clothes*, in the night; instead of which, my coachman conveyed her to an inn, and had great difficulty in making her sleep there. She took my clothes away and seal, which were taken from her. She now calls herself Fain, — her own clothes were marked *E. M.* She left them wet in the laundry or they would have been sent to her that night.

I have, I think, the very person Lady Cloncurry would like; she is about twenty-two, very clever, good, and with a good manner, writes a beautiful hand, knows music thoroughly, both harp and pianoforte. She is attached to an old mathematician in Russia — a Platonic attachment; his name is Wronsky, so that as they are not to marry or meet for ten years, she is very anxious to go into any respectable and comfortable family where she will be well treated; she draws, paints uncommonly well, and, provided she had a room to herself, a fire, pen, ink, and paper, or a book, I dare say she will make herself comfortable anywhere; how far she would like Ireland, I guess not, as her views turned to Italy or Paris: if, however, your lady will communicate with her herself, I will send you her answer; she is a person of strict morals and great propriety — a little high, but excessively sweet-tempered. She is by no means expensive, yet to go to Ireland I think she would ask eighty guineas — is that too much? She would dedicate all her time to the children after ten in the morning to six at night; she would play also on the harp of an evening, read to the lady if she were ill, or write her letters for her.

Ever yours,
CAROLINE LAMB.

There are other letters from the same fascinating and gifted, but most unhappy, lady. They are full of a whimsical grace, and might have been written by a bird of Paradise for all the practical sense they evince. Lady Morgan was very much attached to her, and tried to inspire her with common sense; but of that it holds good, as Rubini said of singing, "*Monsieur le chant ne s'enseigne pas.*" She was full of generous impulses and good instinct; but she was too wilful either to hold or to bind. More than most women, she needed to be wisely guided, and this wise guidance was precisely the "one thing lacking" to her brilliant lot.

Lady Caroline Lamb to Lady Morgan.

September, 1825.

MY DEAR AND MOST AMIABLE LADY MORGAN,

I thank you from my heart for what you said Sir Charles would do; and now, as you say, for business. It is a disagreeable thing to recommend any one, and in particular when the education of children is a point at stake. I therefore shall write you word for the inspection of Lord and Lady Cloncurry, all I know

of Miss Bryan, although the knowledge that my letter
is to be seen by strangers will prevent my writing as
fully as I otherwise should. Pray tell me something
of Lady Charlemont. I feel very much interested for
her. My dearest mother liked her. Lady Abercorn
admired her, and so did Lord Byron. She has, I am
sure, suffered very, very much. Sometime or other,
tell me how Lord Caulfield came to die, and how
Lady Charlewood is. Pray, in your prettiest manner,
remember me to her. I enclose you, upon trust, a letter
of Miss Bryan; but as there are two or three trifling
mistakes in grammar, do not show it. Only see what
her feelings are. I feel interested for her; yet she
and I are not "congenial souls." She is more dignified, tranquil, calm, gentle, and selfpossessed, than I
am; and therefore, if she is made to be all she can be,
she will do better to bring up others. Now as every
one must, will and should fall in love, it is no bad
thing that she should have a happy, Platonic, romantic
attachment to an old mad mathematician several thousand miles off. It will keep her steady, which, in
truth, she is — beyond her years. Added to this, she
plays perfectly; can draw quite well enough to teach;
do beauty work; paint flowers; write and read well;
and teach the harp. For manner, dress, arrangement,
appearance, exactness — do well. What I do not
know about her is this, — I do not know if she is
able to impart her knowledge. I do not know if she
is religious, although I presume she is. Lady Cloncurry must guide her; she is yet but young, and I
advise most particularly that she should begin as
she intends to proceed. Miss Bryan is very gentle,
although proud, and can bear being spoken to; but

she requires to be told the plain truth, whole truth, and all the truth.

She has, certainly, good abilities and considerable knowledge. Of the latter, perhaps rather too much, as it makes her somewhat positive; but there is no conceit: her presumption is in her manner. It appears to me that there is a good chance of her doing well; but Lady Morgan must be aware that the power of instructing is almost a gift of nature; that many of the best instructed themselves are very deficient in it. She must also be aware that much temper and management is necessary to enable a person to like well the situation of a governess, which, in every family, will be beset by some of the difficulties and annoyances which Lady Morgan has well described in *O'Donnel.*

With great regard,
CAROLINE.

Lady Caroline's story of a Governess is continued in her correspondence along with other stories, not so positive in their human interest.

Lady Caroline Lamb to Lady Morgan.

October, 1823.

My dear Lady Morgan,

Thank you and thank Sir Charles for all his kindness about my fairy tale, *Ada Reis*, although I think he uses a rod even whilst he is merciful. I must now tell you about Miss Bryan. She has caught cold, and been very, very ill. I would not, for the world, have Lady Cloncurry wait for her; but if she chances to be without a proper person when well, Miss Bryan would 'assuredly go.   However, it is no loss to the girl, as I feel sure she wishes to die or to marry Wronsky, and therefore do nothing further about her.   She is sensible, handsome, young, good, unsophisticated, independent, true, ladylike, above any deceit or meanness, romantic, very punctual about money, but she has a cold and cough, and is in love, I cannot help it; can you?

Whoever has reviewed *Ada Reis* must not think me discontented, neither unhappy.   The loss of what one adores affects the mind and heart; but I have resigned myself to it, and God knows I am satisfied with all I have and have had.   My husband has been to me as a guardian angel.   I love him most dearly; and my boy, though afflicted, is clever, amiable, and cheerful.

Dear Lady Morgan, let me not be judged by hasty works and hasty letters.   My heart is as calm as a lake on a fine summer day; and I am as grateful to God for his mercy and blessing as it is possible to be. Tell all this to Sir Charles; and pray write to me. Your letters amuse me excessively.   I would I had anything clever or pretty to pay in return.

CAROLINE.

Joseph Hume, then M.P., for Middlesex, was a correspondent of Sir Charles.   The present generation may not know so much of Joseph Hume and his economies as the one that has just passed away.   He was a man who did his duty sturdily, and was a thoroughly honest man, of the stuff that builds up a nation.

Joseph Hume to Sir Charles Morgan.

LONDON,
December 19th, 1823.

DEAR SIR,

As it is my intention to bring the Church Establishment of Ireland before the House of Commons in the ensuing session, I shall be obliged by your sending me any authentic accounts of the value of the Church property, *i. e.*, of the bishops, deans, and chapters of any diocese, that I may lay it before the public as completely as possible.

The cause is so good a one that I wish to be in moderation, and within bounds, as exaggeration always hurts our cause.

The system of tithes ought to be entirely abolished, as every attempt, like that of the last session, to bolster up so preposterous and a bad system must tend to render the change too violent when it shall be made; and the late conduct of some of the church militant will only hasten the event.

Until a radical change takes place in the Church establishment and Church property, there will be no peace in your wretched country, and every aid to effect these changes will be a real benefit to the country.

To expose these evils of the system of tithes as it has been working in the last year, it would be of great use to me if you could cut out of any newspapers all the cases that can be depended upon, where burnings, murders, the interposition of the military, the destruction of cattle, &c., &c., have taken place on account of the tithe system, that they may be brought into array at once; also the conduct of such of the clergy as have taken the law into their own hands, or have behaved harshly so as to produce disturbance or mischief.

Can any account be obtained of the number of persons who have been murdered, hanged, and transported in the last year in Ireland on account of the tithes' disputes?

All these, with documents to enable me to prove them, will be most valuable in forwarding the object I have in view, *an exposure to effect a complete change.*

I shall want as much information of that kind as you can collect for me before the middle of January, to be prepared to agitate the subject by the middle of February. Callous as the ministers are to proceedings that disgrace the country, and regardless as they are to the misery produced in Ireland by their conduct, and indifferent as they are also to the enormous charge on Great Britain to keep a whole nation under military power, I am confident that nothing will rouse the public indignation so much as a proper exposure of all these evils and their causes.

If you will zealously aid me, you will, I trust, aid the best interests of your own country; and in your desire to do that, I hope there cannot be a doubt.

I shall, therefore, expect your early attention to my requests, whilst

I remain,
Your obedient servant,
JOSEPH HUME.

PS. — I this day delivered to the charge of Mr. Felix Fitzpatrick a copy of Mills' Essays on Government, on Jurisprudence, and the Liberty of the Press,

of which we have printed one thousand for circulation;
and I hope you will approve the sound doctrines they
contain.

In October 1823, the *Life and Times of Salvator
Rosa* appeared in two volumes octavo. Lady Morgan
said she wrote the work to the sound of Rossini's
music. It was her favourite of all her works, and was
written because she thought Salvator Rosa had never
received justice from posterity. In her preface to the
first edition she says, "should it be deemed worthy of
enquiring why I selected the Life of Salvator Rosa as
a subject of biographical memoir in preference to that
of any other illustrious painter of the Italian schools, I
answer that I was influenced in my preference more by
the peculiar character of the man than the extraordinary merits of the artist. For admiring the works of
the great Neapolitan master with an enthusiasm unknown perhaps to the sobriety of professed *vertù*, I
estimated still more highly the qualities of the Italian
patriot, who, stepping boldly in advance of a degraded
age, stood in the foreground of his times, like one of
his own spirited and graceful figures when all around
him was timid mannerism, and grovelling subserviency.
I took the opportunity of my residence in Italy to
make some verbal enquiries as to the private character
and story of a man whose powerful intellect and deep
feeling, no less than his wild and gloomy imagination,
came forth even in his most petulant sketches and
careless designs. It was evident that over the name
of Salvator Rosa there hung some spell, dark as one of
his own incantations. I was referred for information
to the Parnasso Italiano, one of the few modern works

published 'with the full approbation of the Grand Inquisitor of the holy office.'   In its consecrated pages I found Salvator Rosa described as being of 'low birth, indigent circumstances — of a subtle organization, and an unregulated mind, one whose life had been disorderly, and whose associates had been chosen among musicians and buffoons.' This discrepancy between the man and his works awakened suspicions which led to further enquiry and deeper research.   It was then I discovered that the sublime painter was in fact precisely the reverse in life and character of all that he had been represented. * * * * As I found, so I have represented him, and if (led by a natural sympathy to make common cause with all who suffer by misrepresentation) I have been the *first* (my only merit) to light a taper at the long neglected shrine, and to raise the veil of calumny from the splendid image of slandered genius, I trust it is still reserved for some compatriot hand to restore the memory of Salvator Rosa to all its original brightness."

Having begun her work with this intention, Lady Morgan carries it through.   She has produced a very clever, romantic biography, obscured by fine phrases and lighted up by exaggerated antitheses, but she has collected her materials with industry, and put them together as carefully and brilliantly as a Roman Mosaic.   She is too much of a partisan to carry her hero out of the quagmire in which she found him, for she fights at every body and every thing that strikes her imagination by any association of ideas, so that Salvator is generally thrown down and lost in the fray.   A more tranquil style and a simpler statement of her facts, with less colouring, and fewer epithets,

would have given her testimony more weight, and
effected her object better, if that were a single-minded
desire to write the true biography of a calumniated
man of genius. But Lady Morgan could never forget
or efface *herself*. In her novels that did not signify;
she kneaded together her characters and her story, and
each had a suitability which gave a charm to the
whole. When she meddled with history and facts she
wrote of them as though they possessed no more substance than scenes in a novel, and this takes away from
the dignity and reality of her historical facts, and
hinders the reader from doing justice to the ardour
and industry with which she sought materials to support every assertion on which she ventured, in spite of
the rash rhetorical exaggerations which marked her
style, — when she was *not* writing works of fiction.

Those who wish to obtain the facts of Salvator
Rosa's life, to form a judgment of his life and labours,
will find Lady Morgan's life of him a good handbook,
for she has bestowed great industry upon it, and she
always gives her authorities and the sources of her information.

Some of the incidental observations in Salvator Rosa
are amusing, as for instance, when speaking of Louis
the Fourteenth, who pensioned Bernini and neglected
Poussin, she said, "this idle prodigality of kings is the
result more of ignorance than of vice. If they usually
know little of the arts, they are still less aware of the
value of money."

Lady Morgan received five hundred pounds for the
copyright. It went into a second edition in 1825,
when it was reprinted in a single volume. It was the
intention of Colburn to have prefixed a portrait of

Lady Morgan; she sat to Lover for the miniature, which has been before referred to. It was to be engraved by Meyer, but between the painter and the engraver, the result was such unmitigated *ugliness*, that Colburn would not let it appear, and he presented Lady Morgan with a beautiful velvet dress, as a peace offering for the annoyance. Colburn and Lady Morgan had many quarrels about this time, chiefly occasioned by Lady Morgan insisting that Colburn made "great gains" out of her works, and did not pay her in proportion, — an imputation which Colburn highly resented. He complained much of her "hard thoughts" of him, and he stoutly maintained that although Lady Morgan had wonderful genius, yet it was to his own good publishing that her works were indebted for their great success; nevertheless, he was dreadfully jealous lest she should leave him for any other publisher.

In spite of the high prices he paid, Colburn seemed to justify Lady Morgan's suspicions of his "great gains," for he this year separated his circulating library from his publishing business, and took a house at No. 8, New Burlington Street, next door to Lady Cork, "who, he feared would be rather angry at his presumption, coming next door to her, shop and all!"

CHAPTER XXII.

CONNEXION WITH THE NEW MONTHLY — 1824.

COLBURN was very anxious to obtain Sir Charles and Lady Morgan as contributors to his Magazine, *The New Monthly.* He wrote to them to say that although the highest terms he {gave were fifteen to sixteen guineas a sheet; yet, to her and to Sir Charles he would give "a bonus of half as much more, according to the quantity." Lady Morgan consented, and set to work on an essay on *Absenteeism*, which the enemies of Ireland were always declaiming against, as the source of all the woes of Ireland. She set herself to show that Absenteeism was but the effect of ill-government and unjust legislation from the earliest period of England's rule.

She began to read up for her materials and she found much help from the *Pacata Hibernia*, of which mention is made in her letters to Sir Charles, when she ran away to Dublin during her engagement, and would not return till she had almost driven him past his patience!

Lady Morgan had seen in her youth so much of the misery of financial irregularity, that she had a sacred horror of all debt; she kept her accounts with a punctuality that would have been creditable to a Chancellor of the Exchequer. One entry has an interest, as showing that literary labour, when well done and industriously followed, is *not* the ungrateful, ill-requited task it has been the fashion to represent it. Lady Morgan worked hard and *drudged*, without feeling degraded by the process.

May 9. — This page is from an old Account-book. — By my earnings, since April 3, 1822, I have added to our joint-stock account, such sums as makes the whole £5,109 7s., from £2,678 11s. 6d., as it stood on that date. The several sums, therefore, vested in the Irish and English Stocks, and *which*, *being my earnings*, I have disposed of according to my marriage settlement, are —

£	s.	d.	
5,109	1	1	Reduced 3 per Cent. Annuities.
680	0	0	Irish 3½ per Cent.
32	13	9	Irish 5 per Cents.
600	0	0	Loan at Interest.
6,421	14	10	

The above is not a despicable sum to have made by her own industry, and saved by her own thrift.

Lady Morgan used to tell an anecdote, that she once took with her to one of the vice-regal balls, during Lord Wellesley's administration of Ireland, a small packet containing a miniature of Lady Morning-ton and a letter. She took the opportunity when his Excellency addressed her, to say —

"I have brought your Excellency an offering, a portrait of the woman you loved best in the world, and a letter that will interest you." Lord Wellesley took it, but not without a look of slight surprise.

'The packet was not of course opened then, but the next morning, before she was up, Lady Morgan received the following letter, accompanied by the gift of a beautiful silver case to hold perfume bottles.

The Marquis of Wellesley to Lady Morgan.

April, 1824.

I am very grateful to Lady Morgan for the perusal of this letter. It is written by Prudentia Trevor (sister to my mother) who was married to Charles Leslie, of Monaghan; it is franked by my grandfather, Arthur Trevor, the first Lord Dungannon. It must have been written from Bryntrinalt, in North Wales, in the year 1761. I was born in Grafton Street, Dublin, 1760; in a large, old house, afterwards pulled down, opposite the Provost's house. I was taken to England, 1767, where my family attended the coronation.

The above note is written in pencil. The essay on *Absenteeism* had become a more important work than Lady Morgan at first contemplated, and she was unwilling to allow it to appear as a mere magazine contribution; but Colburn, after some correspondence, persuaded her to let him have it. On the 10th of May, 1824, he wrote very gratefully to thank her for her acquiescence in his proposal to let it appear in his magazine, expressing a hope that the *notes* would not be too long or too numerous, it being her peculiar tendency to pile up all her loose lying materials into notes as long as the text. *Absenteeism* appeared in the June number of the *New Monthly.* It is written in a florid, declamatory style. It begins with the ancient glories of Ireland, reflecting mournfully on the times "when all in Ireland who were not saints were kings, and many were both, while none were martyrs." In those true Church and State times, the Irish kept in their own country, a pilgrimage to St. Patrick's purgatory — a royal progress of some Toparch of the South to some "Dynasty" of the North, or a morning visit from King Mac Turtell to his close neighbour, King Gillemohalmoghe, (which occasionally resulted in broken heads to both parties) was all the 'absenteeism' of Ireland until the period of our Henry II. King Mac Turtell was king of Dublin; and not far from Dublin there lived an Irish king named Gillemohalmoghe. Of the territories of this prince, Michael's Lane, in Dublin, formed a part; and his kingdom extended as far as Swords, the seat of Sir Compton Domville. Dermont Macmurrough O'Kavenagh, king of Leinster, is the first Irish absentee on record. He took refuge in the court of Henry II., of England; hence the invasion, &c., &c., &c." Sir Charles Morgan, in his preface, gives the pith of the whole book, and says, with a tone of apology, "In taking up the subject of absenteeism, the peculiar bent of Lady Morgan's mind has given a picturesque turn to her ideas, and induced her to view the matter less as an economist than as a poet and as a woman. But the great truth has not escaped her that absenteeism is less a cause than an effect. The whole of Lady Morgan's work goes to prove that English treachery and tyranny first made Ireland uninhabitable, and then punished its inhabitants for trying to leave. Like a true apologist and partisan, whilst she cannot deny the fact of absenteeism, nor the evils which the absence of a resident gentry entailed upon the country, she argues away the blame from the natives and lays it upon the English government. As a treatise of the hour *Absenteeism* did its duty, but it is of little value otherwise.

Sir Charles and Lady Morgan came over to London for the season of 1824; and Lady Morgan described the incidents of her life in letters to her sister.

Lady Morgan to Lady Clarke.

LONDON,
12th July, 1824.

Imprimis, — We have three and ninepence to pay for the last packet, charged overweight; but as I suspect it was the "*chillies bulletins*" that kicked the balance, I am quite satisfied to pay any sum for the productions of the most original writers of the age, only I beg to put my dear little bevy of correspondents on their guard in future. I see you are sick of my *routs and riots*, and, in truth, so am I. The heat is more oppressive than I ever found it in Italy. I have passed such a curious morning that I must describe it to you whilst I remember it. I sat to three artists from ten to one o'clock; then came a delightful person, Mr. Blencoe, by appointment, with a collection of original letters by Algernon Sydney (in his own precious handwriting to his father, Lord Leicester), models of style and full of curious facts that throw new glory on his character, and new light upon the times of Cromwell and Charles II. Mr. Blencoe found also at Penshurst, a journal kept by Lord Leicester which, with Sydney's letters, he is going to publish. He was scarcely gone, when Lord Byron's letters to his mother and others were confided to me. I shall only say, *en bref*, that though Cicero was to rise to plead for him to public opinion, he could say nothing in his behalf so powerfully favorable to his character as these *natural*, *charming*, and interesting letters: warm affections and high morality in every line. Poor fellow! He says, on the death of his mother, "Now she is gone, I have not one friend on earth, and this at twenty-three! What could I have more to say at seventy!" Just as I had devoured them (as I did in a great hurry), came in a packet of Mrs. Piozzi's MSS. letters; but after Byron's, they were sad namby pamby stuff. She says, crying down the French Revolution in 1797, "What do you think, the women have absolutely left off hair-powder! I see nothing but ruin for this unfortunate country!"

We have just got notice that Lord Byron's funeral takes place on Monday. Morgan is to go. His name is on the list; so are all the Whig lords. We could not bring ourselves to go and see him laid in state.

Our dinner at Dick's (*Quintin*) was sumptuous. We had the house of Mulgrave, Lady Cork, Lord and Lady Dillon, Sir Watkin, and others, — Lord Mulgrave's daughter, Lady Murray, is a charming person. They are particularly civil to us, and we dine there next Friday; and, on Wednesday, we are to meet the Duke of Wellington and Lord Hertford at Lady Cork's.

Campbell came to breakfast with Morgan, and they went *together* to the funeral of poor Lord Byron. The public wish was that he should be buried in the abbey, but his sister would have him buried in the *family vault*, and insisted on his funeral being a PEER's funeral, from which the *vulgar public*, the *nation*, was to be excluded. There would not have been a single literary person there, but Rogers and Moore (his personal friends), had not Morgan and Campbell, at the *last moment,* suggested others. All was mean and pompous, yet confusion: hundreds of persons on foot, in deep mourning, who came to pay this respect to one of the greatest geniuses of the age. Thomas Moore takes tea with us this evening, before we go to Lady Cork's *Whig* party. Did I tell you of the *gentilesse* of some of the managers of the theatres? They have sent me *keys* of private boxes?

I can no more. God bless you all, good people; and love me as I love you.

S. MORGAN.

In allusion to Lady Morgan's love of general society, her political friends looked doubtingly on her London season of this year; her friend, the Honourable Mrs. Caulfield, daughter of Sir Capel Molyneux, the fine old Irish gentleman and "patriot," who had registered a vow not to encourage Lord Lieutenants until the act of union should be repealed, — this daughter, as great a patriot as himself, wrote to Lady Morgan, — "I will not affront you by supposing that you will suffer by the ordeal your patriotism and your radicalism are undergoing. I will only say that I shall congratulate you and human nature if you end your gaieties among the Tories without a slight degree of contamination. I am alike enraged at your abuse of Dublin (though as to society, it is just) and at your idea of adding to the number of those *you yourself* write against by becoming an *absentee.* True friendship shows itself most in misfortune; and the riches, the society, the comforts, of London and of England should only attach

an Irish patriot more strongly to his country, — the
land of sorrow and suffering. I trust neither the variety,
scenery, wealth, nor society afforded on the Continent
or in England, will ever tempt us to have a *home* in
either, but that like a captain to his ship, we shall not
abandon poor old Ireland so long as our rulers allow
our lives to be safe and of any use to it."

The *tone* of the "friends of Ireland" was then little
less dangerous to the true welfare of the country than
the ultra-Protestant bitterness of the Tories, who did
not know how to manage either the country or the
people; it is difficult in these days of tranquil politics
to realise how "all faces gathered blackness" when
they touched upon them.

The following letter from Lord Cloncurry is given
as containing the views of an Irish landlord on the
subject of poor laws for Ireland.

Lord Cloncurry, when the Honourable Valentine
Lawless, had been mixed up very actively with the
proceedings of the "United Irishmen." He was arrested in May, 1798, confined for about six weeks in
the house of the king's messenger, in Pimlico, and then
set at liberty with an admonition. On April 14, 1799,
he was again arrested "on suspicion of treasonable
practices." The "*Habeas Corpus*" was at that time
suspended. He was examined before the Privy Council, was committed to the Tower, where he endured a
somewhat rigorous imprisonment, until March, 1801,
when he was discharged on the expiration of the "sus-
pension;" without having had any regular trial. He
suffered much in health; and domestic afflictions fell
heavily upon him during the twenty-two months of his

imprisonment. The lady to whom he was engaged to be married, died of sorrow and anxiety on his account, his father also died, and to avoid the contingency of confiscation, left away from him the sum of seventy thousand pounds; this, together with the disorder that his affairs fell into, made his loss in a pecuniary point of view a sufficiently heavy fine.

Lord Cloncurry to Sir Charles Morgan.

TORQUAY, DEVON,
October 6, 1824.

MY DEAR SIR CHARLES,

I see by the papers that I owe you sixteen shillings and eight pence on the Greek account, which you can either receive from Val. or hold over *in terrorem* against me. Your observations on the Poor Laws, and the prospect of introducing them into Ireland, are founded on the best principles of human political philosophy, and I would only act in opposition to them from a feeling of the utter hopelessness of our situation, and from the idea that they may ultimately be one means of bringing about that change which all parties allow to be necessary. The case of Ireland is so different from that of any other country, that as a mere Irishman I think quite differently from what I would as a citizen of the world. What could be more silly or atrocious than the Corn Laws? An Englishman voting for them should have been sent only to Bethlehem or the hulks, yet I voted for them, as I knew my countrymen *never taste* bread, and the same, bad as it was, gave *us* much English money. Now the Poor Laws will not, I think, ruin the price of land as you expect, but will lower it, and perhaps cost me twelve or fifteen hundred per annum; but as no tenant can pay more than he already does, the landlords must be answerable, as in the case of tithes — thus the Poor Laws will be an indirect absentee tax — the desire to abolish it will join the upper orders to the *corps reformateur*, and ultimately the whole system of iniquity must be put down.

I am truly sorry Lady Morgan should feel one moment's illness. I am interested for her as an Irishman as well as a sincere and grateful friend. We have got a capital house here, and the place is beautiful and pleasant; if you could come to us for a couple of months we could make you and your dear lady very comfortable.

I want to consult you as to an application from Staunton for an advance of one hundred pounds on his security, for the purpose of re-establishing the *Morning Herald*. I would most willingly give one or two hundred pounds for a clever, thorough-going Irish paper, to be managed by a committee; but though I always take the *Evening Herald*, it is too polemical and too personal, and too full of long, drawling, priest-written stuff to do any real good. I have no objection to aid Staunton with fifteen or twenty pounds; but for any farther advance I should like the security of a committee. I wish you and Curran would turn this in your minds, and see whether we could not establish what is so much wanted.

Yours ever,
Most faithfully,
Cloncurry.

PS. Our M.D. here is an Irish Papist, brother to

Councillor Scully. Balls and cards here every week, to the great comfort of Miss Bryan.

CHAPTER XXIII.

LORD BYRON AND LADY CAROLINE LAMB.

THE correspondence between Lady Caroline Lamb and Lady Morgan, on the subject of Lord Byron, together with the noble poet's last letter to Lady Caroline, may now be given. In a rough memorandum, written by Lady Morgan on a loose sheet of paper, in the year before she commenced to keep a regular diary, there is some account of Lady Caroline, taken down from her own mouth. The sentences are but fragments, yet they make a very sad and singular picture of this gifted woman in her youth and early married life. Lady Caroline's account of her first introduction to Byron, and of the impression made on her by the noble poet, will be read with universal interest. The lady's words must be set down in their rough state, exactly as they appear in Lady Morgan's journal.

"Lady Caroline Lamb sent for me. Her story: Her mother had a paralytic stroke: went to Italy: she remained there till nine years old, brought up by a maid called Fanny. She was then taken to Devonshire House, and brought up with her cousins. She gave curious anecdotes of high life, — children neglected by their mothers — children served on silver in the morning, carrying down their plate to the kitchen — no one to attend to them — servants all at variance — ignorance of children on all subjects — thought all people were dukes or beggars — or had never to part with their money — did not know bread, or butter, was made — wondered if horses fed on beef — so neglected in her education, she could not write at ten years old. Lady Georgiana Cavendish took her away, and she was sent to live with her godmother, Spencer, where the house-keeper, in hoop and ruffles, had the rule over seventy servants, and always attended her ladies in the drawing-room. Lady Georgiana's marriage was one *de convenance*. Her delight was hunting butterflies. The house-keeper breaking a lath over her head reconciled her to the match [to become Duchess of Devonshire]. She was ignorant of everything. Lady Spencer had Dr. Warren to examine Lady Caroline. He said she had no tendency to madness, — severity of her governess and indulgence of her parents. Her passion for William Lamb — would not marry him — knew herself to be a fury — wanted to follow him as a clerk, &c. Ill tempers on both sides broke out together after marriage — both loved, hated, quarrelled, and made up. 'He cared nothing for my morals,' she said. 'I might flirt and go about with what men I pleased. He was privy to my affair with Lord Byron, and laughed at it. His indolence rendered him insensible to everything. When I ride, play, and amuse him, he loves me. In sickness and suffering, he deserts me. His violence is as bad as my own.' "

Her account of Lord Byron: —

"Lady Westmoreland knew him in Italy. She took on her to present him. The women suffocated him. I heard nothing of him, till one day Rogers (for he, Moore, and Spencer, were all my lovers, and wrote me up to the skies — I was in the clouds) — Rogers said, 'you should know the new poet,' and he offered me the MS. of *Childe Harold* to read. I read it, and that was enough, Rogers said, 'he has a club-foot, and bites his nails.' I said, 'If he was ugly as Æsop I must know him.' I was one night at Lady Westmoreland's; the women were all throwing their heads at him. Lady Westmoreland led me up to him. I looked earnestly at him, and turned on my heel. My opinion, in my journal was, 'mad — bad — and dangerous to know.' A day or two passed; I was sitting with Lord and Lady Hollond, when he was announced. Lady Holland said, 'I must present Lord Byron to you.' Lord Byron said, 'That offer was made to you before; may I ask why you rejected it?' He begged permission to come and see me. He did so the next day. Rogers and Moore were standing by me: I was on the sofa. I had just come in from riding. I was filthy and heated. When Lord Byron was announced, I flew out of the room to wash myself. When I returned, Rogers said, 'Lord Byron, you are a happy man. Lady Caroline has been sitting here in all her dirt with us, but when you were announced, she flew to beautify herself.' Lord Byron wished to come and see me at eight o'clock, when I was alone; that was my dinner-hour. I said he might. From that moment, for more than nine months, he almost lived at Melbourne House. It was then the centre of all gaiety, at least, in appearance. My cousin Hartington wanted to have waltzes and quadrilles; and, at Devonshire House, it would not be allowed, so we had them in the great drawing-room

of Melbourne House. All the *bon ton* of London assembled here every day. There was nothing so fashionable. Byron contrived to sweep them all away. My
mother grew miserable, and did everything in her
power to break off the connexion. She at last brought
me to consent to go to Ireland with her and papa.
Byron wrote me that letter which I have shown you.
While in Ireland, I received letters constantly, — the
most tender and the most amusing. We had got to
Dublin, on our way home, where my mother brought
me a letter. There was a coronet on the seal. The
initials under the coronet were Lady Oxford's. It was
that cruel letter I have published in *Glenarvon:* it destroyed me: I lost my brain. I was bled, leeched; kept
for a week in the filthy Dolphin Inn, at Rock. On my
return, I was in great prostration of mind and spirit.
Then came my *fracas* with the page, which made such
noise. He was a little *espiègle*, and would throw
detonating balls into the fire. Lord Melbourne always
scolded me for this; and I, the boy. One day I was
playing ball with him. He threw a squib into the fire,
and I threw the ball at his head. It hit him on the
temple, and he bled. He cried out, 'Oh, my lady, you
have killed me!' Out of my senses, I flew into the
hall, and screamed, 'Oh God, I have murdered the
page!' The servants and people in the streets caught
the sound, and it was soon spread about. William
Lamb would live with me no longer. All his family
united in insisting on our separation. Whilst this was
going on, and instruments drawing out — that is, in
one month — I wrote and *sent Glenarvon to the press.* I
wrote it, unknown to all (save a governess, Miss
Welsh), in the middle of the night. It was necessary

to have it copied out. I had heard of a famous copier, an old Mr. Woodhead. I sent to beg he would come to see Lady Caroline Lamb at Melbourne House. I placed Miss Welsh, elegantly dressed, at my harp, and myself at a writing-table, dressed in the page's clothes, looking a boy of fourteen. He addressed Miss Welsh as Lady Caroline. She showed him the 'author. He would not believe that this schoolboy could write such a thing. He came to me again in a few days, and he found me in my own clothes. I told him William Ormond, the young author, was dead. When the work was printed, I sent it to William Lamb. He was delighted with it; and we became united, just as the world thought we were parted for ever. The scene at Brocket Hall (in the novel of *Glenarvon*) was true. Lord Byron's death — the ghost appearing to her — her distraction at his death. Medwin's talk completed her distress."

We may now proceed with the correspondence.

Lady Caroline Lamb to Lady Morgan.

MELBOURNE HOUSE,
June 2.

MY DEAR LADY MORGAN,

I have sent for, and I know not if I shall receive, the portrait you wished to see. I am afraid you have seen me under great irritation, and under circumstances that might try any one. I am too miserable. You have not yet advised me what to do — I know not, care not. Oh, God, it is a punishment severe enough; I never can recover it; it is fair by William Lamb to mention, that since I saw you he has written a kinder letter; but if I am sent to live by myself, let them dread the violence of my despair — better far go away. Every tree, every flower, will awaken bitter reflection. Pity me, for I am too unhappy; I cannot bear it. I would give all I possessed on earth to be again what I once was, and I would now be obedient and gentle; but I shall die of grief.

Think about Ireland — if only for a few months — yet what shall I do at Bessborough alone? God bless you; thanks for your portrait; hearing this, is a sad ending to a too frivolous and far too happy a life. Farewell; if you receive the portrait, return it, and send the letter; it is his parting one when I went to Ireland with mamma (*I mean Lord Byron's*). She was near dying because she thought I was going to leave her. William, at that time, loved me so much that he forgave me all, and only implored me to remain. My life has not been the best possible. The slave of impulse, I have rushed forward to my own destruction. If you like the drawing of me, which Pickett did before he died, I will try and have it copied. I trust faithfully to your returning my letter and both pictures.

Ever with sincere interest,
and affection,
CAROLINE.

Lord Byron's Parting Letter to Lady Caroline Lamb.

[Enclosed in foregoing.]

MY DEAREST CAROLINE,

If tears which you saw and know I am not apt to shed, — if the agitation in which I parted from you, — agitation which you must have perceived through the whole of this most nervous affair, did not commence until the moment of leaving you approached, — if all I have said and done, and am still but too ready to say and do have not sufficiently proved what my real feelings are, and must ever be towards you, my love, I have no other proof to offer. God knows, I wish you happy, and when I quit you, or rather you from a sense of duty to your husband and mother, quit me, you shall acknowledge the truth of what I again promise and vow, that no other in word or deed shall ever hold the place in my affections, which is, and shall be, most sacred to you, till I am nothing. I never knew till that moment the madness of my dearest and most beloved friend; I cannot express myself; this is no time for words, but I shall have a pride, a melancholy pleasure, in suffering what you yourself can scarcely conceive, for you do not know me. I am about to go out with a heavy heart, because my appearing this evening will stop any absurd story which the spite of the day might give rise to. Do you think *now* I am cold, and stern, and wilful? will ever others think so? will your mother ever — that mother to whom we must indeed sacrifice much more, much more on my part than she shall ever know or *can* imagine? "Promise not to love you," ah, Caroline, it is past promising. But I shall attribute all concessions to the proper motive, and never cease to feel all that you have already witnessed, and more than can ever be known but to my own heart, — perhaps to yours.

May God protect, forgive, and bless you ever and ever, more than ever

Your most attached,

BYRON.

PS. — These taunts which have driven you to this, my dearest Caroline, were it not for your mother and the kindness of your connections, is there anything in earth or heaven that would have made me so happy as to have made you mine long ago? and not less *now* than *then*, but more than ever at *this time*. You know I would with pleasure give up all here and beyond the grave for you, and in refraining from this, must my motives be misunderstood? I care not who knows this, what use is made of it, — it is to you and to *you* only that they are, *yourself*. I was and am yours freely and entirely to obey, to honour, love, and fly with you when, where, and how yourself *might* and *may* determine.

From the confession of Lady Caroline, previously given, it will have been seen that Byron continued to write to her while she was in Ireland. How the unhappy woman quarrelled in the last degree with her indulgent husband is not told in these papers. That she parted from him and went abroad, are facts involved in the statements which ensue. The letters must be given without comment.

Lady Caroline Lamb to Lady Morgan.

[No date.]

No, no, not that portrait out of my hands — I cannot bear. I will have it copied for you. I must take it with me to Paris. Thank you, dear Lady Morgan, for your advice, but you do not understand me, and I do not wonder you cannot know me. I had purposed a very pretty little supper for you. I have permission to see all my friends here; it is not William's house; beside, he said he wished me to see every one, and Lady — called and asked me who I wished to see. I shall, therefore, shake hands with the whole Court Guide before I go. The only question I want you to solve is, shall I go abroad? Shall I throw myself upon those who no longer want me, or shall I live a good sort of a half kind of life in some cheap street a little way off, viz., the City Road, Shoreditch, Camberwell, or upon the top of a shop, — or shall I give lectures to little children, and keep a seminary, and thus earn my bread? or shall I write a kind of quiet every day sort of novel, full of wholesome truths, or shall I attempt to be poetical, and failing, beg my friends for a guinea a-piece, and their name, to sell my work, upon the best foolscap paper; or shall I fret, fret, fret, and die; or shall I be dignified and fancy myself, as Richard the Second did when he picked the nettle up — upon a thorn?

Sir Charles Morgan was most agreeable and good-natured. *Faustus* is good in its way, but has not all its sublimity; it is like a rainy shore. I admire it because I *conceive* what I had *heard* translated elsewhere, but the end particularly is in very contemptible taste. The overture tacked to it is magnificent, the scenery beautiful, parts affecting, and not unlike Lord Byron, that dear, that angel, that mis-guided and mis-guiding Byron, whom I adore, although he left that dreadful legacy on me — my memory. Remember thee — and well.

I hope he and William will find better friends; as to myself, I never can love anything better than what I thus tell you: — William Lamb, first; my mother, second; Byron, third; my boy, fourth; my brother William, fifth; my father and godmother, sixth; my uncle and aunt, my cousin Devonshire, my brother Fred., (myself), my cousins next, and last, my *petit* friend, young Russell, because he is my aunt's godson; because when he was but three I nursed him; because he has a hard-to-win, free, and kind heart; but chiefly because he stood by me when no one else did.

I am yours,

C. L.

Send me my portrait. I trust to your kindness and honour.

Lady Caroline Lamb to Lady Morgan.

DEAR LADY MORGAN,   [*No date.*]

You know not what misery and illness I have suffered since last I wrote to you. My brother William — my kind guardian-angel — informed me to-day that you were in town, and as I am too ill to go out, and wish to consult you about publishing my journal, and many other things, would you do me the favour to call here to-morrow evening, or any time you please, between eight and eleven! Unless you meet my brother you will find no one, and, as I have four horses, I can send for you, and send you back when you like.

Yours most sincerely

CAROLINE.

PS. I was rather grieved that you never answered my last imprudent letter; fear not, they have broken my heart — *not my spirit;* and if I will but sign a paper, all my rich relations will protect me, and I shall no doubt, go with an Almack ticket to heaven.

Lady Caroline Lamb to Lady Morgan.

October 16.

MY DEAR LADY MORGAN,

I have a great deal to say to you, and to explain to you, and I will write soon; but I have not been well. Lady Cowper called soon after you left me at Thomas's Hotel, and promised to call on you and say that I could not. I have seen her since, and found she did not; but she wished to do so much, and I now send you her card; pray see William and my son, and write and tell me all you think about them, and Ireland, and when you next will be out. I write this solely to fulfil my engagement — saying, I leave *you when I die Lord Byron's picture,* now under the care of Goddard — the original by Saunders. Pray excuse one more word until I hear from you, and believe me

Ever most sincerely yours,

CAROLINE LAMB.

Lady Caroline Lamb to Lady Morgan.

DOVER.

MY DEAR LADY MORGAN,

It would be charitable in you to write me a letter, and it would be most kind if you would immediately send me Lord Byron's portrait, as far more than the six weeks have expired, and I am again in England. If you will send it for me to Melbourne House, to the care of the porter, I shall be most sincerely obliged to

you. My situation in life, now, is new and strange —
I seem to be left to my fate most completely, and to
take my chance, or rough or smooth, without the
smallest interest being expressed for me. It is for good
purposes, no doubt; besides I must submit to my fate
— it being without remedy. I am now with my maid
at the Ship Tavern, Water Lane, having come over
from Calais. I have no servants, page, carriage, horse,
nor fine rooms — the melancholy of my situation in
this little dreary apartment is roused by the very loud,
jovial laughter of my neighbours, who are smoking in
the next room. Pray send me my invaluable portrait,
and pray think kindly of me; every one in France
talked much of you, and with great enthusiasm. Farewell; remember me to your husband and family, and
believe me

Most truly yours,
CAROLINE LAMB.

PS. Direct to me care of the Honourable William
Ponsonby, St. James's Square, London.

I hope you received a letter from me written before
I left England.

Lady Caroline Lamb to Lady Morgan.

MY DEAREST LADY,

As being a lady whom my adored mother loved,
your kindness about Ada Reis I feel the more, as
everybody wishes to run down and suppress the vital
spark of genius I have, and, in truth, it is but small
(about what one sees a maid gets by excessive beating
on a tinder-box). I am not vain, believe me, nor sel-

fish, nor in love with my authorship; but I am independent, as far as a mite and bit of dust can be. I thank God, being born with all the great names of England around me; I value them alone for what they dare do, and have done, and I fear nobody except the devil, who certainly has all along been very particular in his attentions to me, and has sent me as many baits as he did Job. I, however, am, happily for myself, in as ill a state of health as he was, so I trust in God I shall ever more resist temptation. My history, if you ever care and like to read it, is this — My mother, having boys, wished ardently for a girl; and I, who evidently ought to have been a soldier, was found a naughty girl — forward, talking like Richard the Third.

I was a trouble, not a pleasure, all my childhood, for which reason, after my return from Italy, where I was from the age of four until nine, I was ordered by the late Dr. Warren neither to learn anything nor see any one, for fear the violent passions and strange whims they found in me should lead to madness; of which, however, he assured every one there were no symptoms. I differ, but the end was, that until fifteen I learned nothing. My instinct — for we all have instincts — was for music — in it I delighted; I cried when it was pathetic, and did all that Dryden's ode made Alexander do — of course I was not allowed to follow it up. My angel mother's ill-health prevented my living at home; my kind aunt Devonshire took me; the present Duke loved me better than himself, and every one paid me those compliments shown to children who are precious to their parents, or delicate and likely to die. I wrote not, spelt not; but I made verses, which they all thought beautiful — for myself, I preferred washing a dog, or polishing a piece of Derbyshire spar, or breaking in a horse, to any accomplishment in the world. Drawing-room (shall I say withdrawing-room, as they now say?) looking-glasses, finery, or dress-company for ever were my abhorrence. I was, I am, religious; I was loving (?) but I was and am unkind. I fell in love when only twelve years old, with a friend of Charles Fox — a friend of liberty whose poems I had read, whose self I had never seen, and when I did see him, at thirteen, could I change? No, I was more attached than ever. William Lamb was beautiful, and far the cleverest person then about, and the most daring in his opinions, in his love of liberty and independence. He thought of me but as a child, yet he liked me much; afterwards he offered to marry me, and I refused him because of my temper, which was too violent; he, however, asked twice, and was not refused the second time, and the reason was that I adored him. I had three children; two died; my only child is afflicted; it is the will of God. I have wandered from right, and been punished. I have suffered what you can hardly believe; I have lost my mother, whose gentleness and good sense guided me. I have received more kindness than I can ever repay. I have suffered, also, but I deserved it. My power of mind and of body are gone; I am like the shade of what I was; to write was once my resource and pleasure; but since the only eyes that ever admired most poor and humble productions are closed, wherefore should I indulge the propensity! God bless you; I write from my heart. You are one like me, who, perhaps, have not taken the right road. I am on my death-bed; say, I might have died by a diamond, I die now by a brickbat; but remember, the only noble fellow I ever met with is William Lamb; he is to me what Shore was to Jane Shore. I saw it once; I am as grateful, but as unhappy. Pray excuse the sorrows this sad, strange letter will cause you; could you be in time I would be glad to see you — to you alone would I give up Byron's letters — much else, but all like the note you have. Pray excuse this being not written as clearly as you can write. I speak as I hope you do, from the heart.

C. L.

END OF VOL. II.

PRINTING OFFICE OF THE PUBLISHER.